AW YEAH
COMICS!™

Time for...ADVENTURE!

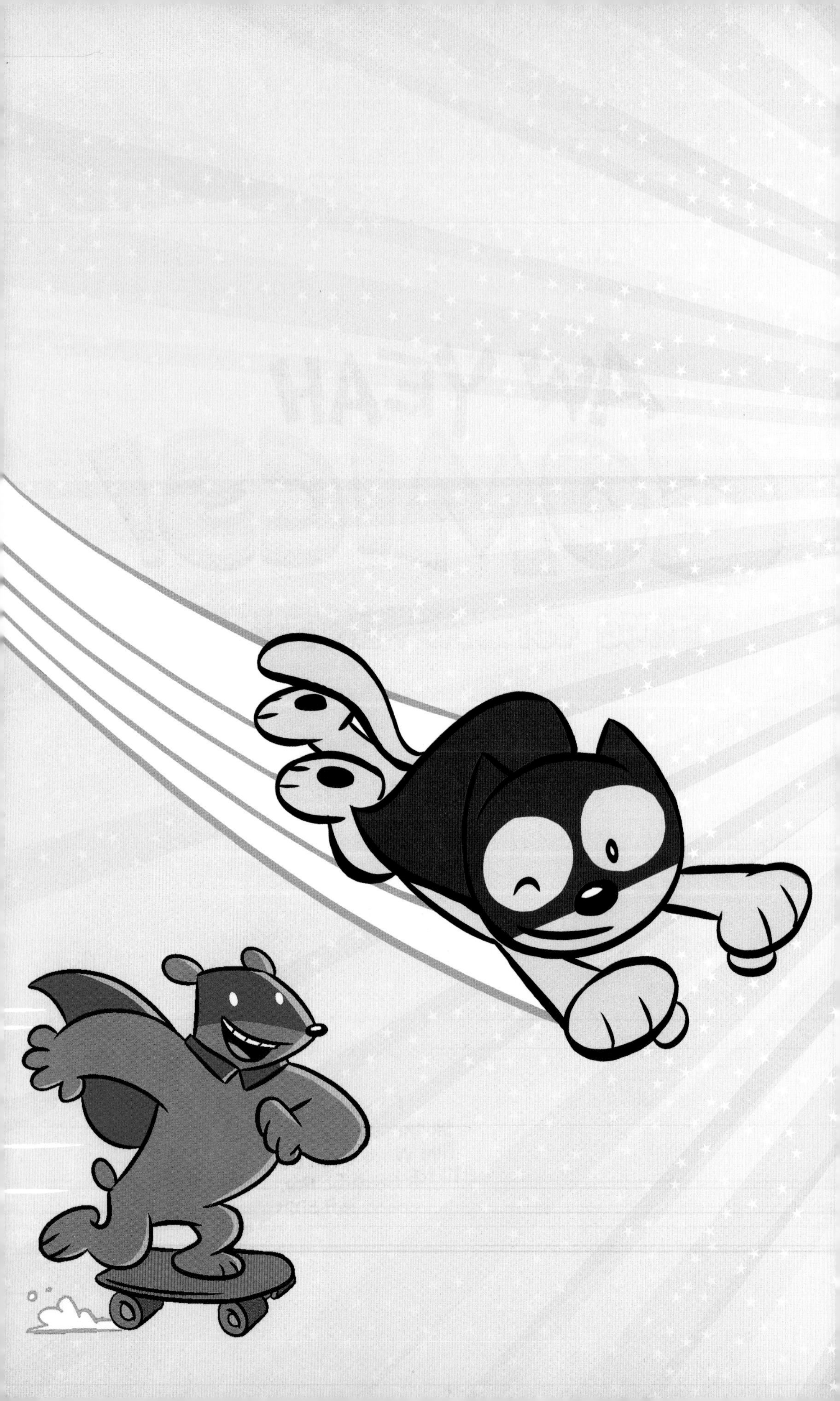

AW YEAH COMICS! ™

Time for... ADVENTURE!

STORY AND ARTWORK BY **ART BALTAZAR** AND **FRANCO**

Chapter break artwork by Art Baltazar

FEATURING

Nicolas Aureliani, Gordon Baltazar, Denver Brubaker,
"the Catman," Chris Giarrusso, Marc Hammond, Stephen Mayer,
Scoot McMahon, Chris Roberson, Georgia Roberson,
Alejandro Rosado, Chris Zod Smits, David Wolfgang von Ehrlicher,
Mr. Whitmore, Judd Winick, Kurt Wood, and Zac

Dark Horse Books

Designer KAT LARSON
Assistant Editor JEMIAH JEFFERSON
Editor BRENDAN WRIGHT
Publisher MIKE RICHARDSON

Published by
Dark Horse Books
A division of Dark Horse Comics, Inc.
10956 SE Main Street
Milwaukie, OR 97222

DarkHorse.com ★ AwYeahComics.com

First edition: JUNE 2015
ISBN 978-1-61655-689-1

13 5 7 9 10 8 6 4 2
Printed in China

This volume collects *Aw Yeah Comics!* #5–#8, originally published by
Aw Yeah Comics! Publishing, as well as new material created for this volume.

AW YEAH COMICS! TIME FOR . . . ADVENTURE!

★ CHAPTER ONE ★

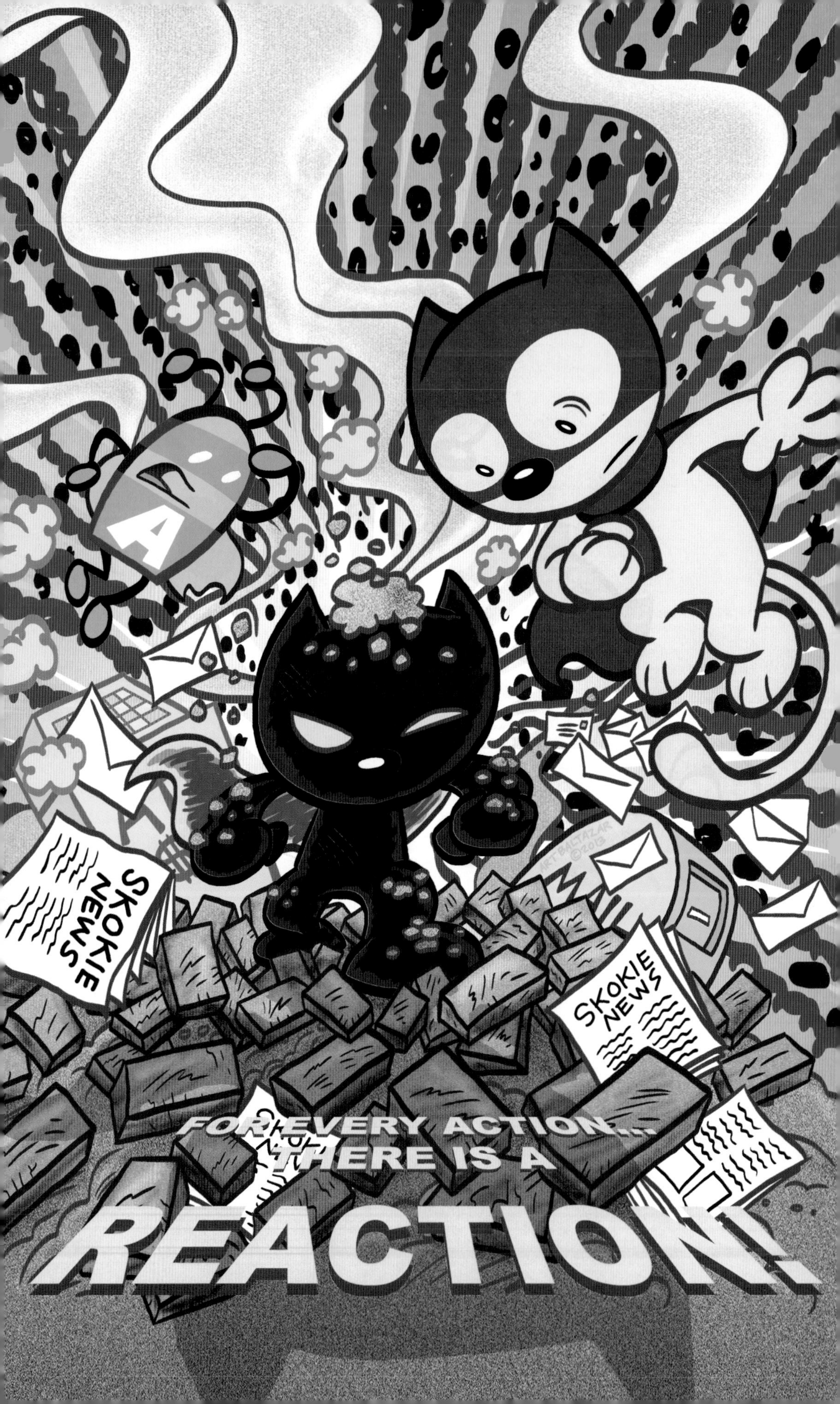
SKOKIE NEWS
SKOKIE NEWS
ART BALTAZAR ©2013
FOR EVERY ACTION...
THERE IS A
REACTION!

AW YEAH COMICS PRESENTS...

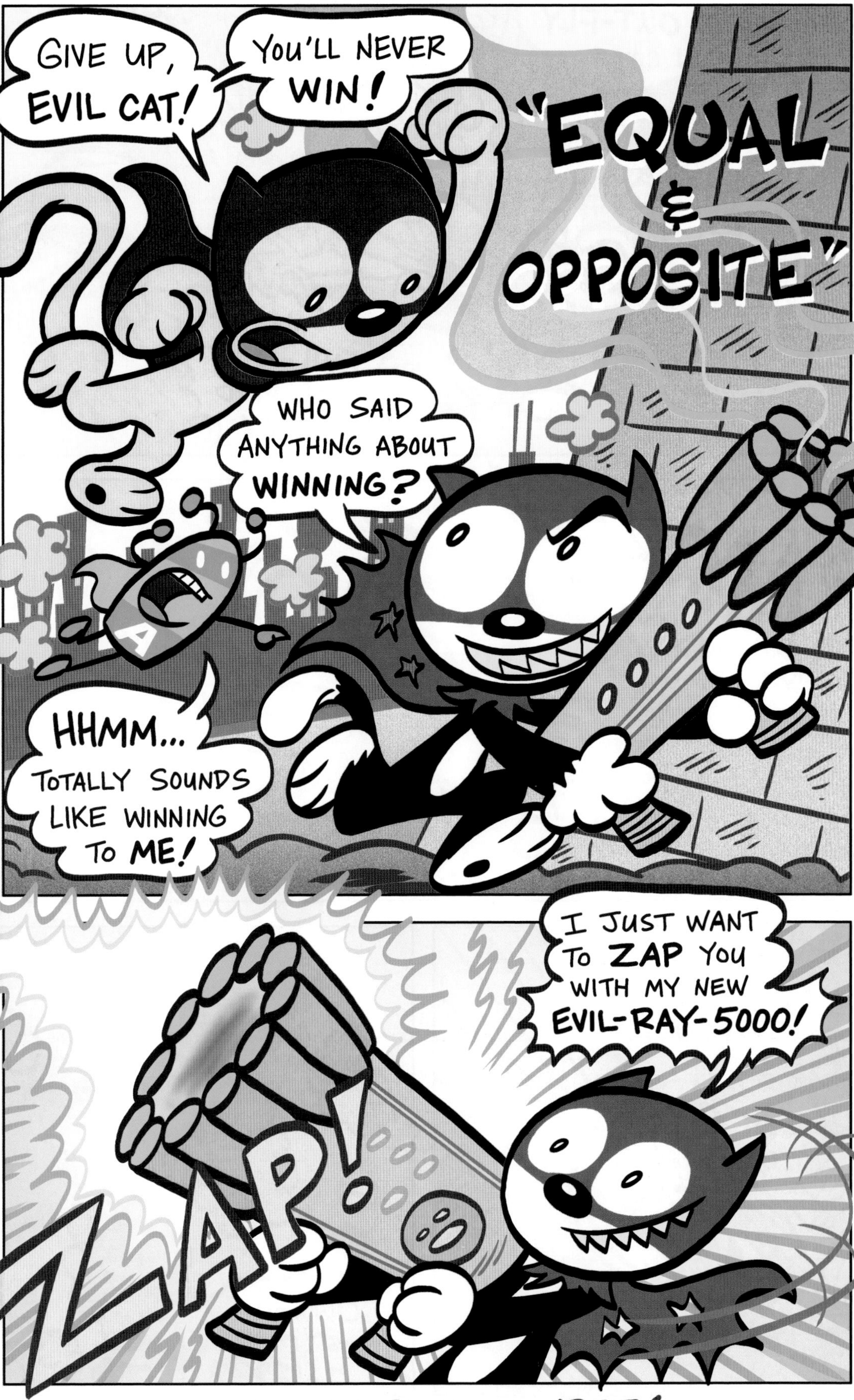

GIVE UP, EVIL CAT!
YOU'LL NEVER WIN!
"EQUAL & OPPOSITE"
WHO SAID ANYTHING ABOUT WINNING?
HHMM... TOTALLY SOUNDS LIKE WINNING TO ME!
I JUST WANT TO ZAP YOU WITH MY NEW EVIL-RAY-5000!
ZAP!

BY BROTHER BEAR AND ARTIE!

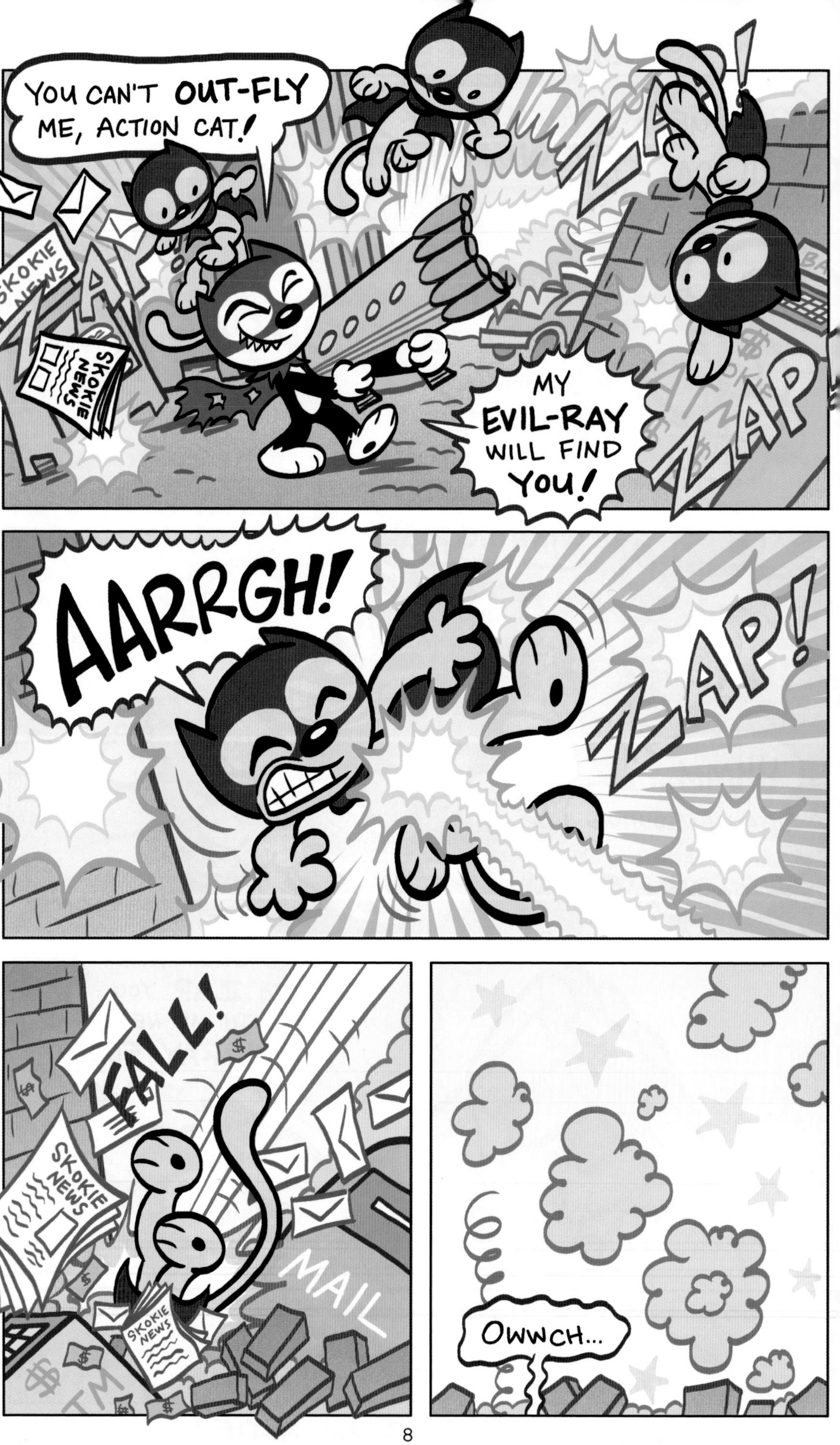
YOU CAN'T OUT-FLY ME, ACTION CAT!
SKOKIE NEWS
ZAP!
SKOKIE NEWS
ZAP!
MY EVIL-RAY WILL FIND YOU!
ZAP!
AARRGH!
ZAP!
FALL!
SKOKIE NEWS
MAIL
SKOKIE NEWS
ATM
OWWCH...

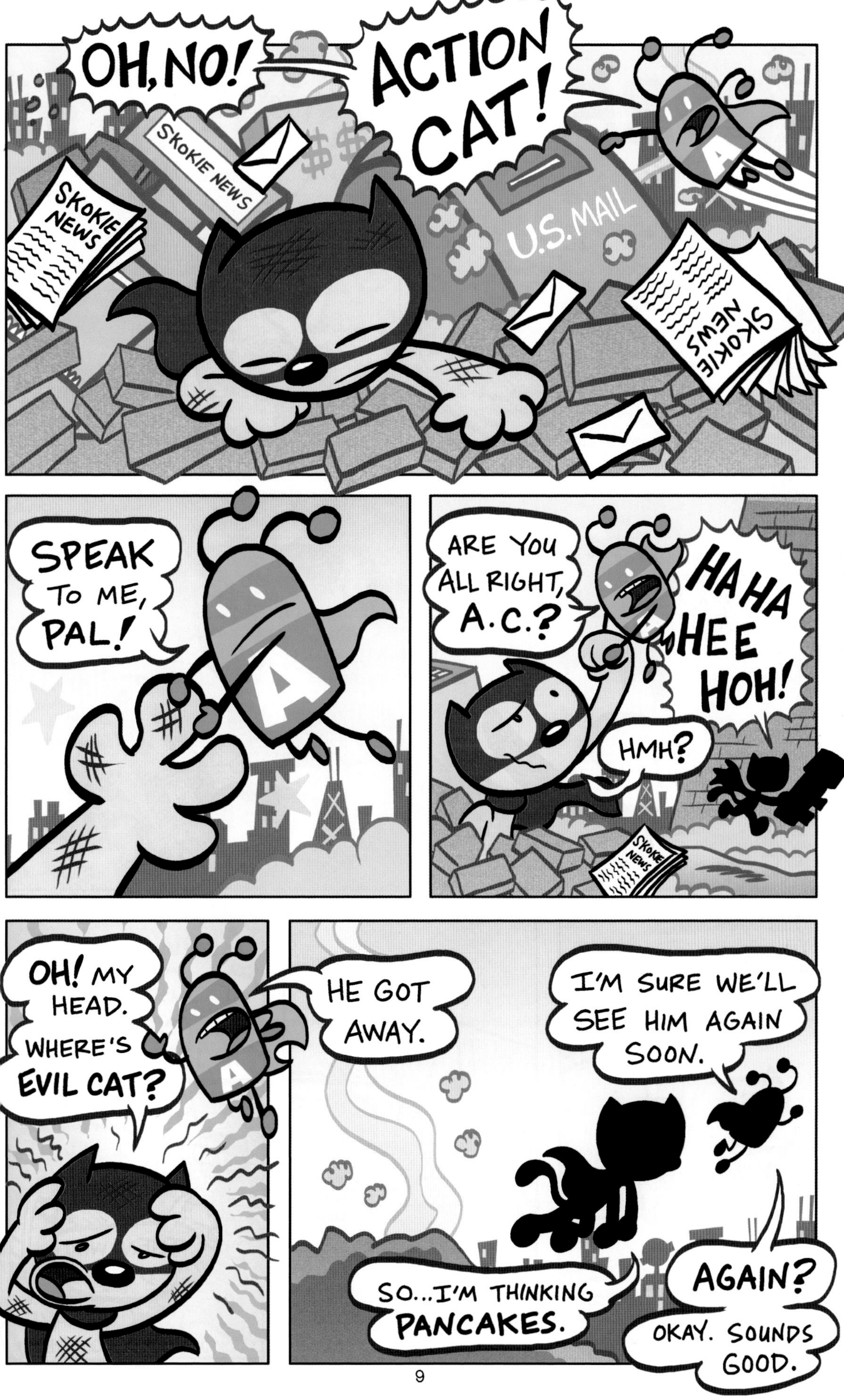
OH, NO!
ACTION CAT!
SKOKIE NEWS
SKOKIE NEWS
U.S. MAIL
SKOKIE NEWS
SPEAK TO ME, PAL!
ARE YOU ALL RIGHT, A.C.?
HA HA HEE HOH!
HMH?
SKOKIE NEWS
OH! MY HEAD. WHERE'S EVIL CAT?
HE GOT AWAY.
I'M SURE WE'LL SEE HIM AGAIN SOON.
SO... I'M THINKING PANCAKES.
AGAIN?
OKAY. SOUNDS GOOD.

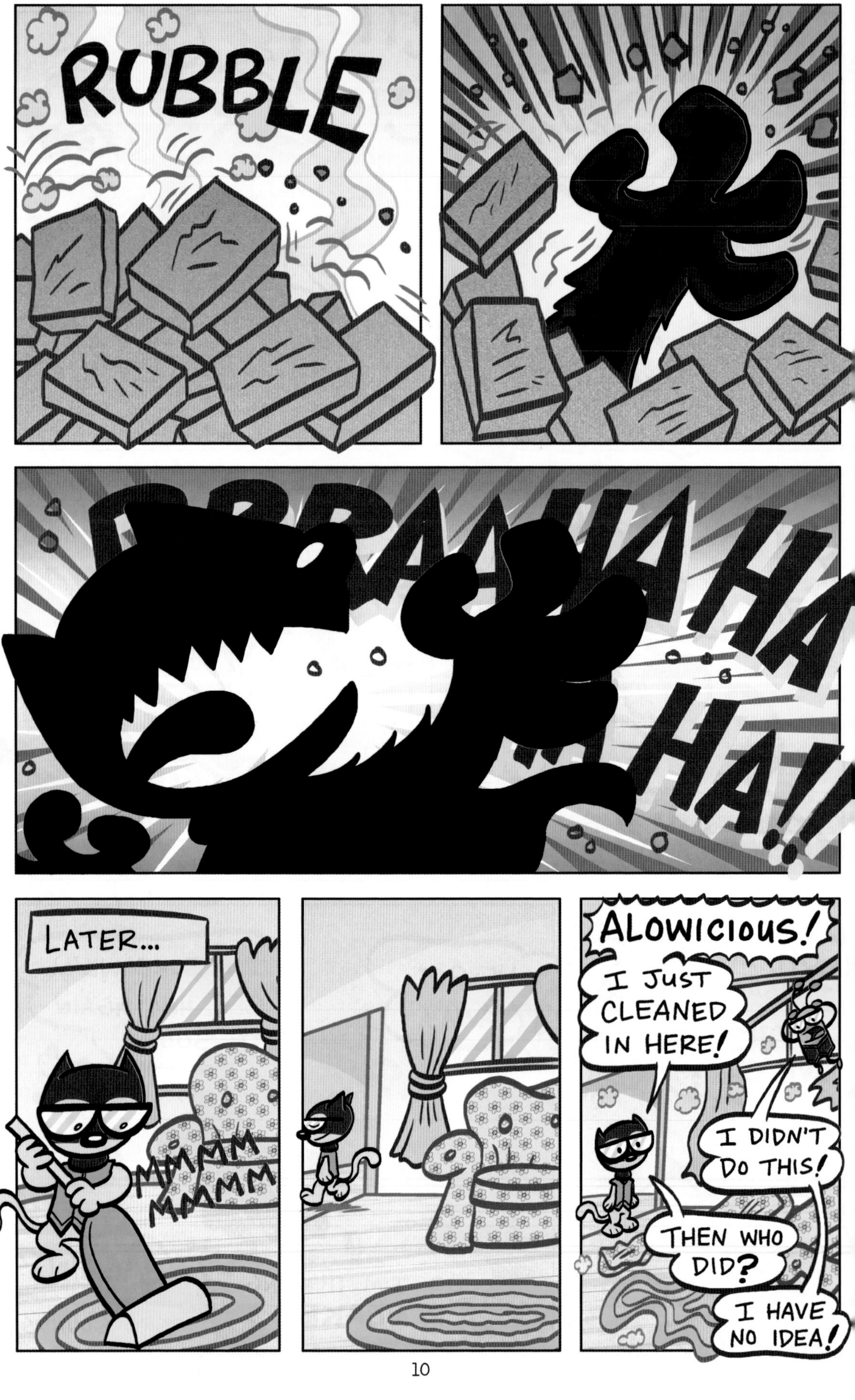
RUBBLE
BRRAAHAHAHA HA!!
LATER...
MMMM MMMM
ALOWICIOUS!
I JUST CLEANED IN HERE!
I DIDN'T DO THIS!
THEN WHO DID?
I HAVE NO IDEA!

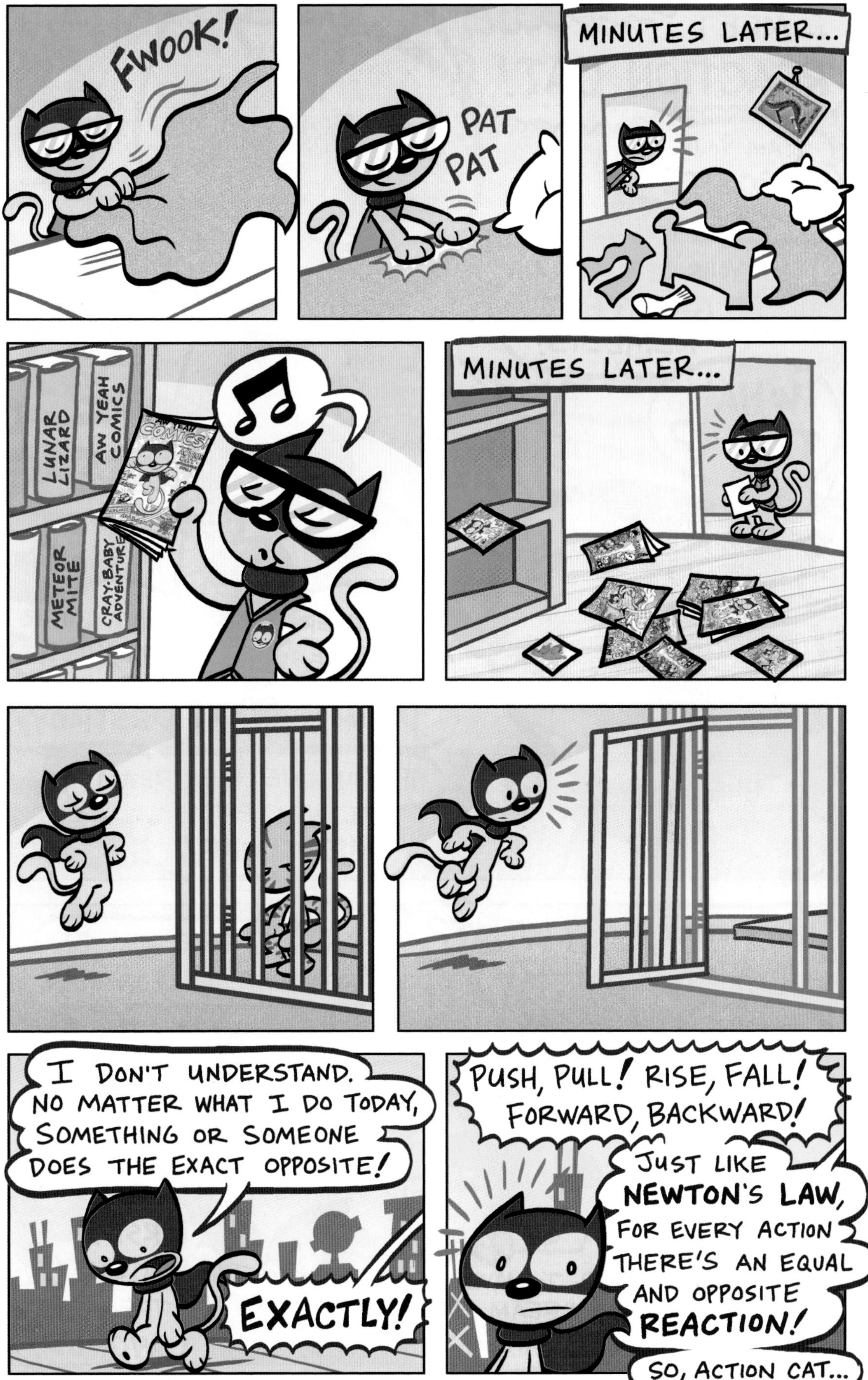
FWOOK!
PAT PAT
MINUTES LATER...
LUNAR LIZARD
AW YEAH COMICS
METEOR MITE
CRAY-BABY ADVENTURE
AW YEAH COMICS!
MINUTES LATER...
I DON'T UNDERSTAND. NO MATTER WHAT I DO TODAY, SOMETHING OR SOMEONE DOES THE EXACT OPPOSITE!
EXACTLY!
PUSH, PULL! RISE, FALL! FORWARD, BACKWARD!
JUST LIKE NEWTON'S LAW, FOR EVERY ACTION THERE'S AN EQUAL AND OPPOSITE REACTION!
SO, ACTION CAT...

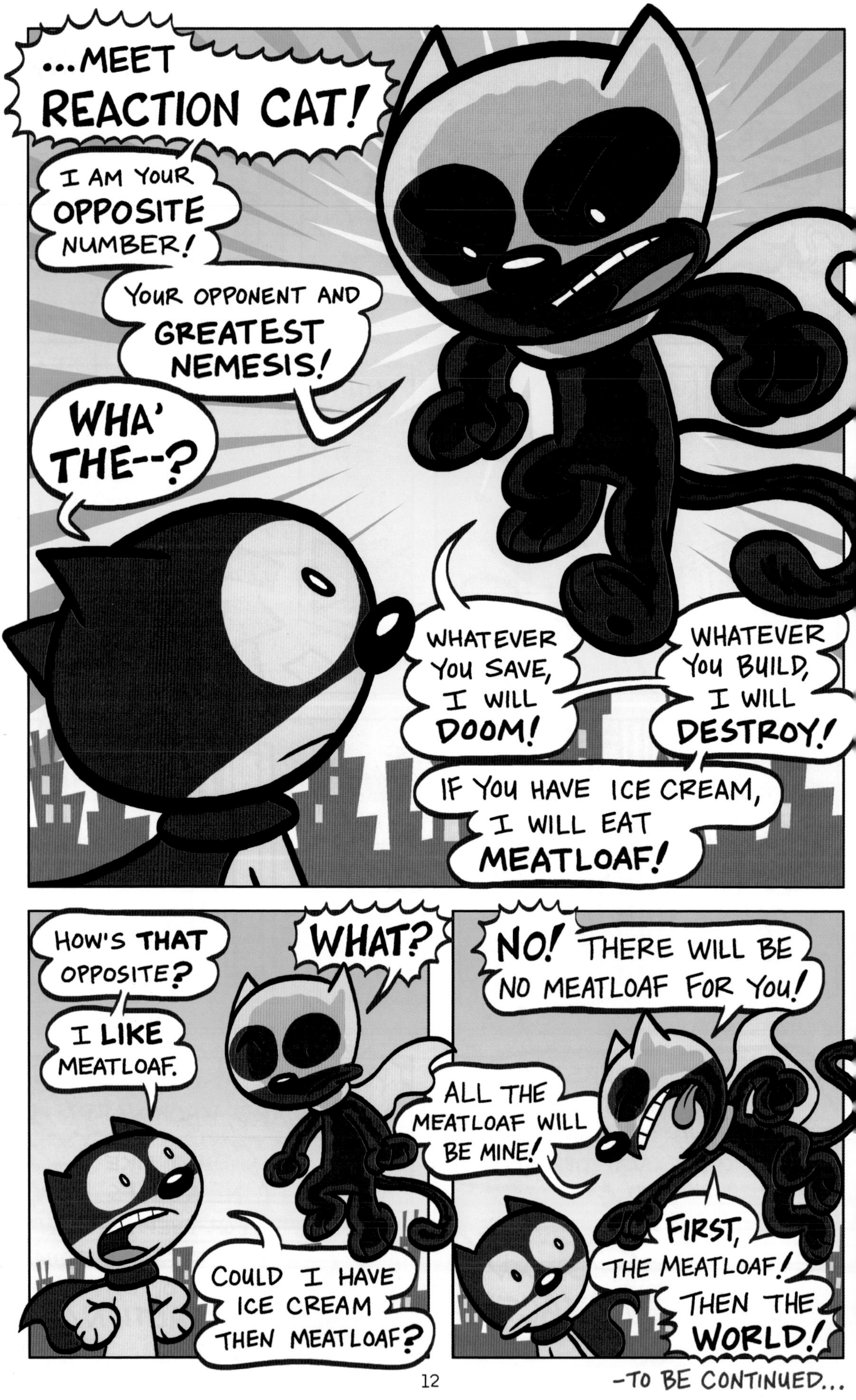

...MEET REACTION CAT!
I AM YOUR OPPOSITE NUMBER!
YOUR OPPONENT AND GREATEST NEMESIS!
WHA' THE--?
WHATEVER YOU SAVE, I WILL DOOM!
WHATEVER YOU BUILD, I WILL DESTROY!
IF YOU HAVE ICE CREAM, I WILL EAT MEATLOAF!
HOW'S THAT OPPOSITE?
I LIKE MEATLOAF.
WHAT?
COULD I HAVE ICE CREAM THEN MEATLOAF?
NO! THERE WILL BE NO MEATLOAF FOR YOU!
ALL THE MEATLOAF WILL BE MINE!
FIRST, THE MEATLOAF! THEN THE WORLD!

-TO BE CONTINUED...

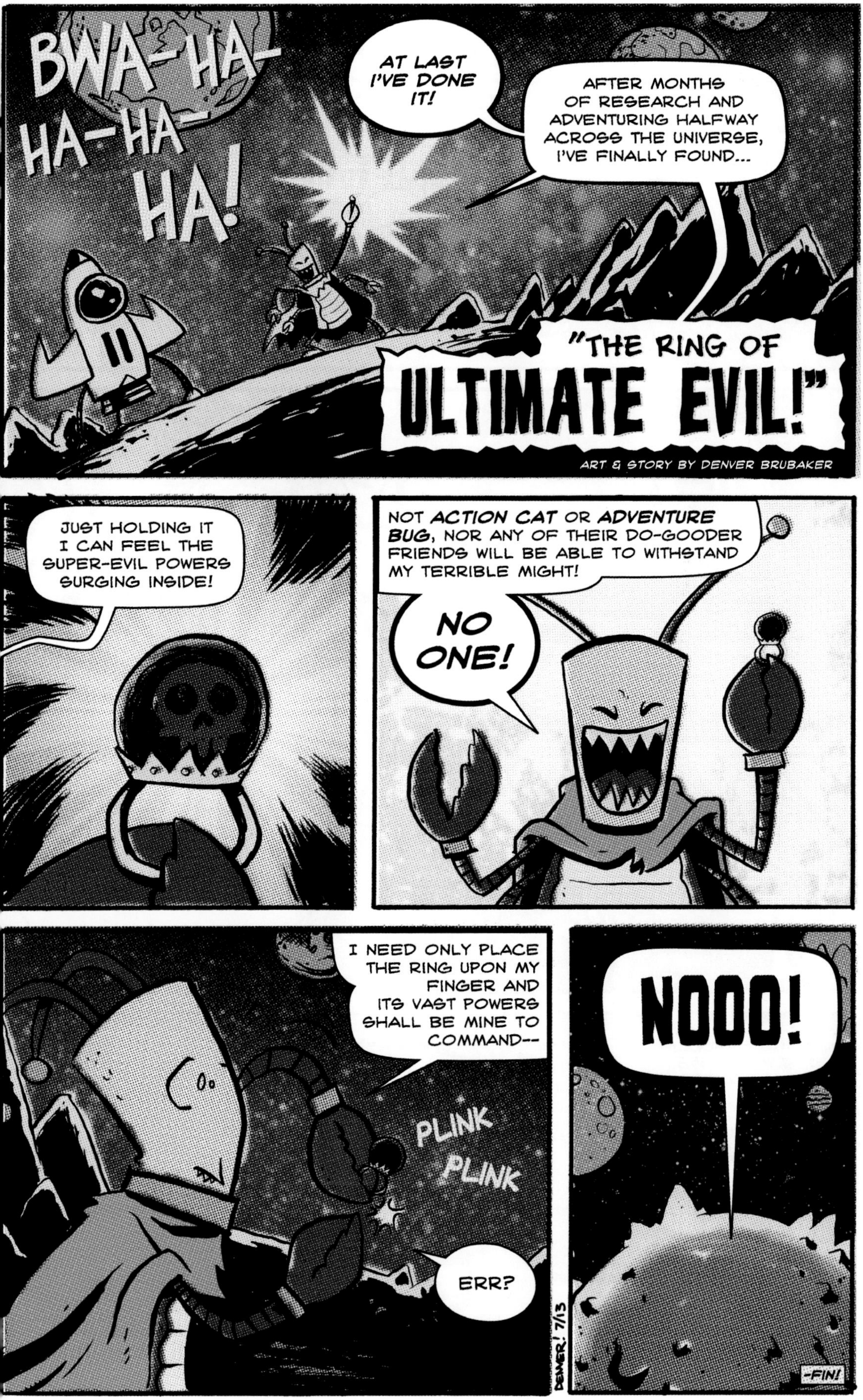
BWA-HA-HA-HA-HA!
AT LAST I'VE DONE IT!
AFTER MONTHS OF RESEARCH AND ADVENTURING HALFWAY ACROSS THE UNIVERSE, I'VE FINALLY FOUND...
"THE RING OF ULTIMATE EVIL!"
ART & STORY BY DENVER BRUBAKER
JUST HOLDING IT I CAN FEEL THE SUPER-EVIL POWERS SURGING INSIDE!
NOT ACTION CAT OR ADVENTURE BUG, NOR ANY OF THEIR DO-GOODER FRIENDS WILL BE ABLE TO WITHSTAND MY TERRIBLE MIGHT!
NO ONE!
I NEED ONLY PLACE THE RING UPON MY FINGER AND ITS VAST POWERS SHALL BE MINE TO COMMAND--
PLINK
PLINK
ERR?
DENVER! 7/13
NOOO!
-FIN!

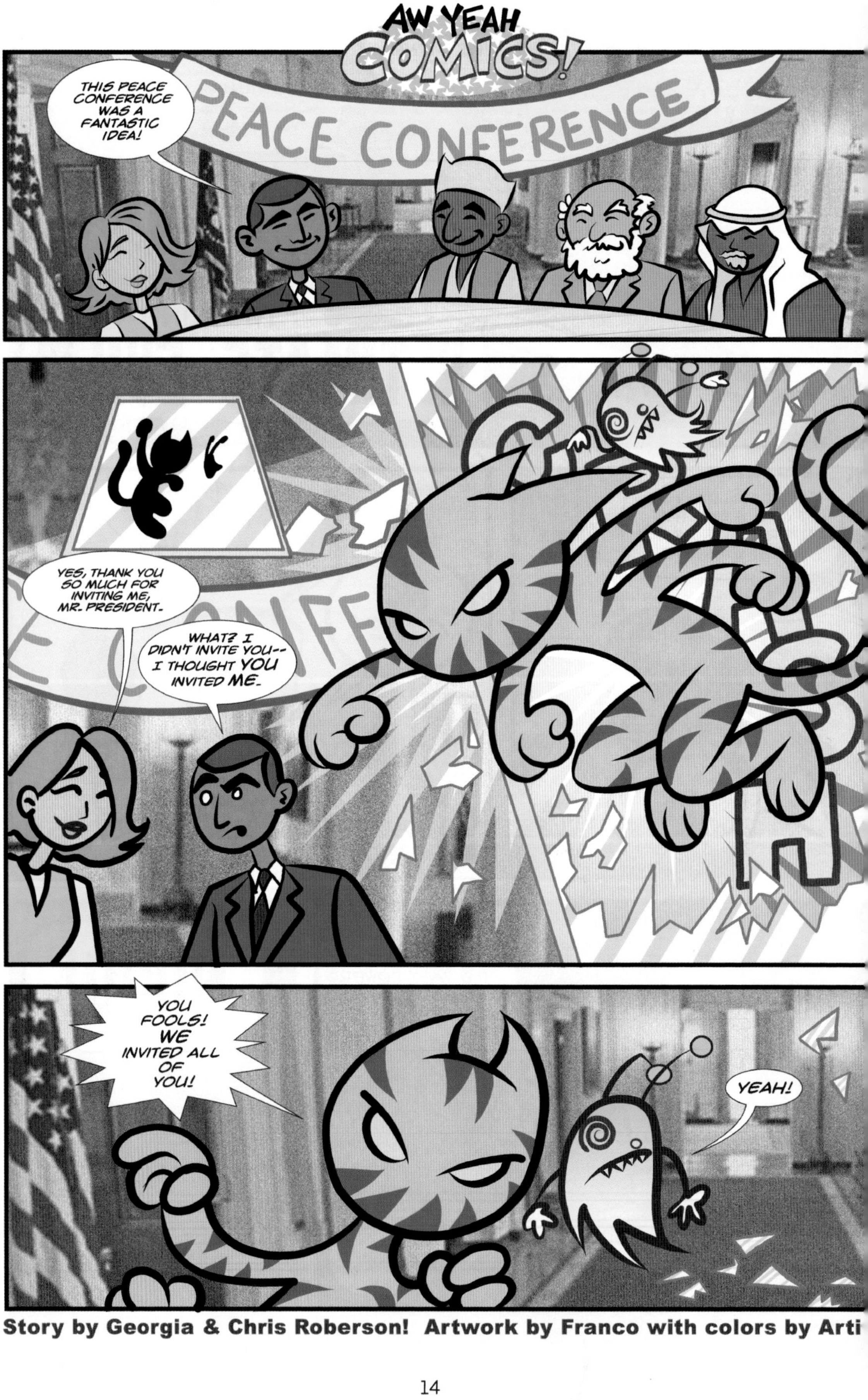
AW YEAH COMICS!
THIS PEACE CONFERENCE WAS A FANTASTIC IDEA!
PEACE CONFERENCE
YES, THANK YOU SO MUCH FOR INVITING ME, MR. PRESIDENT.
WHAT? I DIDN'T INVITE YOU-- I THOUGHT YOU INVITED ME.
YOU FOOLS! WE INVITED ALL OF YOU!
YEAH!

Story by Georgia & Chris Roberson! Artwork by Franco with colors by Arti

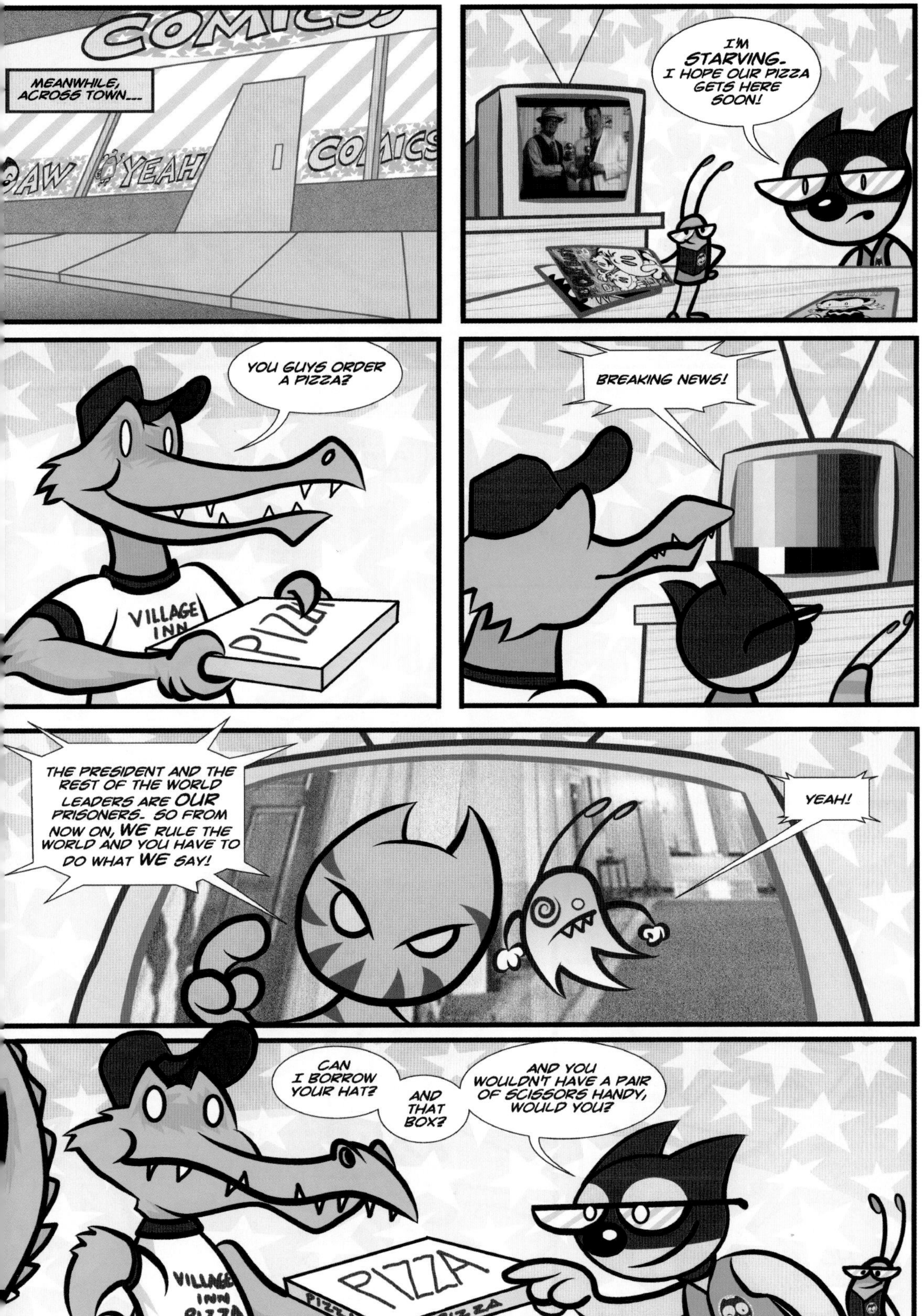
COMICS
MEANWHILE, ACROSS TOWN...
AW YEAH COMICS
I'M STARVING. I HOPE OUR PIZZA GETS HERE SOON!
YOU GUYS ORDER A PIZZA?
VILLAGE INN
PIZZA
BREAKING NEWS!
THE PRESIDENT AND THE REST OF THE WORLD LEADERS ARE OUR PRISONERS. SO FROM NOW ON, WE RULE THE WORLD AND YOU HAVE TO DO WHAT WE SAY!
YEAH!
CAN I BORROW YOUR HAT?
AND THAT BOX?
AND YOU WOULDN'T HAVE A PAIR OF SCISSORS HANDY, WOULD YOU?
VILLAGE INN PIZZA
PIZZA

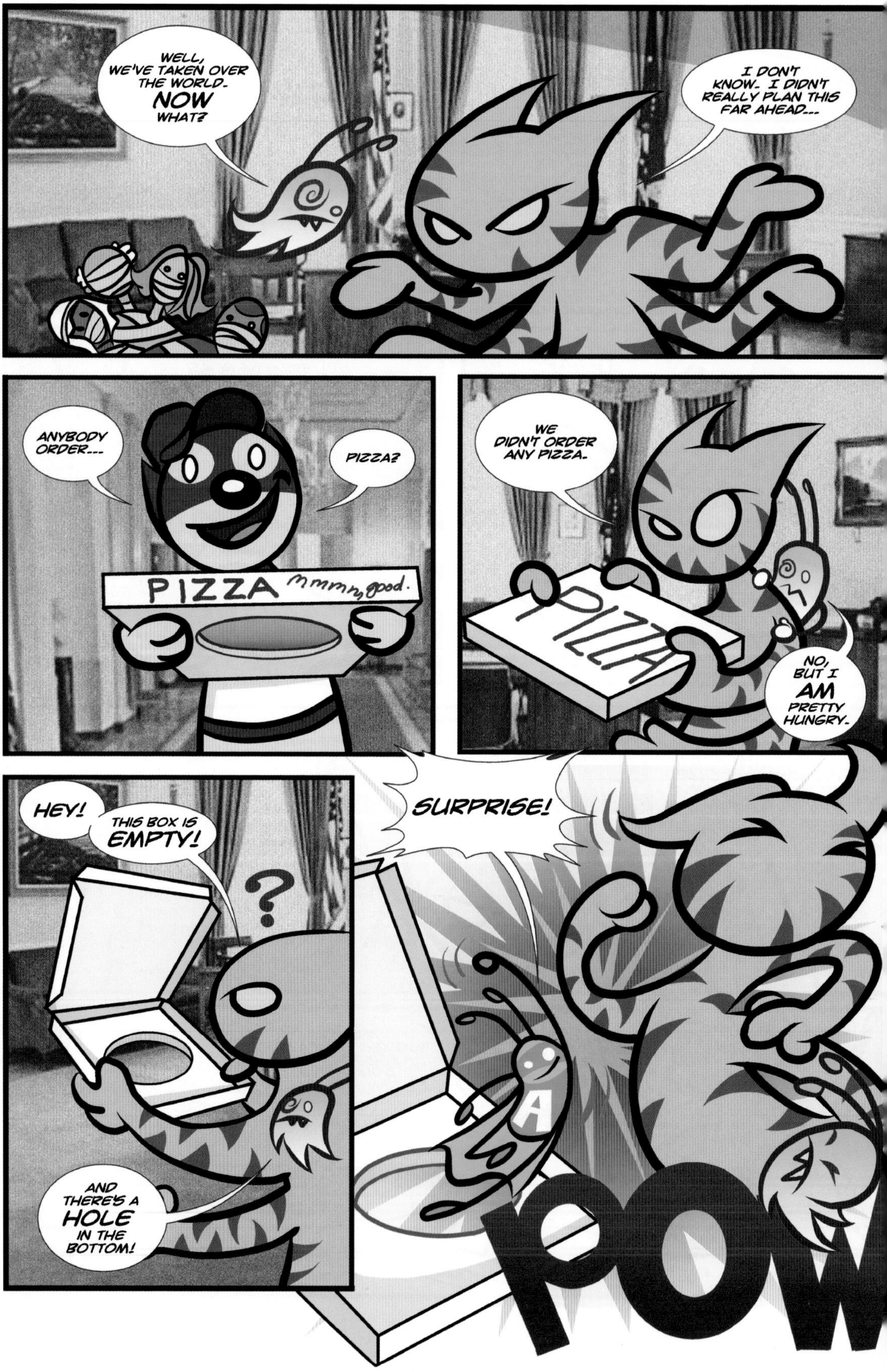
WELL, WE'VE TAKEN OVER THE WORLD. NOW WHAT?
I DON'T KNOW. I DIDN'T REALLY PLAN THIS FAR AHEAD...
ANYBODY ORDER...
PIZZA?
PIZZA mmmm, good.
WE DIDN'T ORDER ANY PIZZA.
PIZZA
NO, BUT I AM PRETTY HUNGRY.
HEY!
THIS BOX IS EMPTY!
?
AND THERE'S A HOLE IN THE BOTTOM!
SURPRISE!
A
POW

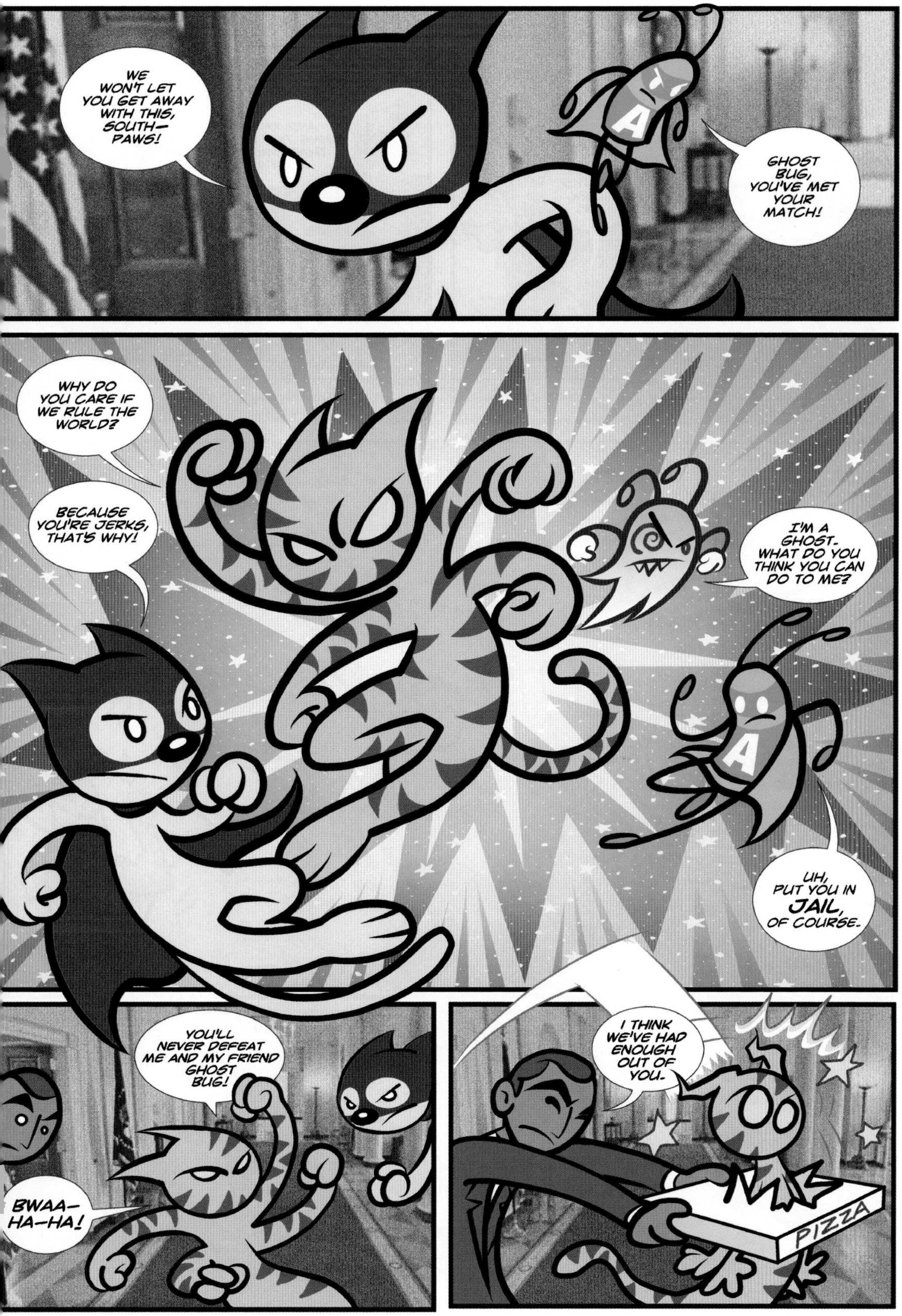

WE WON'T LET YOU GET AWAY WITH THIS, SOUTH-PAWS!
GHOST BUG, YOU'VE MET YOUR MATCH!
WHY DO YOU CARE IF WE RULE THE WORLD?
BECAUSE YOU'RE JERKS, THAT'S WHY!
I'M A GHOST- WHAT DO YOU THINK YOU CAN DO TO ME?
UH, PUT YOU IN JAIL, OF COURSE.
YOU'LL NEVER DEFEAT ME AND MY FRIEND GHOST BUG!
BWAA-HA-HA!
I THINK WE'VE HAD ENOUGH OUT OF YOU.
PIZZA

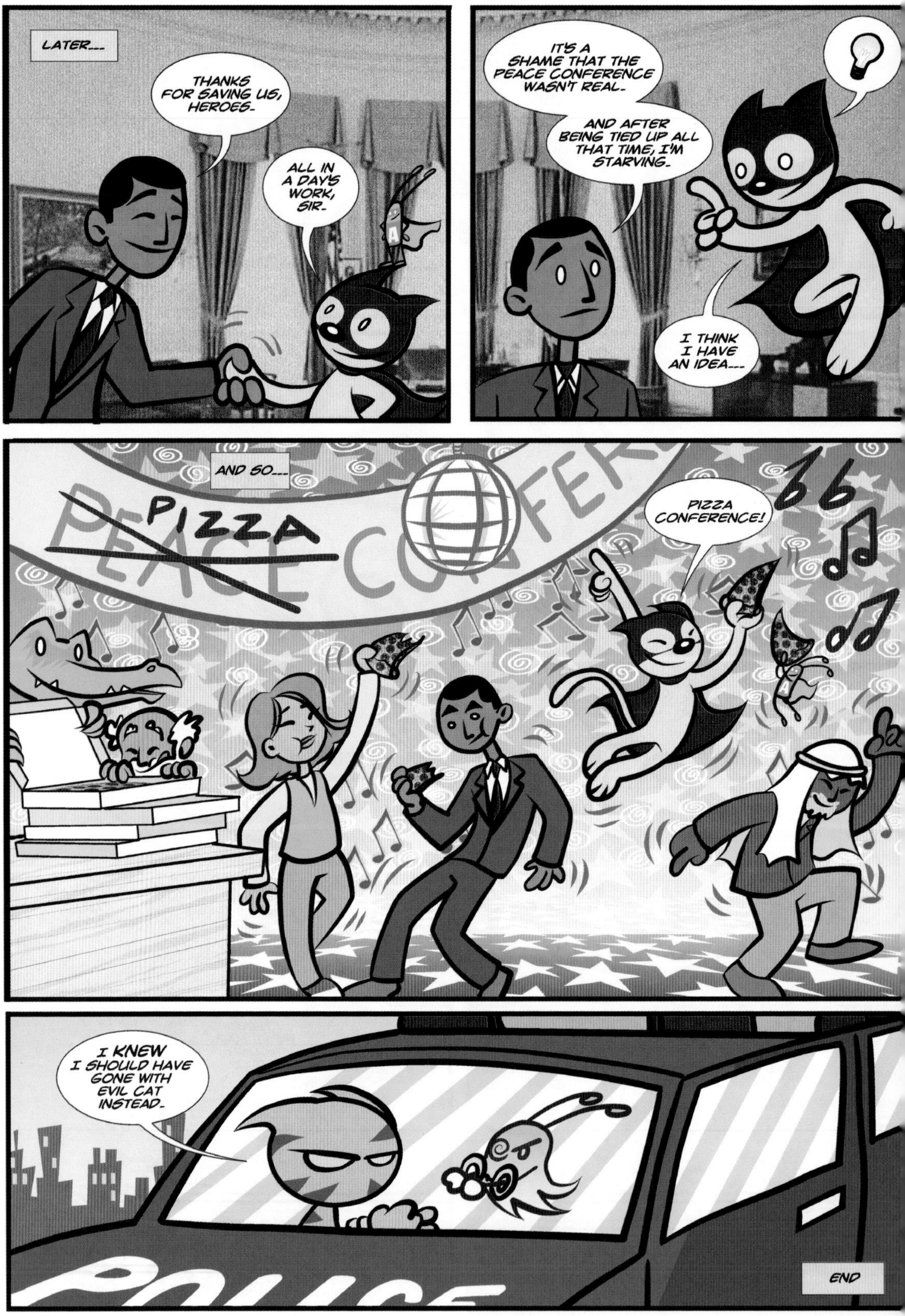
LATER...
THANKS FOR SAVING US, HEROES.
ALL IN A DAY'S WORK, SIR.
IT'S A SHAME THAT THE PEACE CONFERENCE WASN'T REAL.
AND AFTER BEING TIED UP ALL THAT TIME, I'M STARVING.
I THINK I HAVE AN IDEA...
AND SO...
PEACE PIZZA CONFER
PIZZA CONFERENCE!
I KNEW I SHOULD HAVE GONE WITH EVIL CAT INSTEAD.
POLICE
END

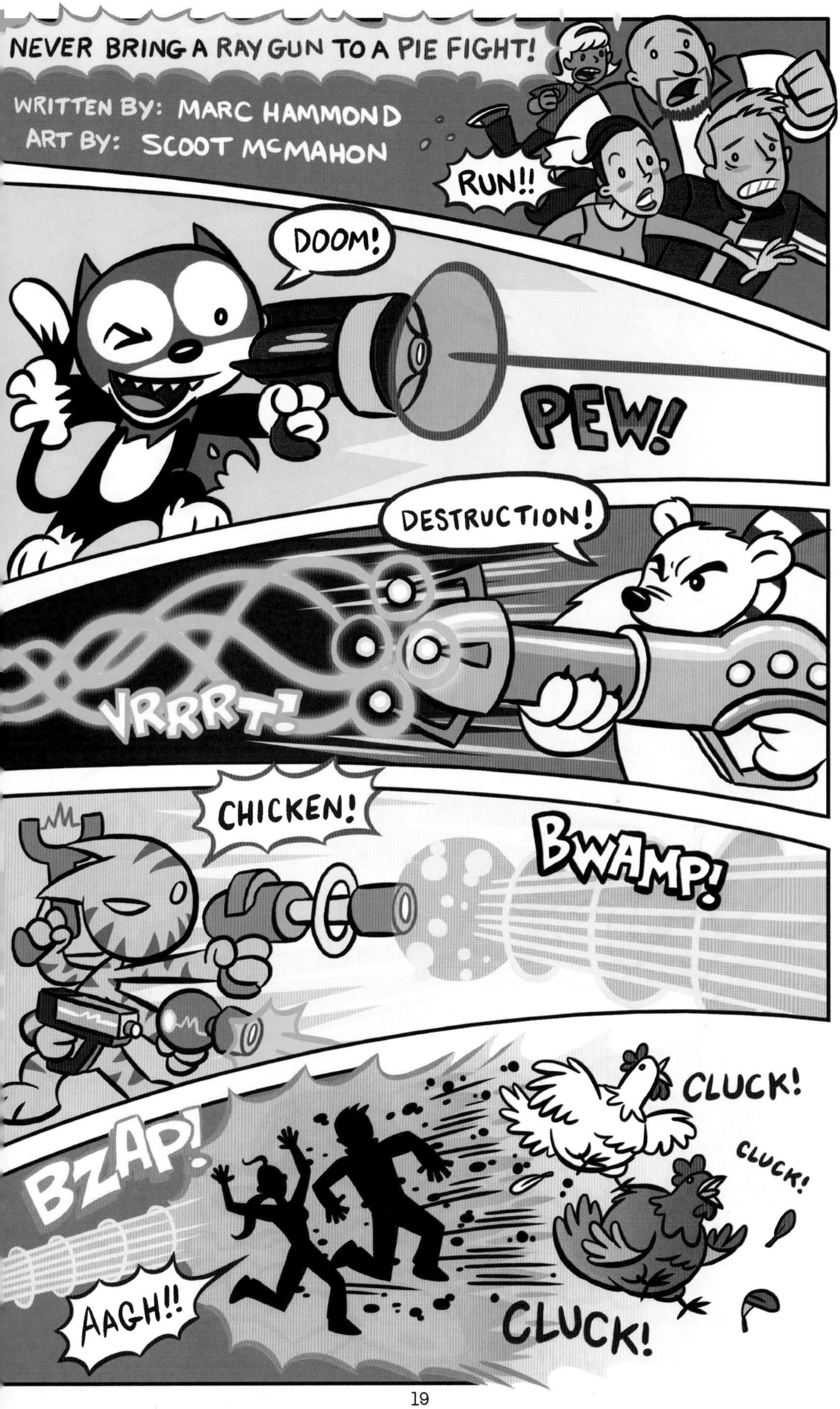

NEVER BRING A RAY GUN TO A PIE FIGHT!
WRITTEN BY: MARC HAMMOND
ART BY: SCOOT MCMAHON
RUN!!
DOOM!
PEW!
DESTRUCTION!
VRRRT!
CHICKEN!
BWAMP!
BZAP!
CLUCK!
CLUCK!
AAGH!!
CLUCK!

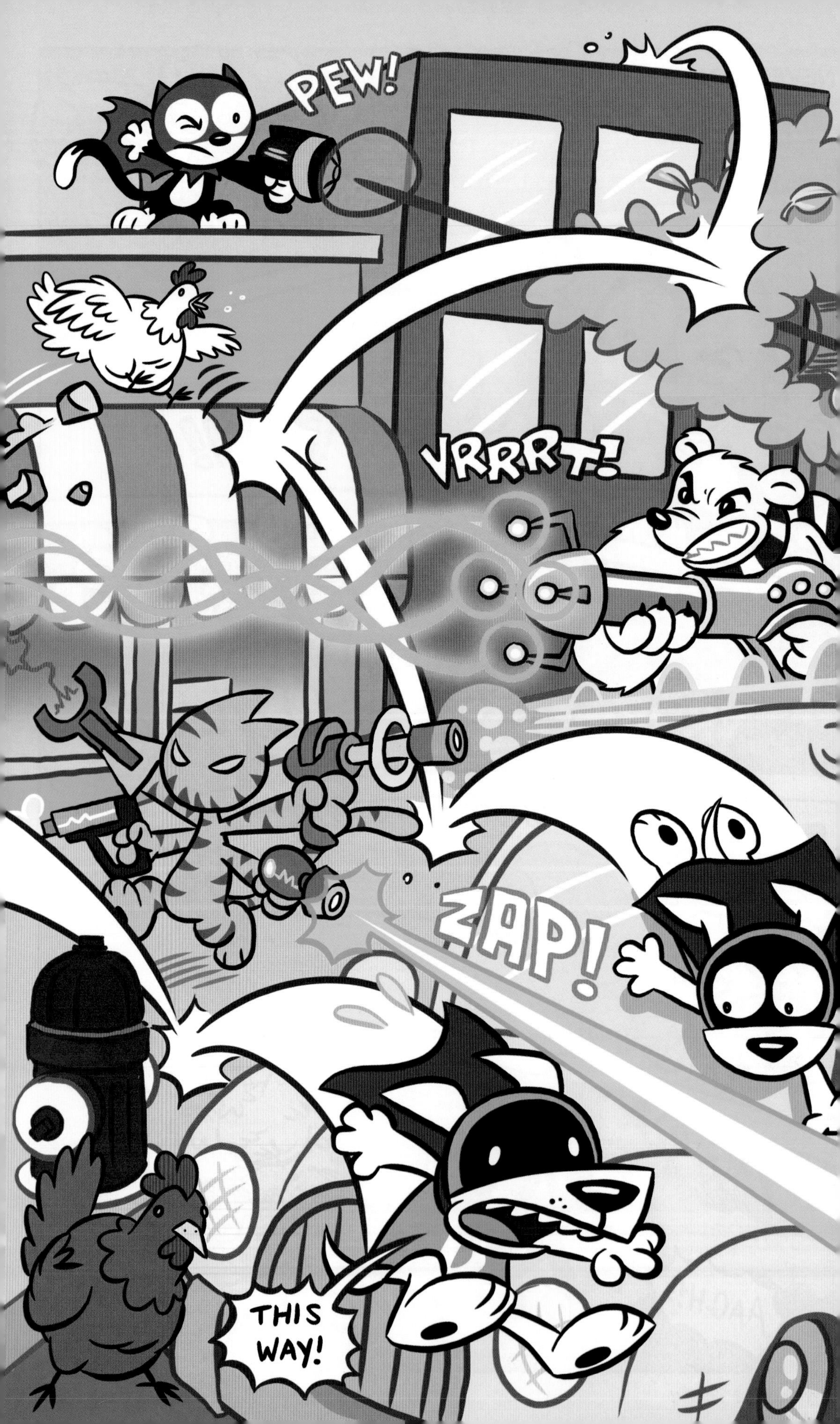
PEW!
VRRRT!
ZAP!
THIS WAY!

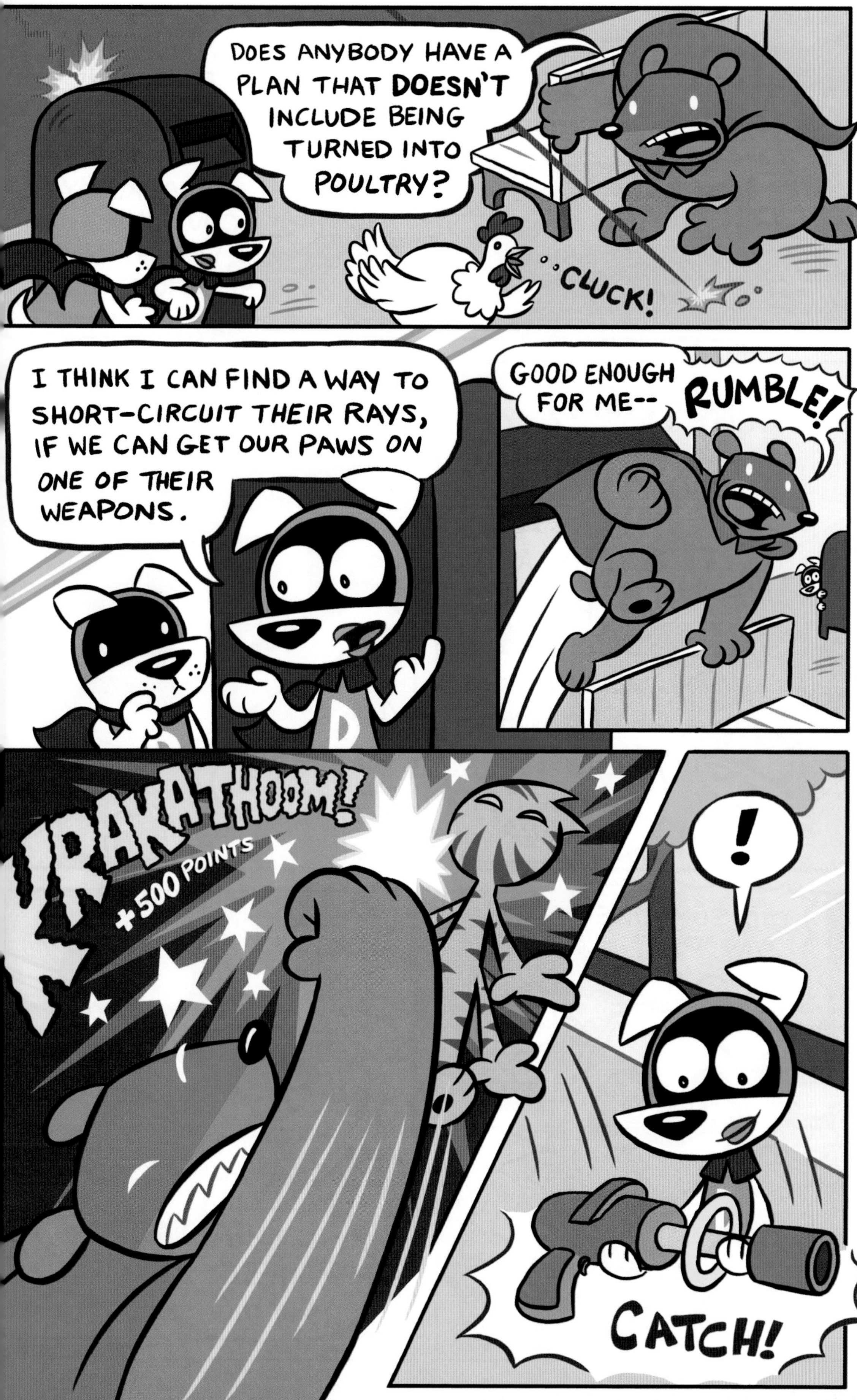
DOES ANYBODY HAVE A PLAN THAT **DOESN'T** INCLUDE BEING TURNED INTO POULTRY?
CLUCK!
I THINK I CAN FIND A WAY TO SHORT-CIRCUIT THEIR RAYS, IF WE CAN GET OUR PAWS ON ONE OF THEIR WEAPONS.
GOOD ENOUGH FOR ME--
RUMBLE!
KRAKATHOOM!
+500 POINTS
!
CATCH!

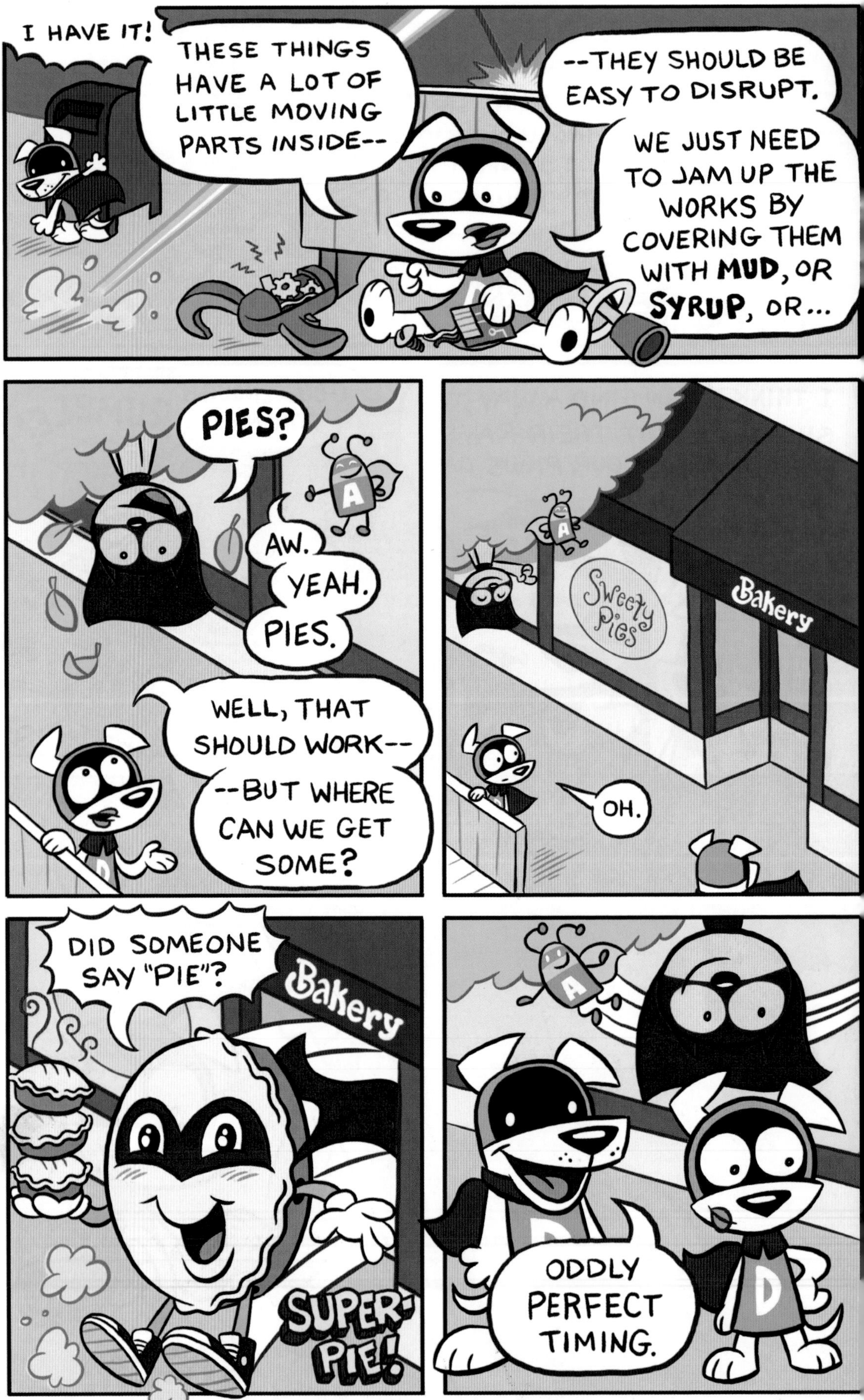
I HAVE IT!
THESE THINGS HAVE A LOT OF LITTLE MOVING PARTS INSIDE--
--THEY SHOULD BE EASY TO DISRUPT.
WE JUST NEED TO JAM UP THE WORKS BY COVERING THEM WITH MUD, OR SYRUP, OR...
PIES?
AW.
YEAH.
PIES.
WELL, THAT SHOULD WORK--
--BUT WHERE CAN WE GET SOME?
Sweety Pies
Bakery
OH.
DID SOMEONE SAY "PIE"?
Bakery
SUPER-PIE!
ODDLY PERFECT TIMING.

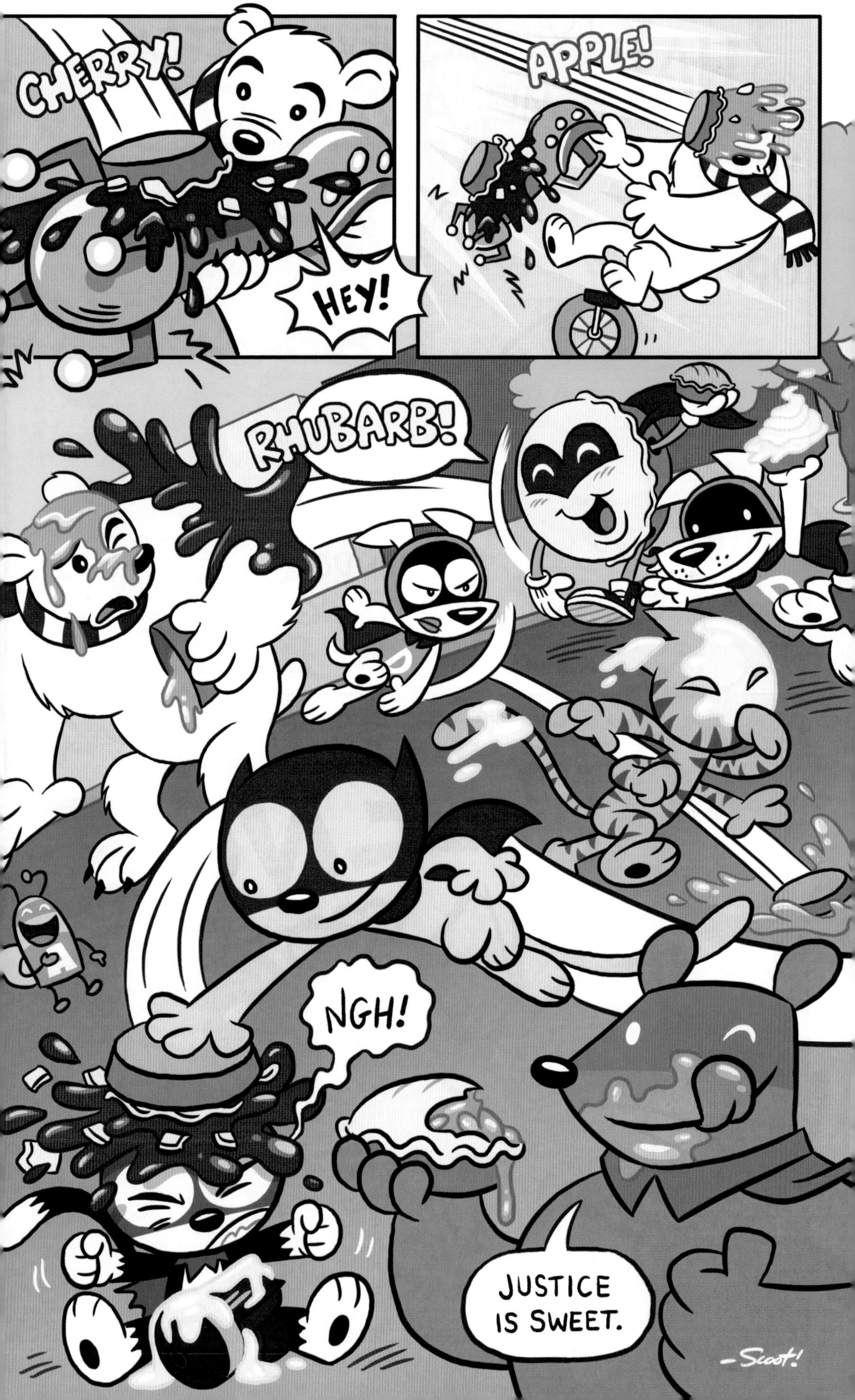
CHERRY!
HEY!
APPLE!
RHUBARB!
NGH!
JUSTICE IS SWEET.
-Scoot!

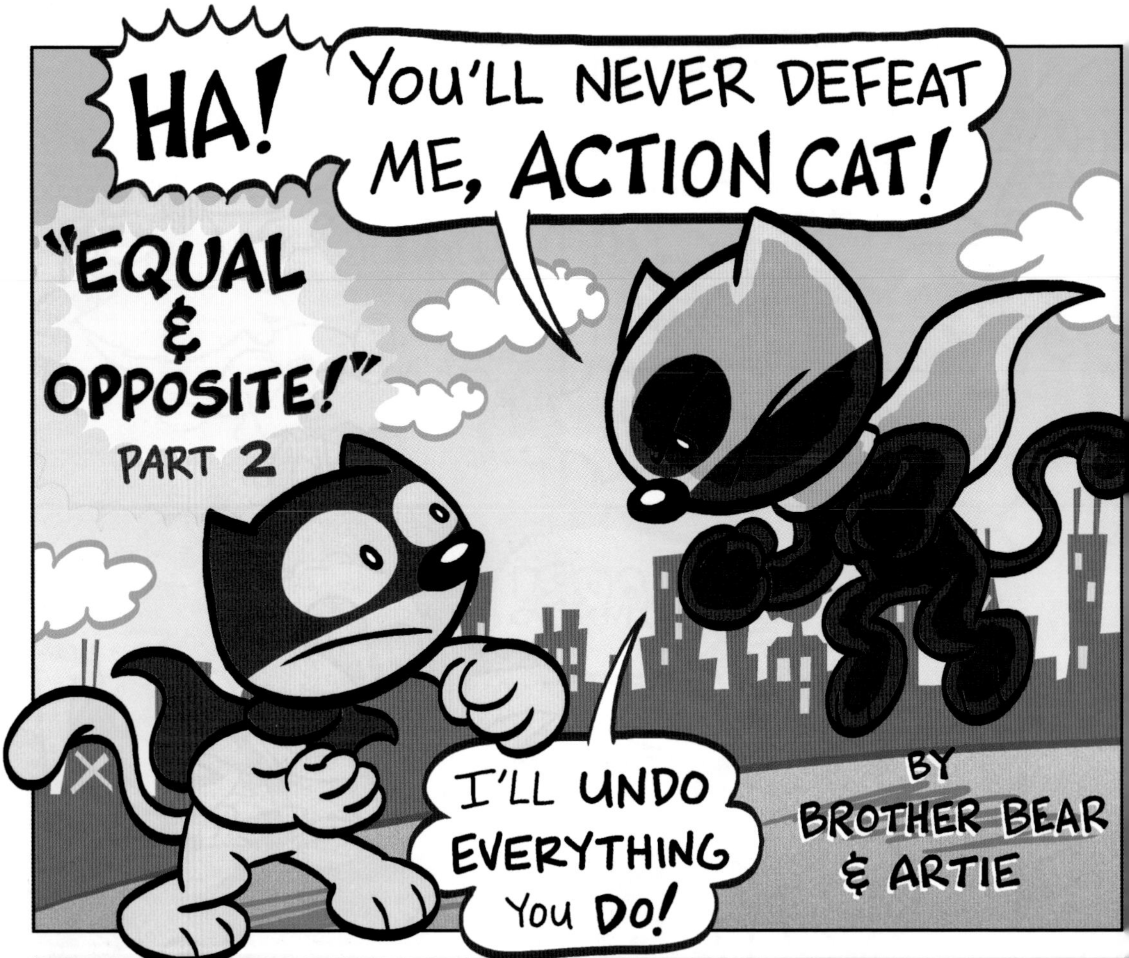
HA!
YOU'LL NEVER DEFEAT ME, ACTION CAT!
"EQUAL & OPPOSITE!"
PART 2
I'LL UNDO EVERYTHING YOU DO!
BY BROTHER BEAR & ARTIE

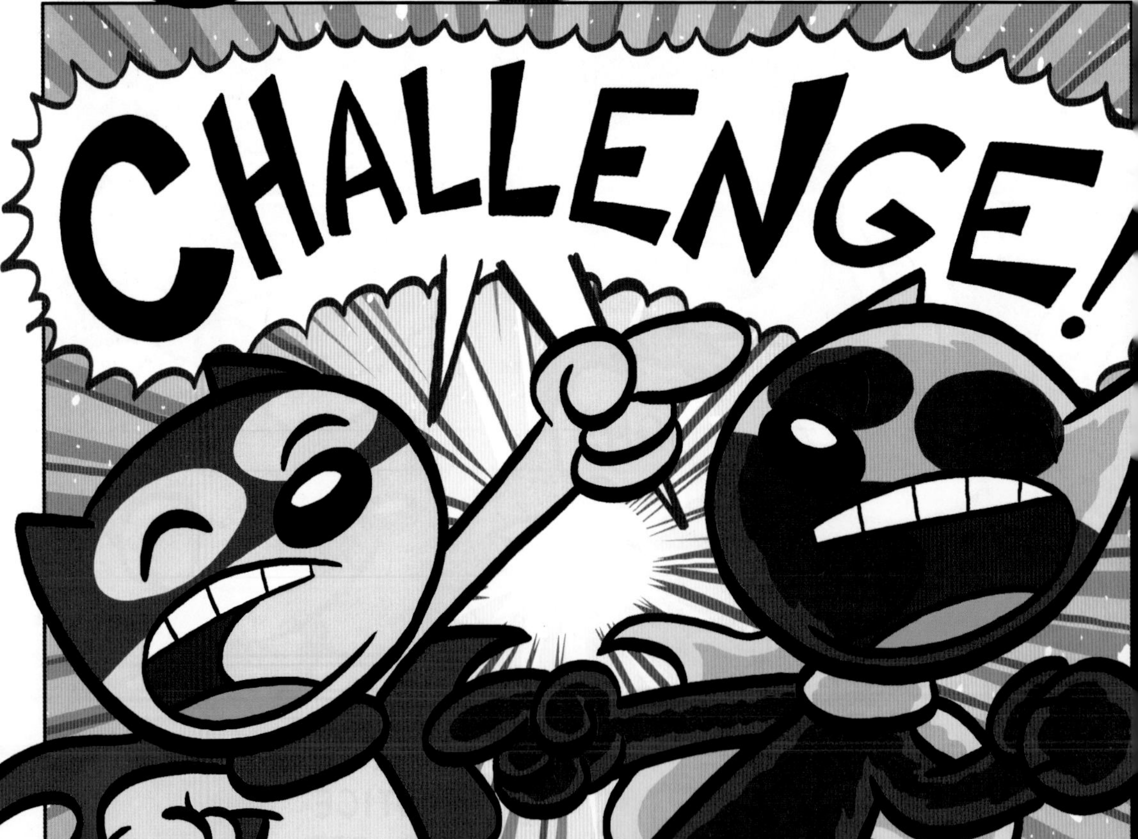
CHALLENGE!

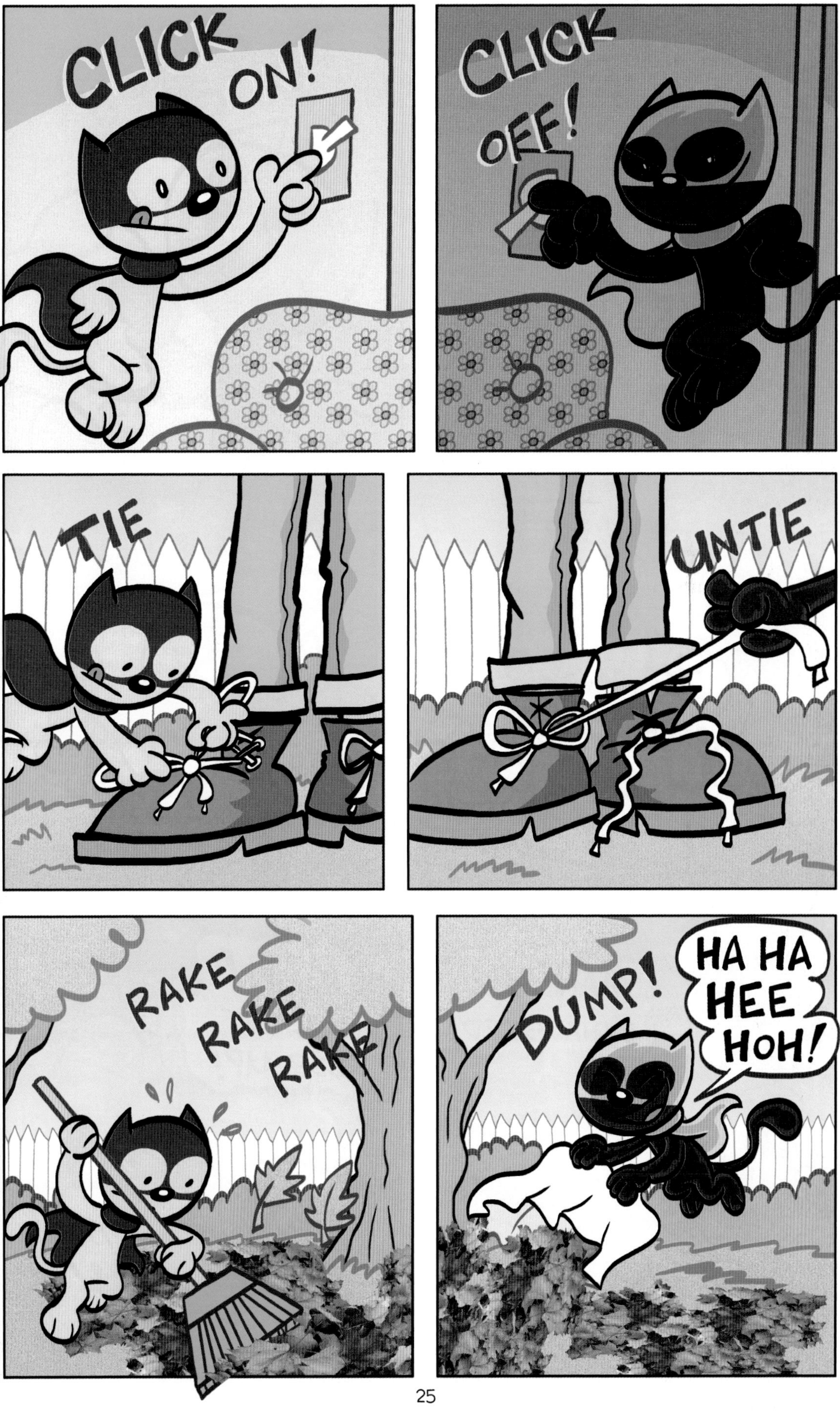
CLICK ON!
CLICK OFF!
TIE
UNTIE
RAKE RAKE RAKE
DUMP!
HA HA HEE HOH!

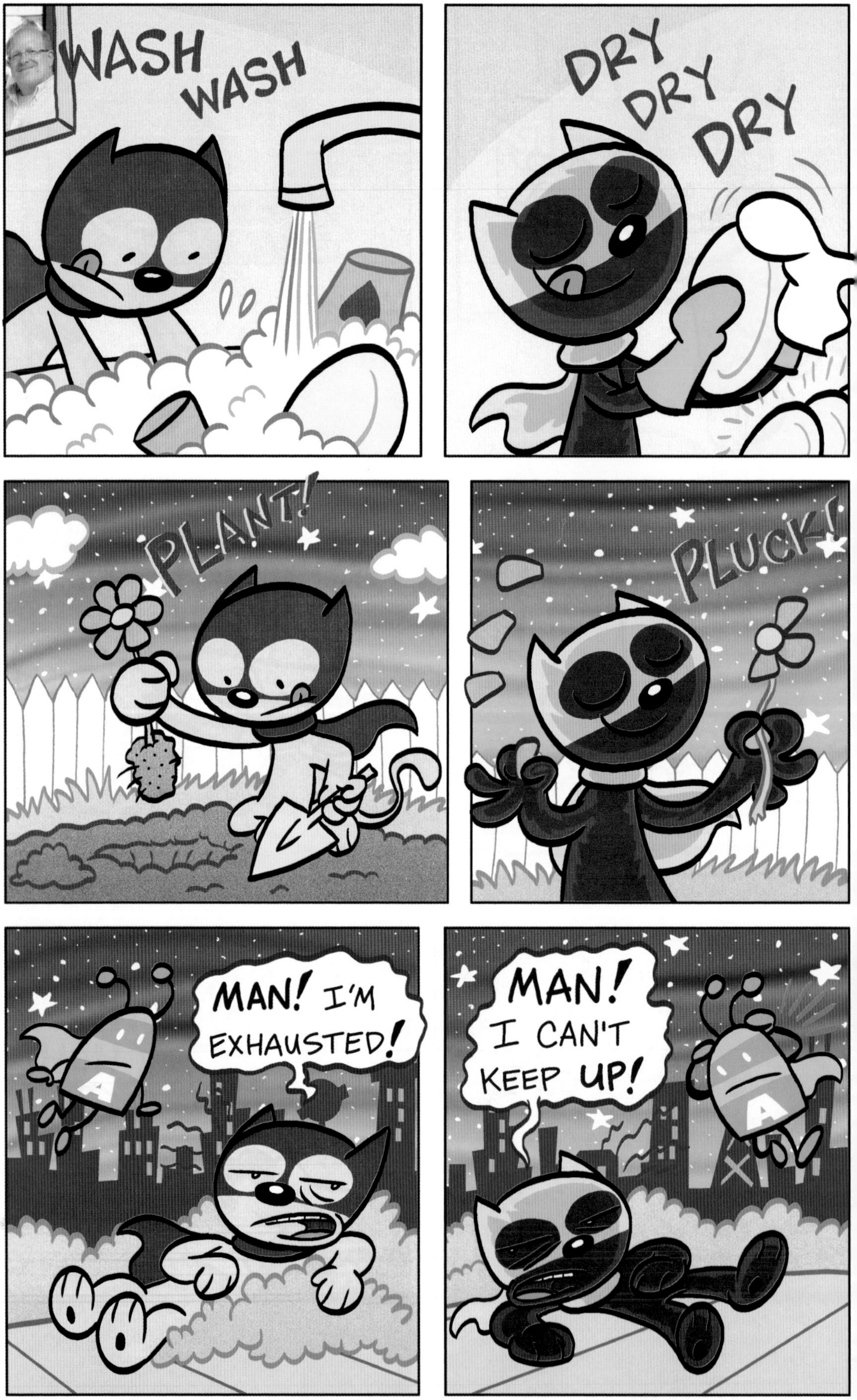
WASH
WASH
DRY
DRY
DRY
PLANT!
PLUCK!
MAN! I'M EXHAUSTED!
MAN! I CAN'T KEEP UP!

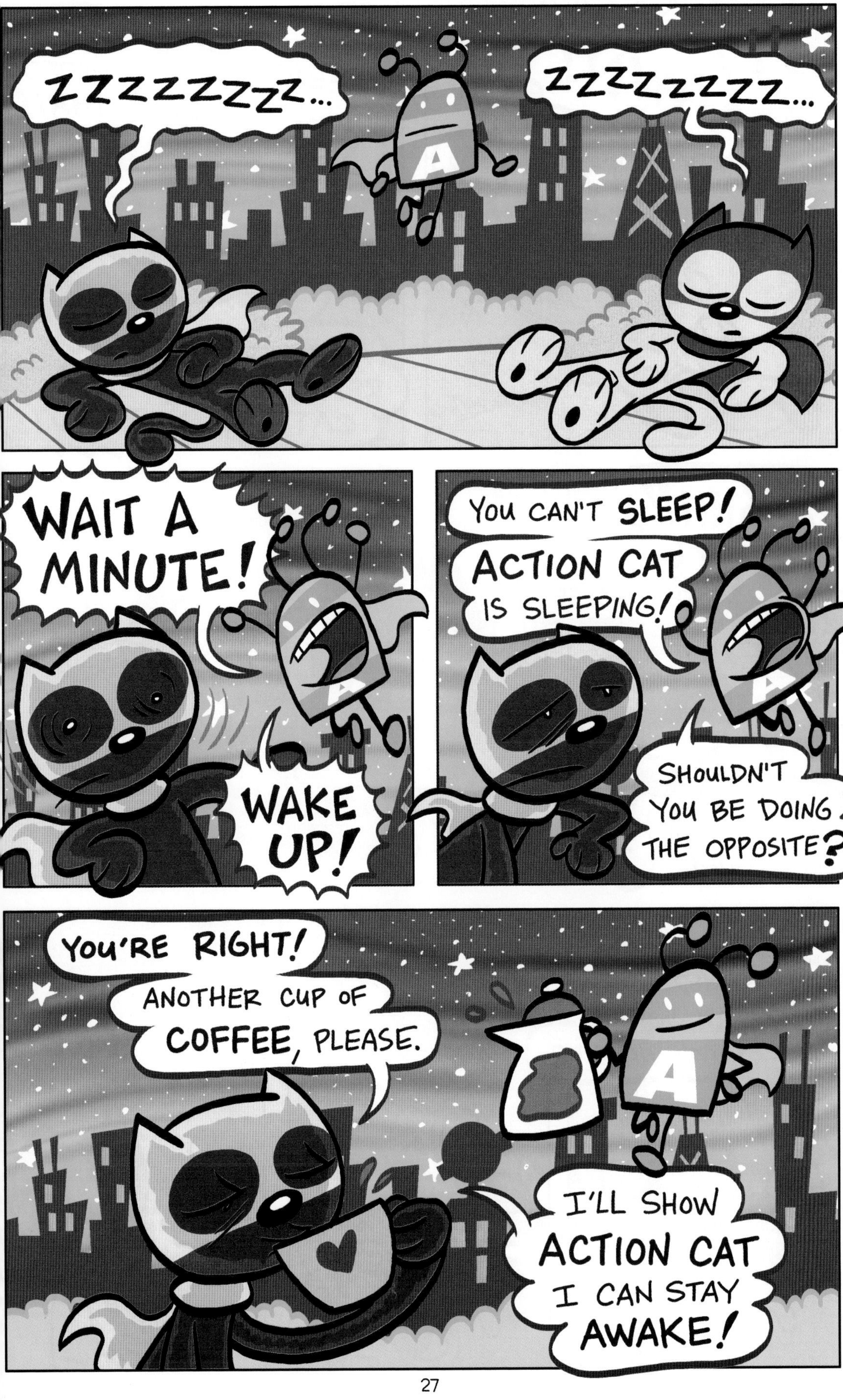
ZZZZZZZZ...
ZZZZZZZZ...
WAIT A MINUTE!
WAKE UP!
YOU CAN'T SLEEP!
ACTION CAT IS SLEEPING!
SHOULDN'T YOU BE DOING THE OPPOSITE?
YOU'RE RIGHT!
ANOTHER CUP OF COFFEE, PLEASE.
I'LL SHOW ACTION CAT I CAN STAY AWAKE!

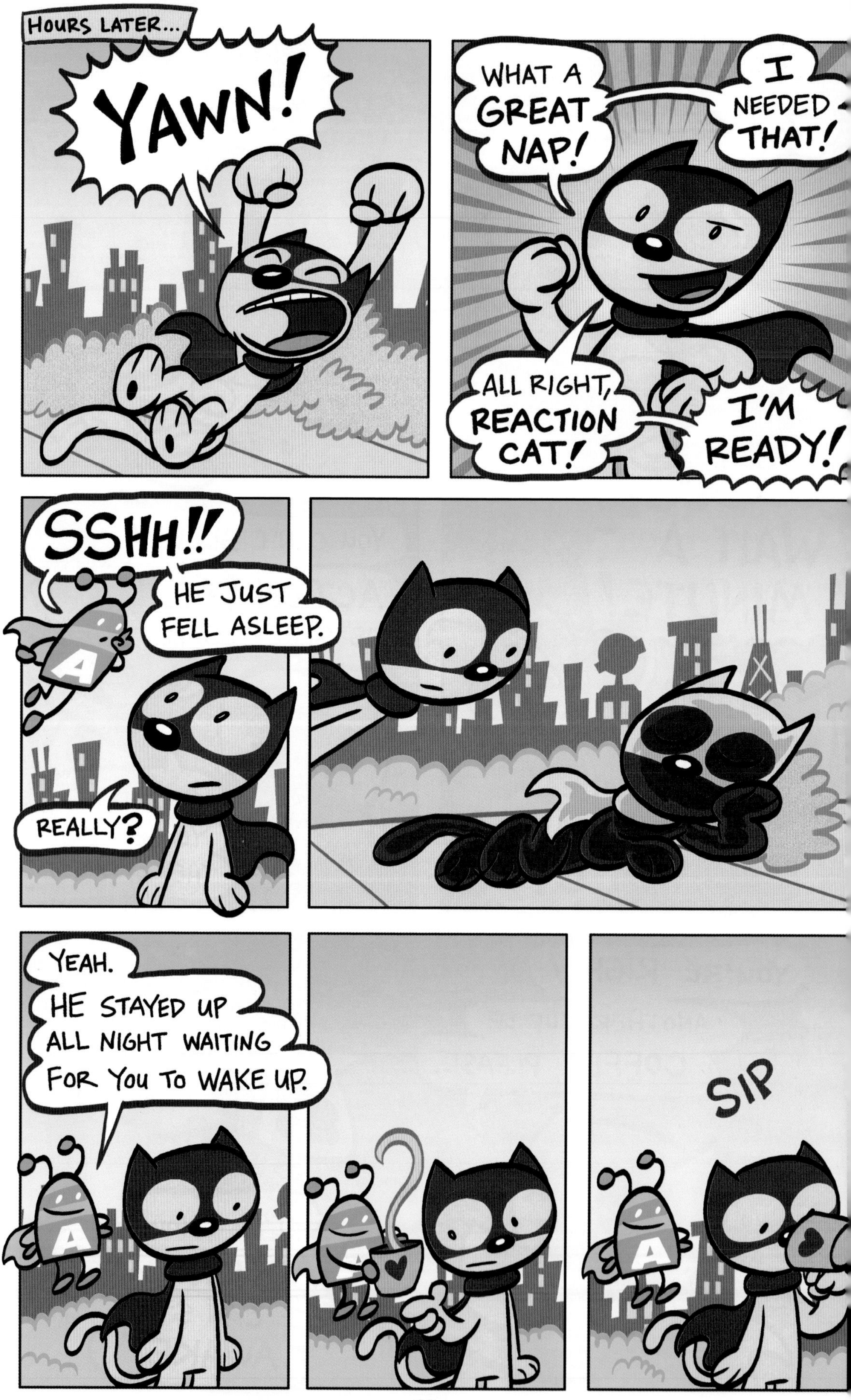
HOURS LATER...
YAWN!
WHAT A GREAT NAP!
I NEEDED THAT!
ALL RIGHT, REACTION CAT!
I'M READY!
SSHH!!
HE JUST FELL ASLEEP.
REALLY?
YEAH.
HE STAYED UP ALL NIGHT WAITING FOR YOU TO WAKE UP.
SIP

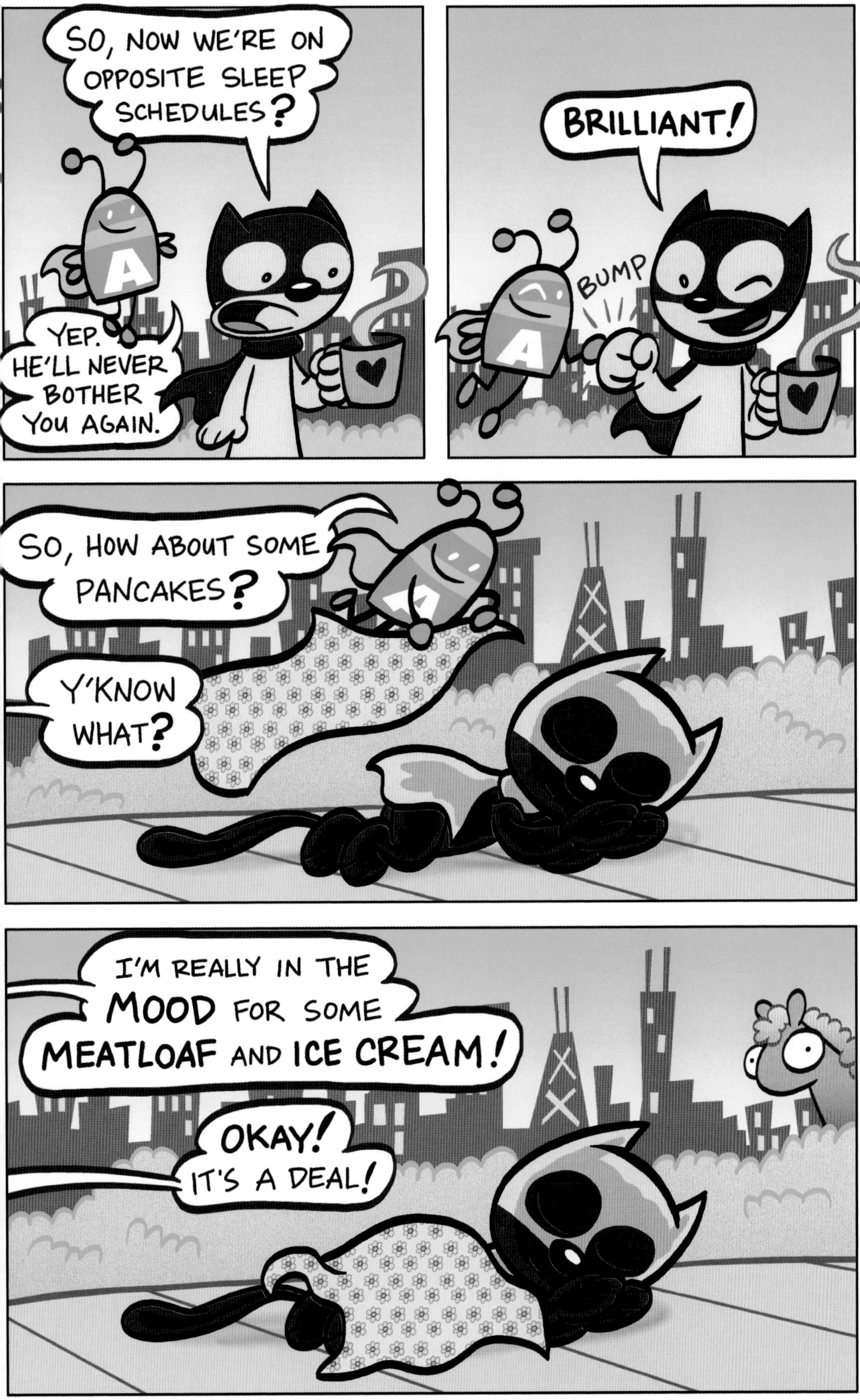
SO, NOW WE'RE ON OPPOSITE SLEEP SCHEDULES?
YEP. HE'LL NEVER BOTHER YOU AGAIN.
BRILLIANT!
BUMP
SO, HOW ABOUT SOME PANCAKES?
Y'KNOW WHAT?
I'M REALLY IN THE MOOD FOR SOME MEATLOAF AND ICE CREAM!
OKAY! IT'S A DEAL!

-SSSHH...

★ CHAPTER TWO ★

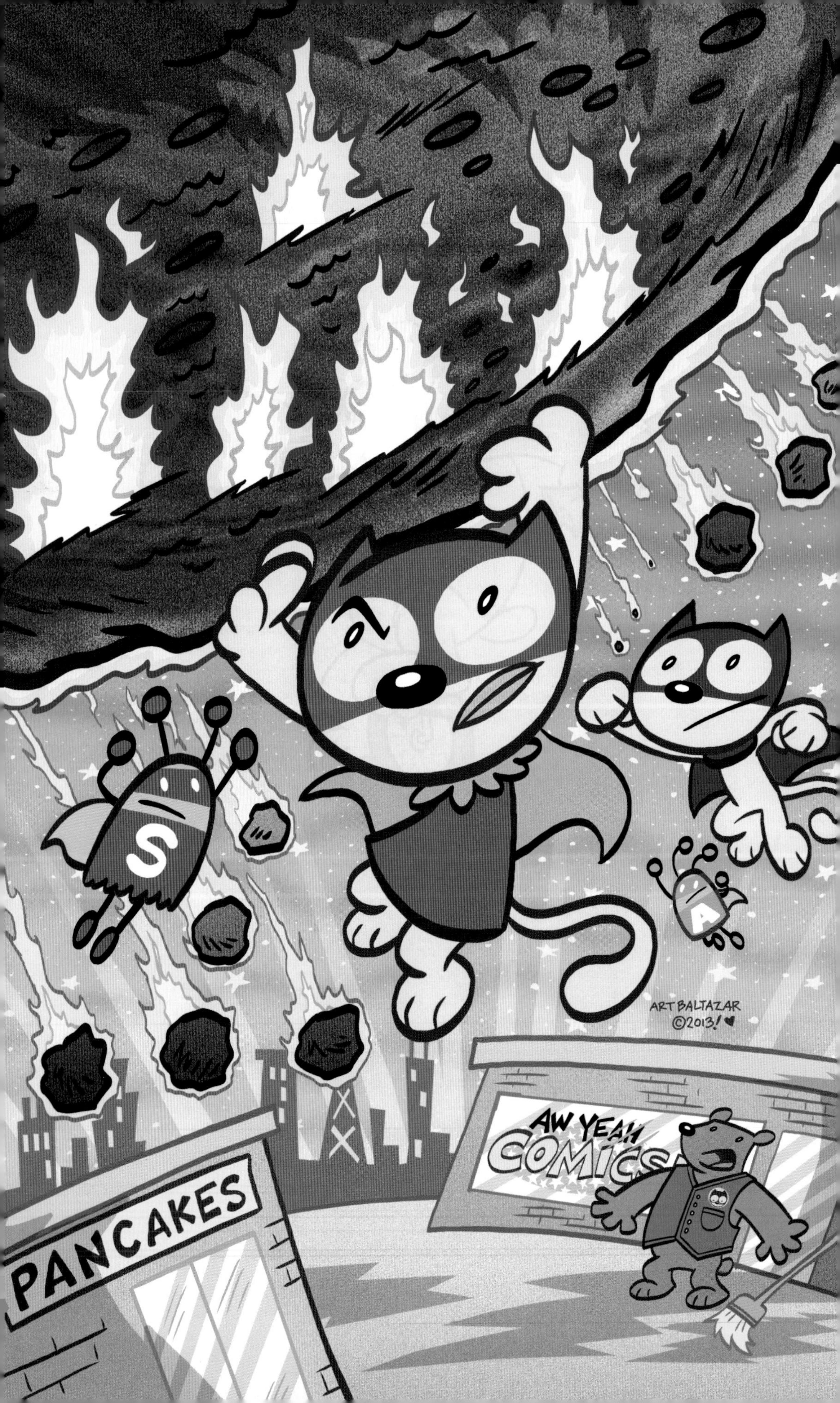

S
A
ART BALTAZAR
©2013!
AW YEAH
COMICS
PANCAKES

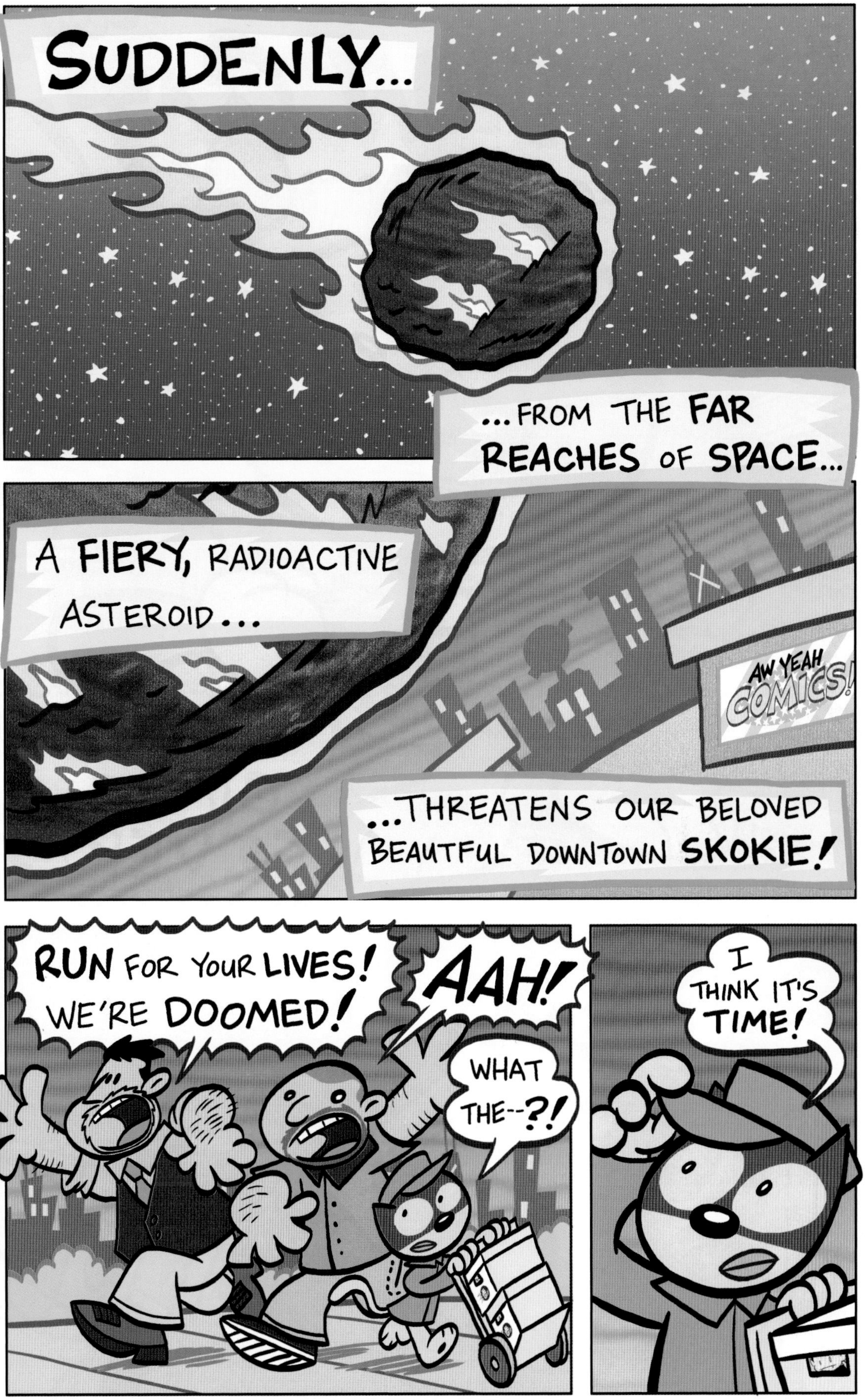
SUDDENLY...
...FROM THE FAR REACHES OF SPACE...
A FIERY, RADIOACTIVE ASTEROID...
AW YEAH COMICS!
...THREATENS OUR BELOVED BEAUTIFUL DOWNTOWN SKOKIE!
RUN FOR YOUR LIVES! WE'RE DOOMED!
AAH!
WHAT THE--?!
I THINK IT'S TIME!

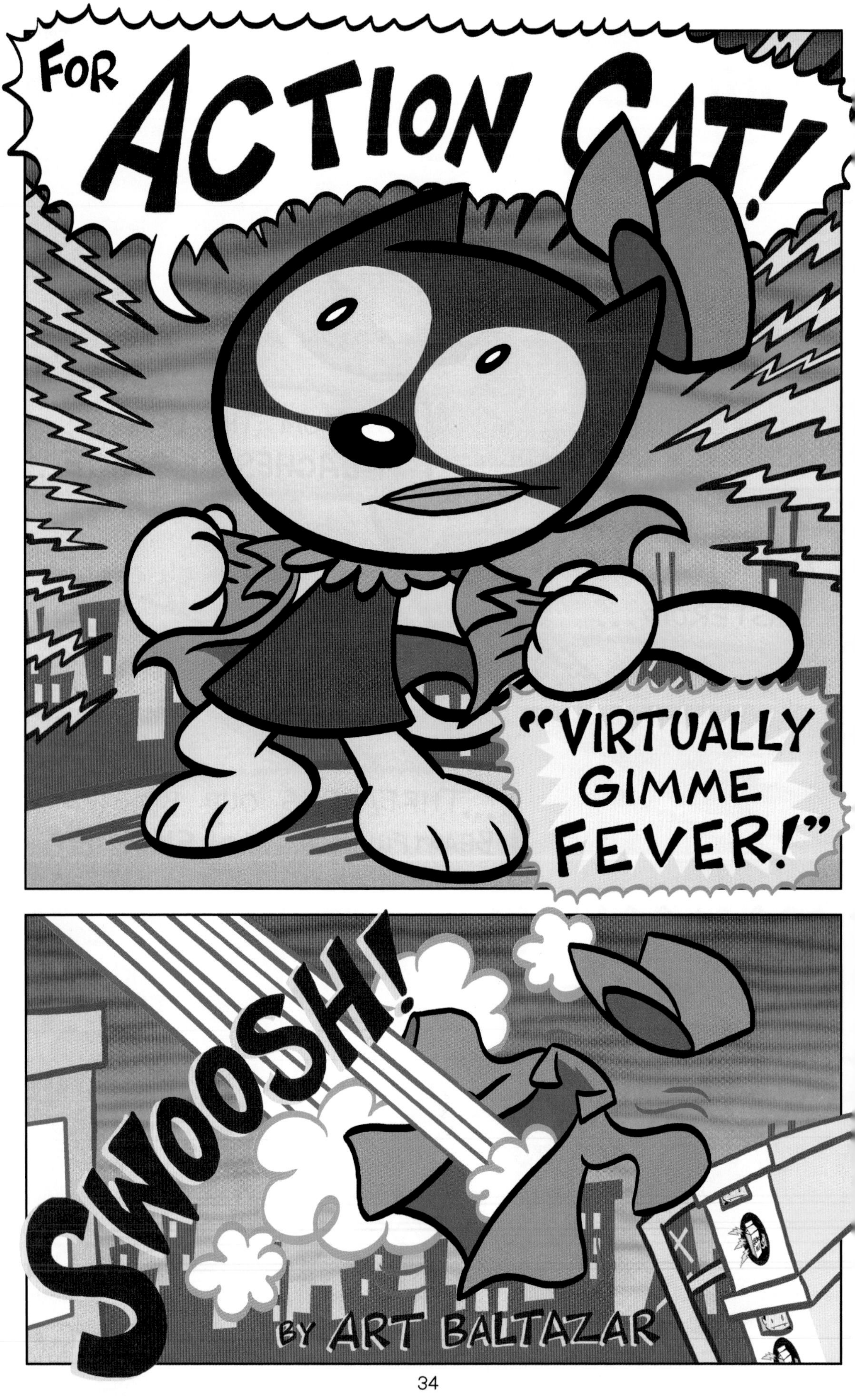
FOR ACTION CAT!
"VIRTUALLY GIMME FEVER!"
SWOOSH!
BY ART BALTAZAR

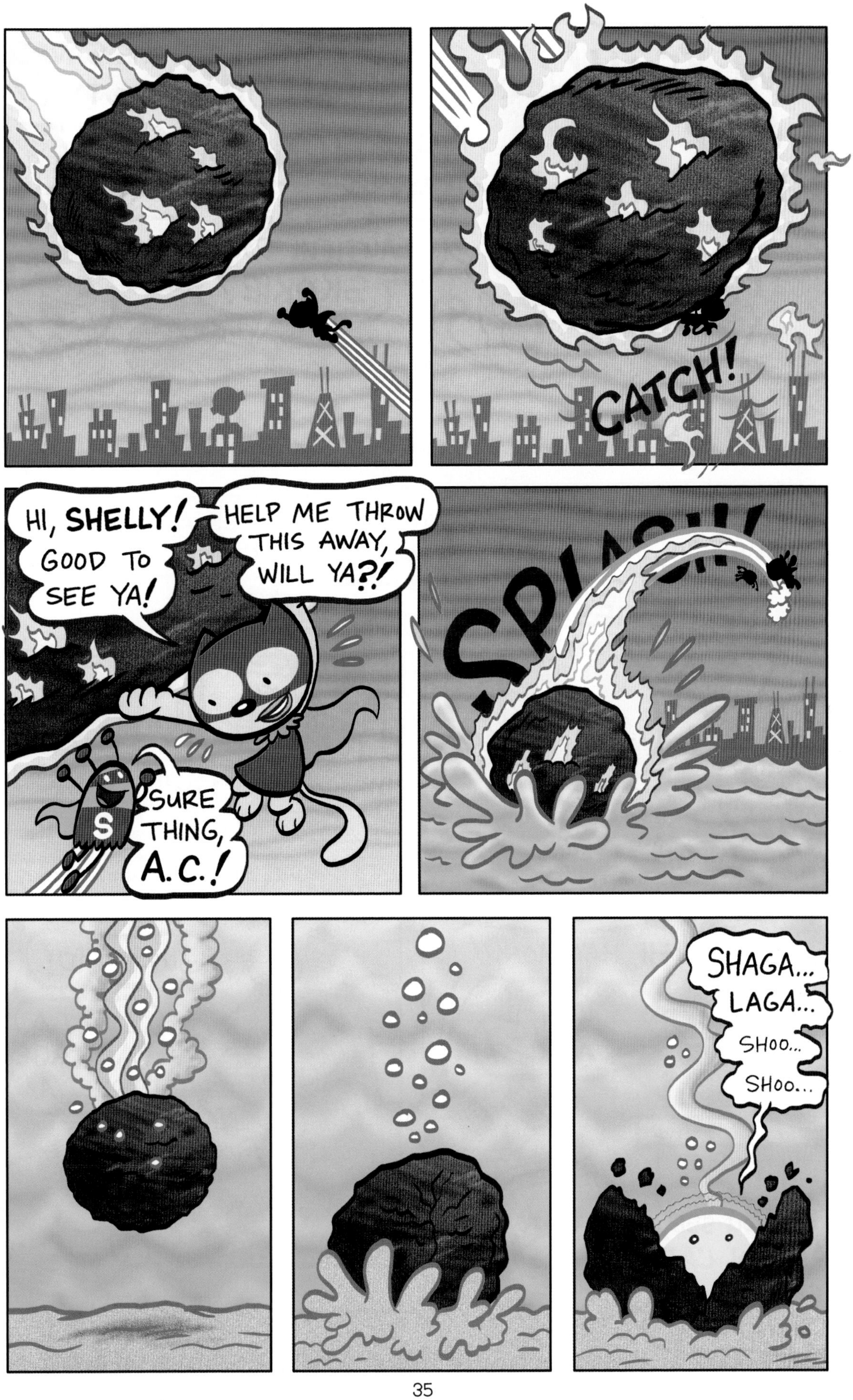
CATCH!
HI, SHELLY! GOOD TO SEE YA!
HELP ME THROW THIS AWAY, WILL YA?!
SURE THING, A.C.!
SPLASH!
SHAGA... LAGA... SHOO... SHOO...

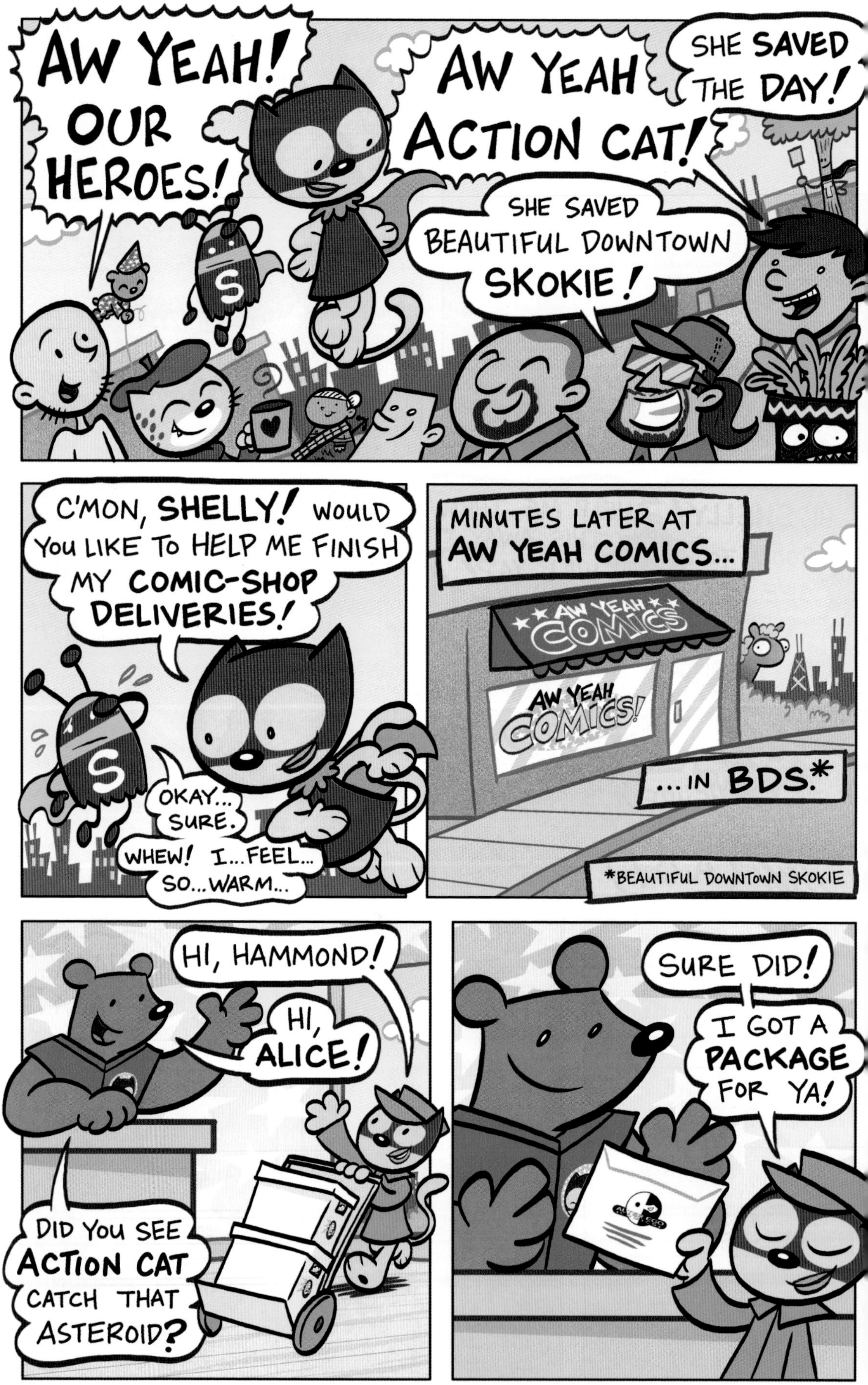
AW YEAH! OUR HEROES!
AW YEAH ACTION CAT!
SHE SAVED THE DAY!
SHE SAVED BEAUTIFUL DOWNTOWN SKOKIE!
C'MON, SHELLY! WOULD YOU LIKE TO HELP ME FINISH MY COMIC-SHOP DELIVERIES!
OKAY... SURE.
WHEW! I...FEEL... SO...WARM...
MINUTES LATER AT AW YEAH COMICS...
AW YEAH COMICS
AW YEAH COMICS!
...IN BDS.*
*BEAUTIFUL DOWNTOWN SKOKIE
HI, HAMMOND!
HI, ALICE!
DID YOU SEE ACTION CAT CATCH THAT ASTEROID?
SURE DID!
I GOT A PACKAGE FOR YA!

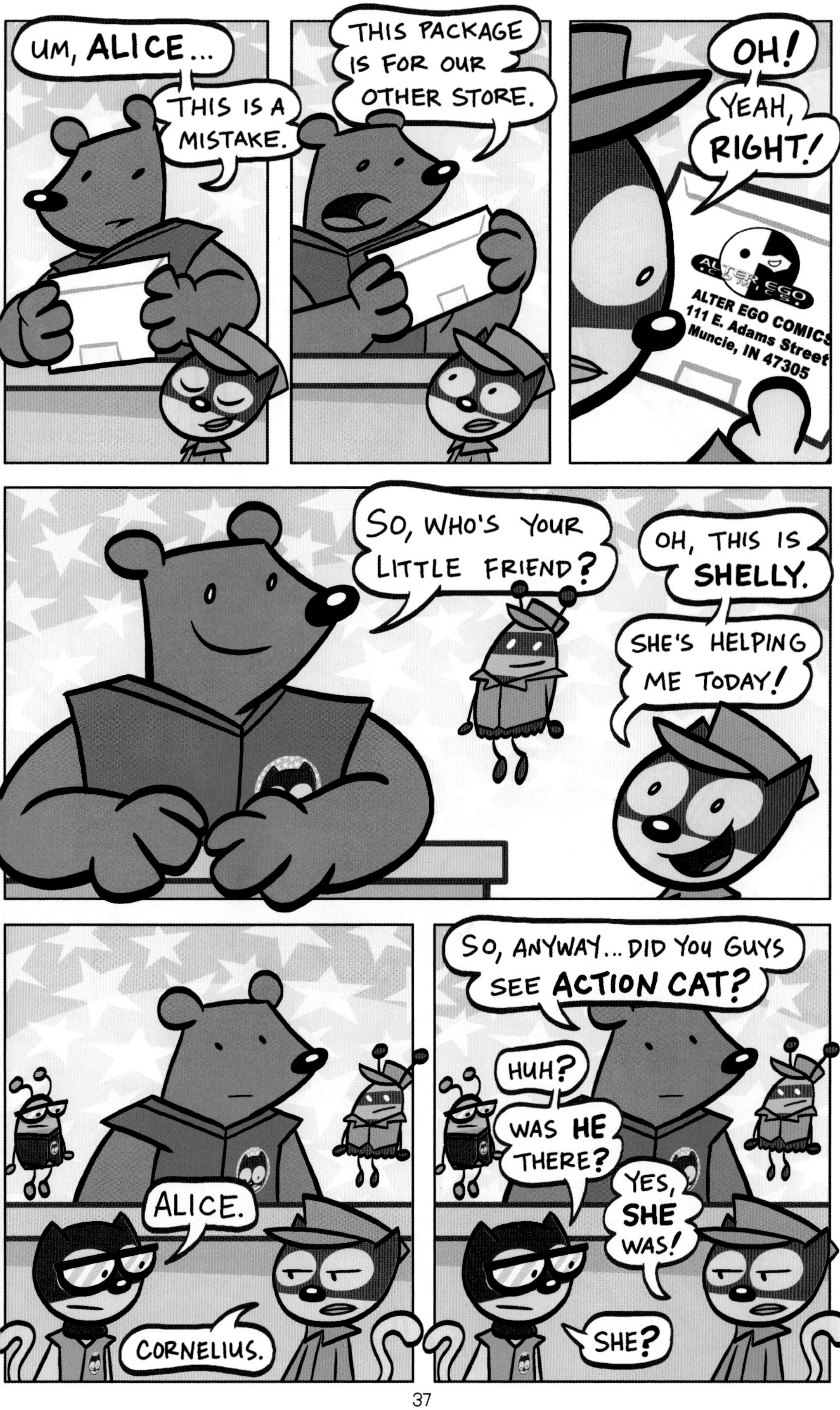
UM, ALICE...
THIS IS A MISTAKE.
THIS PACKAGE IS FOR OUR OTHER STORE.
OH!
YEAH, RIGHT!
ALTER EGO COMICS
ALTER EGO COMICS
111 E. Adams Street
Muncie, IN 47305
SO, WHO'S YOUR LITTLE FRIEND?
OH, THIS IS SHELLY.
SHE'S HELPING ME TODAY!
ALICE.
CORNELIUS.
SO, ANYWAY... DID YOU GUYS SEE ACTION CAT?
HUH?
WAS HE THERE?
YES, SHE WAS!
SHE?

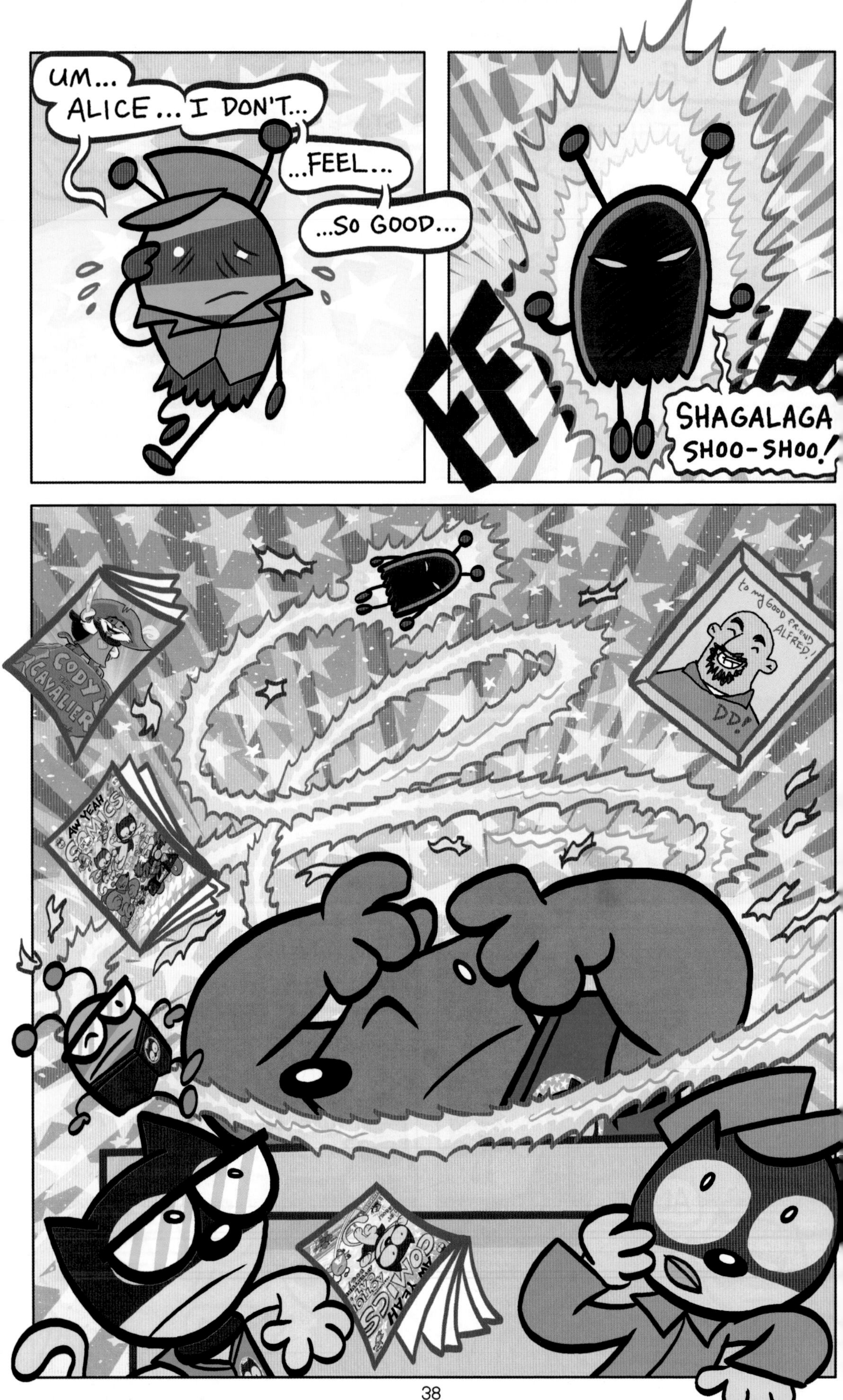

UM... ALICE... I DON'T...
...FEEL...
...SO GOOD...
SHAGALAGA SHOO-SHOO!
CODY THE CAVALIER
AW YEAH COMICS
to my GOOD FRIEND ALFRED!
DD!
AW YEAH COMICS

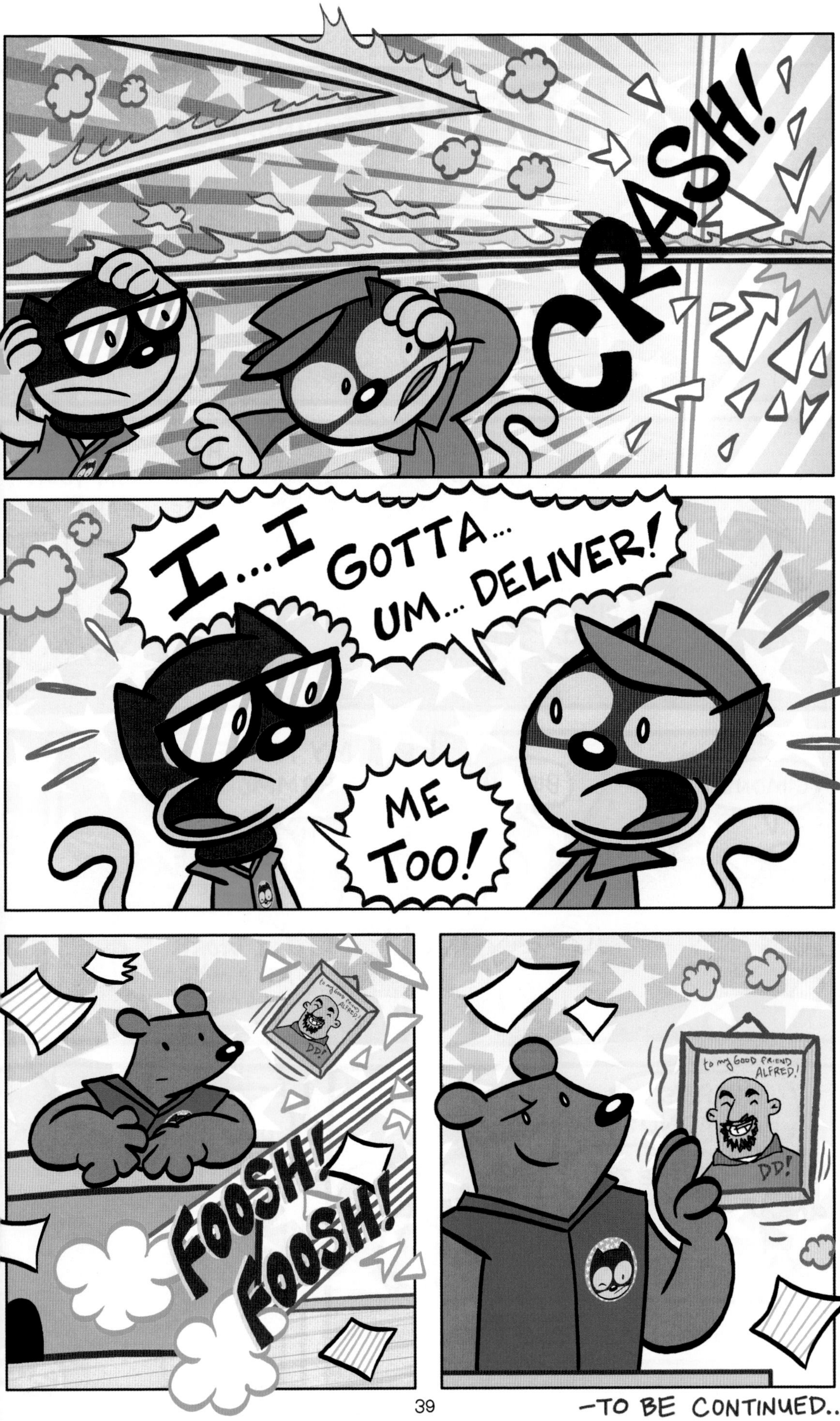
CRASH!
I...I GOTTA... UM... DELIVER!
ME TOO!
to my GOOD FRIEND ALFRED!
DD!
FOOSH! FOOSH!
to my GOOD FRIEND ALFRED!
DD!

–TO BE CONTINUED...

AWESOME BEAR in: MISTAKEN IDENTITY!

by: SCOOT

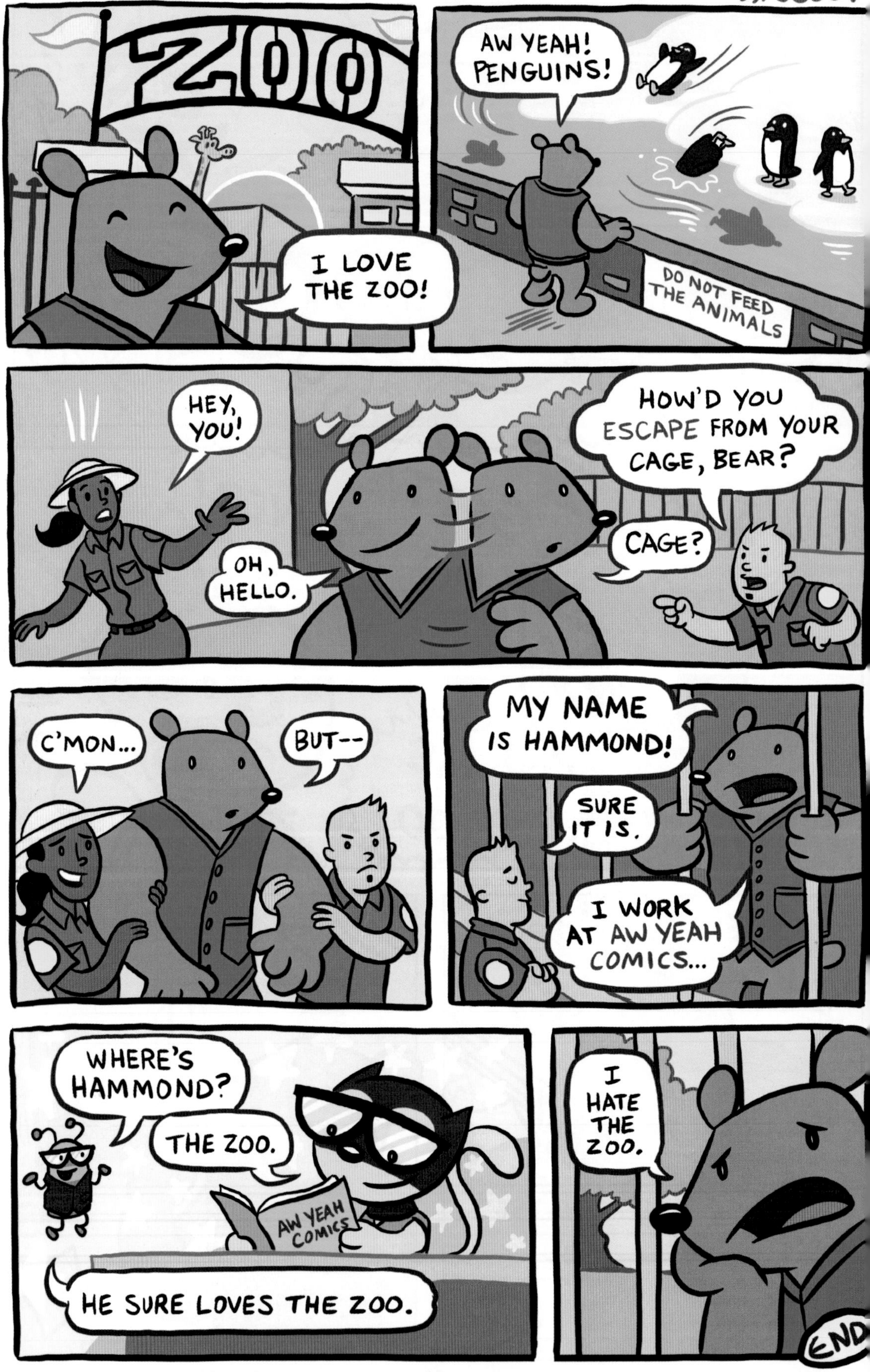
ZOO
I LOVE THE ZOO!
AW YEAH! PENGUINS!
DO NOT FEED THE ANIMALS
HEY, YOU!
OH, HELLO.
HOW'D YOU ESCAPE FROM YOUR CAGE, BEAR?
CAGE?
C'MON...
BUT--
MY NAME IS HAMMOND!
SURE IT IS.
I WORK AT AW YEAH COMICS...
WHERE'S HAMMOND?
THE ZOO.
AW YEAH COMICS
HE SURE LOVES THE ZOO.
I HATE THE ZOO.
END

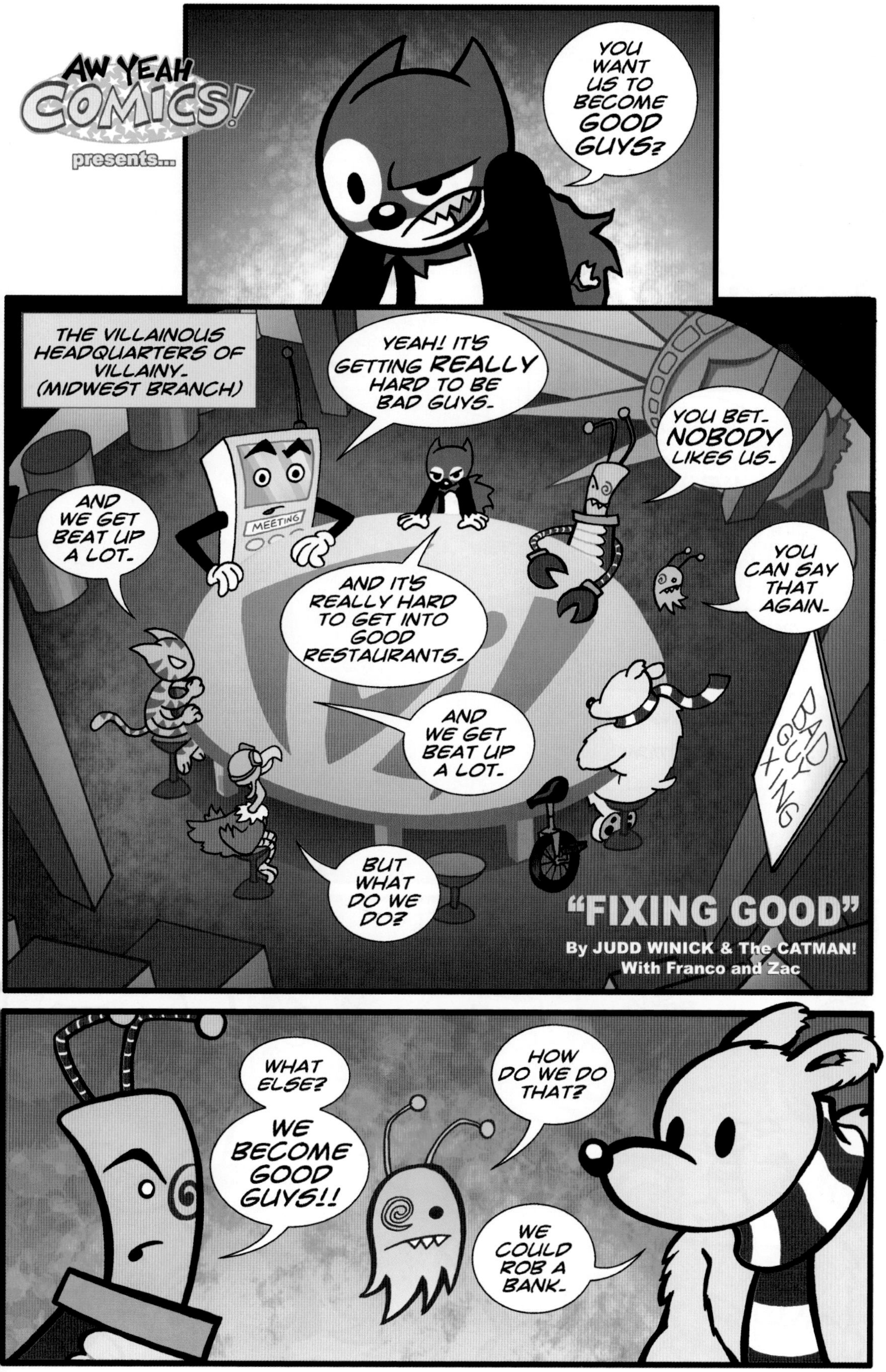
AW YEAH COMICS! presents...
YOU WANT US TO BECOME GOOD GUYS?
THE VILLAINOUS HEADQUARTERS OF VILLAINY. (MIDWEST BRANCH)
YEAH! IT'S GETTING REALLY HARD TO BE BAD GUYS.
YOU BET. NOBODY LIKES US.
AND WE GET BEAT UP A LOT.
MEETING
AND IT'S REALLY HARD TO GET INTO GOOD RESTAURANTS.
YOU CAN SAY THAT AGAIN.
AND WE GET BEAT UP A LOT.
BAD GUY XING
BUT WHAT DO WE DO?
"FIXING GOOD"
By JUDD WINICK & The CATMAN!
With Franco and Zac
WHAT ELSE?
WE BECOME GOOD GUYS!!
HOW DO WE DO THAT?
WE COULD ROB A BANK.

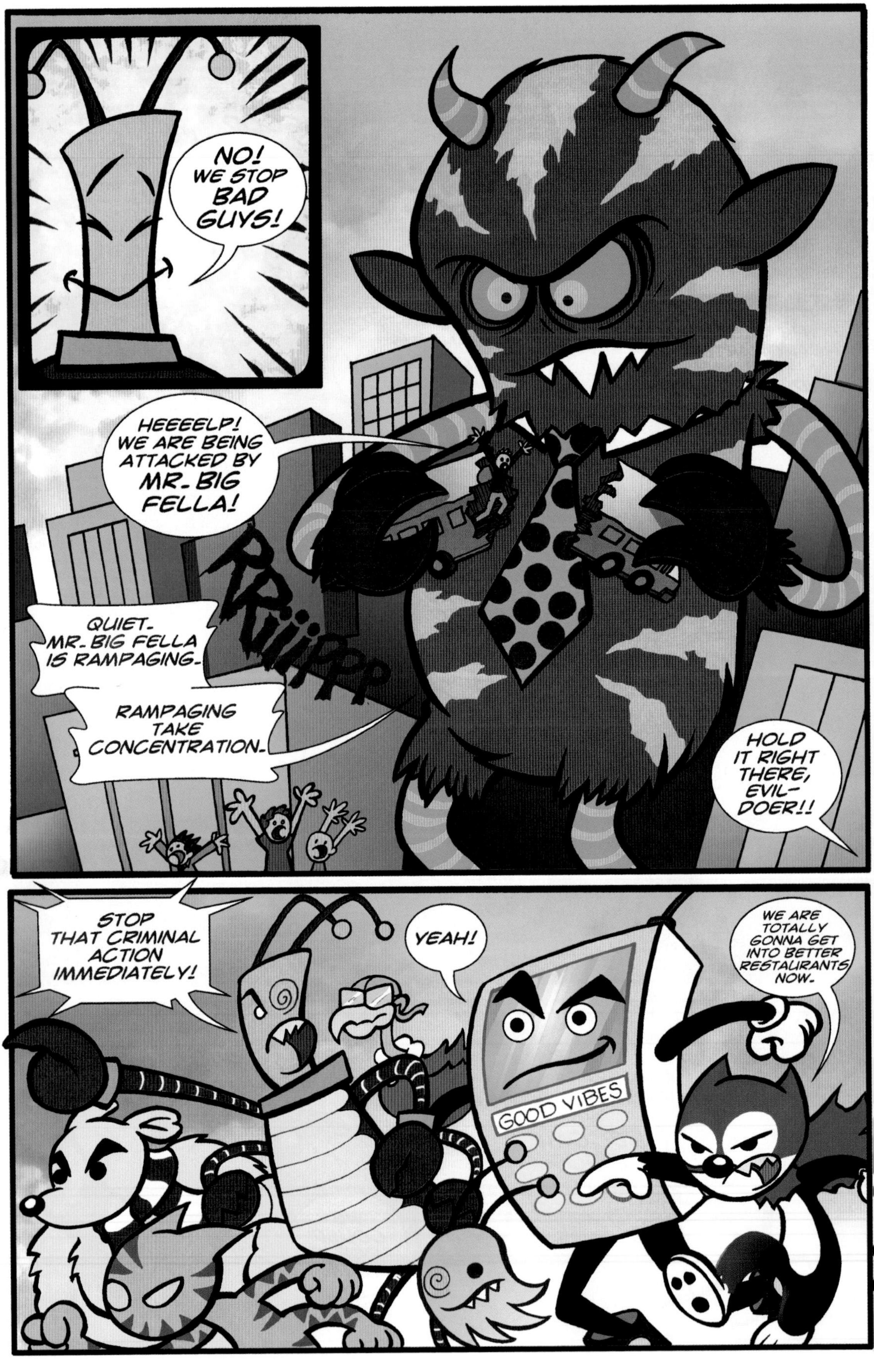
NO! WE STOP BAD GUYS!
HEEEELP! WE ARE BEING ATTACKED BY MR. BIG FELLA!
RRIIIPPP
QUIET. MR. BIG FELLA IS RAMPAGING.
RAMPAGING TAKE CONCENTRATION.
HOLD IT RIGHT THERE, EVIL-DOER!!
STOP THAT CRIMINAL ACTION IMMEDIATELY!
YEAH!
WE ARE TOTALLY GONNA GET INTO BETTER RESTAURANTS NOW.
GOOD VIBES

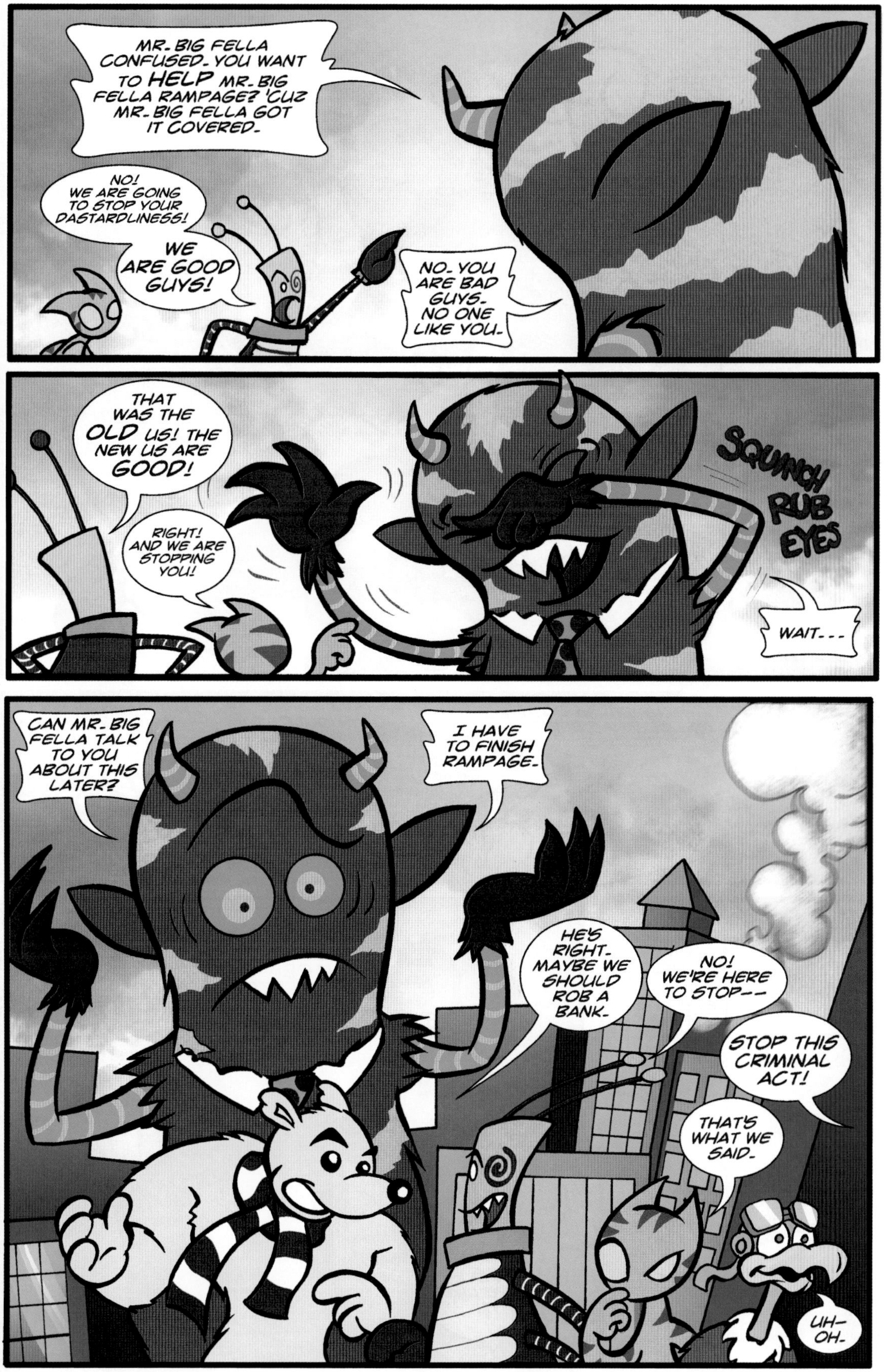
MR. BIG FELLA CONFUSED. YOU WANT TO HELP MR. BIG FELLA RAMPAGE? 'CUZ MR. BIG FELLA GOT IT COVERED.
NO! WE ARE GOING TO STOP YOUR DASTARDLINESS!
WE ARE GOOD GUYS!
NO. YOU ARE BAD GUYS. NO ONE LIKE YOU.
THAT WAS THE OLD US! THE NEW US ARE GOOD!
RIGHT! AND WE ARE STOPPING YOU!
SQUINCH
RUB
EYES
WAIT...
CAN MR. BIG FELLA TALK TO YOU ABOUT THIS LATER?
I HAVE TO FINISH RAMPAGE.
HE'S RIGHT. MAYBE WE SHOULD ROB A BANK.
NO! WE'RE HERE TO STOP--
STOP THIS CRIMINAL ACT!
THAT'S WHAT WE SAID.
UH-OH.

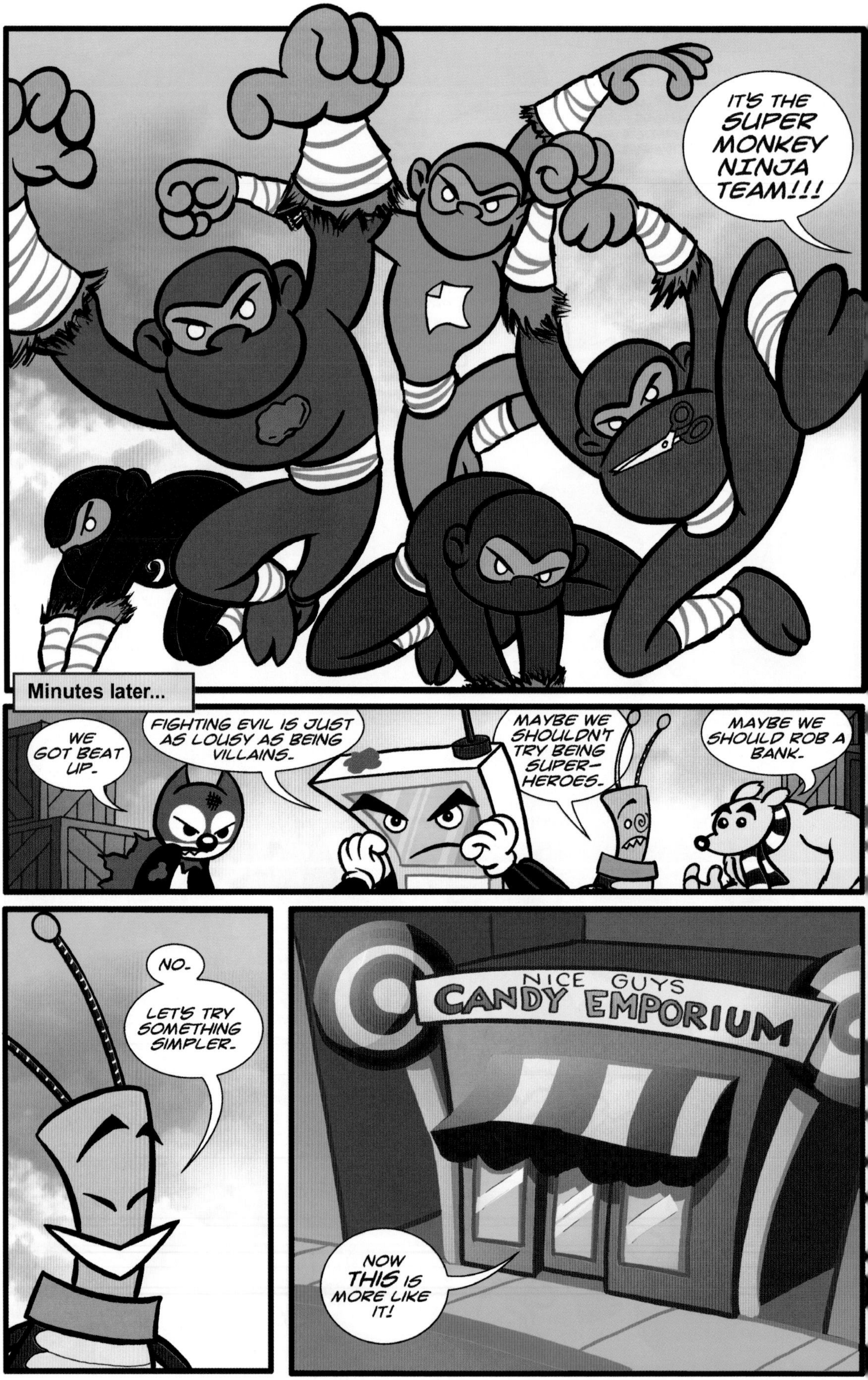

IT'S THE SUPER MONKEY NINJA TEAM!!!
Minutes later...
WE GOT BEAT UP.
FIGHTING EVIL IS JUST AS LOUSY AS BEING VILLAINS.
MAYBE WE SHOULDN'T TRY BEING SUPER-HEROES.
MAYBE WE SHOULD ROB A BANK.
NO.
LET'S TRY SOMETHING SIMPLER.
NICE GUYS CANDY EMPORIUM
NOW THIS IS MORE LIKE IT!

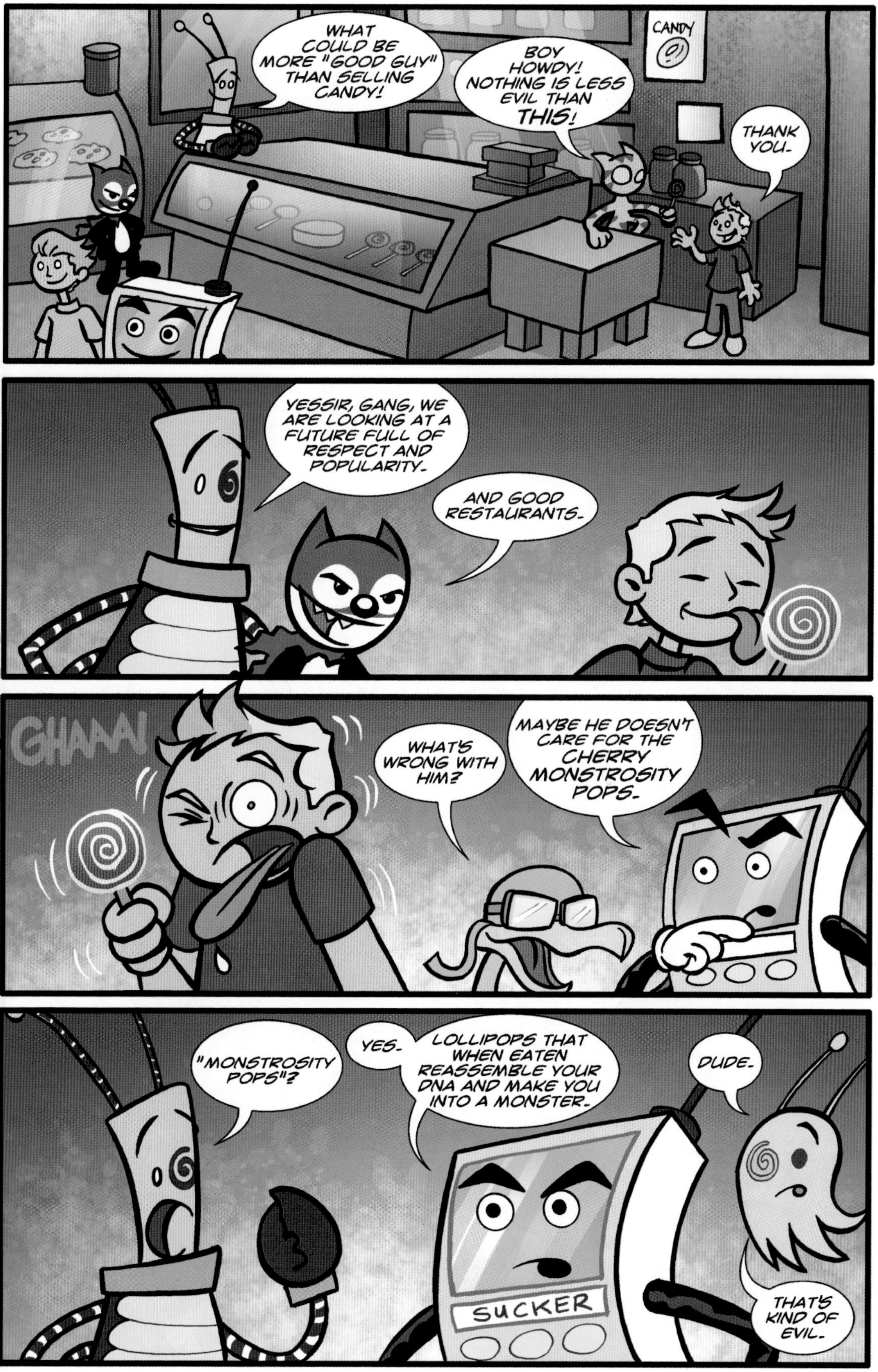
WHAT COULD BE MORE "GOOD GUY" THAN SELLING CANDY!
BOY HOWDY! NOTHING IS LESS EVIL THAN THIS!
CANDY
THANK YOU.
YESSIR, GANG, WE ARE LOOKING AT A FUTURE FULL OF RESPECT AND POPULARITY.
AND GOOD RESTAURANTS.
GHAAA!
WHAT'S WRONG WITH HIM?
MAYBE HE DOESN'T CARE FOR THE CHERRY MONSTROSITY POPS.
"MONSTROSITY POPS"?
YES.
LOLLIPOPS THAT WHEN EATEN REASSEMBLE YOUR DNA AND MAKE YOU INTO A MONSTER.
DUDE.
SUCKER
THAT'S KIND OF EVIL.

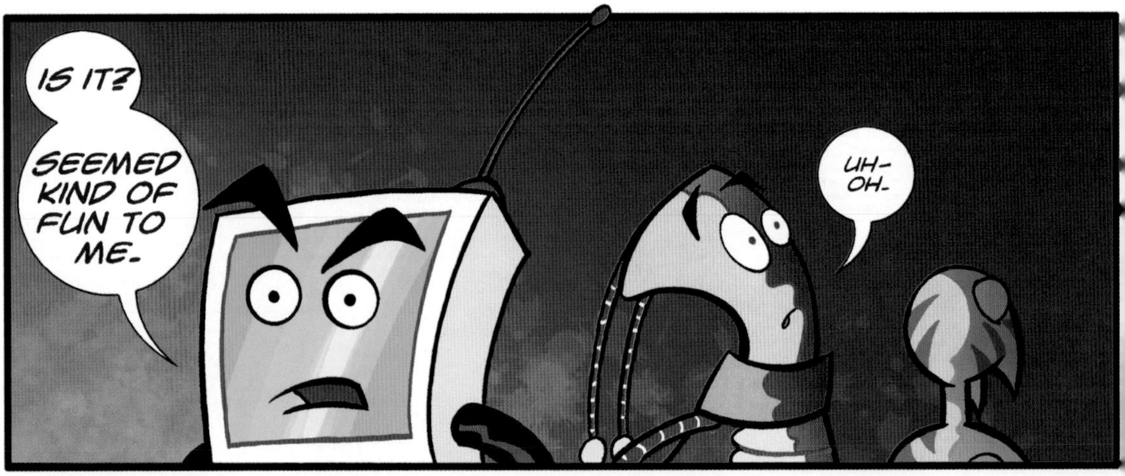
IS IT?
SEEMED KIND OF FUN TO ME.
UH-OH.

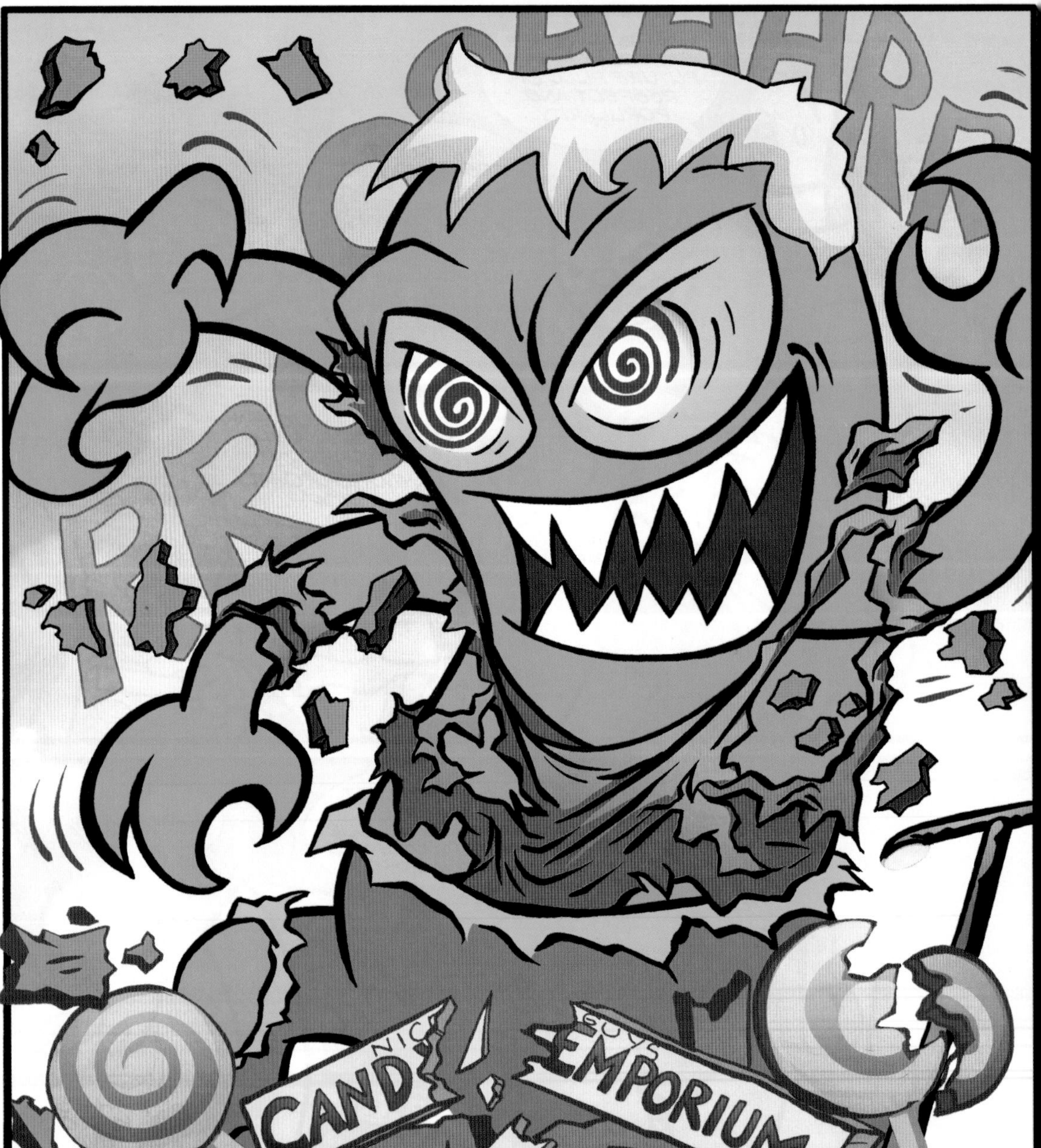
RRROOAAARR
NICE GUYS CAND EMPORIUM

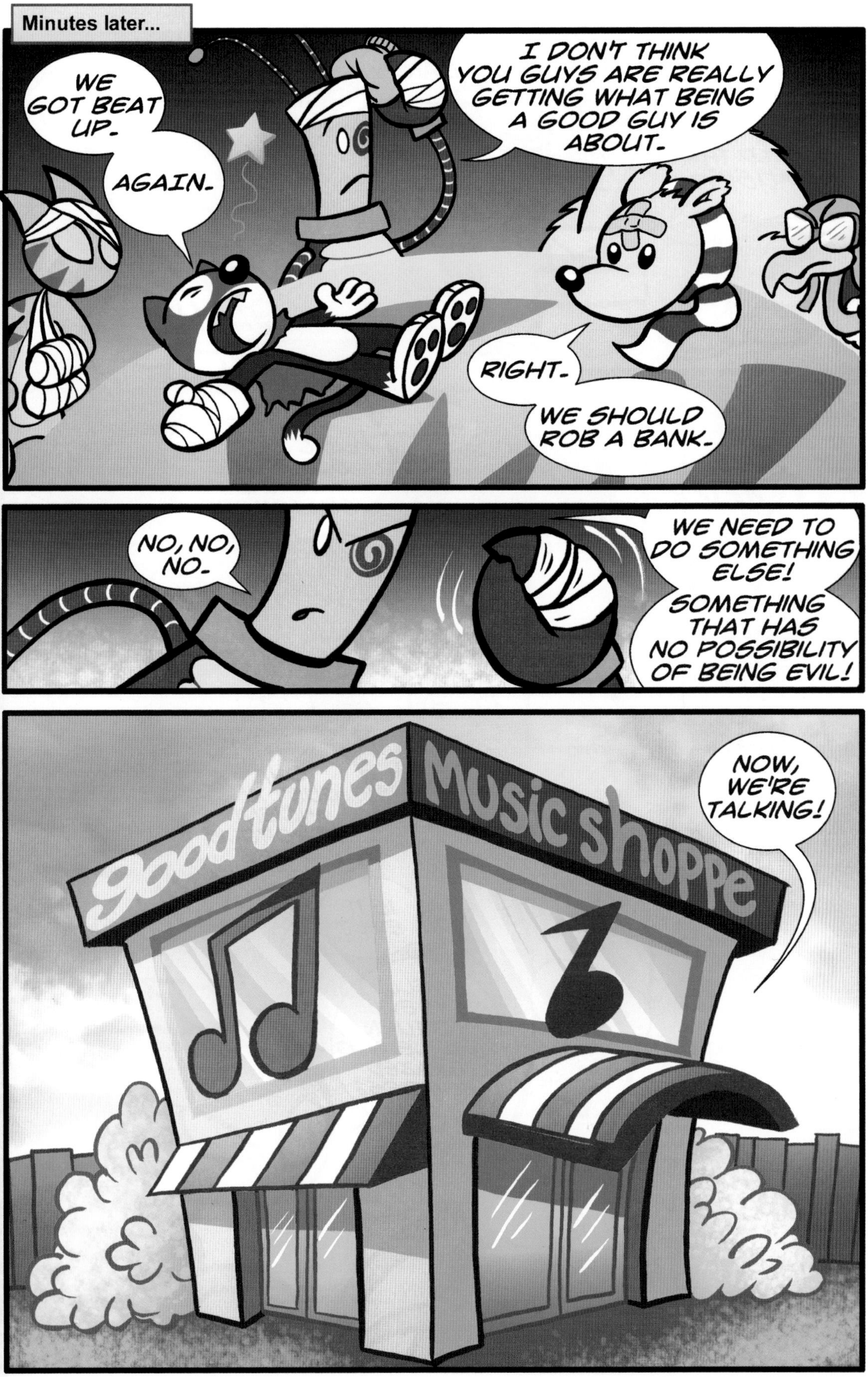
Minutes later...
WE GOT BEAT UP.
AGAIN.
I DON'T THINK YOU GUYS ARE REALLY GETTING WHAT BEING A GOOD GUY IS ABOUT.
RIGHT.
WE SHOULD ROB A BANK.
NO, NO, NO.
WE NEED TO DO SOMETHING ELSE!
SOMETHING THAT HAS NO POSSIBILITY OF BEING EVIL!
good tunes Music shoppe
NOW, WE'RE TALKING!

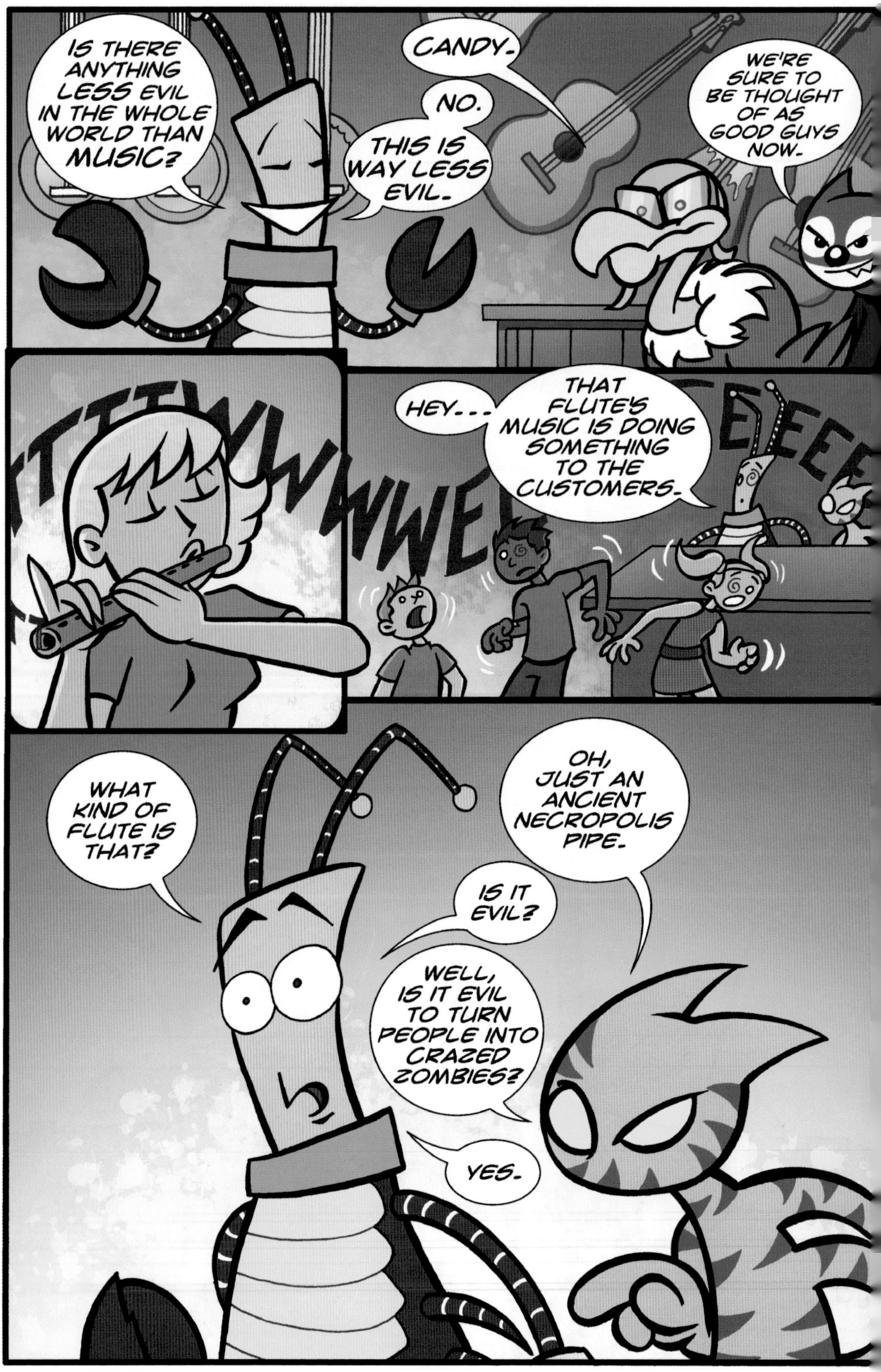
IS THERE ANYTHING LESS EVIL IN THE WHOLE WORLD THAN MUSIC?
CANDY.
NO.
THIS IS WAY LESS EVIL.
WE'RE SURE TO BE THOUGHT OF AS GOOD GUYS NOW.
HEY...
THAT FLUTE'S MUSIC IS DOING SOMETHING TO THE CUSTOMERS.
WHAT KIND OF FLUTE IS THAT?
OH, JUST AN ANCIENT NECROPOLIS PIPE.
IS IT EVIL?
WELL, IS IT EVIL TO TURN PEOPLE INTO CRAZED ZOMBIES?
YES.

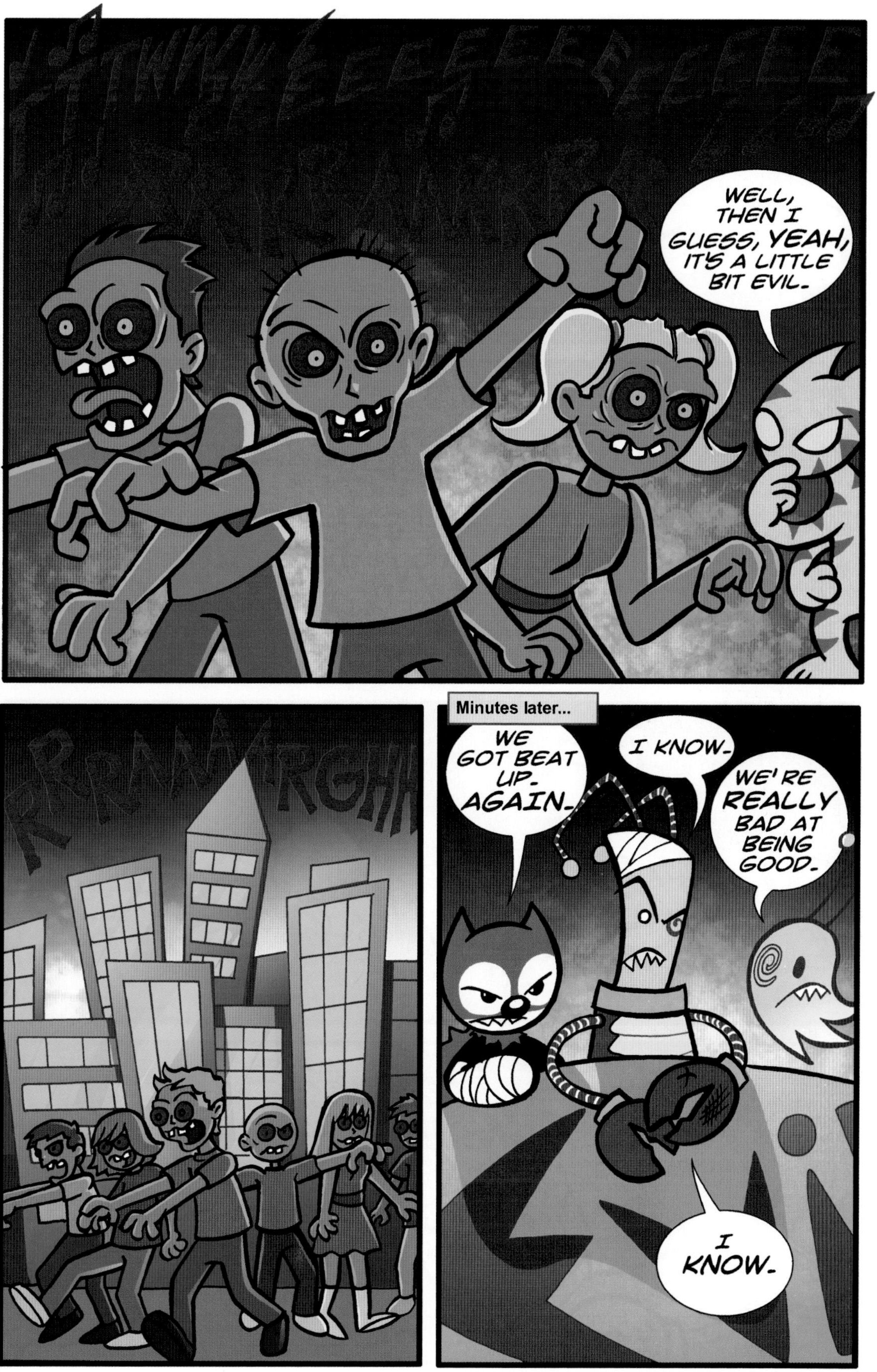
WELL, THEN I GUESS, YEAH, IT'S A LITTLE BIT EVIL.
RRRAWWRGHH
Minutes later...
WE GOT BEAT UP. AGAIN.
I KNOW.
WE'RE REALLY BAD AT BEING GOOD.
I KNOW.

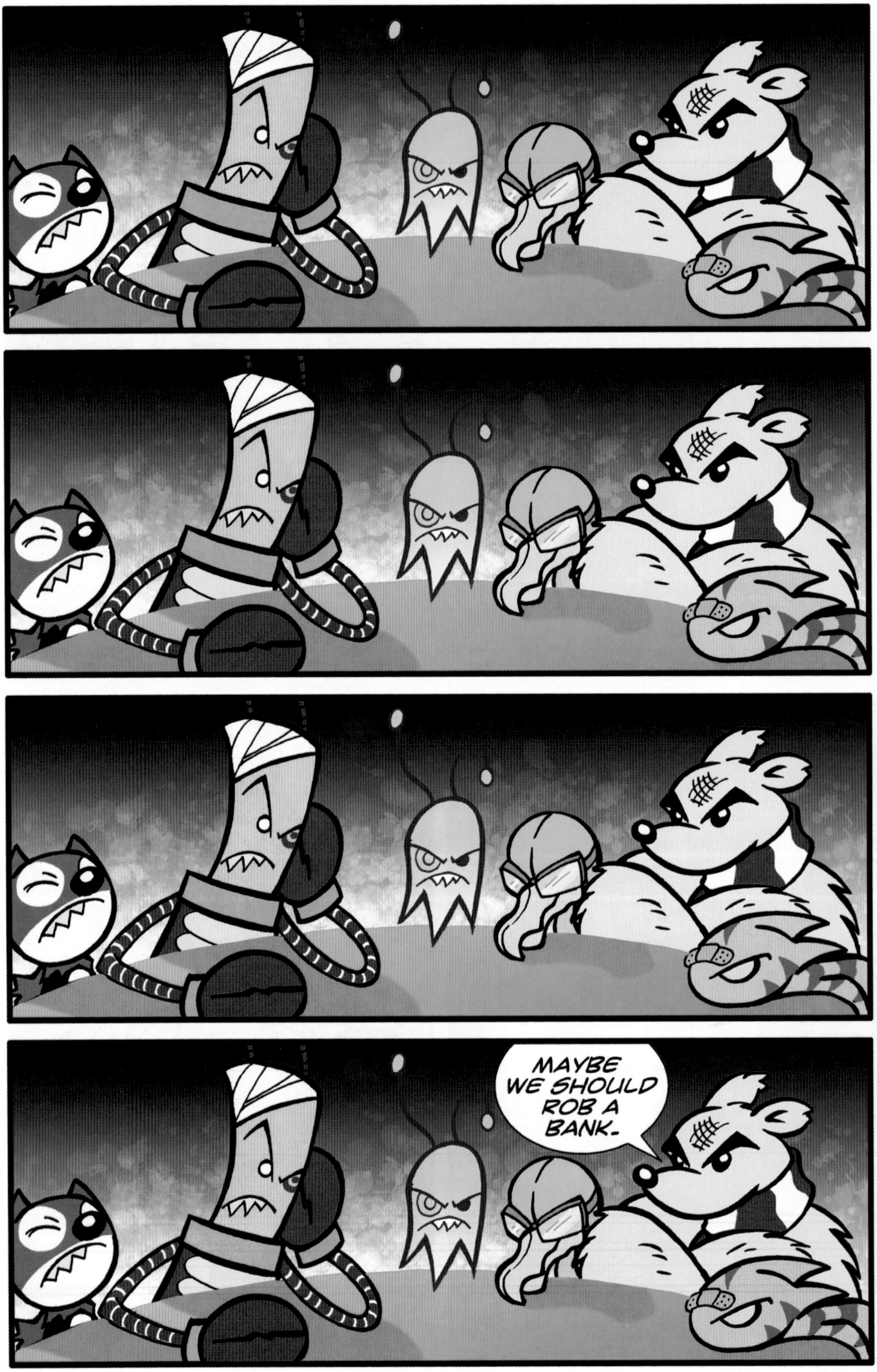
MAYBE WE SHOULD ROB A BANK.

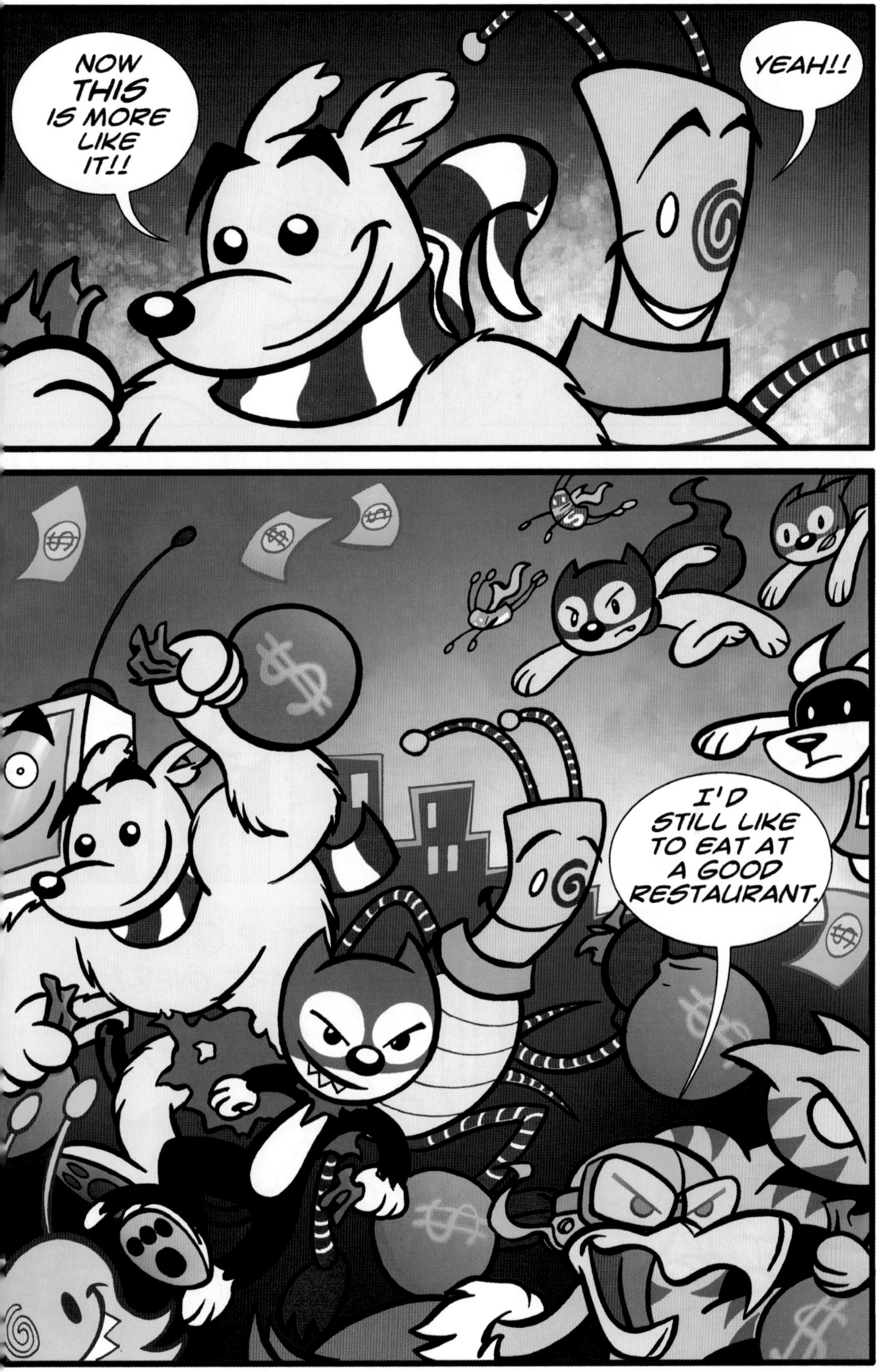
NOW THIS IS MORE LIKE IT!!
YEAH!!
I'D STILL LIKE TO EAT AT A GOOD RESTAURANT.

--GOOD at EVIL is GOOD.

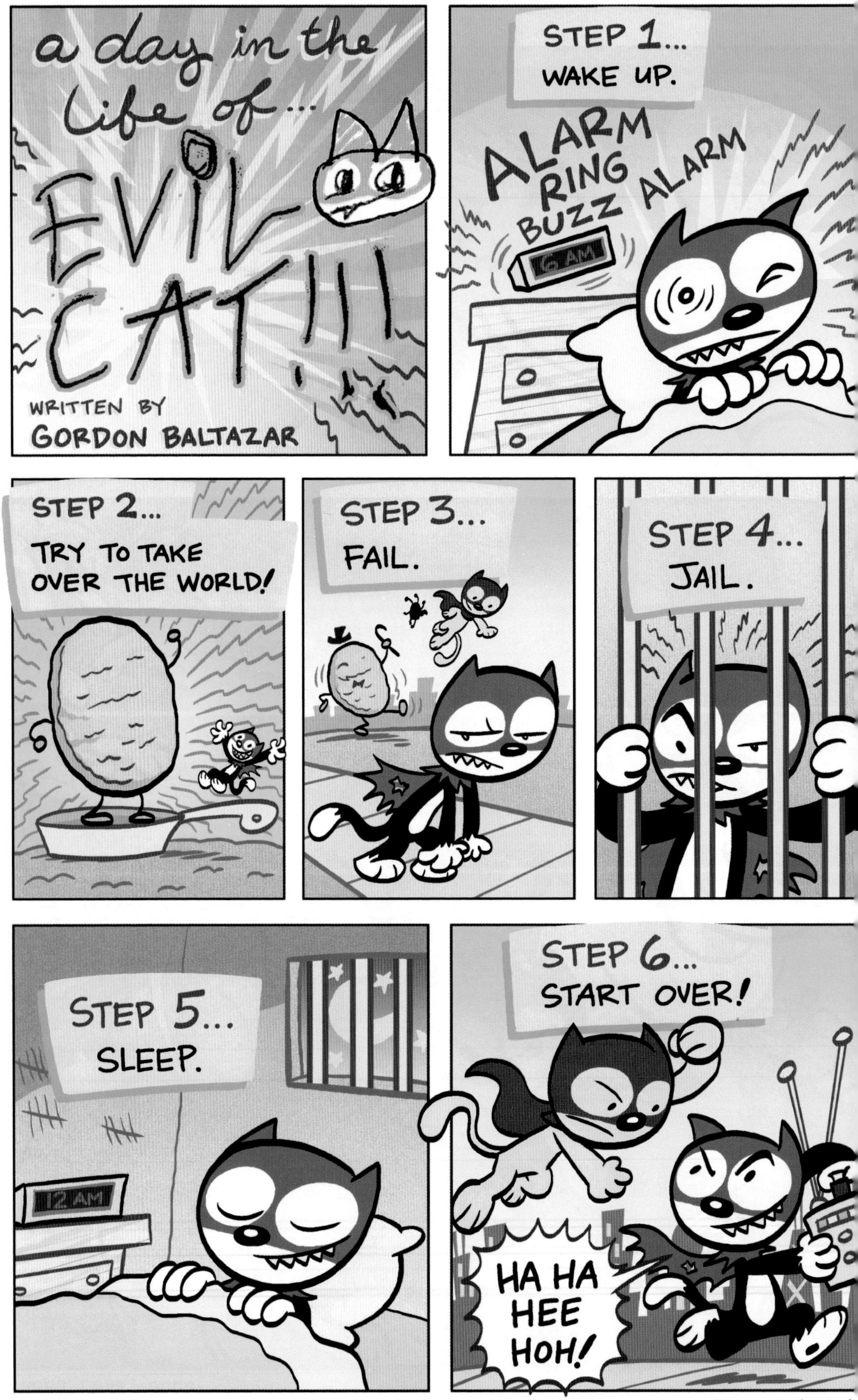

a day in the life of...
EVIL CAT!!!
WRITTEN BY
GORDON BALTAZAR
STEP 1...
WAKE UP.
ALARM
RING
BUZZ
ALARM
6 AM
STEP 2...
TRY TO TAKE OVER THE WORLD!
STEP 3...
FAIL.
STEP 4...
JAIL.
STEP 5...
SLEEP.
12 AM
STEP 6...
START OVER!
HA HA
HEE
HOH!

—IT'S A NEW DAY.

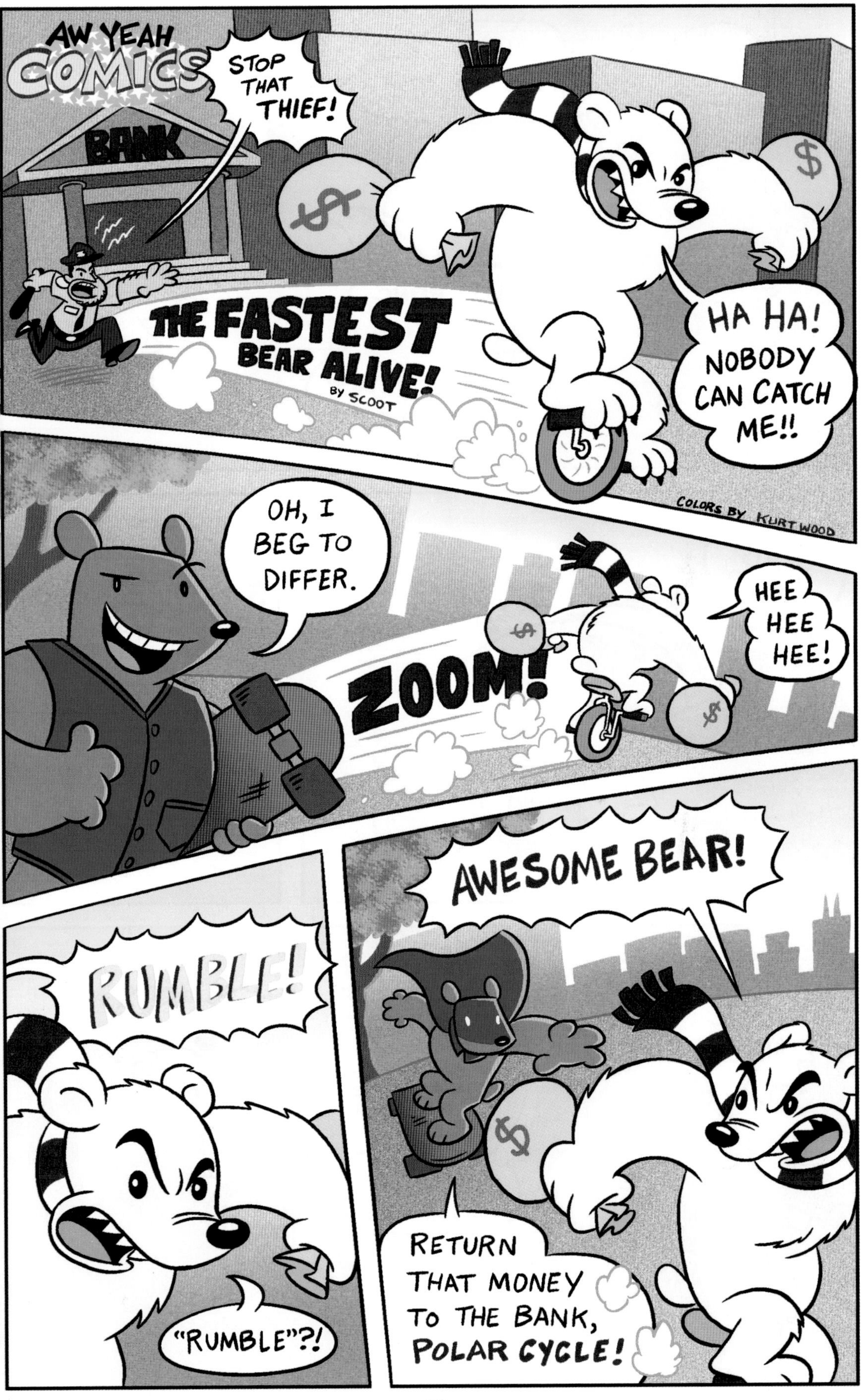
AW YEAH COMICS
STOP THAT THIEF!
BANK
THE FASTEST BEAR ALIVE!
BY SCOOT
HA HA! NOBODY CAN CATCH ME!!
COLORS BY KURTWOOD
OH, I BEG TO DIFFER.
ZOOM!
HEE HEE HEE!
RUMBLE!
"RUMBLE"?!
AWESOME BEAR!
RETURN THAT MONEY TO THE BANK, POLAR CYCLE!

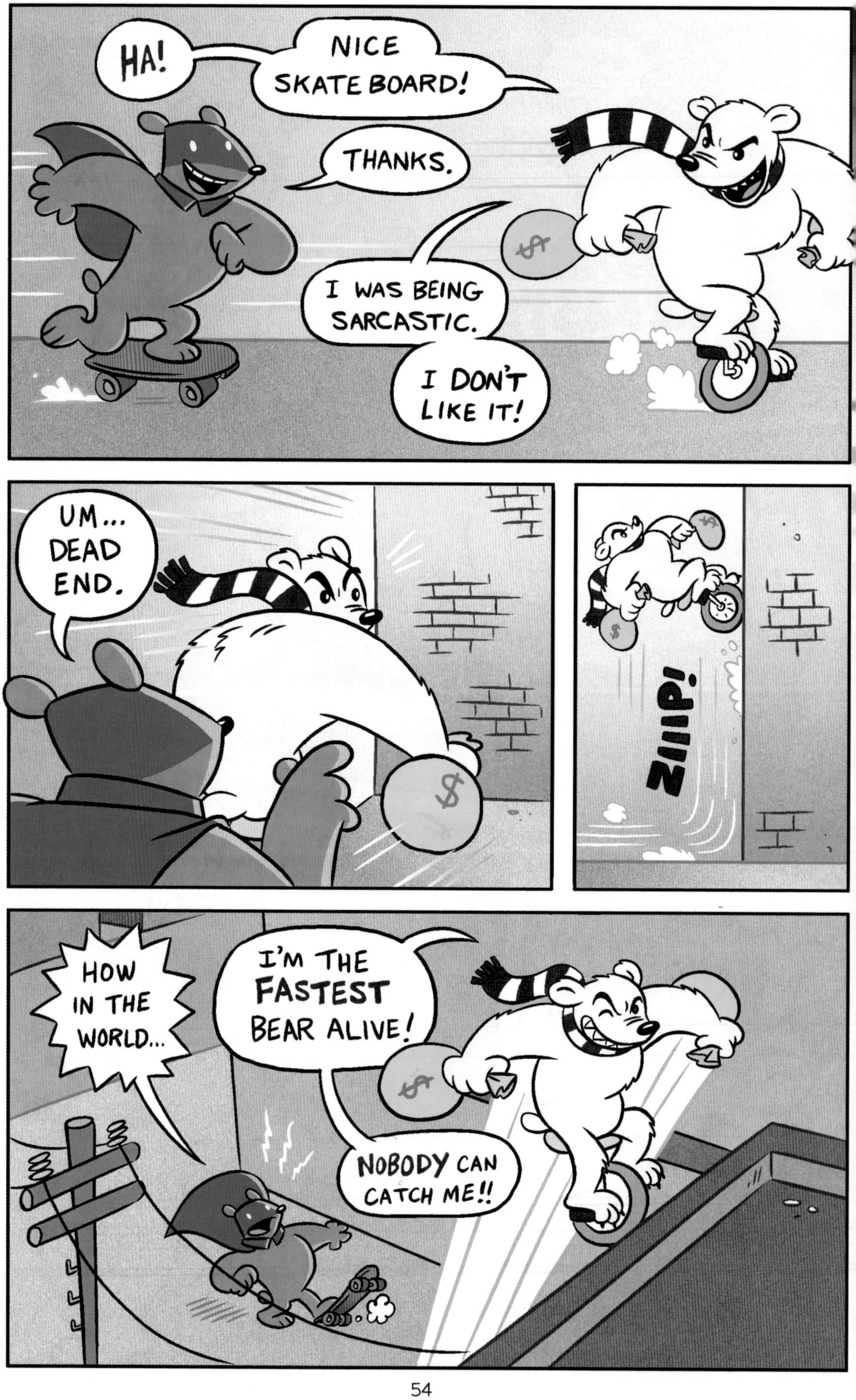
HA!
NICE SKATE BOARD!
THANKS.
I WAS BEING SARCASTIC.
I DON'T LIKE IT!
UM... DEAD END.
ZIIIP!
HOW IN THE WORLD...
I'M THE FASTEST BEAR ALIVE!
NOBODY CAN CATCH ME!!

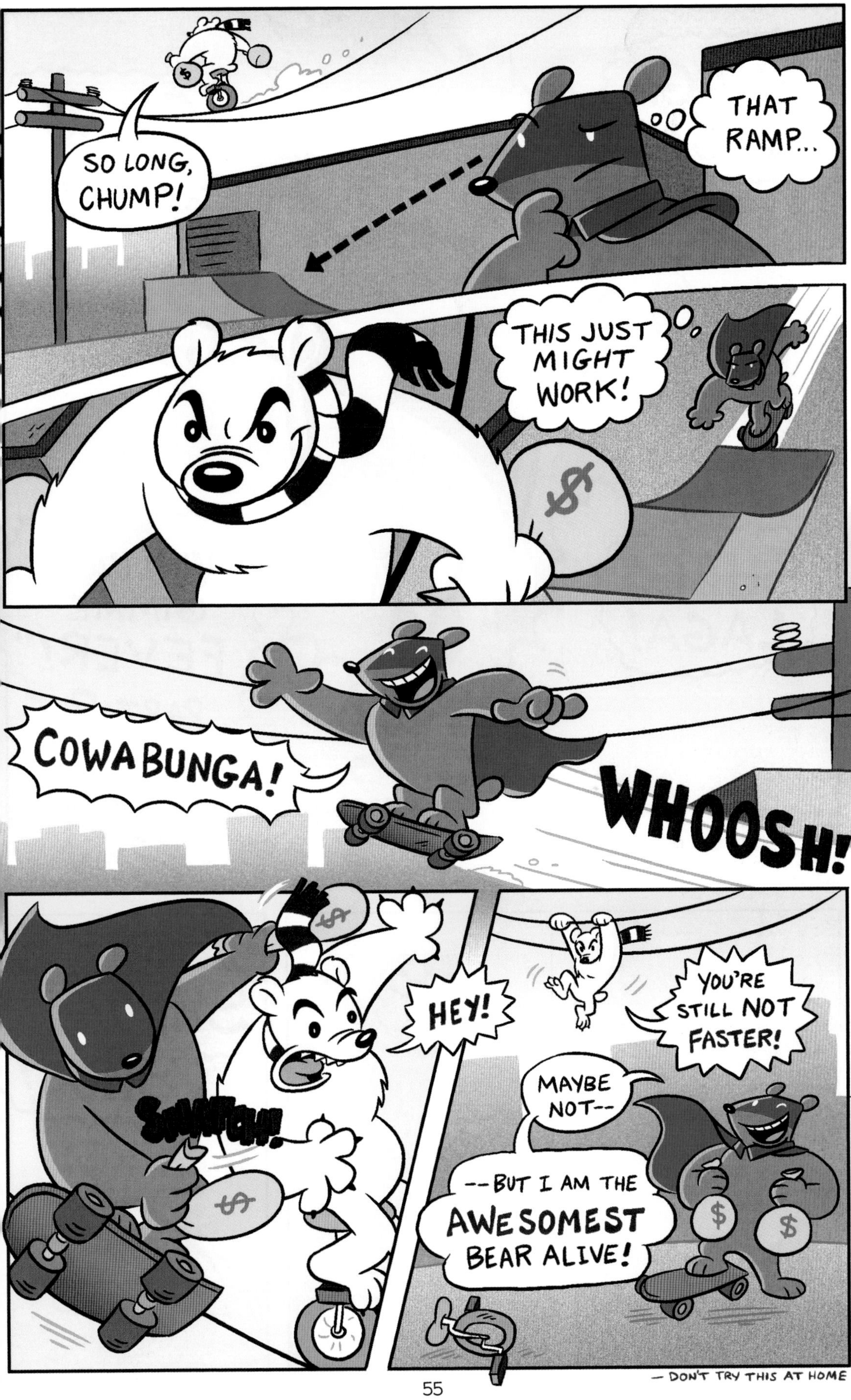
SO LONG, CHUMP!
THAT RAMP...
THIS JUST MIGHT WORK!
COWABUNGA!
WHOOSH!
HEY!
YOU'RE STILL NOT FASTER!
MAYBE NOT--
--BUT I AM THE AWESOMEST BEAR ALIVE!

— DON'T TRY THIS AT HOME

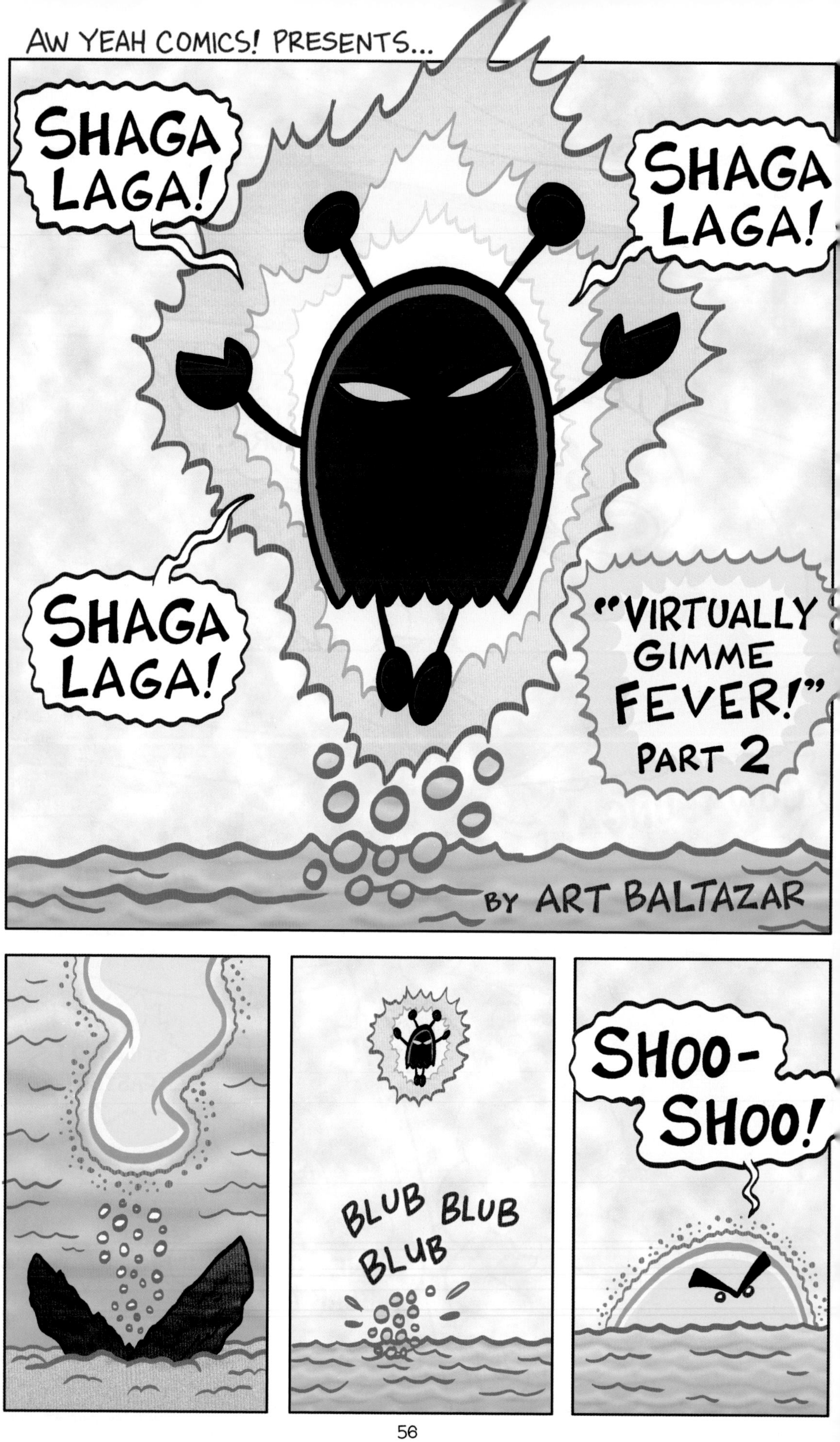
SHAGA LAGA!
SHAGA LAGA!
SHAGA LAGA!
"VIRTUALLY GIMME FEVER!" PART 2
BY ART BALTAZAR
BLUB BLUB
BLUB
SHOO-SHOO!

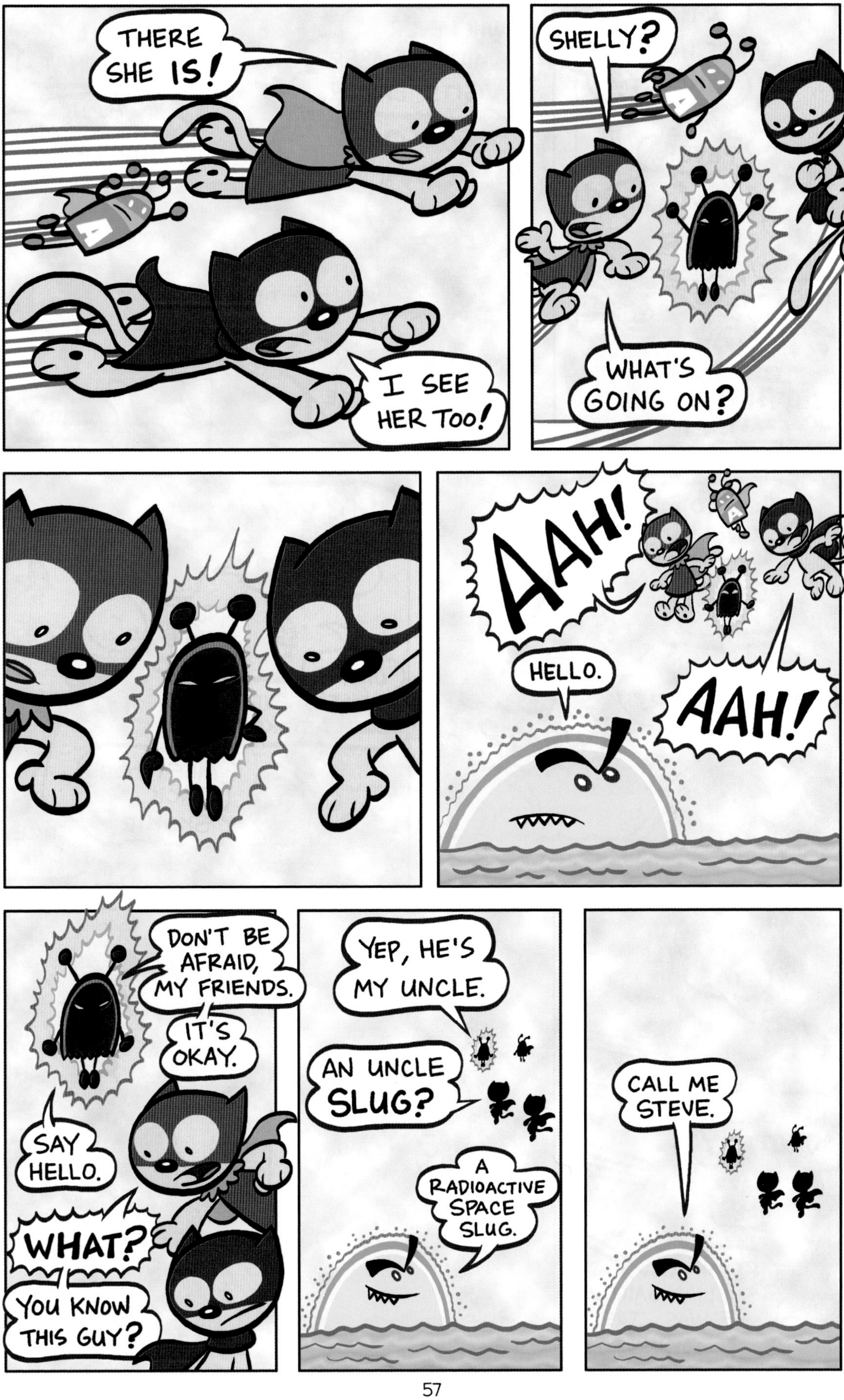
THERE SHE IS!
I SEE HER TOO!
SHELLY?
WHAT'S GOING ON?
AAH!
HELLO.
AAH!
DON'T BE AFRAID, MY FRIENDS.
IT'S OKAY.
SAY HELLO.
WHAT?
YOU KNOW THIS GUY?
YEP, HE'S MY UNCLE.
AN UNCLE SLUG?
A RADIOACTIVE SPACE SLUG.
CALL ME STEVE.

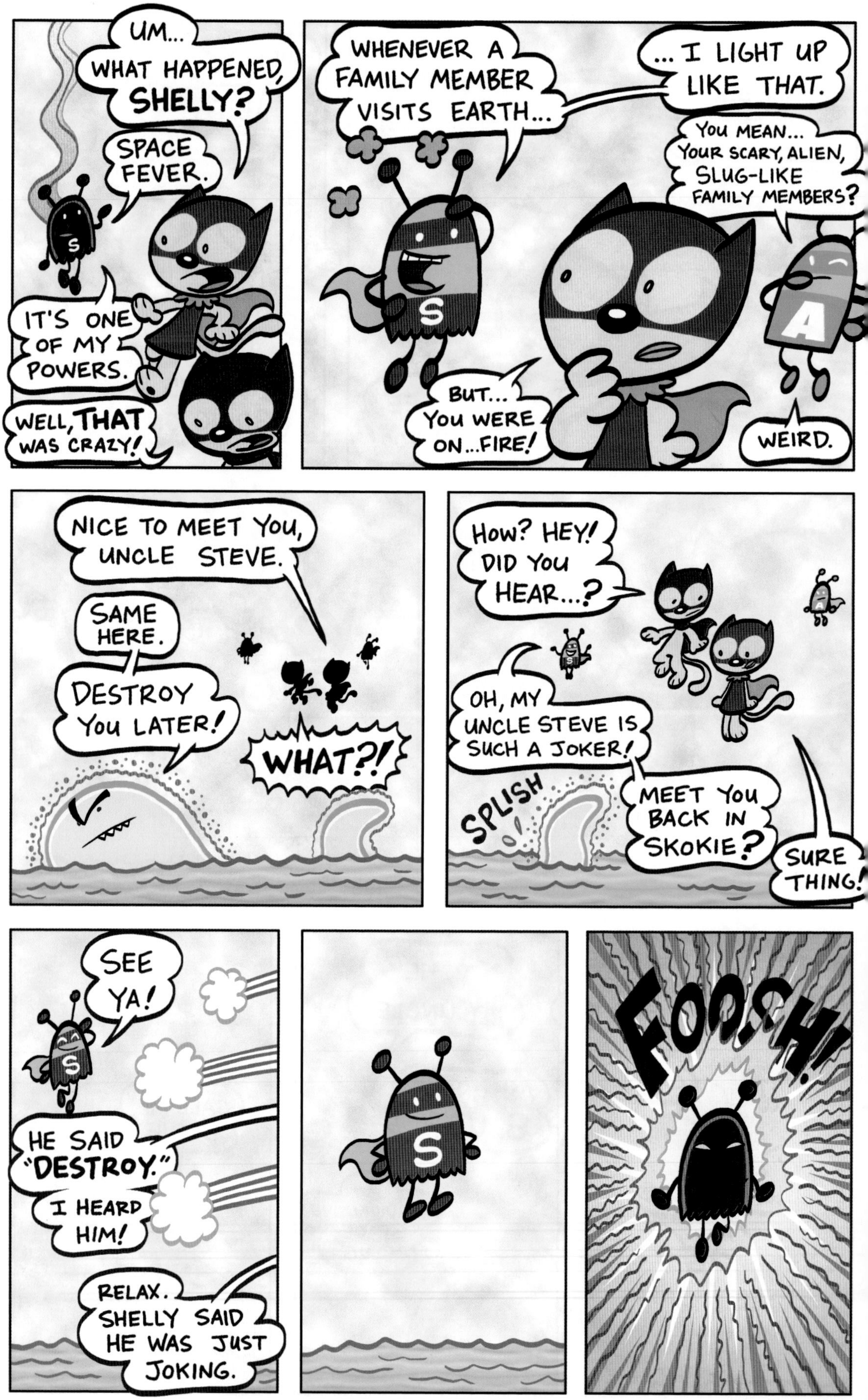
UM... WHAT HAPPENED, SHELLY?
SPACE FEVER.
IT'S ONE OF MY POWERS.
WELL, THAT WAS CRAZY!
WHENEVER A FAMILY MEMBER VISITS EARTH...
... I LIGHT UP LIKE THAT.
BUT... YOU WERE ON...FIRE!
YOU MEAN... YOUR SCARY, ALIEN, SLUG-LIKE FAMILY MEMBERS?
WEIRD.
NICE TO MEET YOU, UNCLE STEVE.
SAME HERE.
DESTROY YOU LATER!
WHAT?!
HOW? HEY! DID YOU HEAR...?
OH, MY UNCLE STEVE IS SUCH A JOKER!
SPLISH
MEET YOU BACK IN SKOKIE?
SURE THING!
SEE YA!
HE SAID "DESTROY."
I HEARD HIM!
RELAX. SHELLY SAID HE WAS JUST JOKING.
FOOSH!

-WHAT? ANOTHER ONE? SO, IT BEGINS!

ZOMBIE Cat

STORY BY KURT WOOD

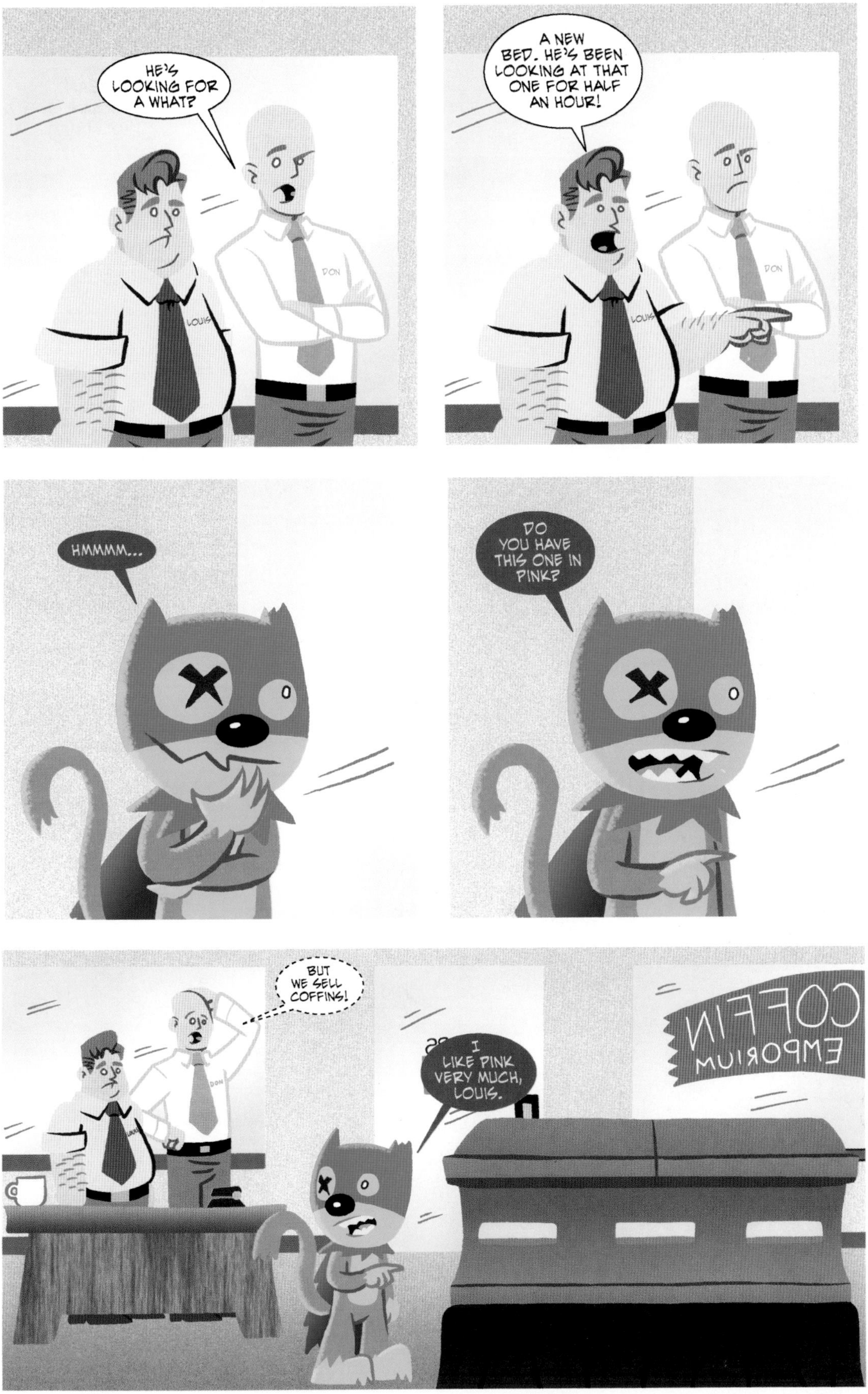

HE'S LOOKING FOR A WHAT?
DON
LOUIS
A NEW BED. HE'S BEEN LOOKING AT THAT ONE FOR HALF AN HOUR!
HMMMM...
DO YOU HAVE THIS ONE IN PINK?
BUT WE SELL COFFINS!
I LIKE PINK VERY MUCH, LOUIS.
COFFIN EMPORIUM

THE END!

★ CHAPTER THREE ★

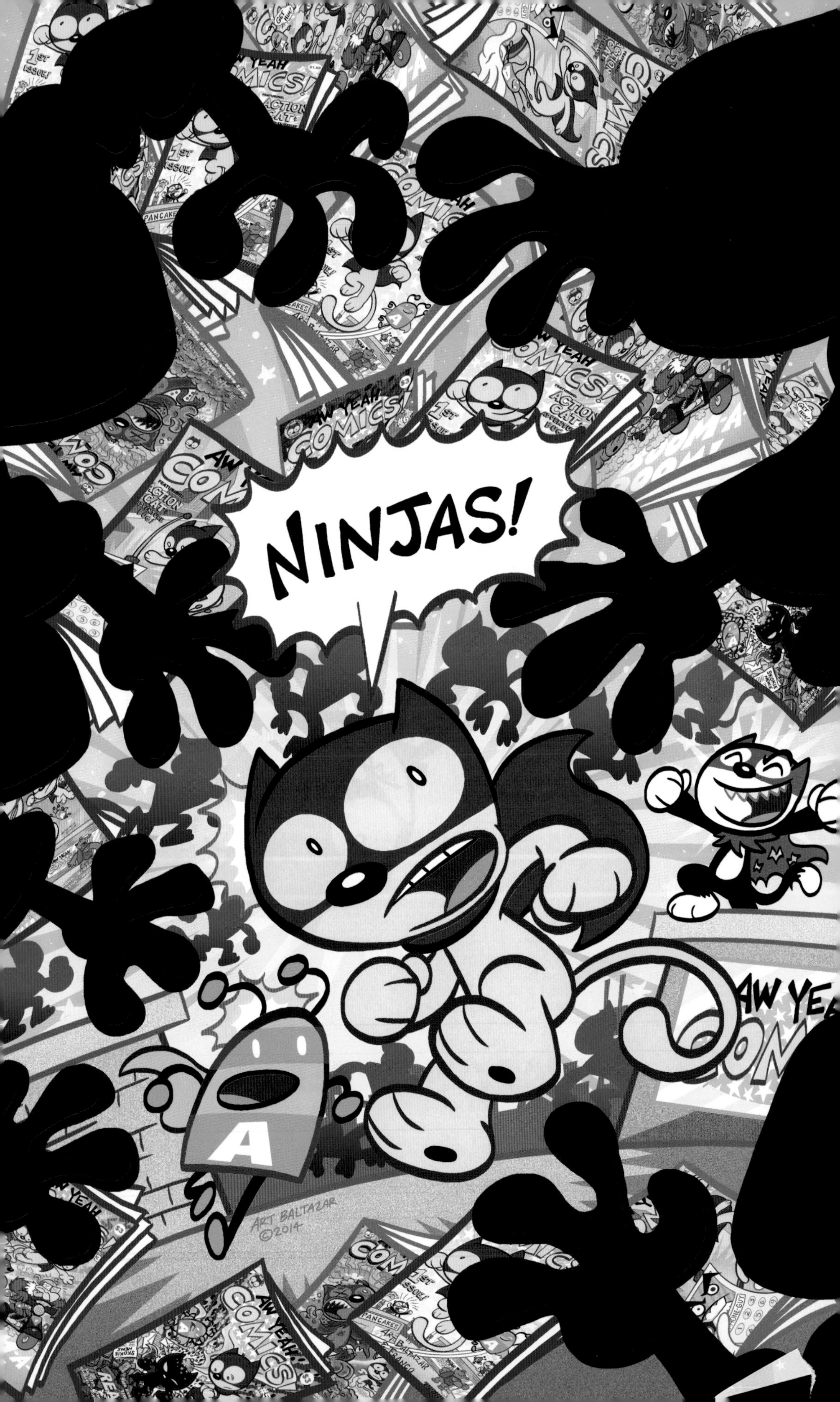
NINJAS!
ART BALTAZAR
©2014

AW YEAH COMICS! PRESENTS...

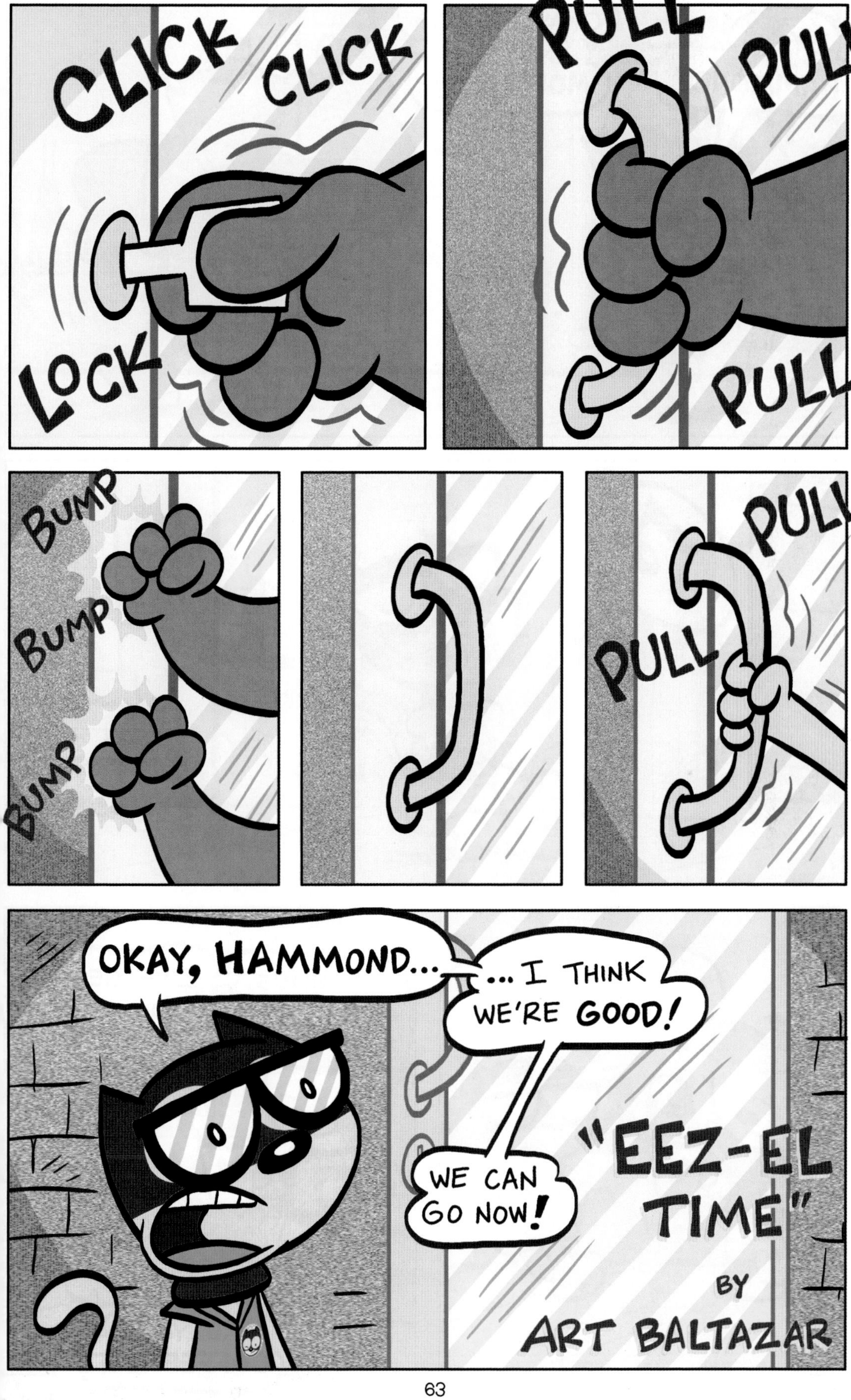
CLICK
CLICK
LOCK
PULL
PULL
PULL
BUMP
BUMP
BUMP
PULL
PULL
OKAY, HAMMOND...
... I THINK WE'RE GOOD!
WE CAN GO NOW!
"EEZ-EL TIME"
BY
ART BALTAZAR

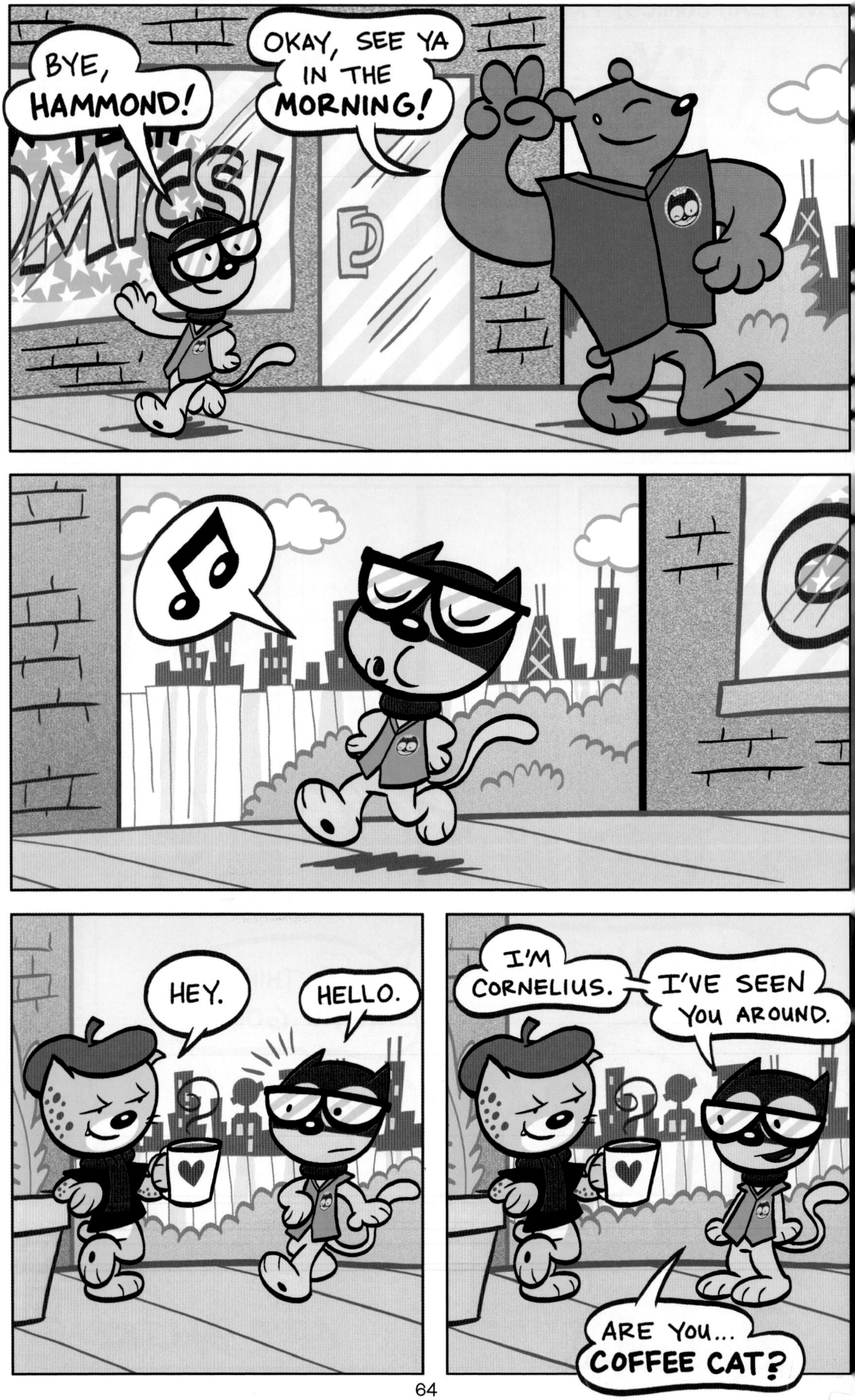
BYE, HAMMOND!
OKAY, SEE YA IN THE MORNING!
HEY.
HELLO.
I'M CORNELIUS.
I'VE SEEN YOU AROUND.
ARE YOU... COFFEE CAT?

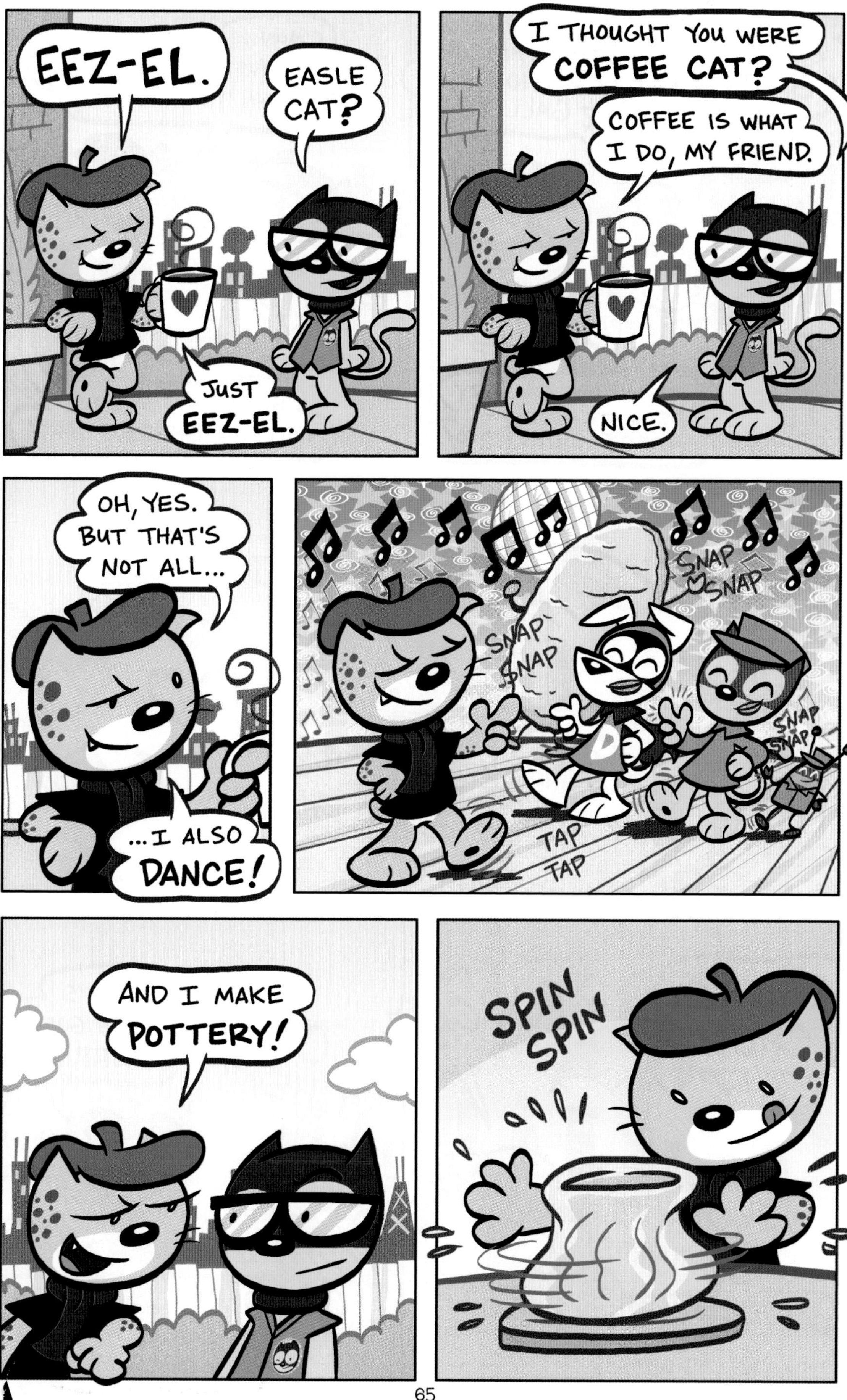
EEZ-EL.
EASLE CAT?
JUST EEZ-EL.
I THOUGHT YOU WERE COFFEE CAT?
COFFEE IS WHAT I DO, MY FRIEND.
NICE.
OH, YES. BUT THAT'S NOT ALL...
...I ALSO DANCE!
SNAP SNAP
SNAP SNAP
SNAP SNAP
TAP TAP
AND I MAKE POTTERY!
SPIN SPIN

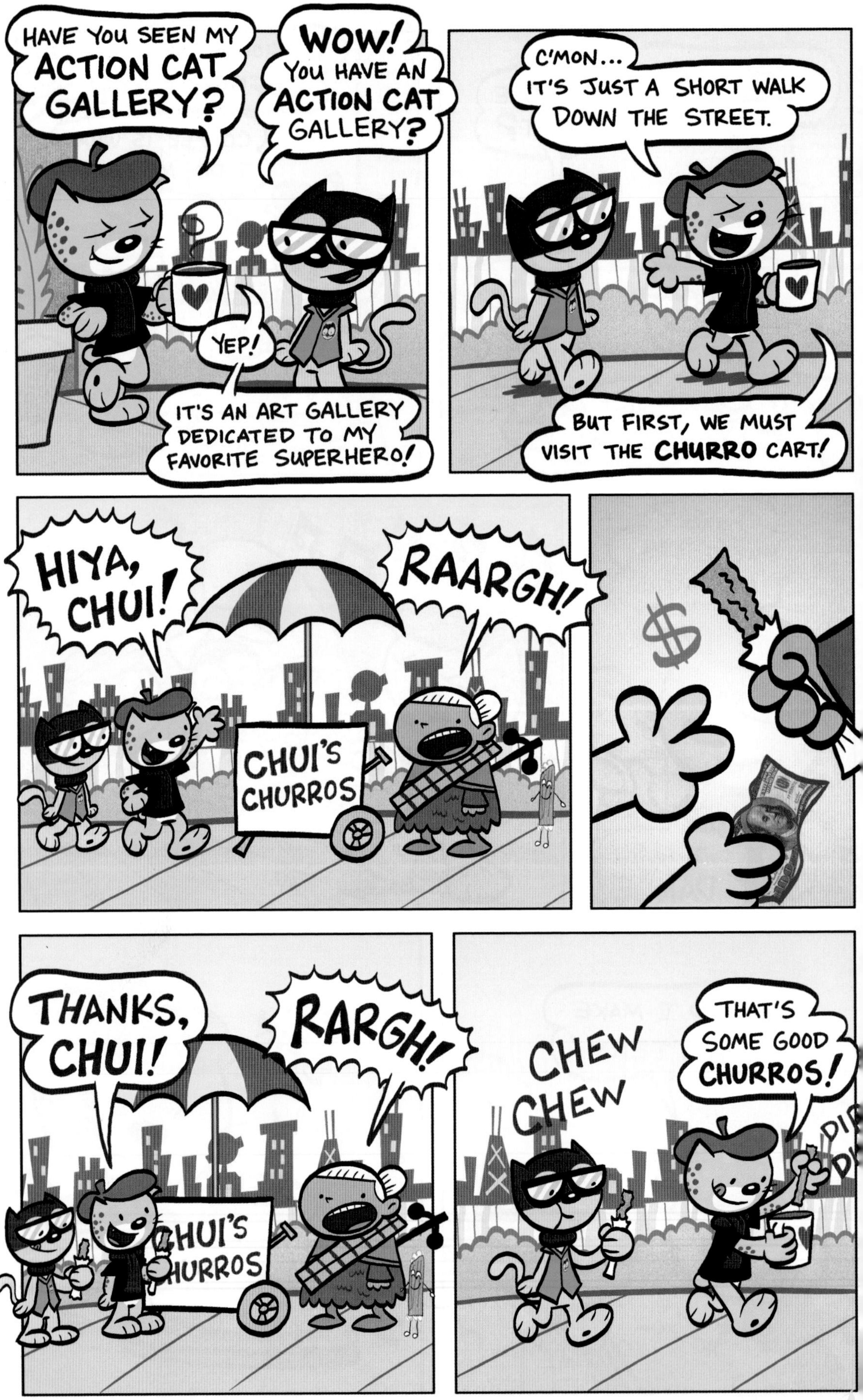
HAVE YOU SEEN MY ACTION CAT GALLERY?
WOW! YOU HAVE AN ACTION CAT GALLERY?
YEP!
IT'S AN ART GALLERY DEDICATED TO MY FAVORITE SUPERHERO!
C'MON... IT'S JUST A SHORT WALK DOWN THE STREET.
BUT FIRST, WE MUST VISIT THE CHURRO CART!
HIYA, CHUI!
RAARGH!
CHUI'S CHURROS
THANKS, CHUI!
RARGH!
CHUI'S CHURROS
CHEW CHEW
THAT'S SOME GOOD CHURROS!

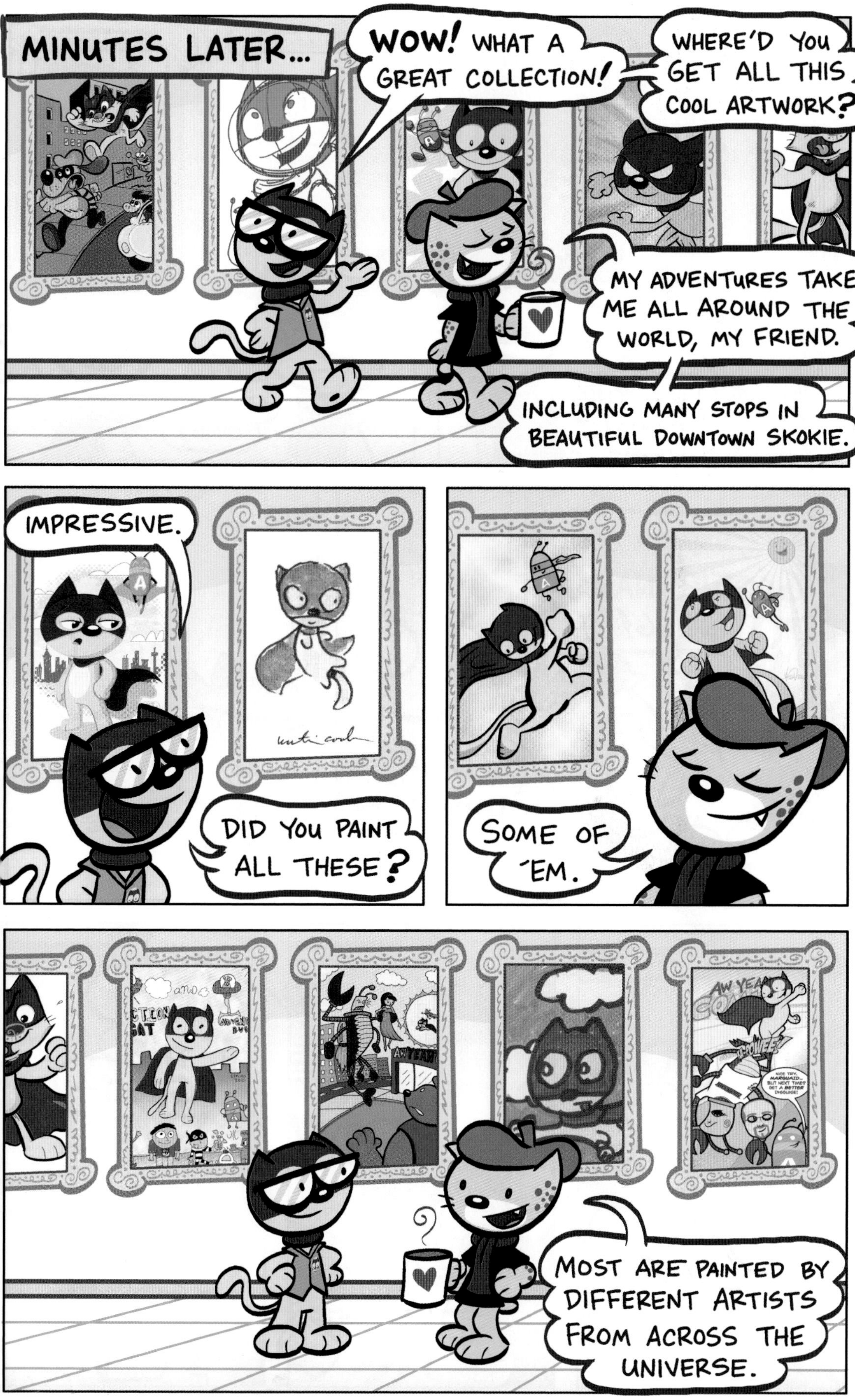
MINUTES LATER...
WOW! WHAT A GREAT COLLECTION!
WHERE'D YOU GET ALL THIS COOL ARTWORK?
MY ADVENTURES TAKE ME ALL AROUND THE WORLD, MY FRIEND.
INCLUDING MANY STOPS IN BEAUTIFUL DOWNTOWN SKOKIE.
IMPRESSIVE.
DID YOU PAINT ALL THESE?
SOME OF 'EM.
MOST ARE PAINTED BY DIFFERENT ARTISTS FROM ACROSS THE UNIVERSE.

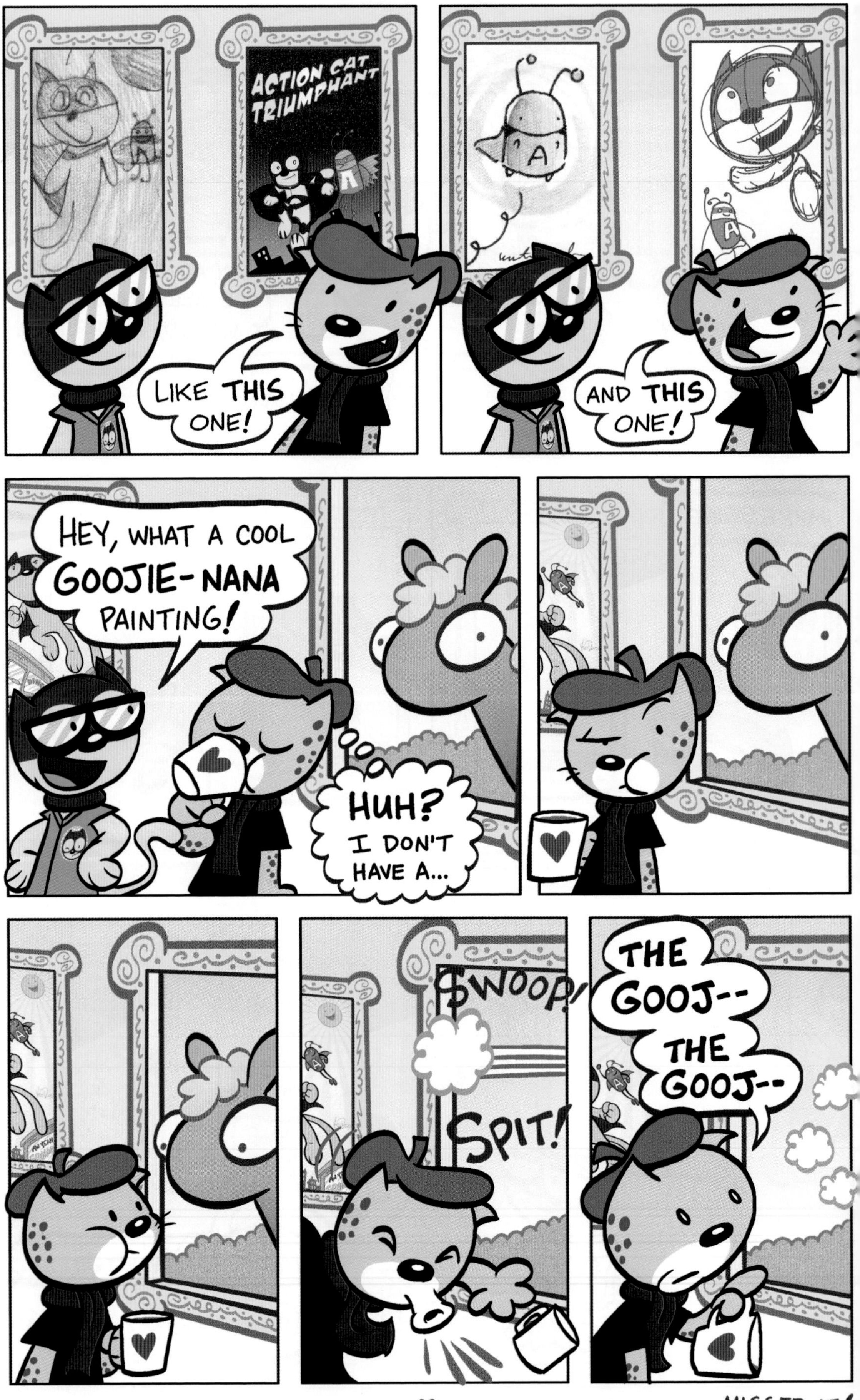
ACTION CAT TRIUMPHANT
LIKE THIS ONE!
AND THIS ONE!
HEY, WHAT A COOL GOOJIE-NANA PAINTING!
HUH? I DON'T HAVE A...
SWOOP!
SPIT!
THE GOOJ--
THE GOOJ--

AW YEAH COMICS PRESENTS:

ADVENTURE GEAR!

BY DENVER BRUBAKER

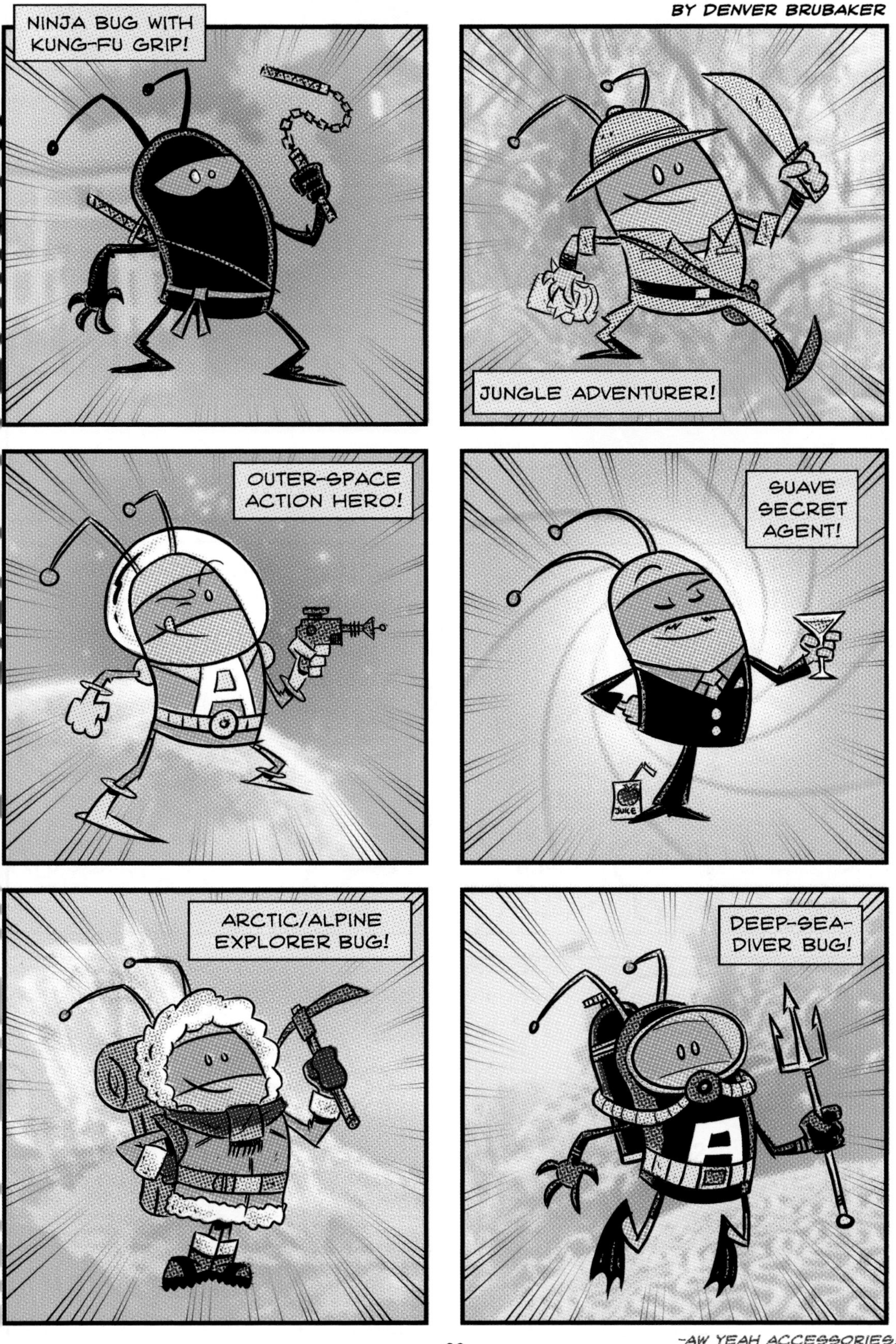

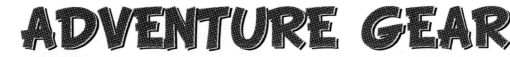

NINJA BUG WITH KUNG-FU GRIP!
JUNGLE ADVENTURER!
OUTER-SPACE ACTION HERO!
SUAVE SECRET AGENT!
ARCTIC/ALPINE EXPLORER BUG!
DEEP-SEA-DIVER BUG!

-AW YEAH ACCESSORIES!

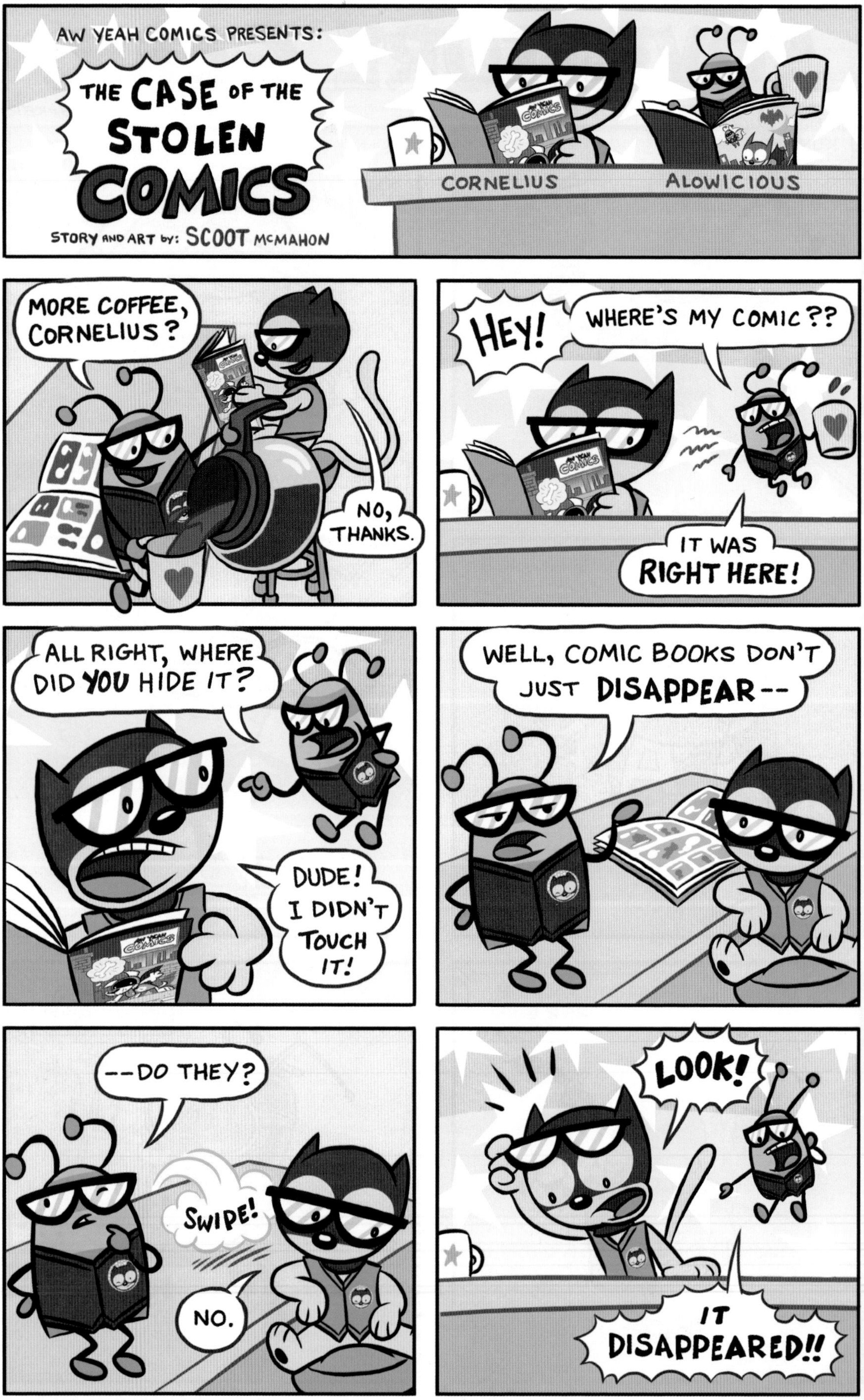
AW YEAH COMICS PRESENTS:
THE CASE OF THE STOLEN COMICS
STORY AND ART BY: SCOOT MCMAHON
AW YEAH COMICS
CORNELIUS
ALOWICIOUS
MORE COFFEE, CORNELIUS?
NO, THANKS.
HEY!
WHERE'S MY COMIC??
IT WAS RIGHT HERE!
ALL RIGHT, WHERE DID YOU HIDE IT?
DUDE! I DIDN'T TOUCH IT!
WELL, COMIC BOOKS DON'T JUST DISAPPEAR--
--DO THEY?
SWIPE!
NO.
LOOK!
IT DISAPPEARED!!

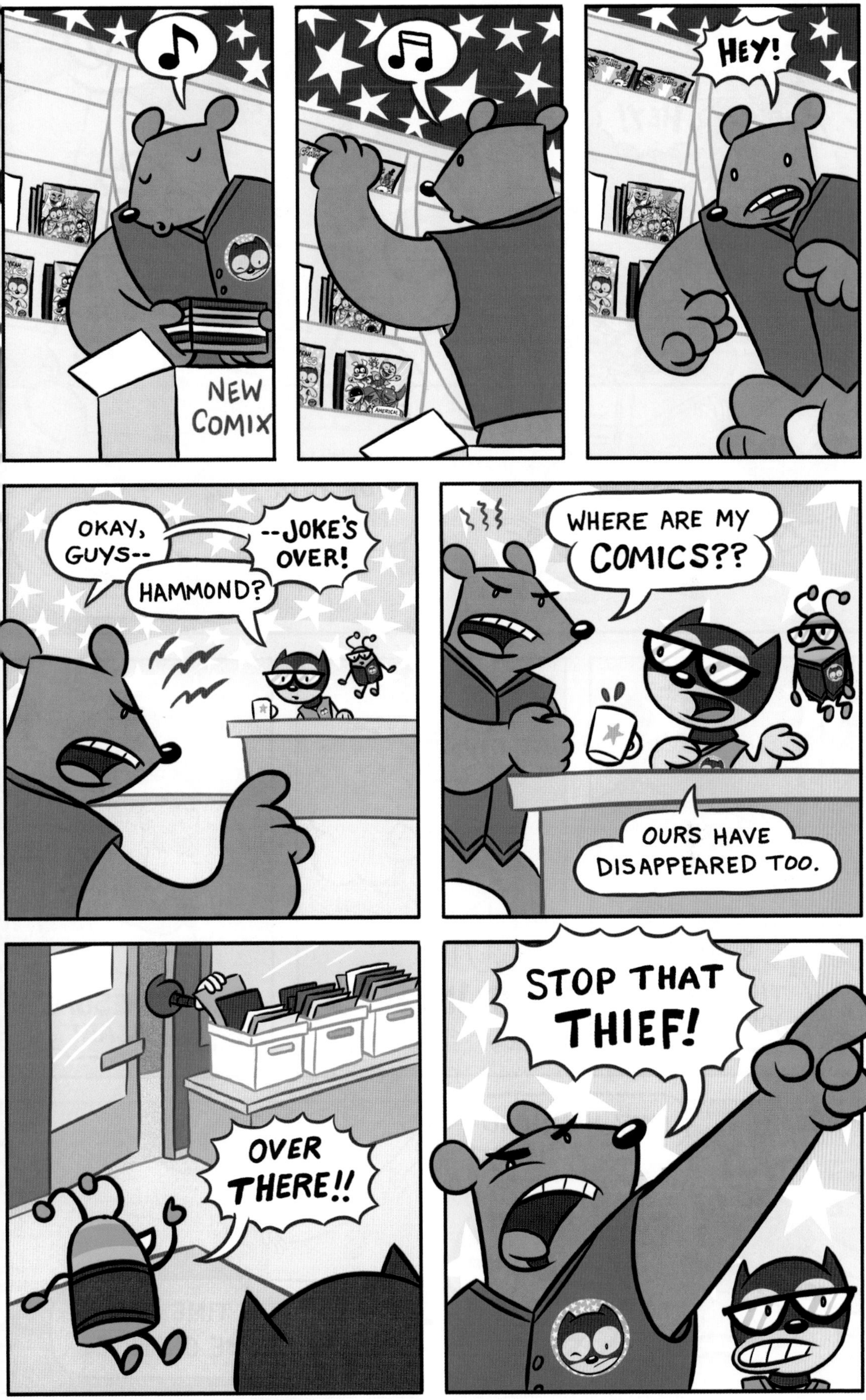
♪
♫
HEY!
NEW COMIX
OKAY, GUYS--
--JOKE'S OVER!
HAMMOND?
WHERE ARE MY COMICS??
OURS HAVE DISAPPEARED TOO.
OVER THERE!!
STOP THAT THIEF!

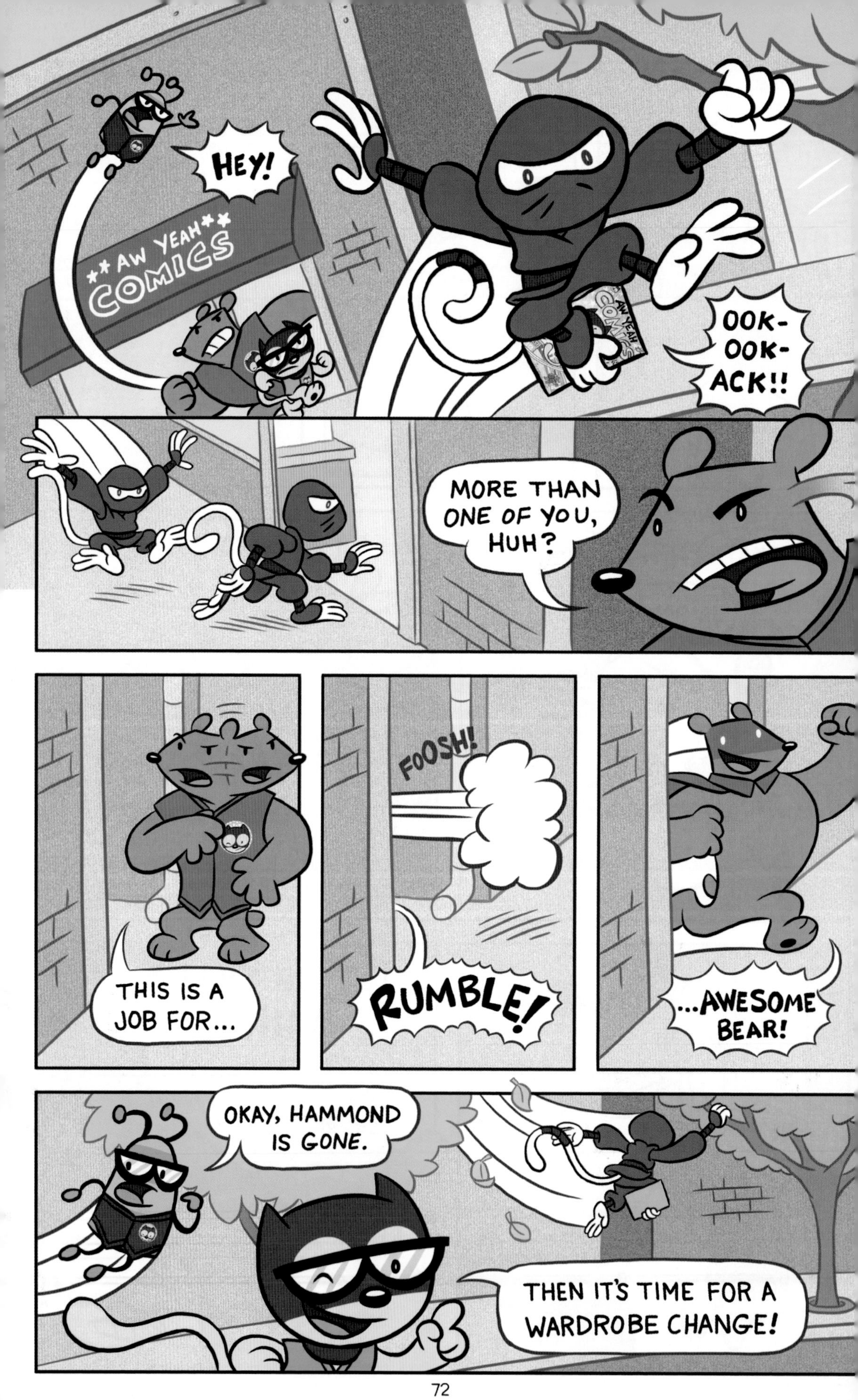
HEY!
** AW YEAH ** COMICS
AW YEAH COMICS
OOK-OOK-ACK!!
MORE THAN ONE OF YOU, HUH?
THIS IS A JOB FOR...
FOOSH!
RUMBLE!
...AWESOME BEAR!
OKAY, HAMMOND IS GONE.
THEN IT'S TIME FOR A WARDROBE CHANGE!

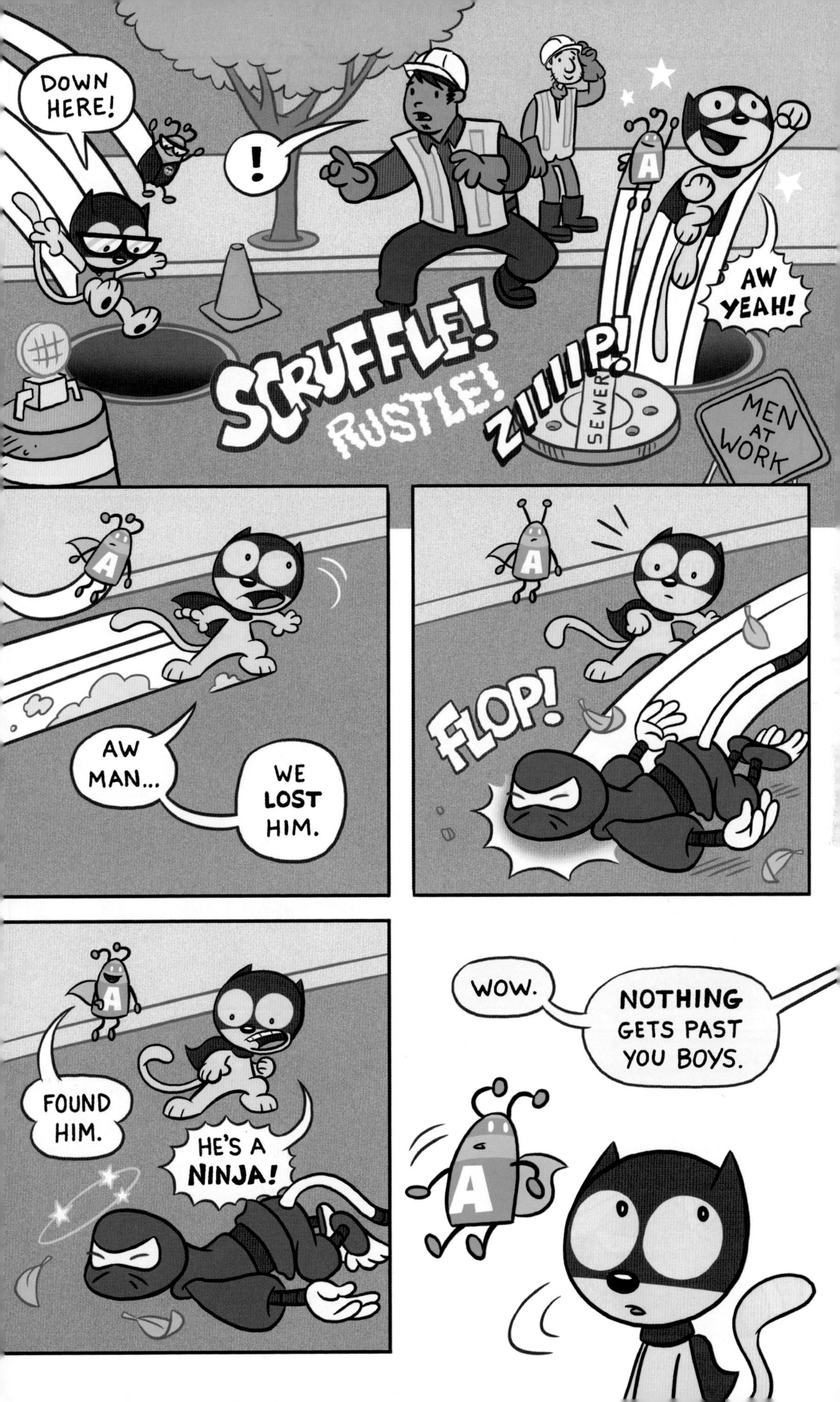
DOWN HERE!
!
SCRUFFLE!
RUSTLE!
ZIIIIIP!
SEWER
AW YEAH!
MEN AT WORK
AW MAN...
WE LOST HIM.
FLOP!
FOUND HIM.
HE'S A NINJA!
WOW.
NOTHING GETS PAST YOU BOYS.

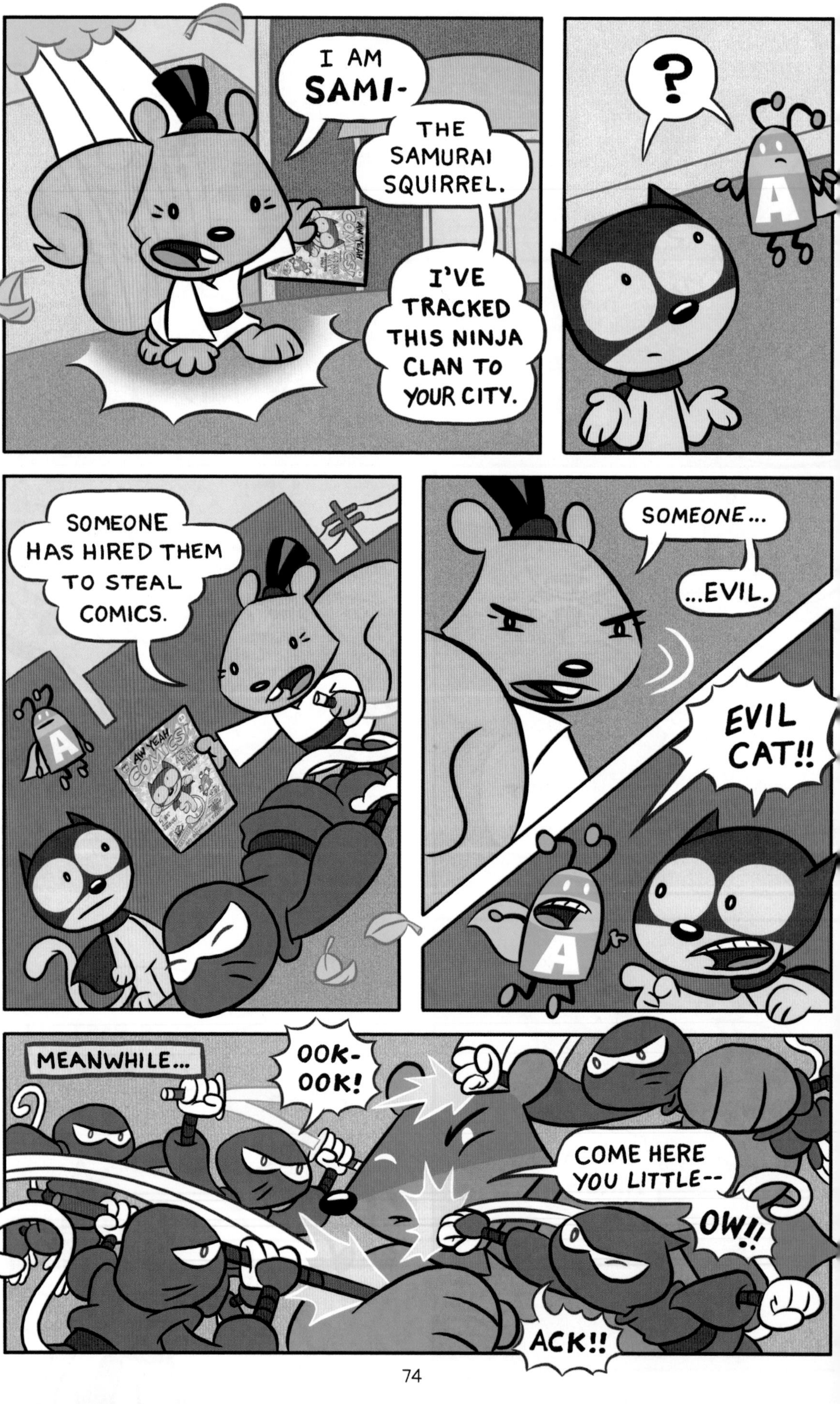
I AM SAMI-
THE SAMURAI SQUIRREL.
I'VE TRACKED THIS NINJA CLAN TO YOUR CITY.
?
SOMEONE HAS HIRED THEM TO STEAL COMICS.
SOMEONE...
...EVIL.
EVIL CAT!!
MEANWHILE...
OOK-OOK!
COME HERE YOU LITTLE--
OW!!
ACK!!

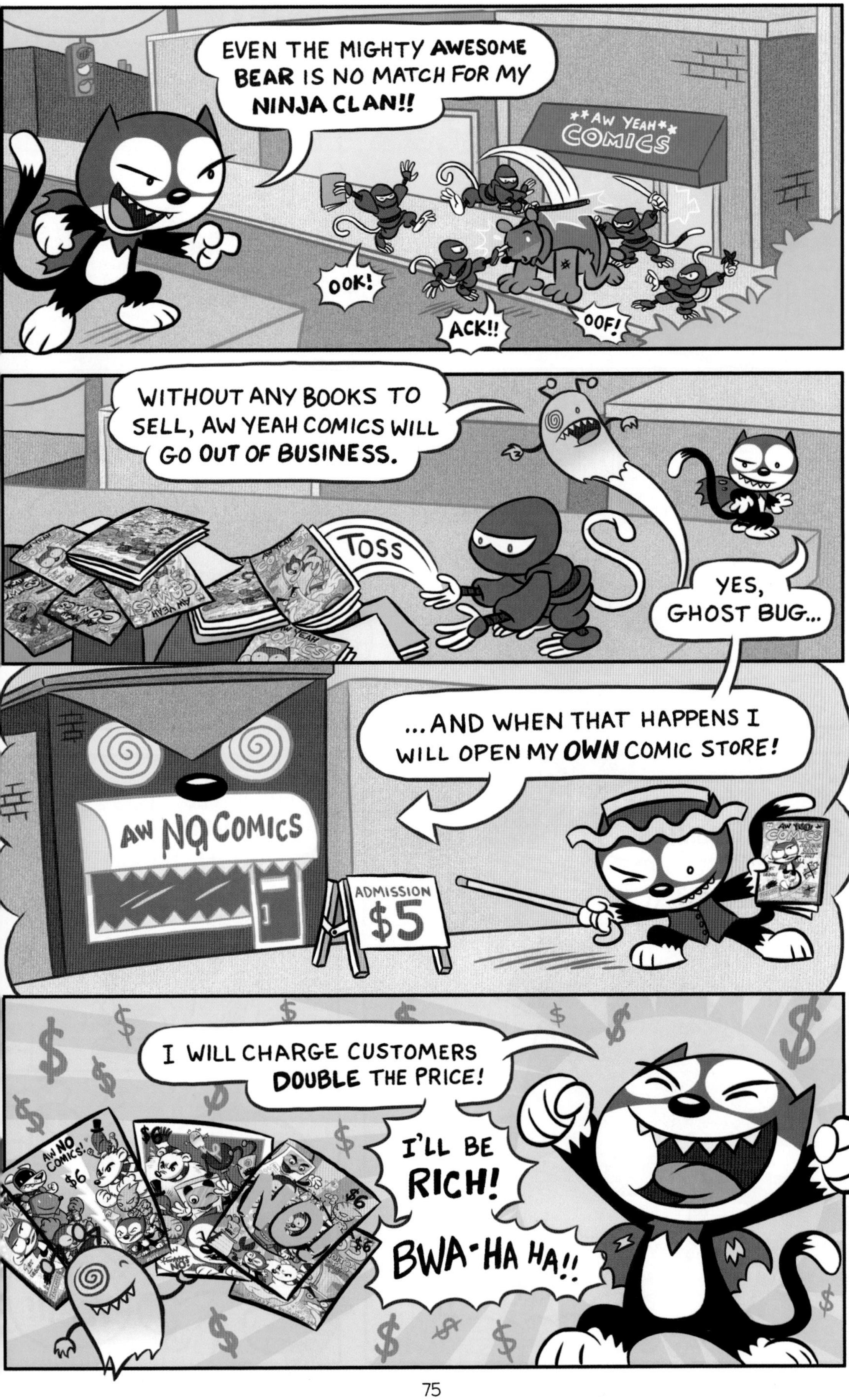

EVEN THE MIGHTY AWESOME BEAR IS NO MATCH FOR MY NINJA CLAN!!
AW YEAH COMICS
OOK!
ACK!!
OOF!
WITHOUT ANY BOOKS TO SELL, AW YEAH COMICS WILL GO OUT OF BUSINESS.
TOSS
YES, GHOST BUG...
...AND WHEN THAT HAPPENS I WILL OPEN MY OWN COMIC STORE!
AW NO COMICS
ADMISSION $5
I WILL CHARGE CUSTOMERS DOUBLE THE PRICE!
I'LL BE RICH!
BWA-HA HA!!
AW NO COMICS! $6

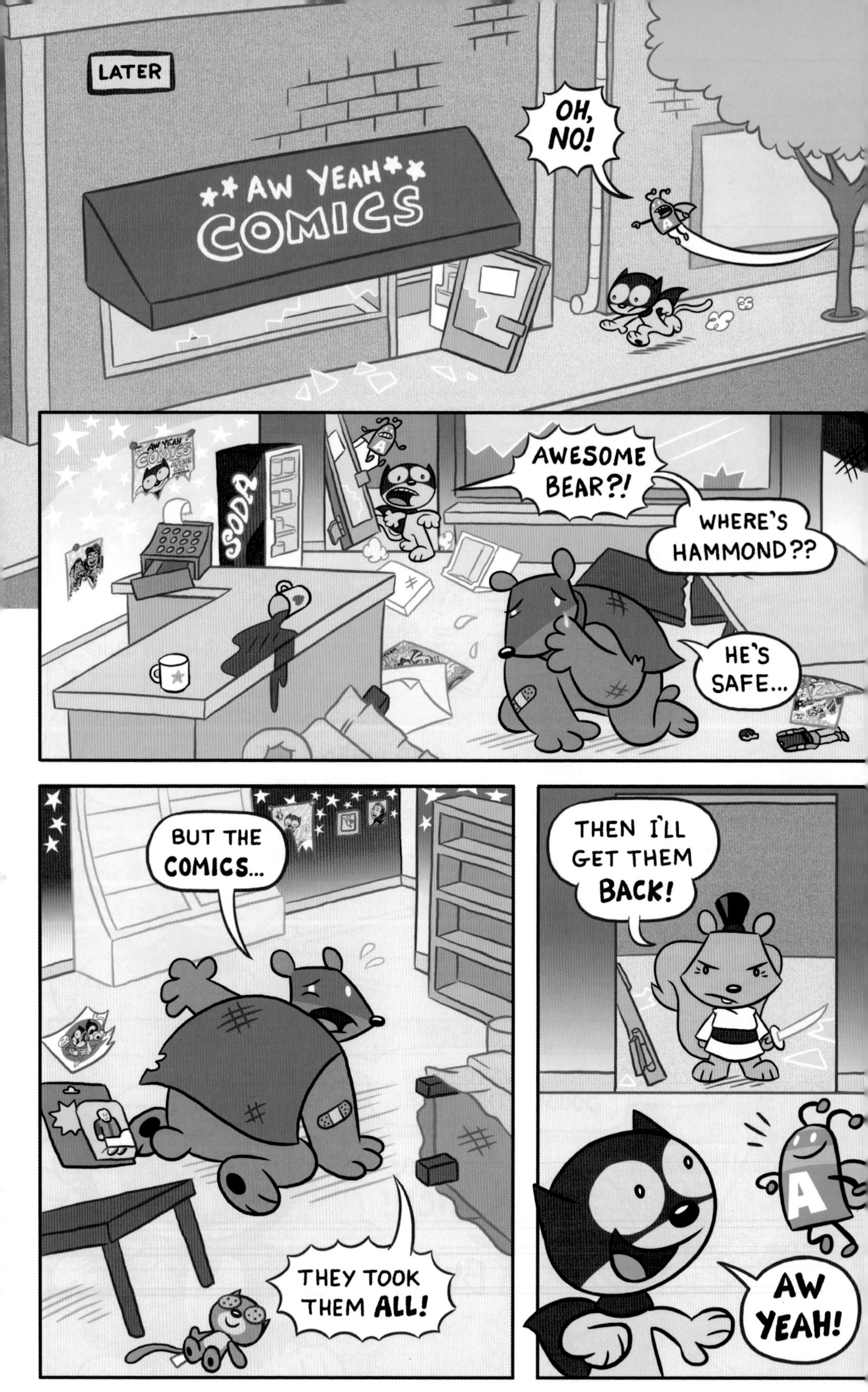
LATER
AW YEAH COMICS
OH, NO!
AWESOME BEAR?!
WHERE'S HAMMOND??
HE'S SAFE...
SODA
BUT THE COMICS...
THEY TOOK THEM ALL!
THEN I'LL GET THEM BACK!
AW YEAH!

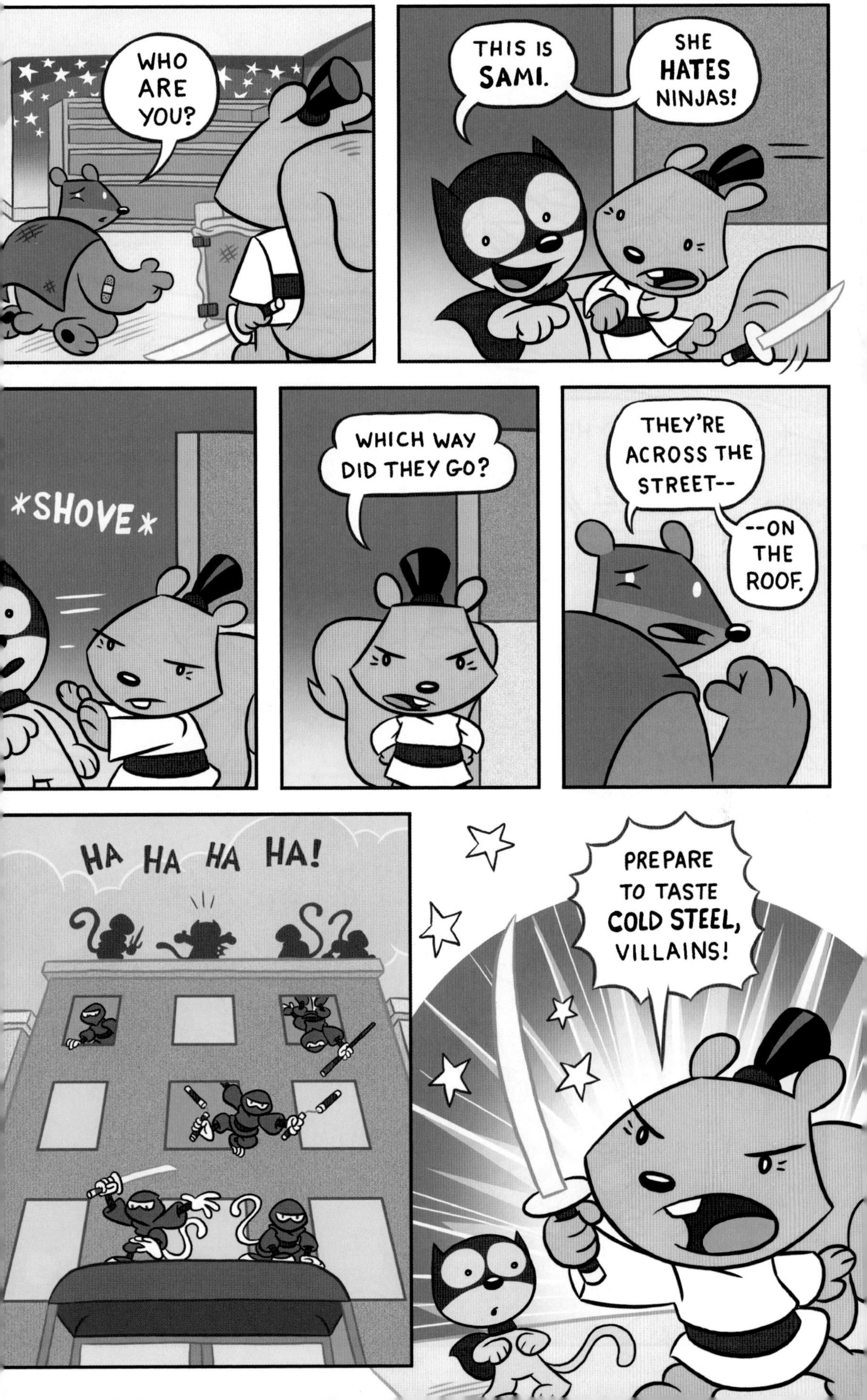
WHO ARE YOU?
THIS IS SAMI.
SHE HATES NINJAS!
SHOVE
WHICH WAY DID THEY GO?
THEY'RE ACROSS THE STREET--
--ON THE ROOF.
HA HA HA HA!
PREPARE TO TASTE COLD STEEL, VILLAINS!

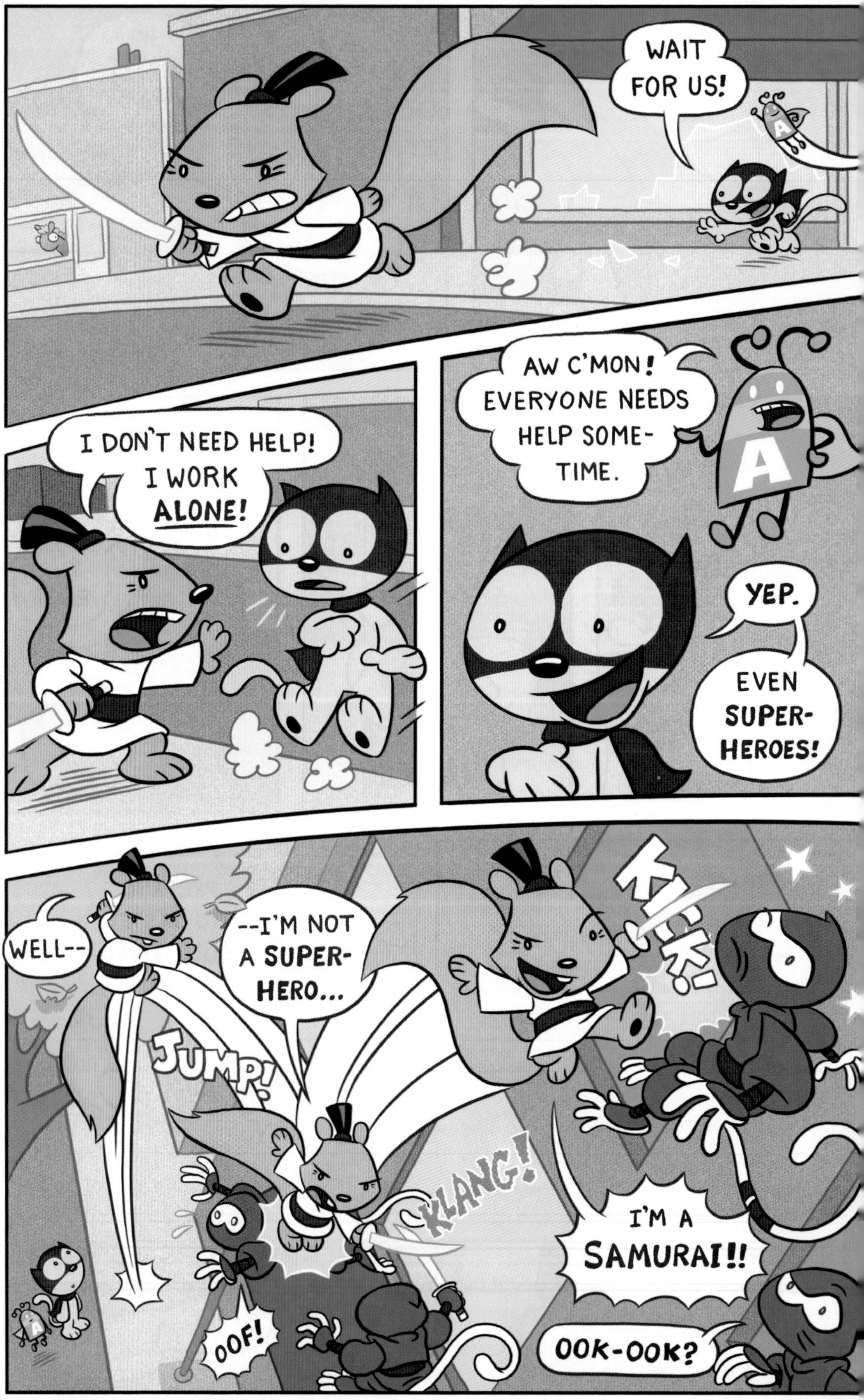
WAIT FOR US!
I DON'T NEED HELP! I WORK ALONE!
AW C'MON! EVERYONE NEEDS HELP SOME-TIME.
YEP.
EVEN SUPER-HEROES!
WELL--
--I'M NOT A SUPER-HERO...
KICK!
JUMP!
KLANG!
I'M A SAMURAI!!
OOF!
OOK-OOK?

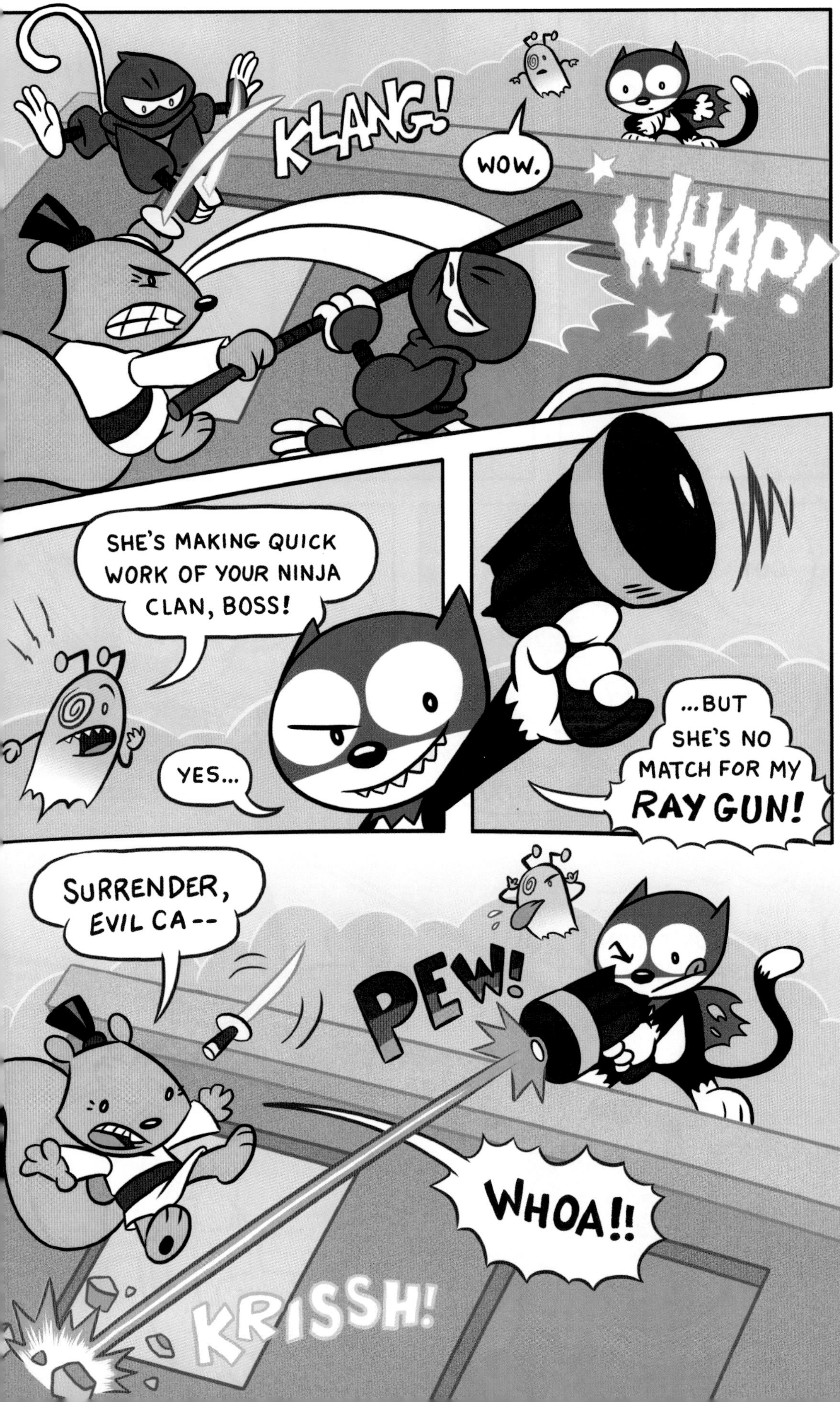
KLANG!
WOW.
WHAP!
SHE'S MAKING QUICK WORK OF YOUR NINJA CLAN, BOSS!
YES...
...BUT SHE'S NO MATCH FOR MY RAY GUN!
SURRENDER, EVIL CA--
PEW!
WHOA!!
KRISSH!

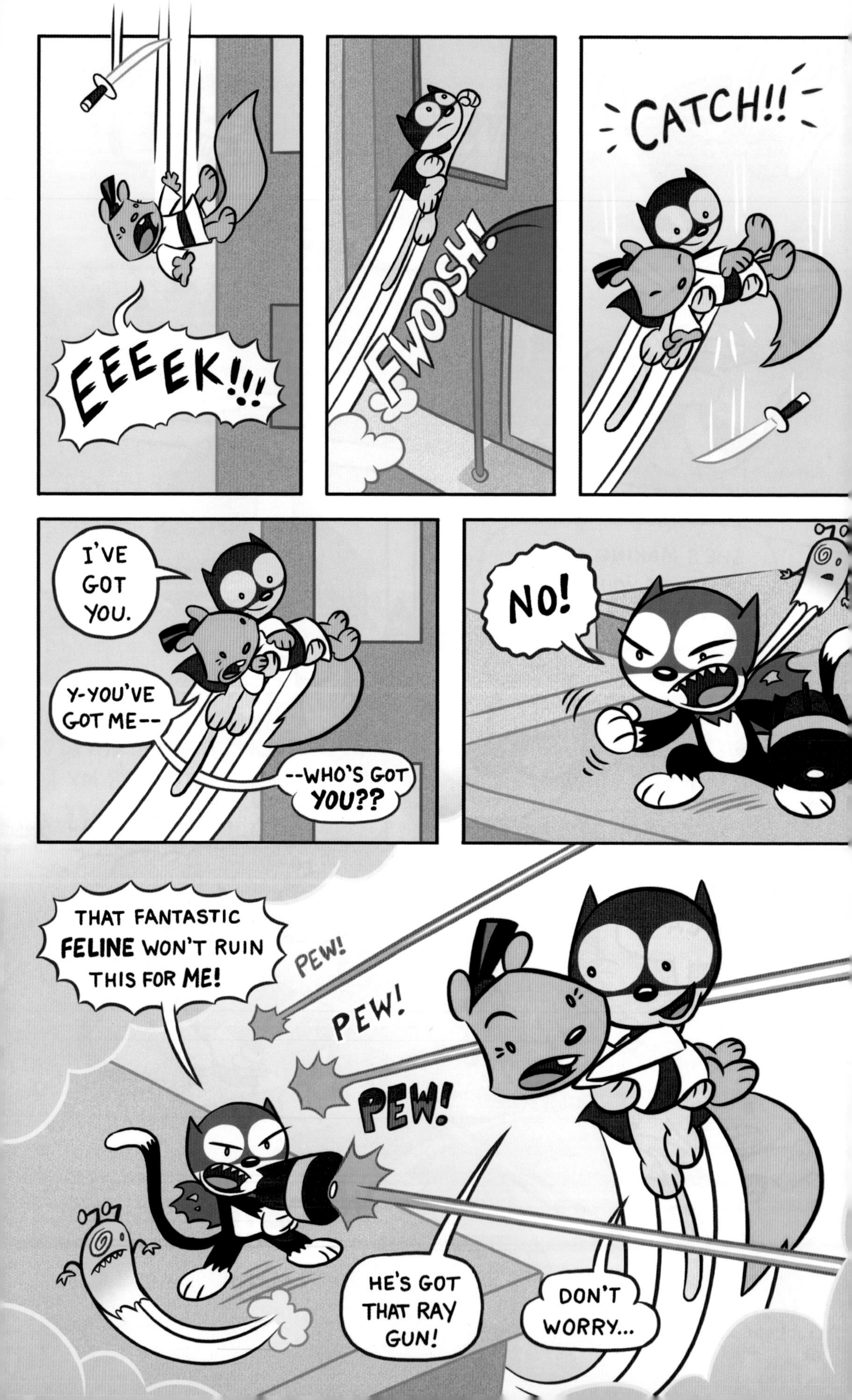
EEEEK!!!
FWOOSH!
CATCH!!
I'VE GOT YOU.
Y-YOU'VE GOT ME--
--WHO'S GOT YOU??
NO!
THAT FANTASTIC FELINE WON'T RUIN THIS FOR ME!
PEW!
PEW!
PEW!
HE'S GOT THAT RAY GUN!
DON'T WORRY...

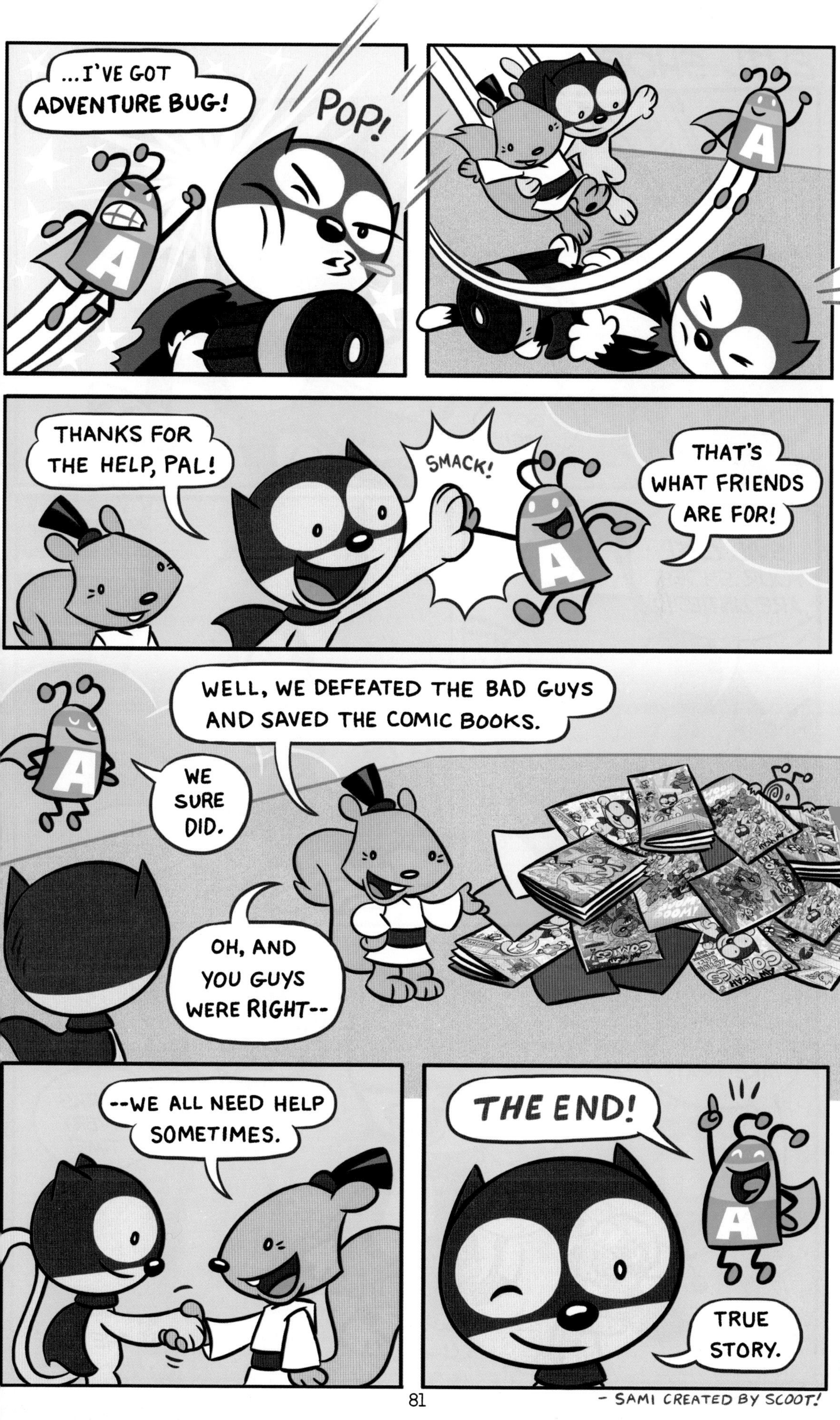
...I'VE GOT ADVENTURE BUG!
POP!
THANKS FOR THE HELP, PAL!
SMACK!
THAT'S WHAT FRIENDS ARE FOR!
WELL, WE DEFEATED THE BAD GUYS AND SAVED THE COMIC BOOKS.
WE SURE DID.
OH, AND YOU GUYS WERE RIGHT--
--WE ALL NEED HELP SOMETIMES.
THE END!
TRUE STORY.

- SAMI CREATED BY SCOOT!

EVIL SHOES!

BY: ALEJANDRO ROSADO

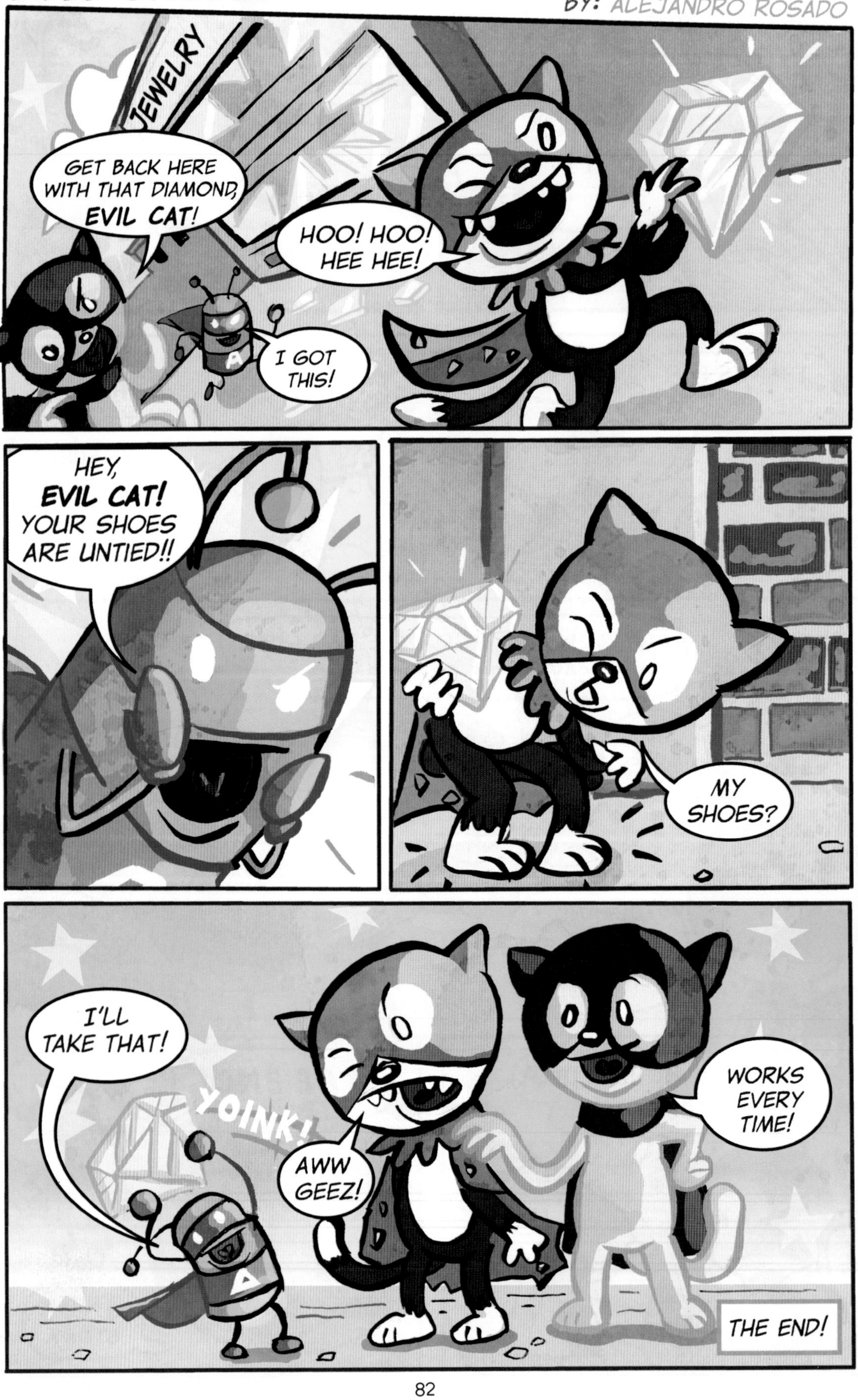
JEWELRY
GET BACK HERE WITH THAT DIAMOND, EVIL CAT!
HOO! HOO! HEE HEE!
I GOT THIS!
HEY, EVIL CAT! YOUR SHOES ARE UNTIED!!
MY SHOES?
I'LL TAKE THAT!
YOINK!
AWW GEEZ!
WORKS EVERY TIME!
THE END!

ACTION CAT in..."IT'S A TRAP!" by ZOD & Franco & Mr. Whitmore

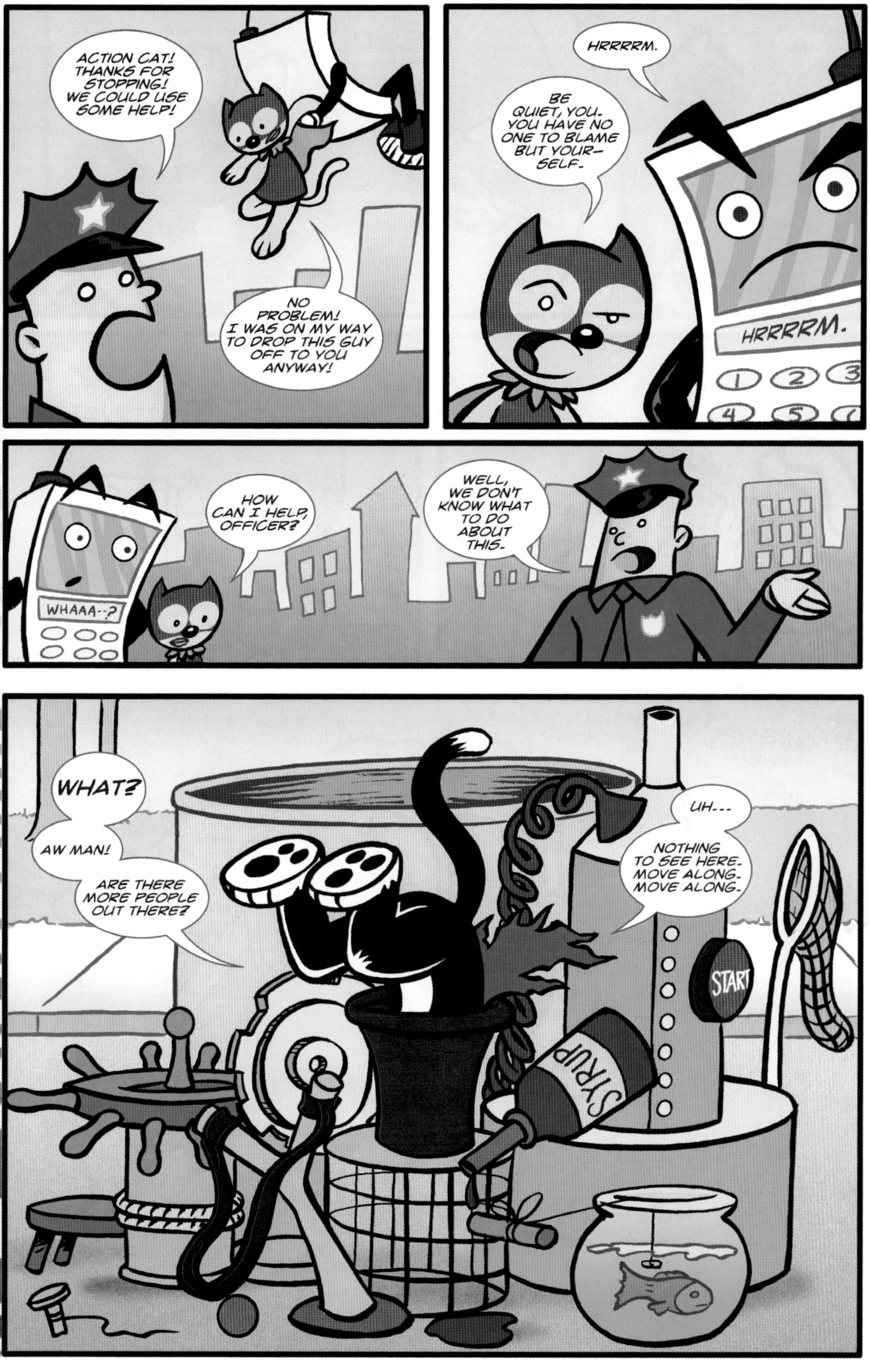
ACTION CAT! THANKS FOR STOPPING! WE COULD USE SOME HELP!
NO PROBLEM! I WAS ON MY WAY TO DROP THIS GUY OFF TO YOU ANYWAY!
HRRRRM.
BE QUIET, YOU. YOU HAVE NO ONE TO BLAME BUT YOURSELF.
HRRRRM.
1 2 3
4 5
WHAAA--?
HOW CAN I HELP, OFFICER?
WELL, WE DON'T KNOW WHAT TO DO ABOUT THIS.
WHAT?
AW MAN!
ARE THERE MORE PEOPLE OUT THERE?
UH---
NOTHING TO SEE HERE. MOVE ALONG. MOVE ALONG.
START
SYRUP

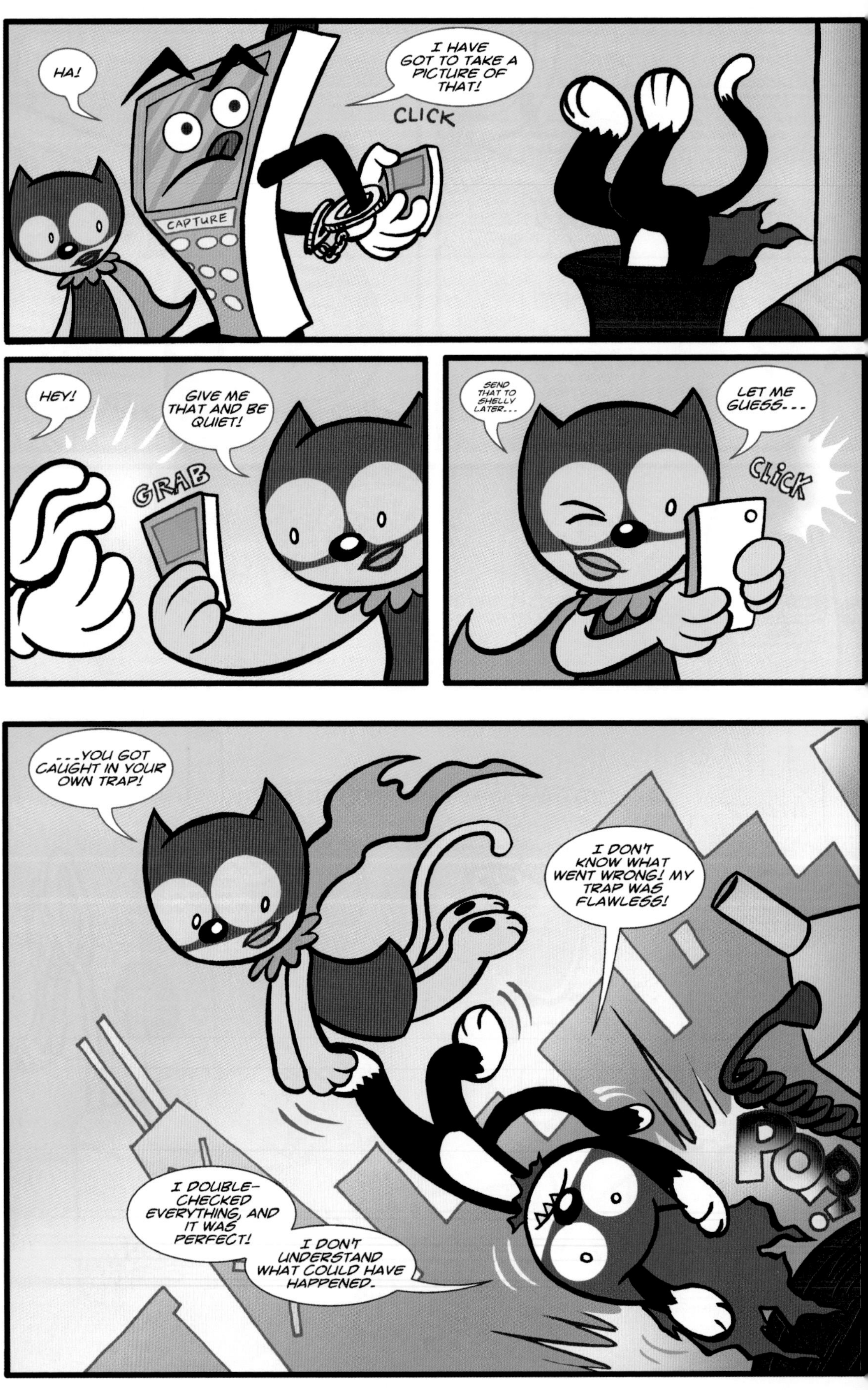
HA!
I HAVE GOT TO TAKE A PICTURE OF THAT!
CLICK
CAPTURE
HEY!
GIVE ME THAT AND BE QUIET!
GRAB
SEND THAT TO SHELLY LATER...
LET ME GUESS...
CLICK
...YOU GOT CAUGHT IN YOUR OWN TRAP!
I DON'T KNOW WHAT WENT WRONG! MY TRAP WAS FLAWLESS!
I DOUBLE-CHECKED EVERYTHING, AND IT WAS PERFECT!
I DON'T UNDERSTAND WHAT COULD HAVE HAPPENED.
POP!

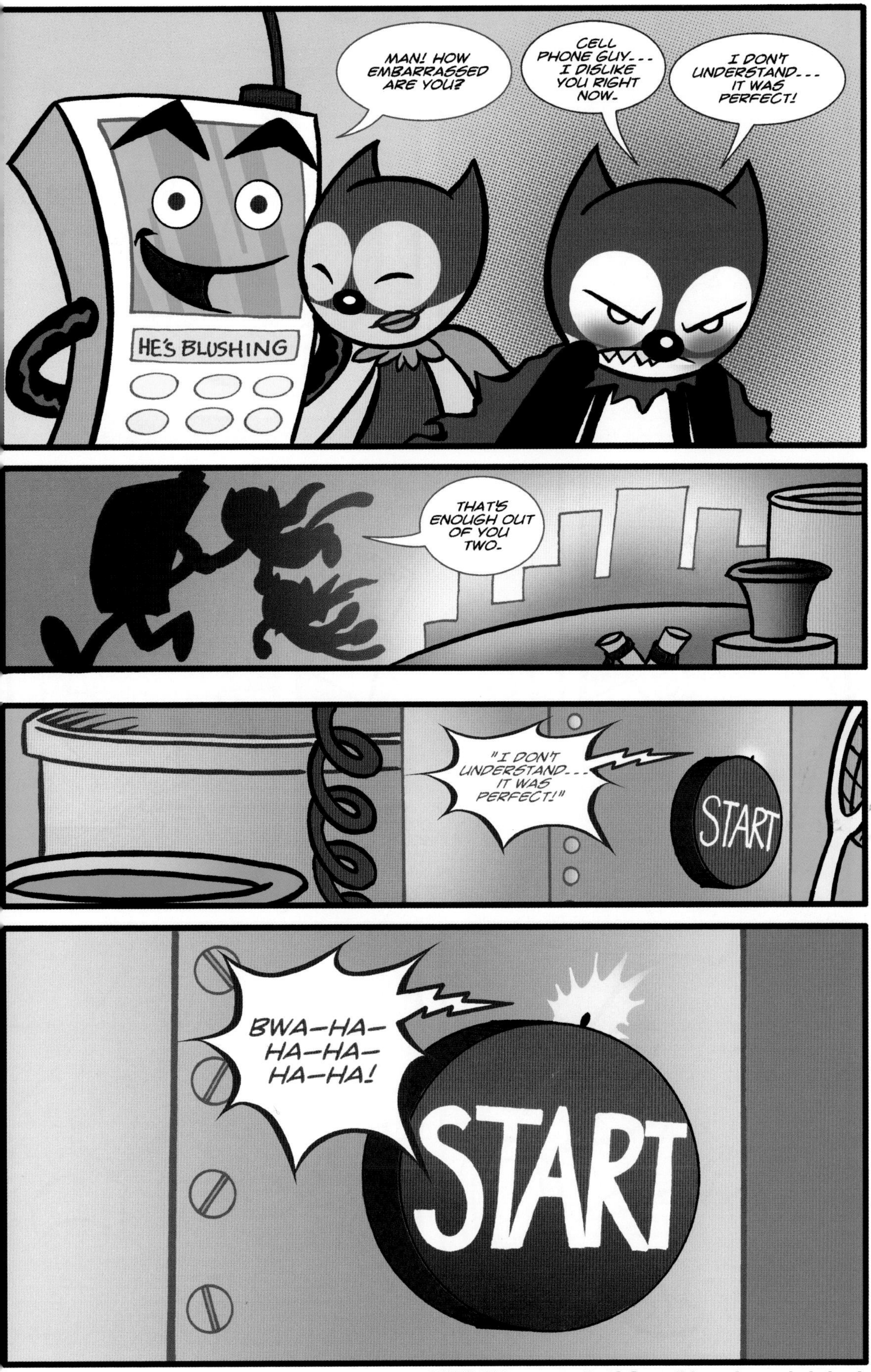
MAN! HOW EMBARRASSED ARE YOU?
CELL PHONE GUY... I DISLIKE YOU RIGHT NOW.
I DON'T UNDERSTAND... IT WAS PERFECT!
HE'S BLUSHING
THAT'S ENOUGH OUT OF YOU TWO.
"I DON'T UNDERSTAND... IT WAS PERFECT!"
START
BWA-HA-HA-HA-HA-HA!
START

-HUH? Did you see that? Something minuscule indeed.

ZOMBIE CAT AND GHOST BUG: TIC-TAC-TOE BY KURT WOOD

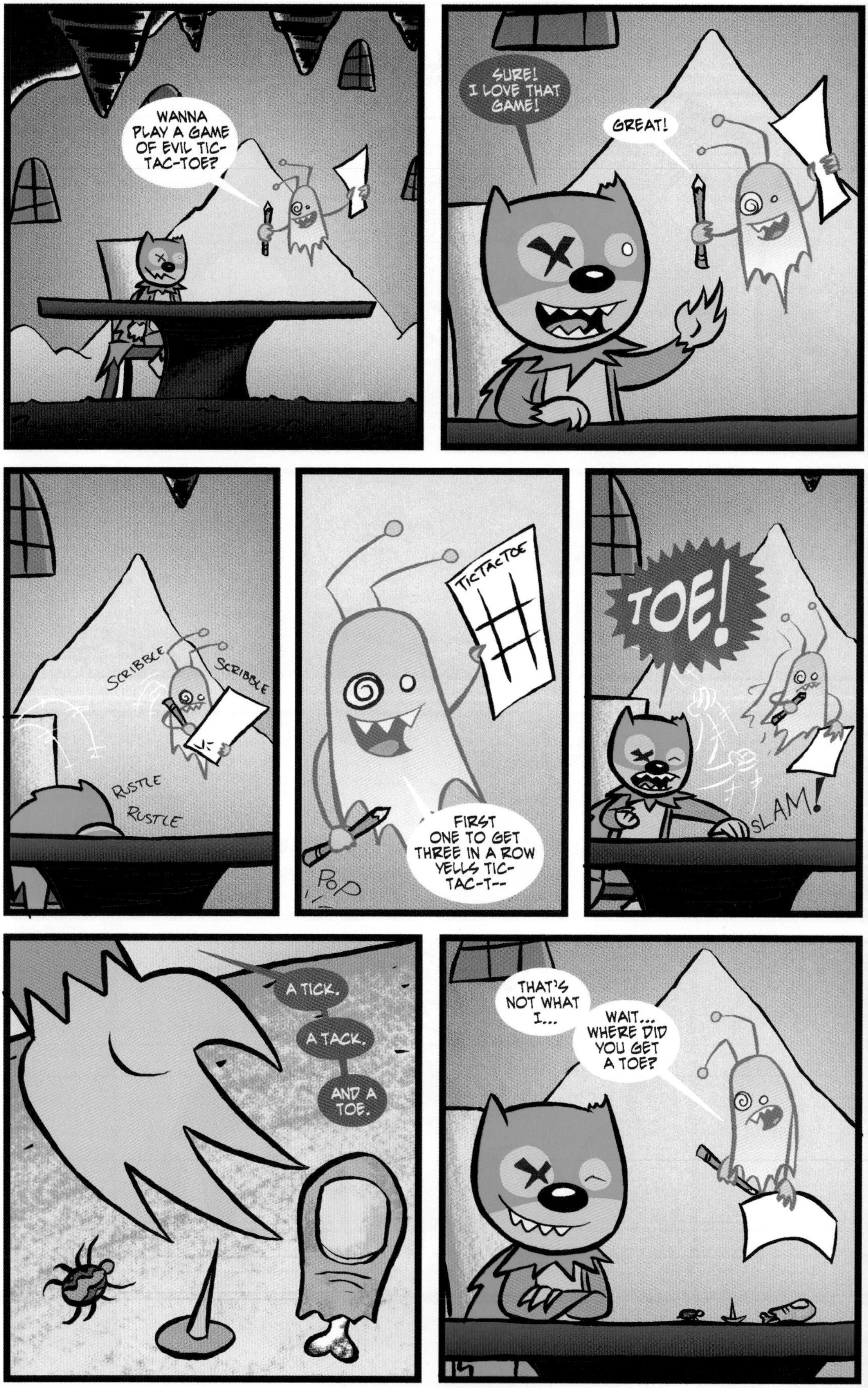
WANNA PLAY A GAME OF EVIL TIC-TAC-TOE?
SURE! I LOVE THAT GAME!
GREAT!
SCRIBBLE
SCRIBBLE
RUSTLE
RUSTLE
TICTACTOE
FIRST ONE TO GET THREE IN A ROW YELLS TIC-TAC-T--
POP
TOE!
SLAM!
A TICK.
A TACK.
AND A TOE.
THAT'S NOT WHAT I...
WAIT... WHERE DID YOU GET A TOE?

THE END!

★ CHAPTER FOUR ★

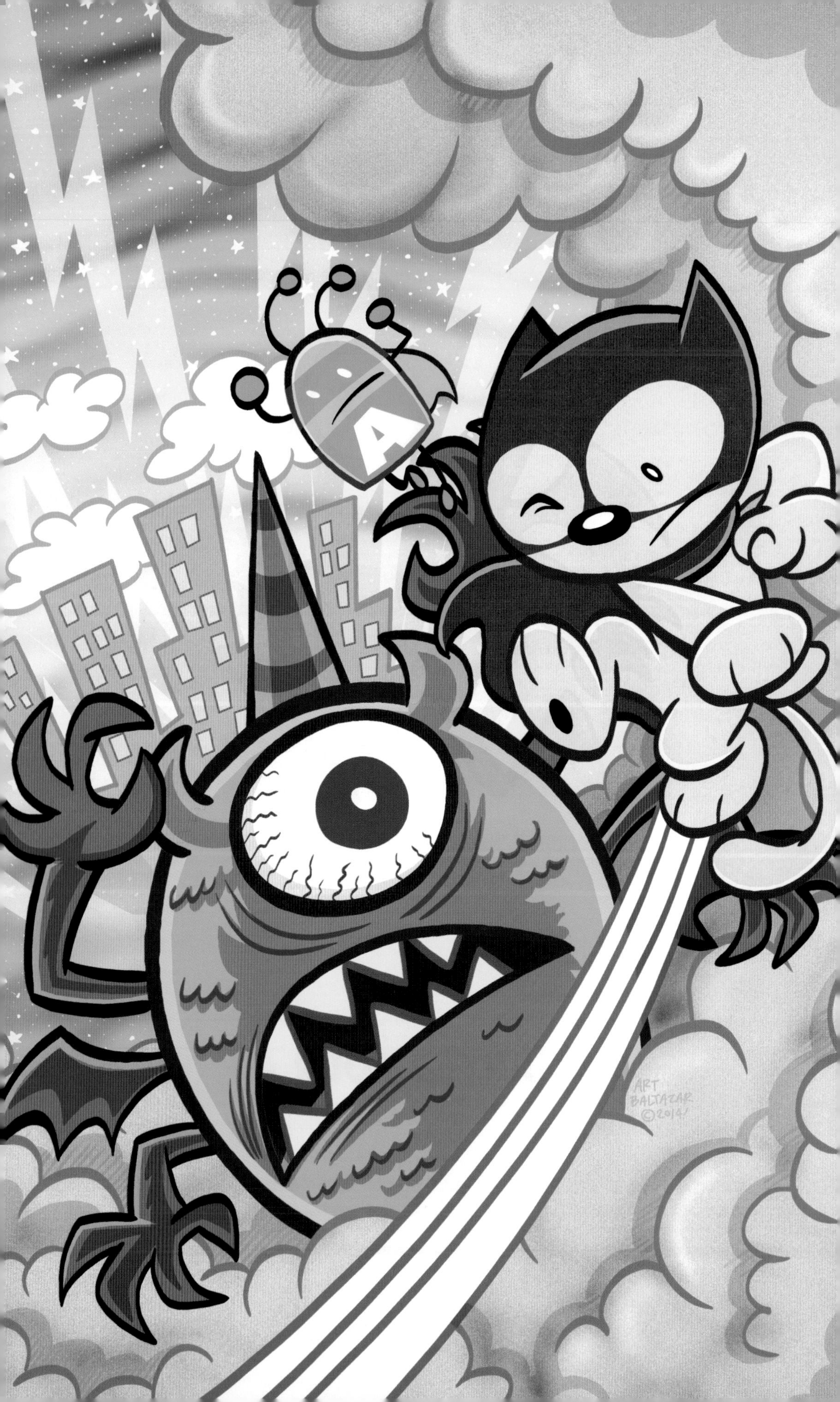
ART BALTAZAR ©2014

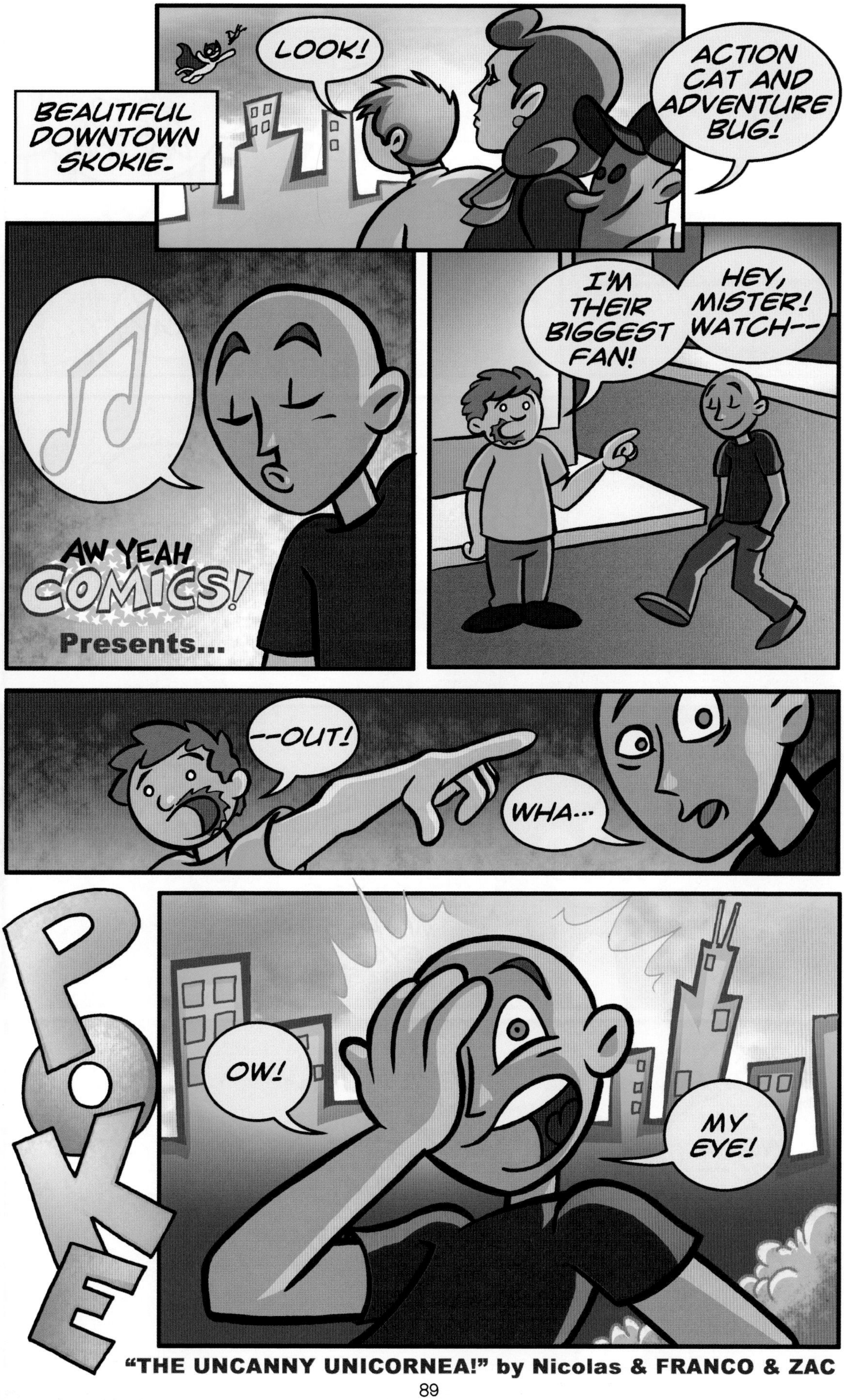
BEAUTIFUL DOWNTOWN SKOKIE-
LOOK!
ACTION CAT AND ADVENTURE BUG!
AW YEAH COMICS!
Presents...
I'M THEIR BIGGEST FAN!
HEY, MISTER! WATCH--
--OUT!
WHA...
POKE
OW!
MY EYE!

"THE UNCANNY UNICORNEA!" by Nicolas & FRANCO & ZAC

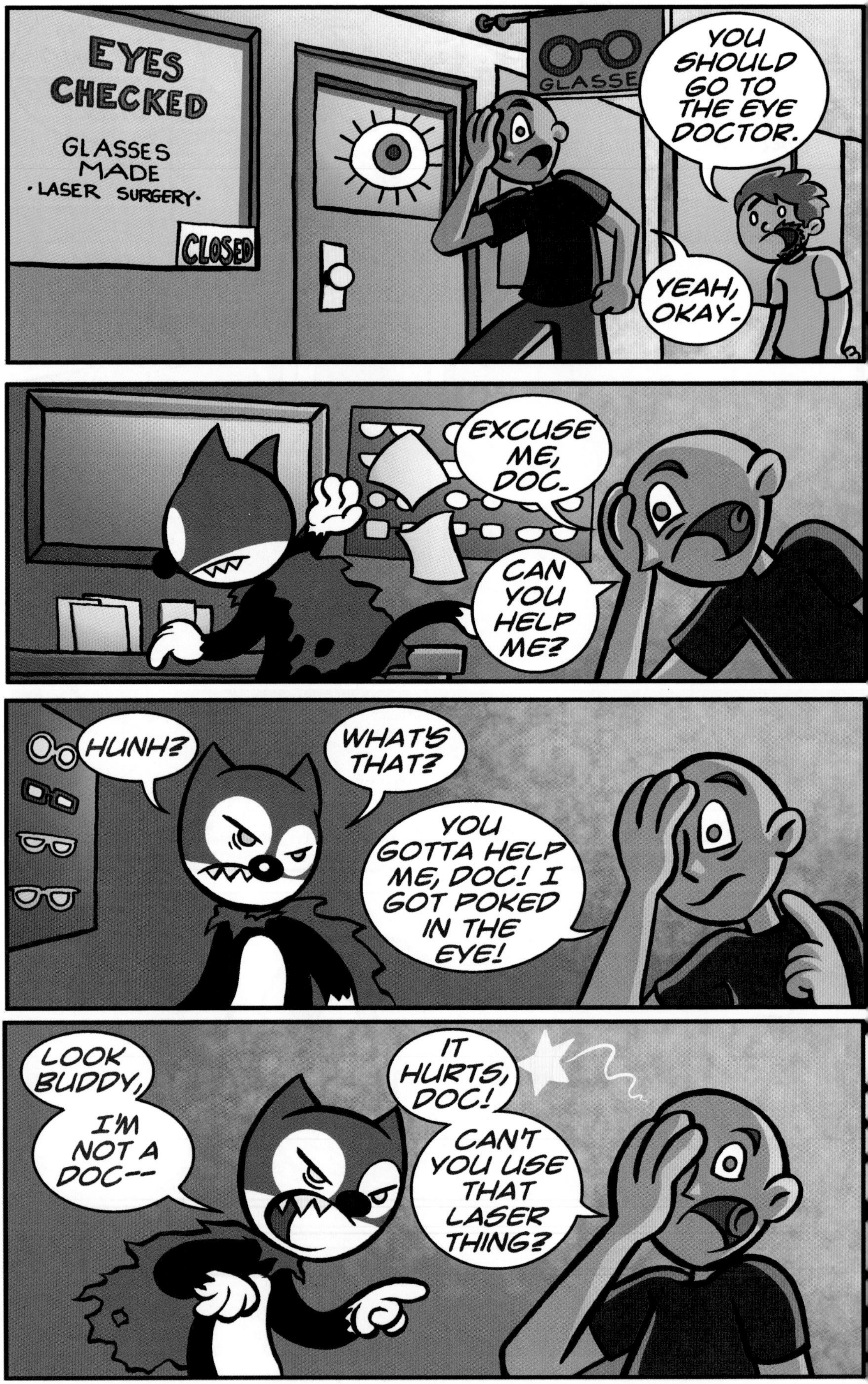
EYES CHECKED
GLASSES MADE
·LASER SURGERY·
CLOSED
GLASSE
YOU SHOULD GO TO THE EYE DOCTOR.
YEAH, OKAY.
EXCUSE ME, DOC.
CAN YOU HELP ME?
HUNH?
WHAT'S THAT?
YOU GOTTA HELP ME, DOC! I GOT POKED IN THE EYE!
LOOK BUDDY,
I'M NOT A DOC--
IT HURTS, DOC!
CAN'T YOU USE THAT LASER THING?

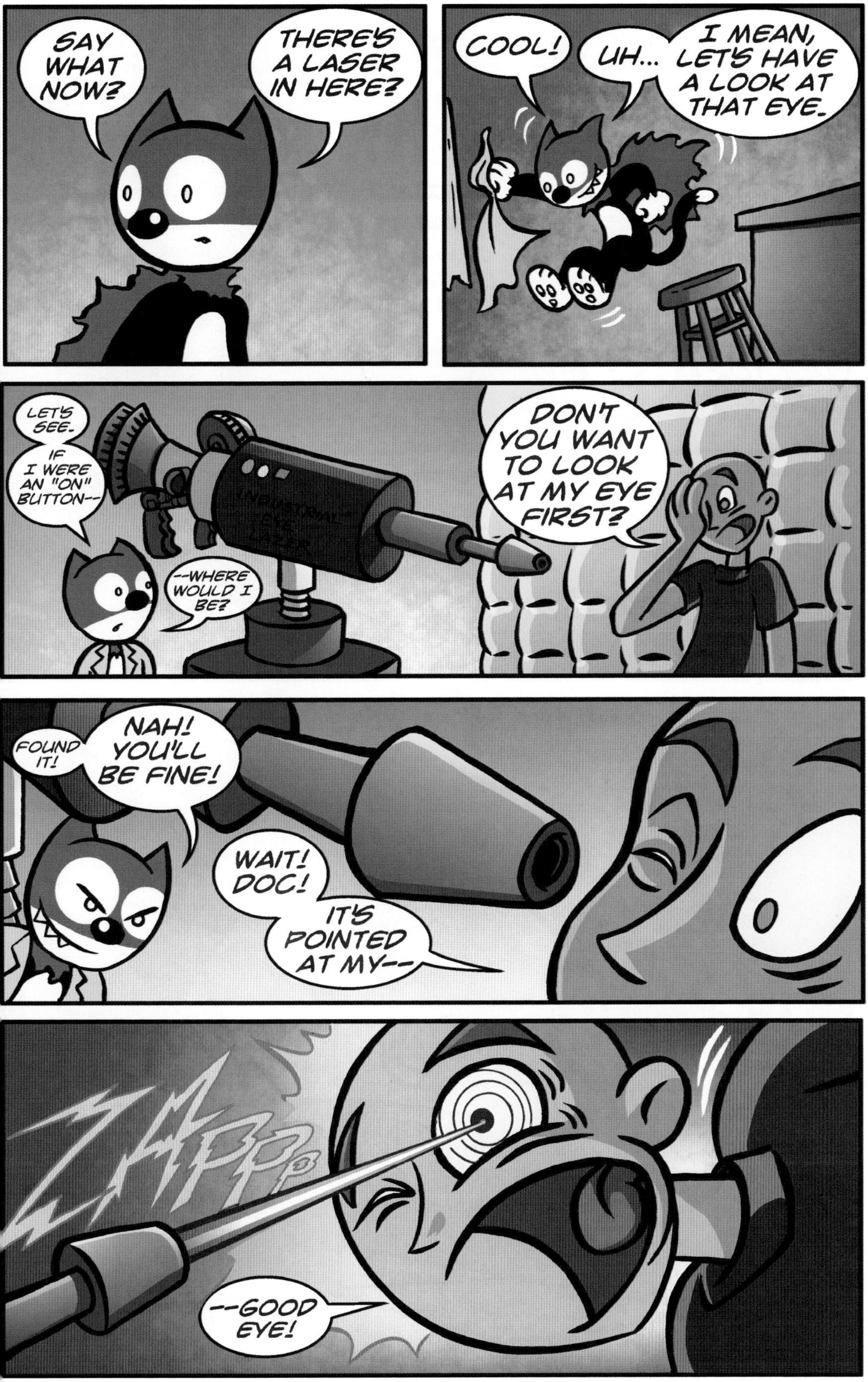
SAY WHAT NOW?
THERE'S A LASER IN HERE?
COOL!
UH... I MEAN, LET'S HAVE A LOOK AT THAT EYE.
LET'S SEE.
IF I WERE AN "ON" BUTTON--
--WHERE WOULD I BE?
DON'T YOU WANT TO LOOK AT MY EYE FIRST?
FOUND IT!
NAH! YOU'LL BE FINE!
WAIT! DOC!
IT'S POINTED AT MY--
ZAPPP
--GOOD EYE!

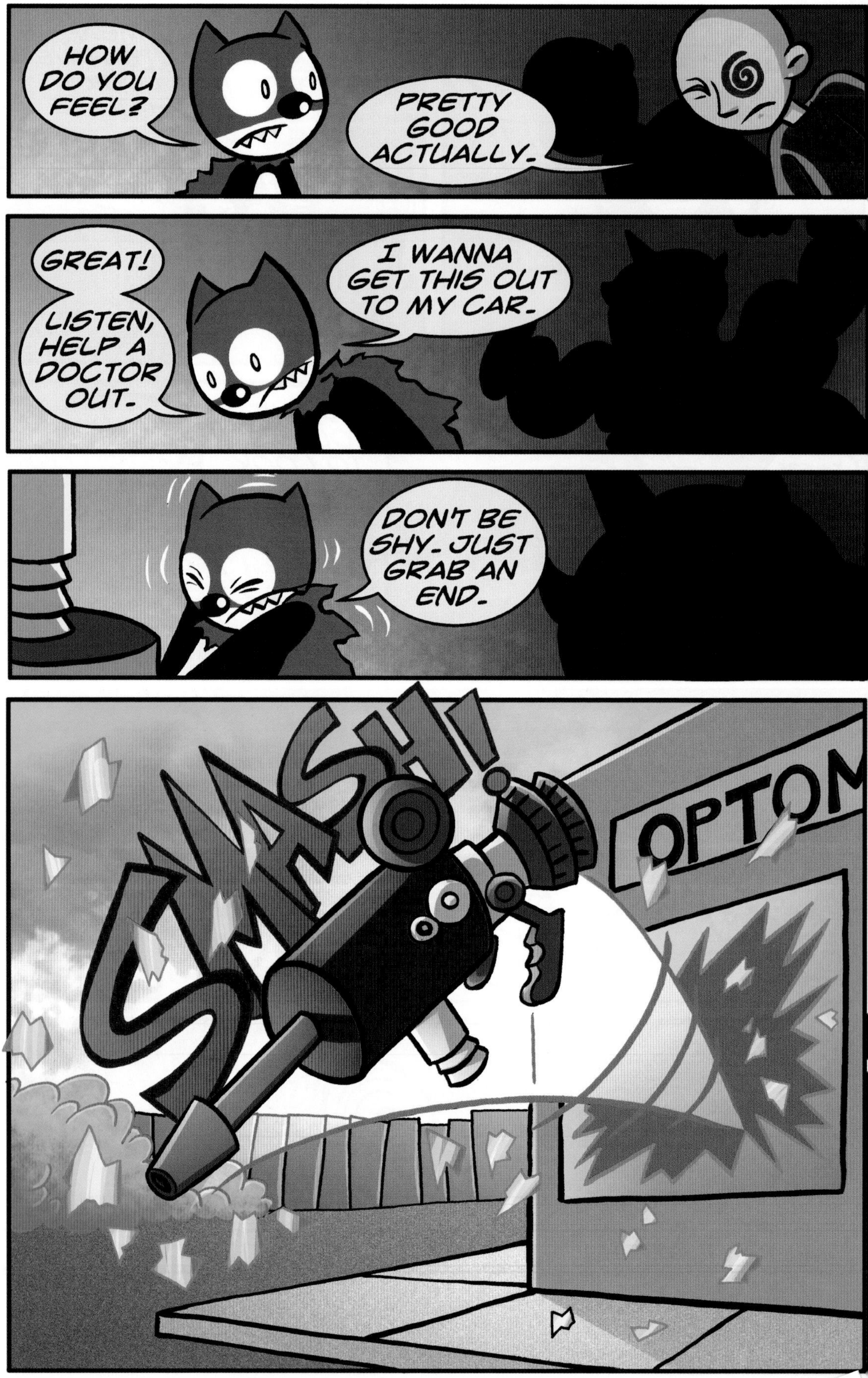
HOW DO YOU FEEL?
PRETTY GOOD ACTUALLY...
GREAT!
LISTEN, HELP A DOCTOR OUT.
I WANNA GET THIS OUT TO MY CAR.
DON'T BE SHY. JUST GRAB AN END.
SMASH!
OPTOM

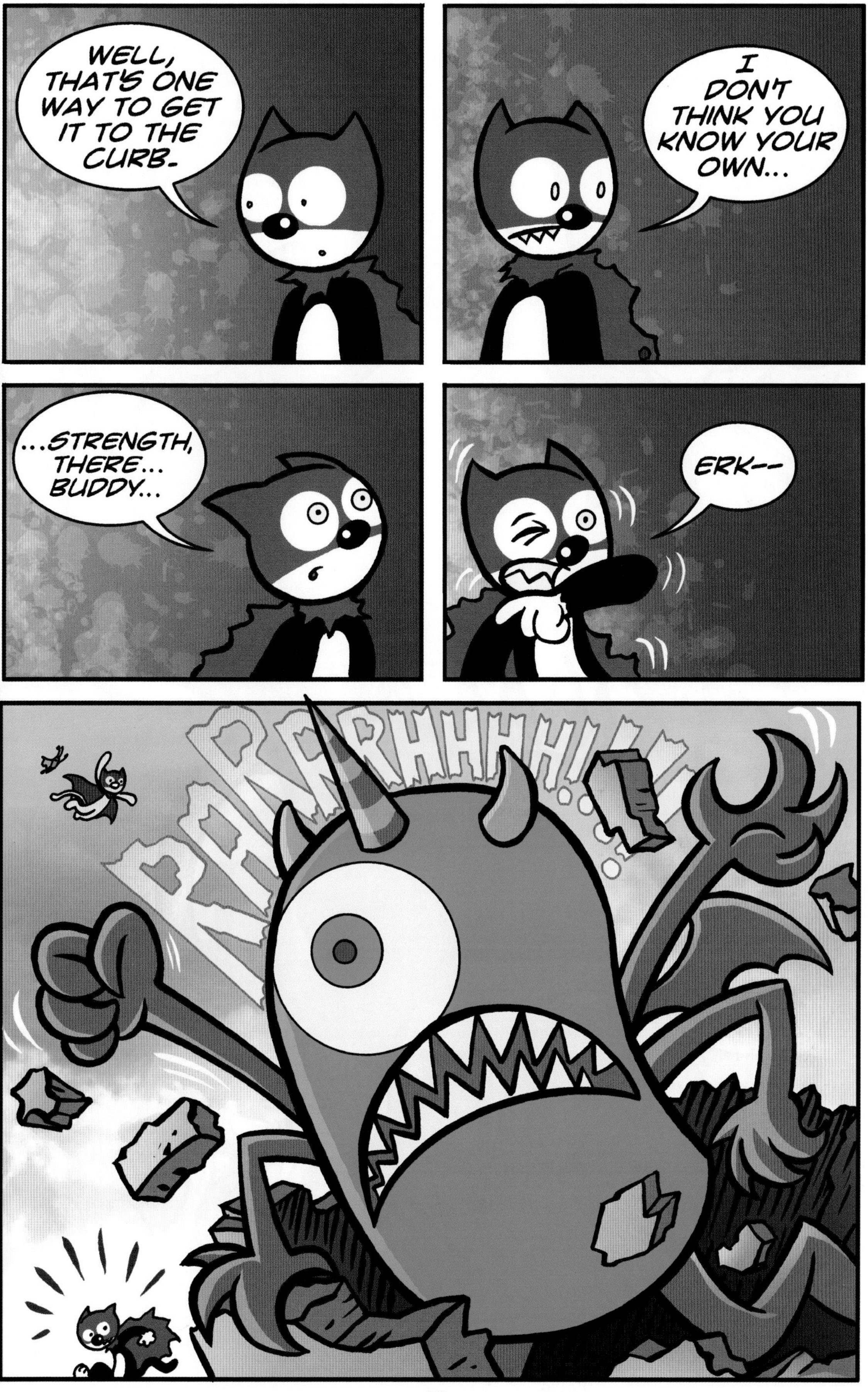
WELL, THAT'S ONE WAY TO GET IT TO THE CURB.
I DON'T THINK YOU KNOW YOUR OWN...
...STRENGTH, THERE... BUDDY...
ERK--
RRAARRHHHH!!!

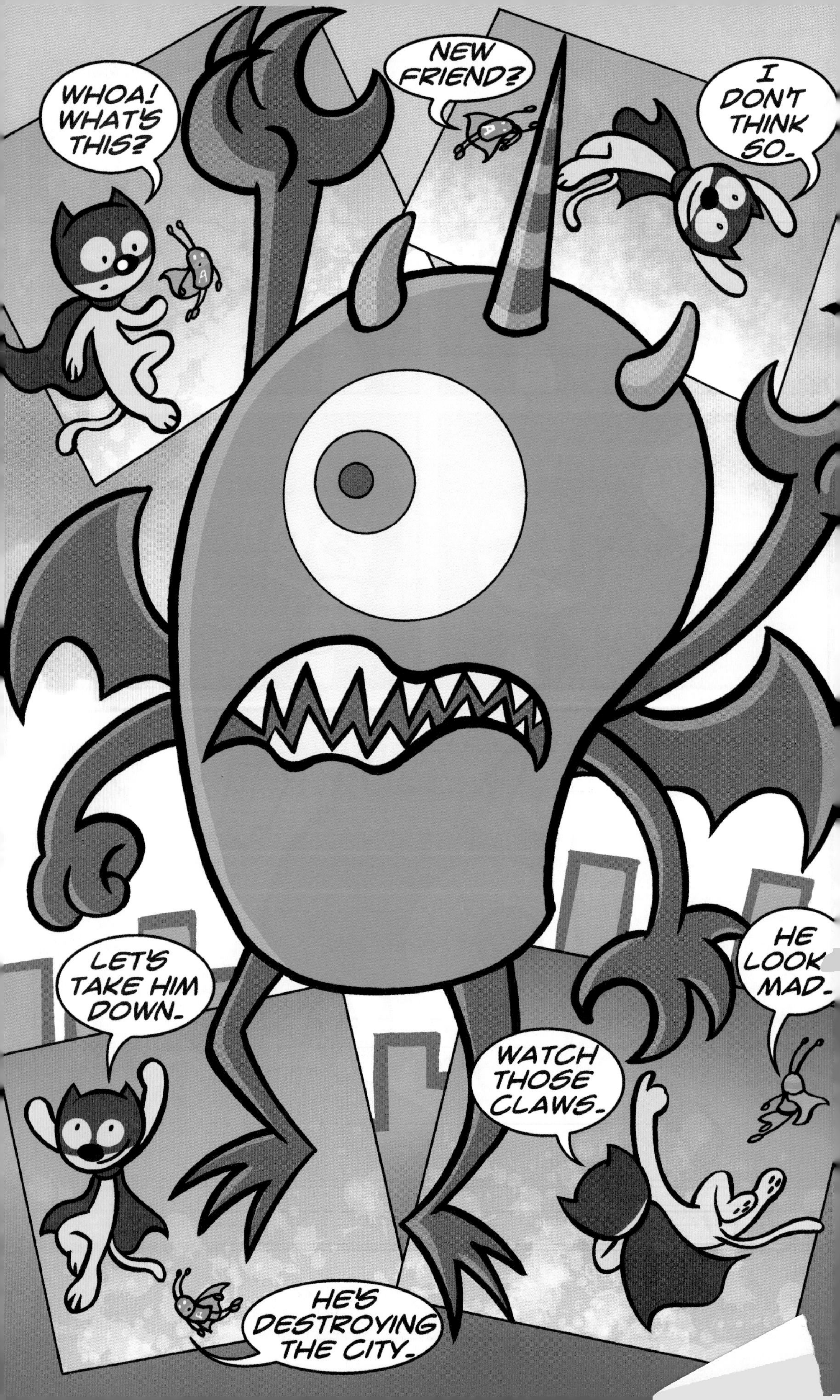
WHOA! WHAT'S THIS?
NEW FRIEND?
I DON'T THINK SO.
LET'S TAKE HIM DOWN.
HE'S DESTROYING THE CITY.
WATCH THOSE CLAWS.
HE LOOK MAD.

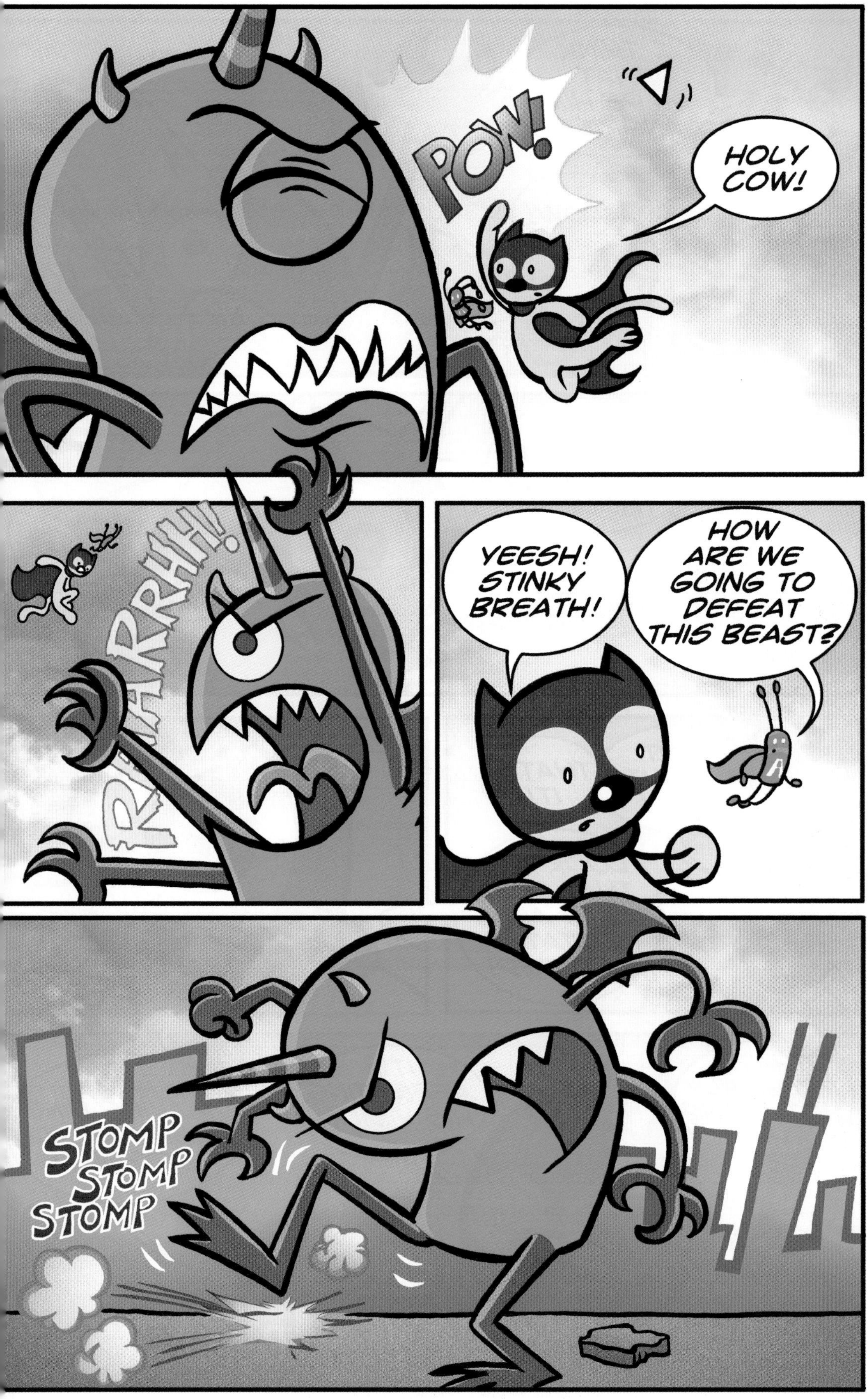
POW!
HOLY COW!
RARRH!!
YEESH! STINKY BREATH!
HOW ARE WE GOING TO DEFEAT THIS BEAST?
STOMP STOMP STOMP

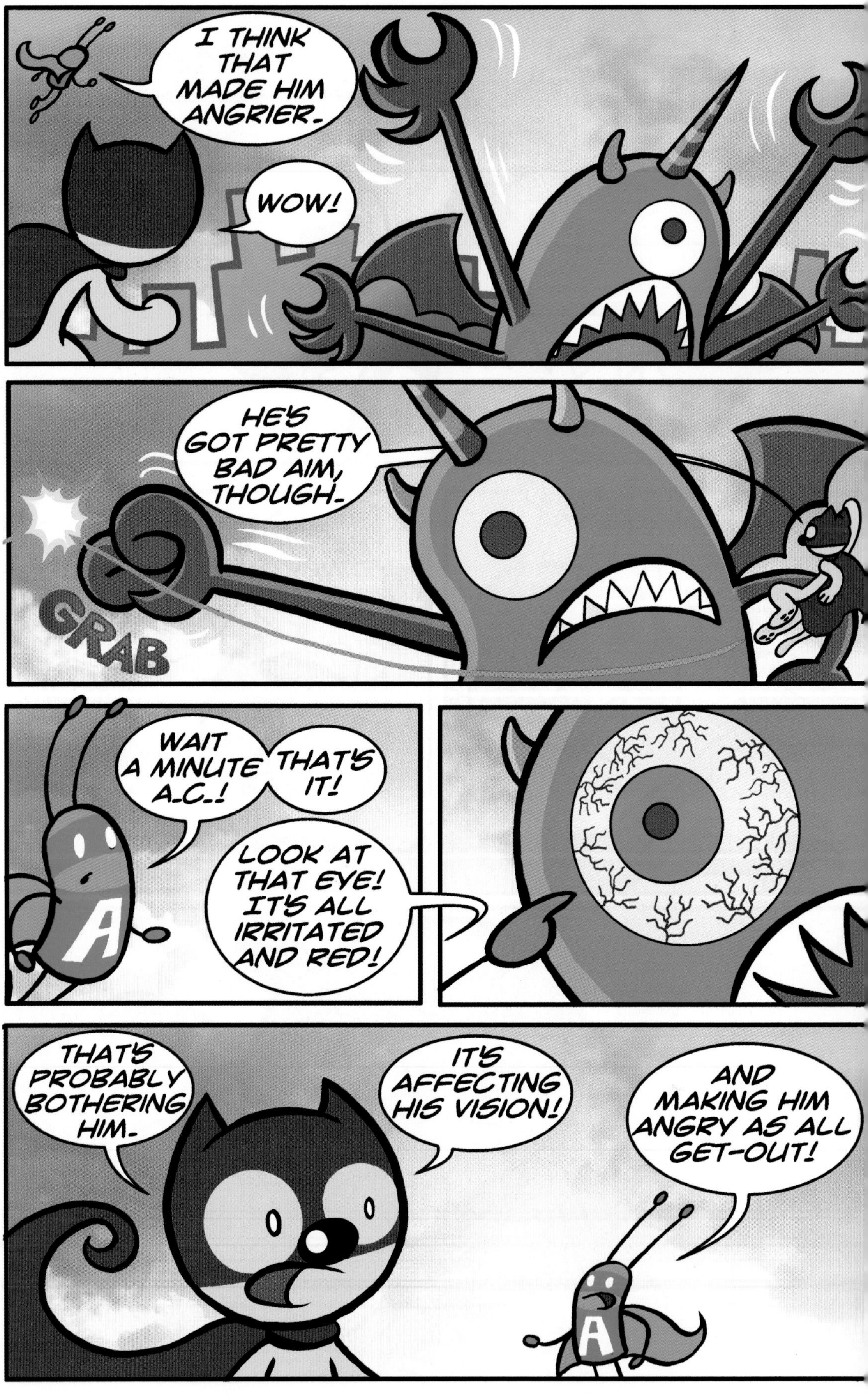

I THINK THAT MADE HIM ANGRIER.
WOW!
HE'S GOT PRETTY BAD AIM, THOUGH.
GRAB
WAIT A MINUTE A.C.!
THAT'S IT!
LOOK AT THAT EYE! IT'S ALL IRRITATED AND RED!
THAT'S PROBABLY BOTHERING HIM.
IT'S AFFECTING HIS VISION!
AND MAKING HIM ANGRY AS ALL GET-OUT!

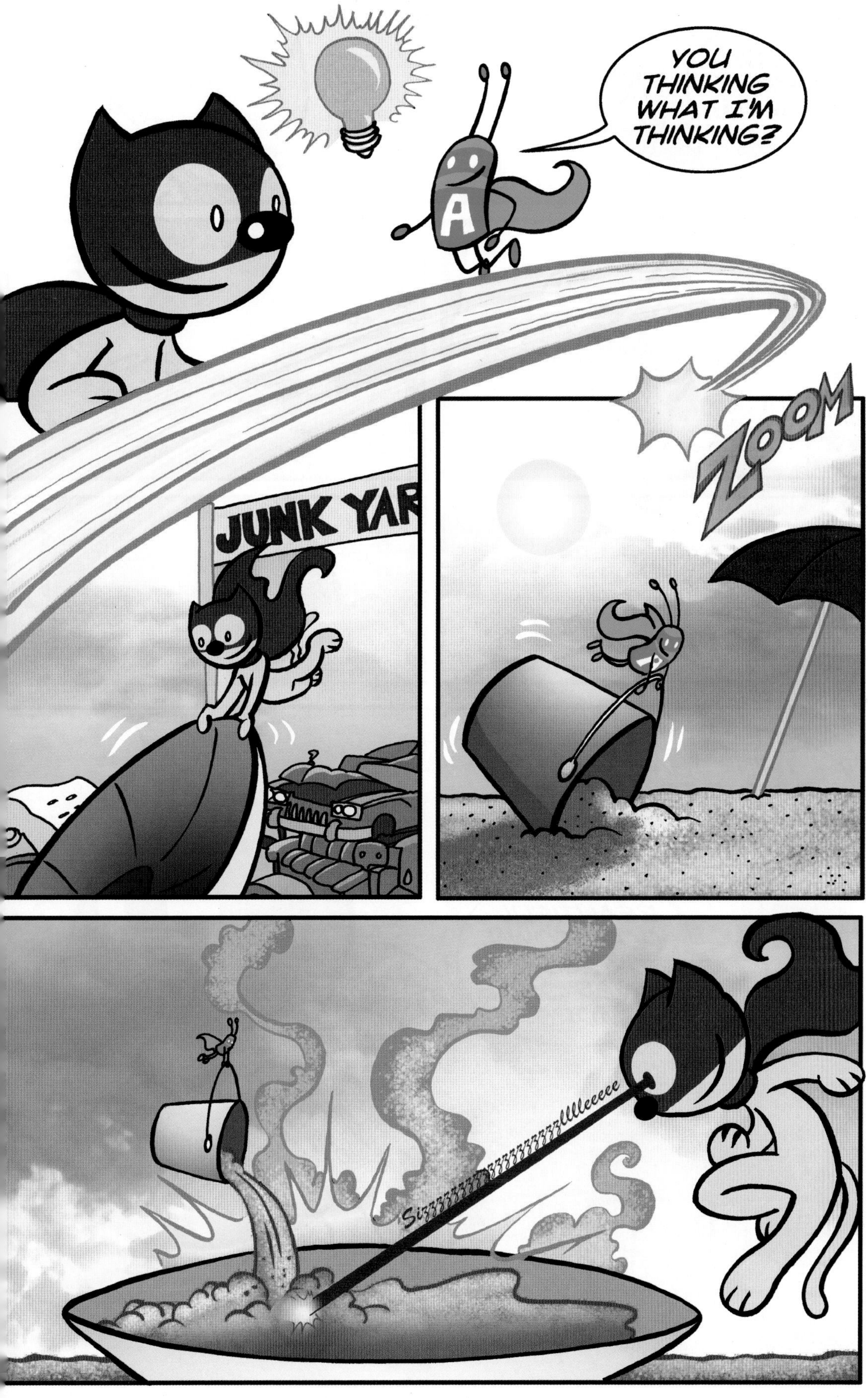

YOU THINKING WHAT I'M THINKING?
JUNK YAR
ZOOM
Sizzzzzzzzzzzzzzzzzzzzzllleeeee

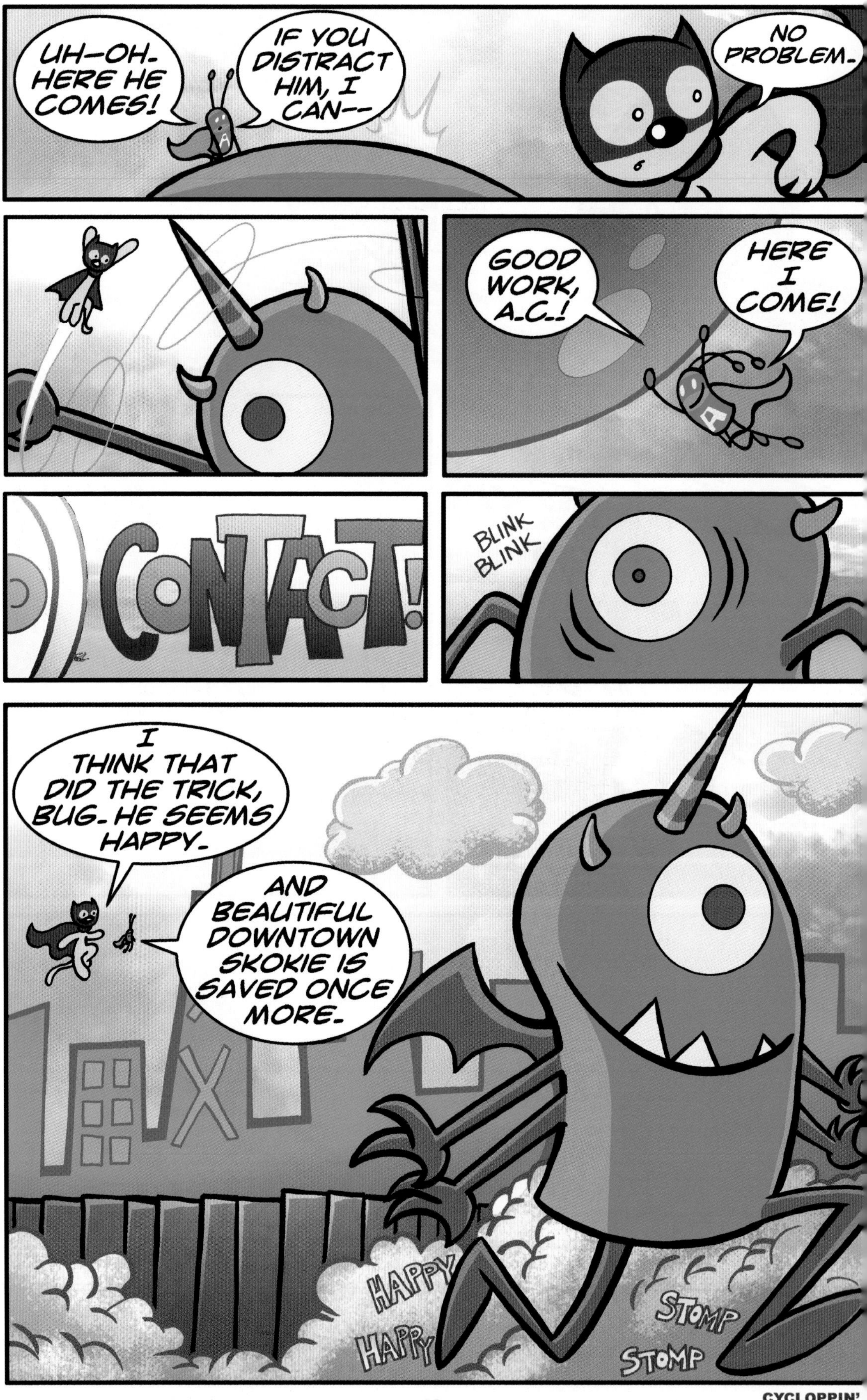
UH-OH. HERE HE COMES!
IF YOU DISTRACT HIM, I CAN--
NO PROBLEM.
GOOD WORK, A.C.!
HERE I COME!
CONTACT!
BLINK BLINK
I THINK THAT DID THE TRICK, BUG. HE SEEMS HAPPY.
AND BEAUTIFUL DOWNTOWN SKOKIE IS SAVED ONCE MORE.
HAPPY HAPPY
STOMP STOMP

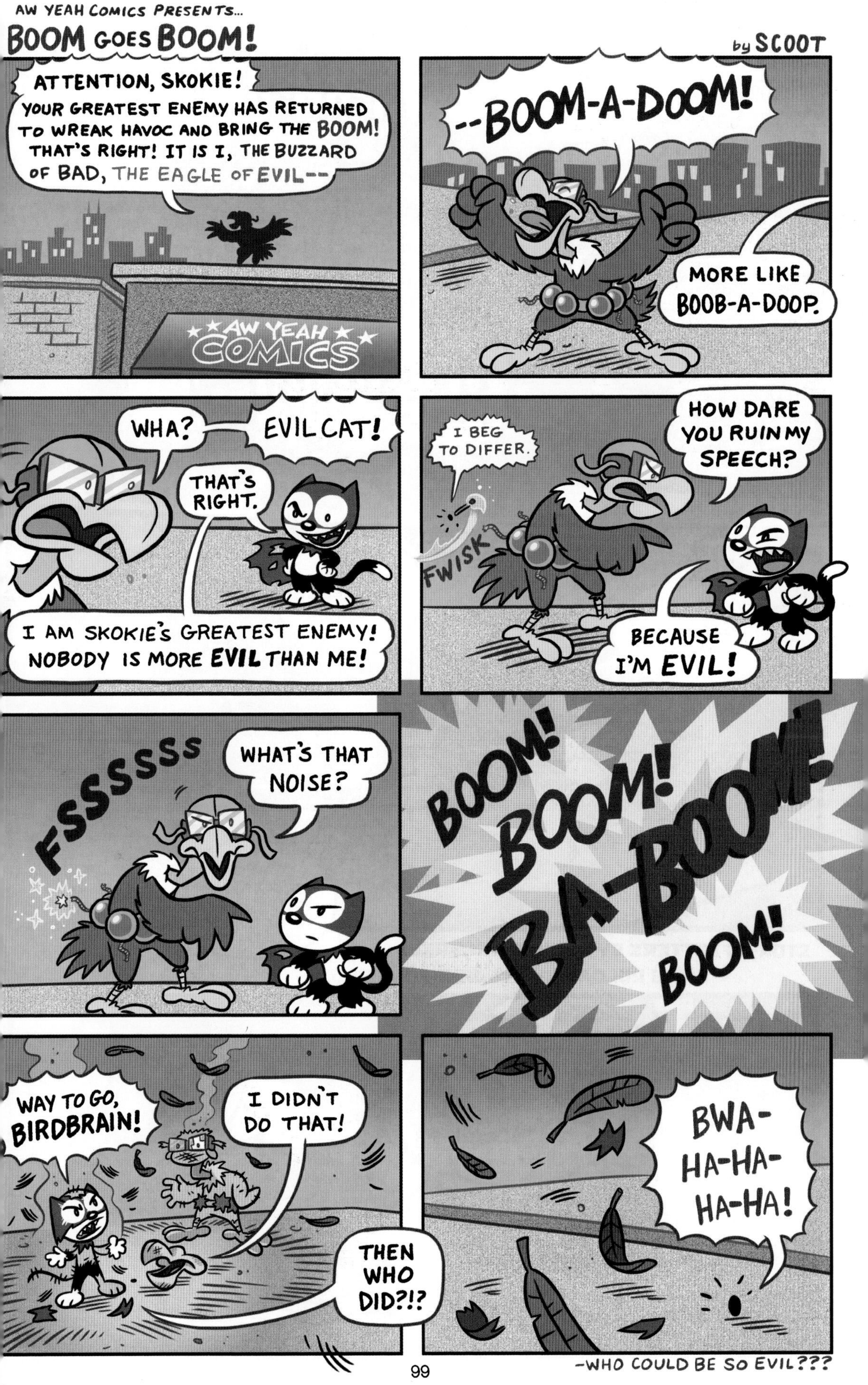

AW YEAH COMICS PRESENTS...
BOOM GOES BOOM!
by SCOOT
ATTENTION, SKOKIE!
YOUR GREATEST ENEMY HAS RETURNED TO WREAK HAVOC AND BRING THE BOOM! THAT'S RIGHT! IT IS I, THE BUZZARD OF BAD, THE EAGLE OF EVIL--
AW YEAH COMICS
--BOOM-A-DOOM!
MORE LIKE BOOB-A-DOOP.
WHA?
EVIL CAT!
THAT'S RIGHT.
I AM SKOKIE'S GREATEST ENEMY! NOBODY IS MORE EVIL THAN ME!
I BEG TO DIFFER.
HOW DARE YOU RUIN MY SPEECH?
FWISK
BECAUSE I'M EVIL!
FSSSSSS
WHAT'S THAT NOISE?
BOOM! BOOM! BA-BOOM! BOOM!
WAY TO GO, BIRDBRAIN!
I DIDN'T DO THAT!
THEN WHO DID?!?
BWA-HA-HA-HA-HA!
-WHO COULD BE SO EVIL???

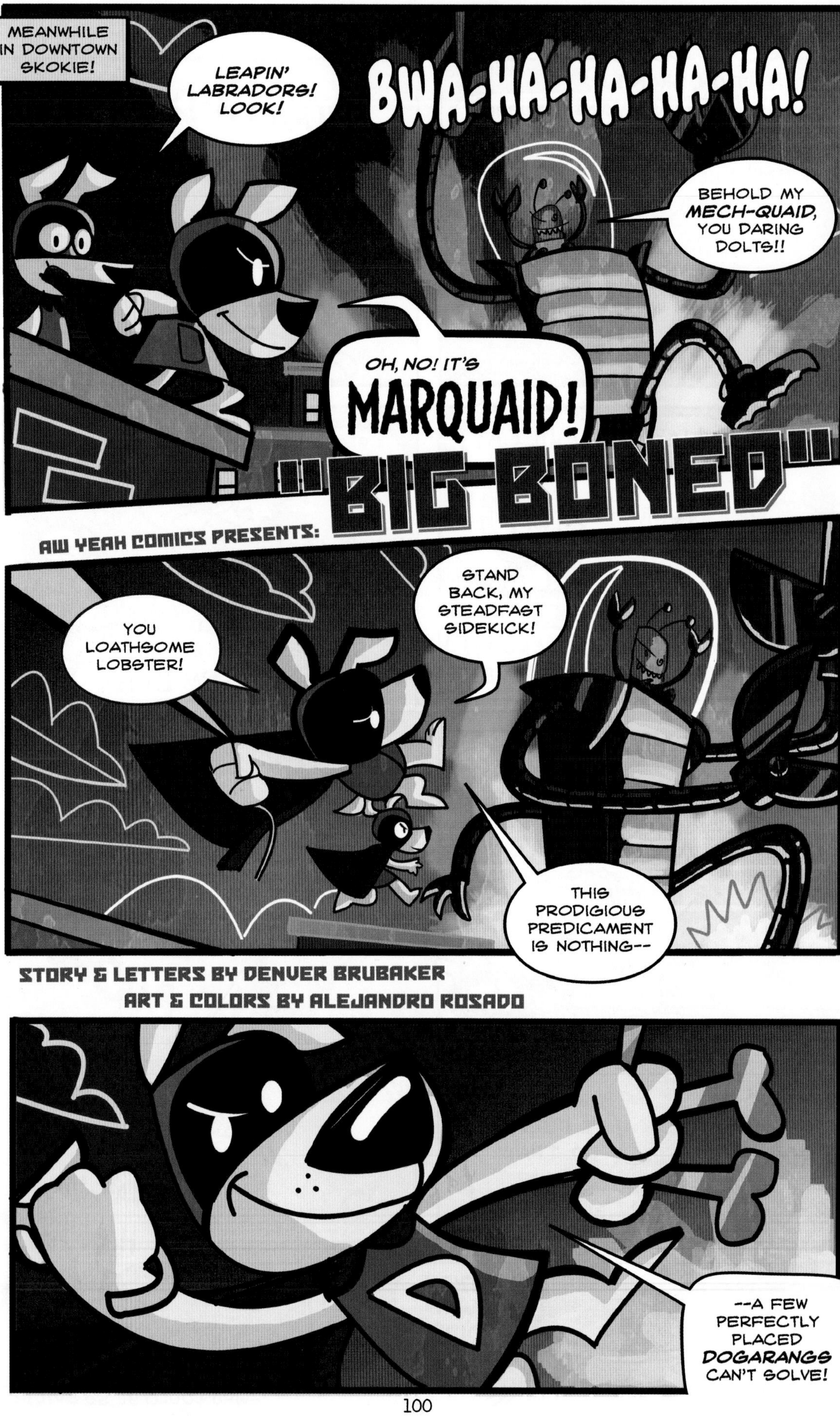

MEANWHILE IN DOWNTOWN SKOKIE!
LEAPIN' LABRADORS! LOOK!
BWA-HA-HA-HA-HA!
BEHOLD MY *MECH-QUAID*, YOU DARING DOLTS!!
OH, NO! IT'S MARQUAID!
AW YEAH COMICS PRESENTS: "BIG BONED"
YOU LOATHSOME LOBSTER!
STAND BACK, MY STEADFAST SIDEKICK!
THIS PRODIGIOUS PREDICAMENT IS NOTHING--
STORY & LETTERS BY DENVER BRUBAKER
ART & COLORS BY ALEJANDRO ROSADO
--A FEW PERFECTLY PLACED *DOGARANGS* CAN'T SOLVE!

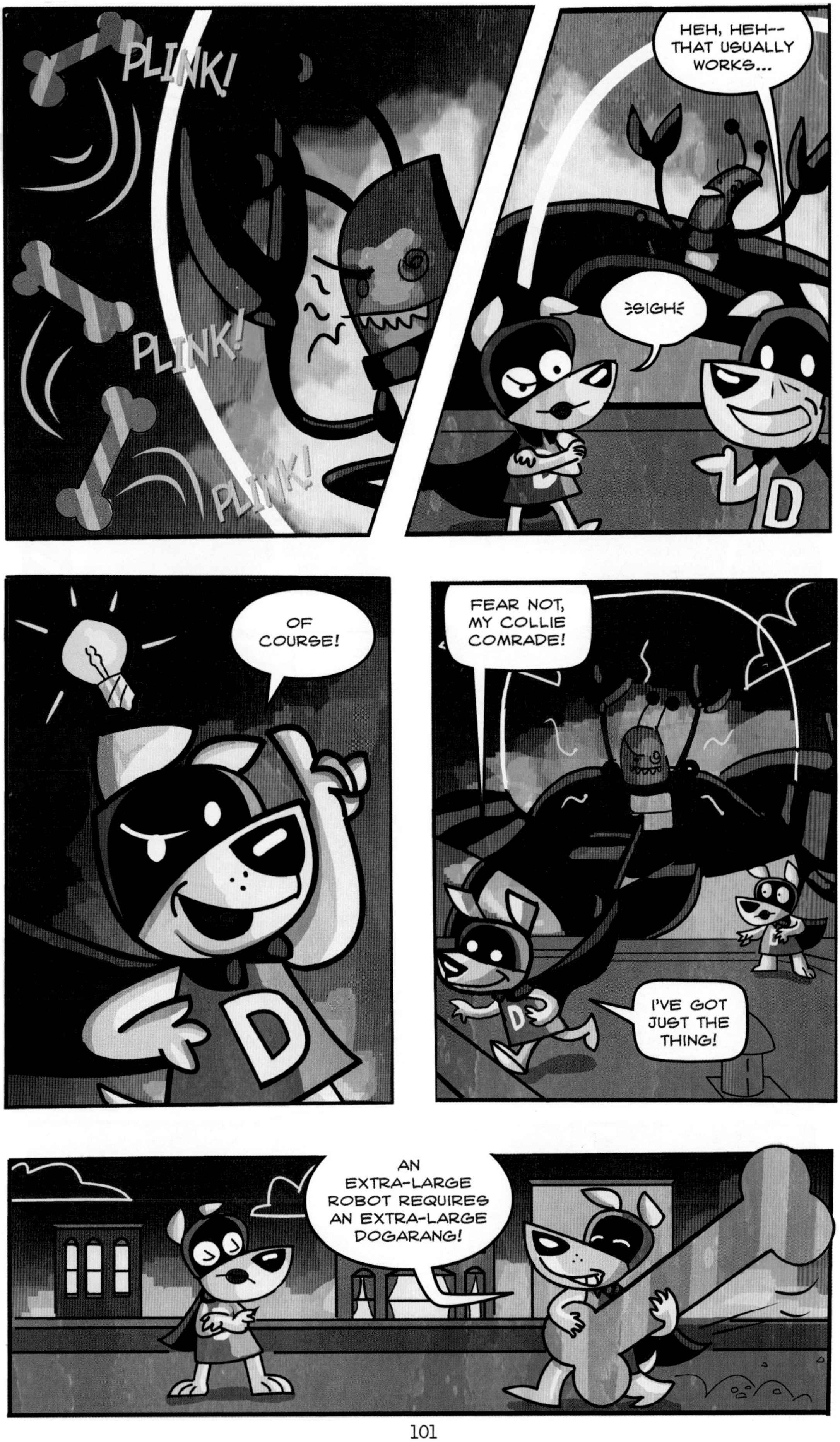
PLINK!
PLINK!
PLINK!
HEH, HEH-- THAT USUALLY WORKS...
SIGH
OF COURSE!
FEAR NOT, MY COLLIE COMRADE!
I'VE GOT JUST THE THING!
AN EXTRA-LARGE ROBOT REQUIRES AN EXTRA-LARGE DOGARANG!

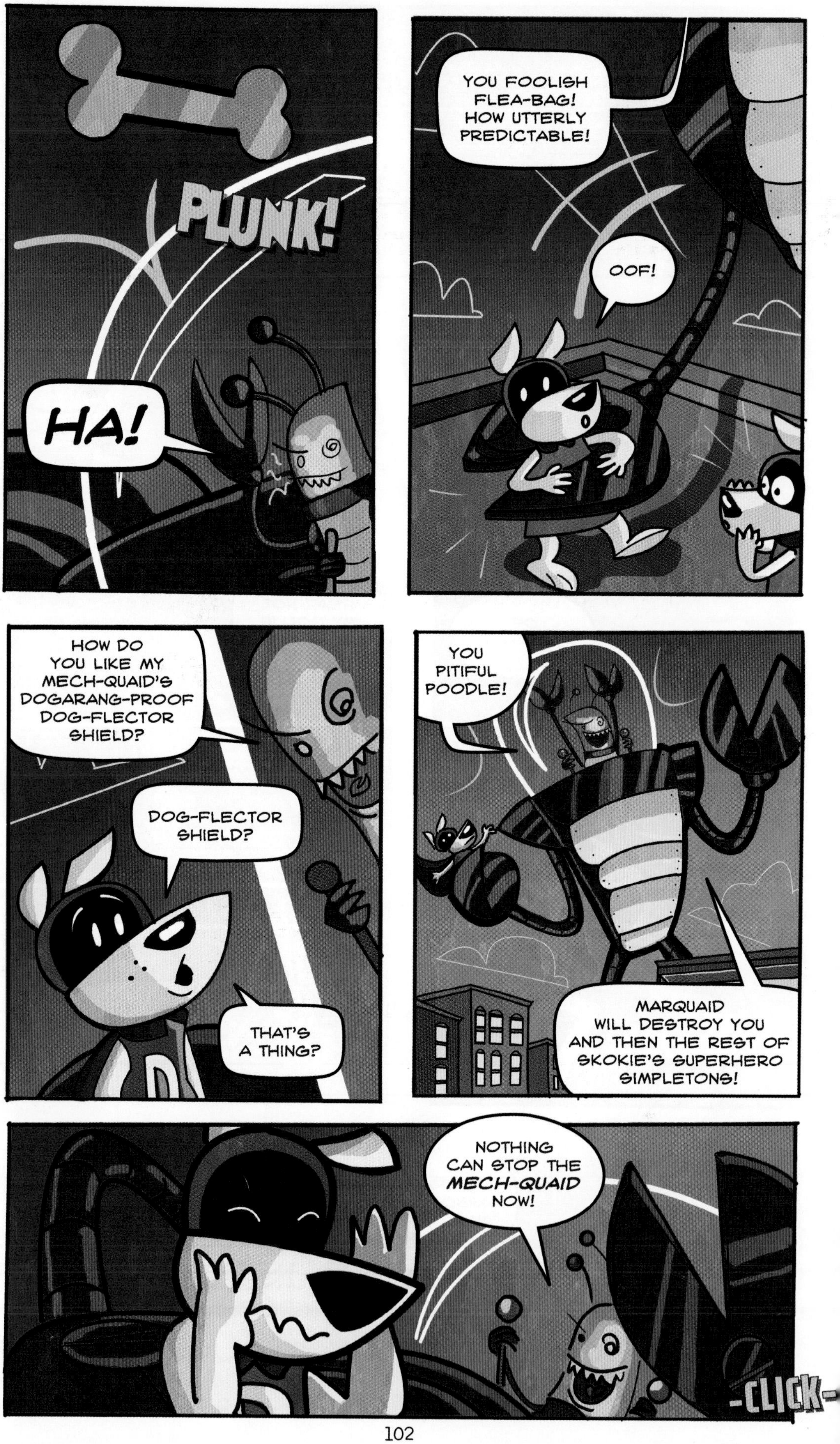
PLUNK!
HA!
YOU FOOLISH FLEA-BAG! HOW UTTERLY PREDICTABLE!
OOF!
HOW DO YOU LIKE MY MECH-QUAID'S DOGARANG-PROOF DOG-FLECTOR SHIELD?
DOG-FLECTOR SHIELD?
THAT'S A THING?
YOU PITIFUL POODLE!
MARQUAID WILL DESTROY YOU AND THEN THE REST OF SKOKIE'S SUPERHERO SIMPLETONS!
NOTHING CAN STOP THE *MECH-QUAID* NOW!
-CLICK-

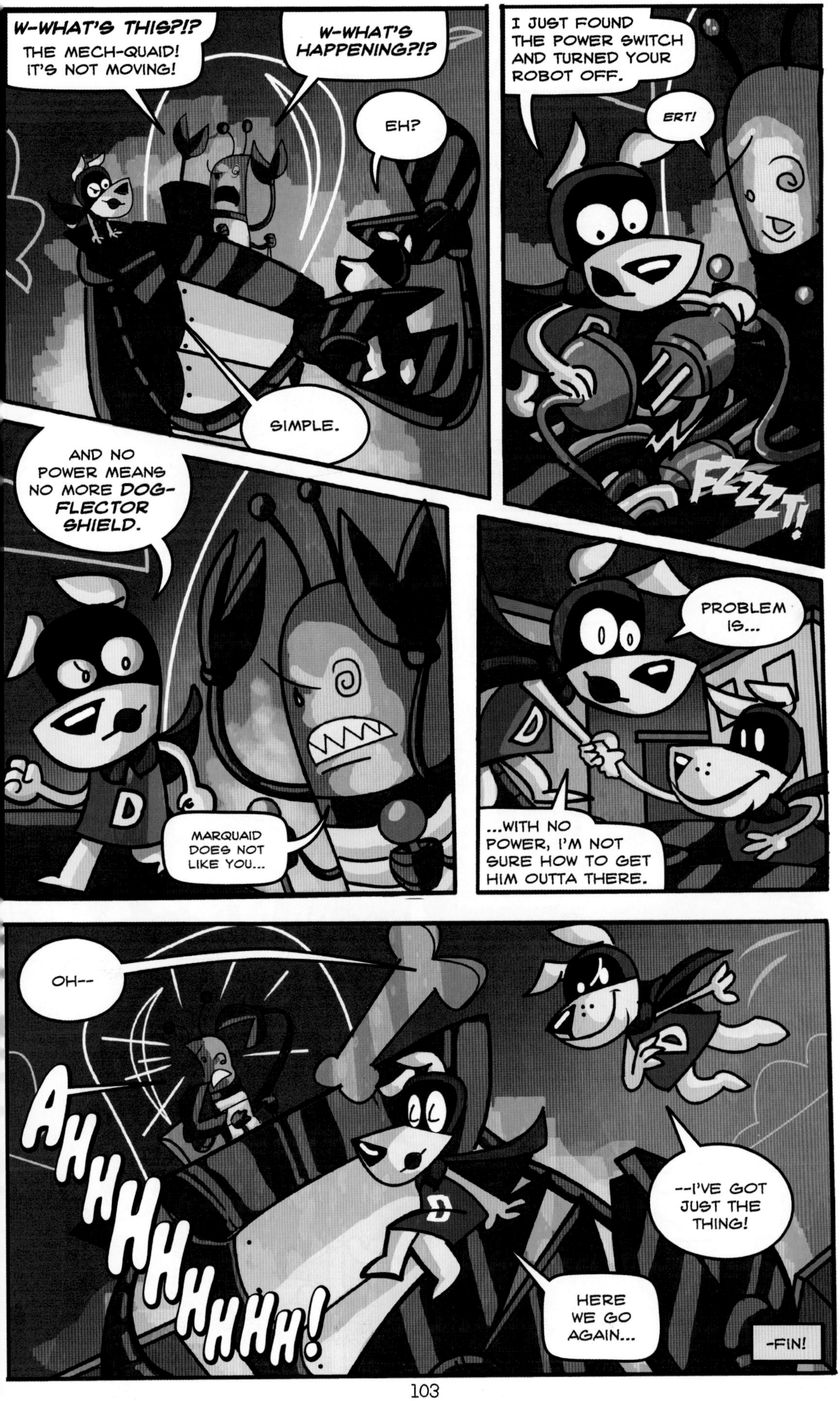
W-WHAT'S THIS?!? THE MECH-QUAID! IT'S NOT MOVING!
W-WHAT'S HAPPENING?!?
EH?
SIMPLE.
I JUST FOUND THE POWER SWITCH AND TURNED YOUR ROBOT OFF.
ERT!
FZZZT!
AND NO POWER MEANS NO MORE DOG-FLECTOR SHIELD.
MARQUAID DOES NOT LIKE YOU...
PROBLEM IS...
...WITH NO POWER, I'M NOT SURE HOW TO GET HIM OUTTA THERE.
OH--
AHHHHHHHHHHH!
--I'VE GOT JUST THE THING!
HERE WE GO AGAIN...
-FIN!

AN ACME NOVELTY

WRITTEN BY **STEPHEN MAYER**
ART BY **CHRIS GIARRUSSO**

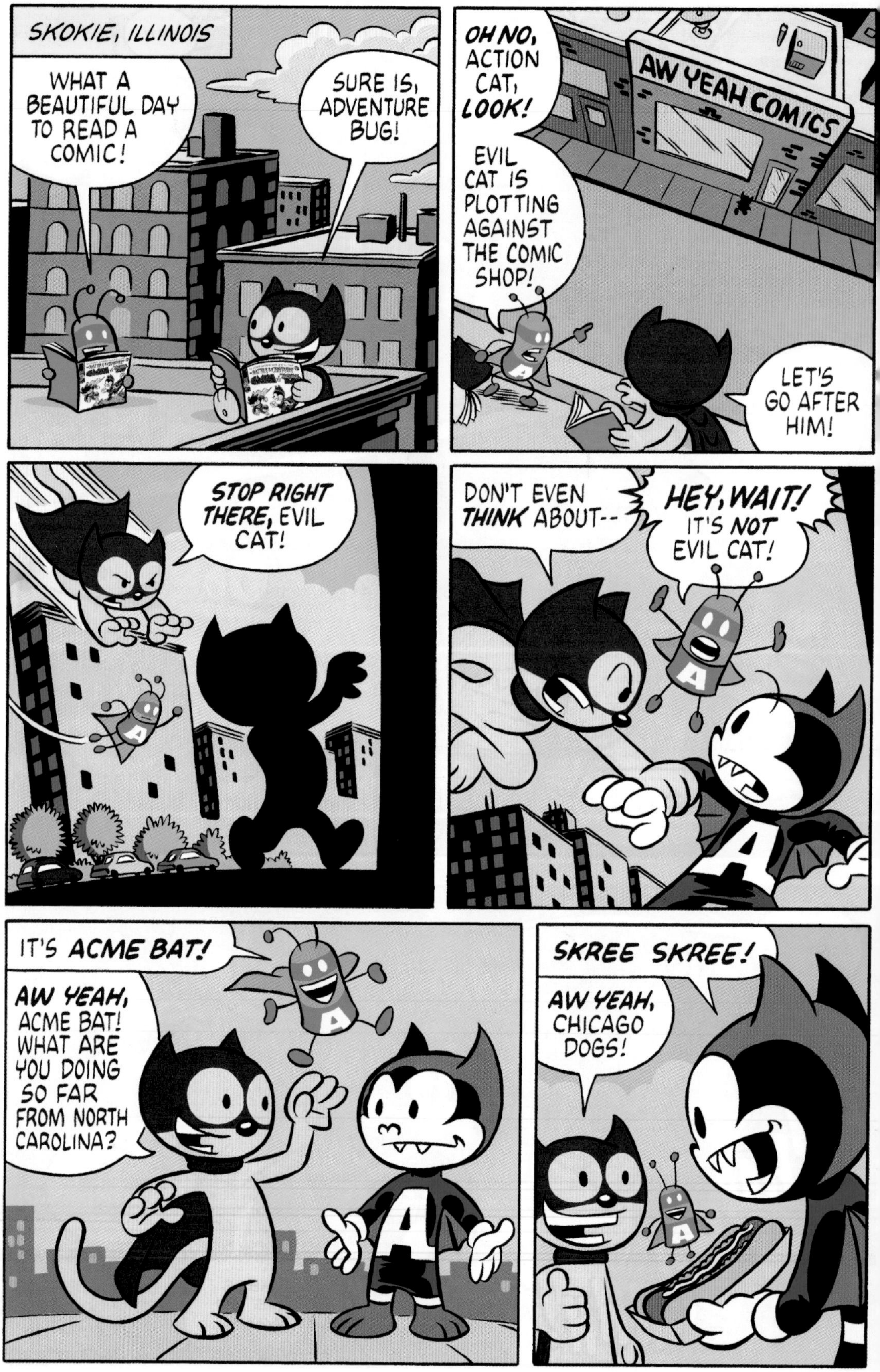
SKOKIE, ILLINOIS
WHAT A BEAUTIFUL DAY TO READ A COMIC!
SURE IS, ADVENTURE BUG!
AW YEAH COMICS
OH NO, ACTION CAT, LOOK!
EVIL CAT IS PLOTTING AGAINST THE COMIC SHOP!
LET'S GO AFTER HIM!
STOP RIGHT THERE, EVIL CAT!
DON'T EVEN THINK ABOUT--
HEY, WAIT! IT'S NOT EVIL CAT!
IT'S ACME BAT!
AW YEAH, ACME BAT! WHAT ARE YOU DOING SO FAR FROM NORTH CAROLINA?
SKREE SKREE!
AW YEAH, CHICAGO DOGS!

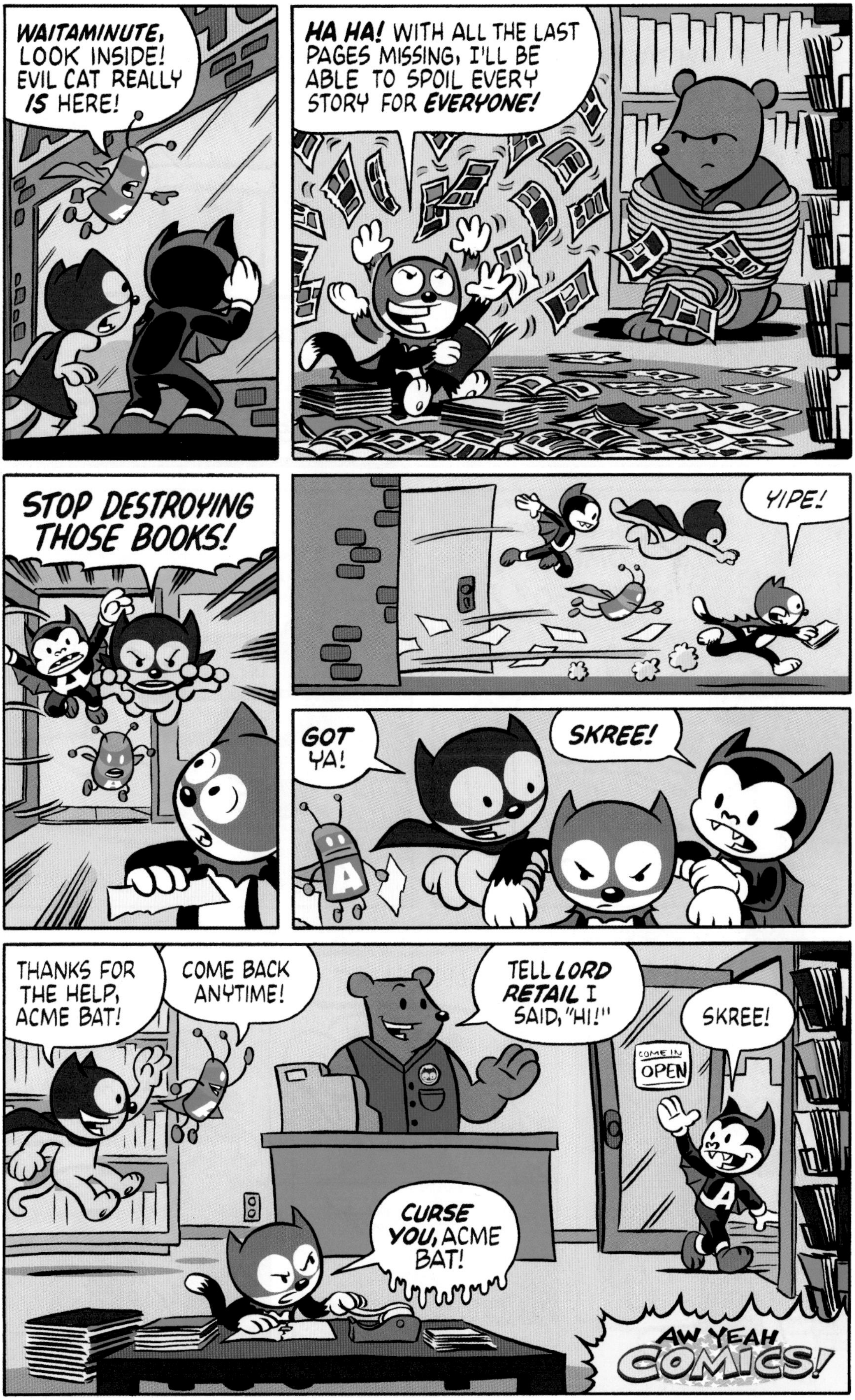
WAITAMINUTE, LOOK INSIDE! EVIL CAT REALLY IS HERE!
HA HA! WITH ALL THE LAST PAGES MISSING, I'LL BE ABLE TO SPOIL EVERY STORY FOR EVERYONE!
STOP DESTROYING THOSE BOOKS!
YIPE!
GOT YA!
SKREE!
THANKS FOR THE HELP, ACME BAT!
COME BACK ANYTIME!
TELL LORD RETAIL I SAID, "HI!"
SKREE!
COME IN
OPEN
CURSE YOU, ACME BAT!
AW YEAH COMICS!

AW YEAH COMICS PRESENTS...

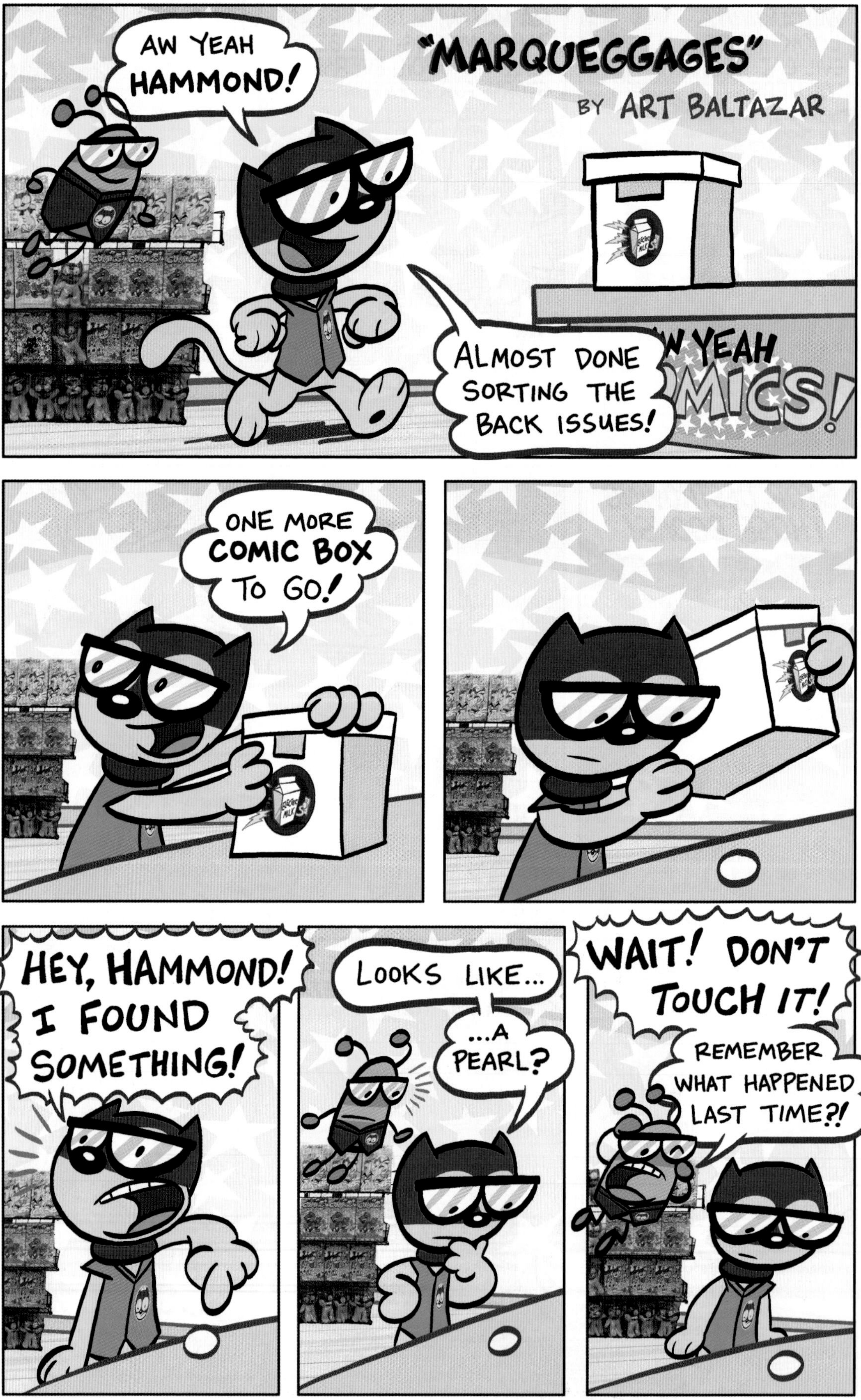

AW YEAH HAMMOND!
"MARQUEGGAGES"
BY ART BALTAZAR
ALMOST DONE SORTING THE BACK ISSUES!
ONE MORE COMIC BOX TO GO!
HEY, HAMMOND! I FOUND SOMETHING!
LOOKS LIKE...
...A PEARL?
WAIT! DON'T TOUCH IT!
REMEMBER WHAT HAPPENED LAST TIME?!

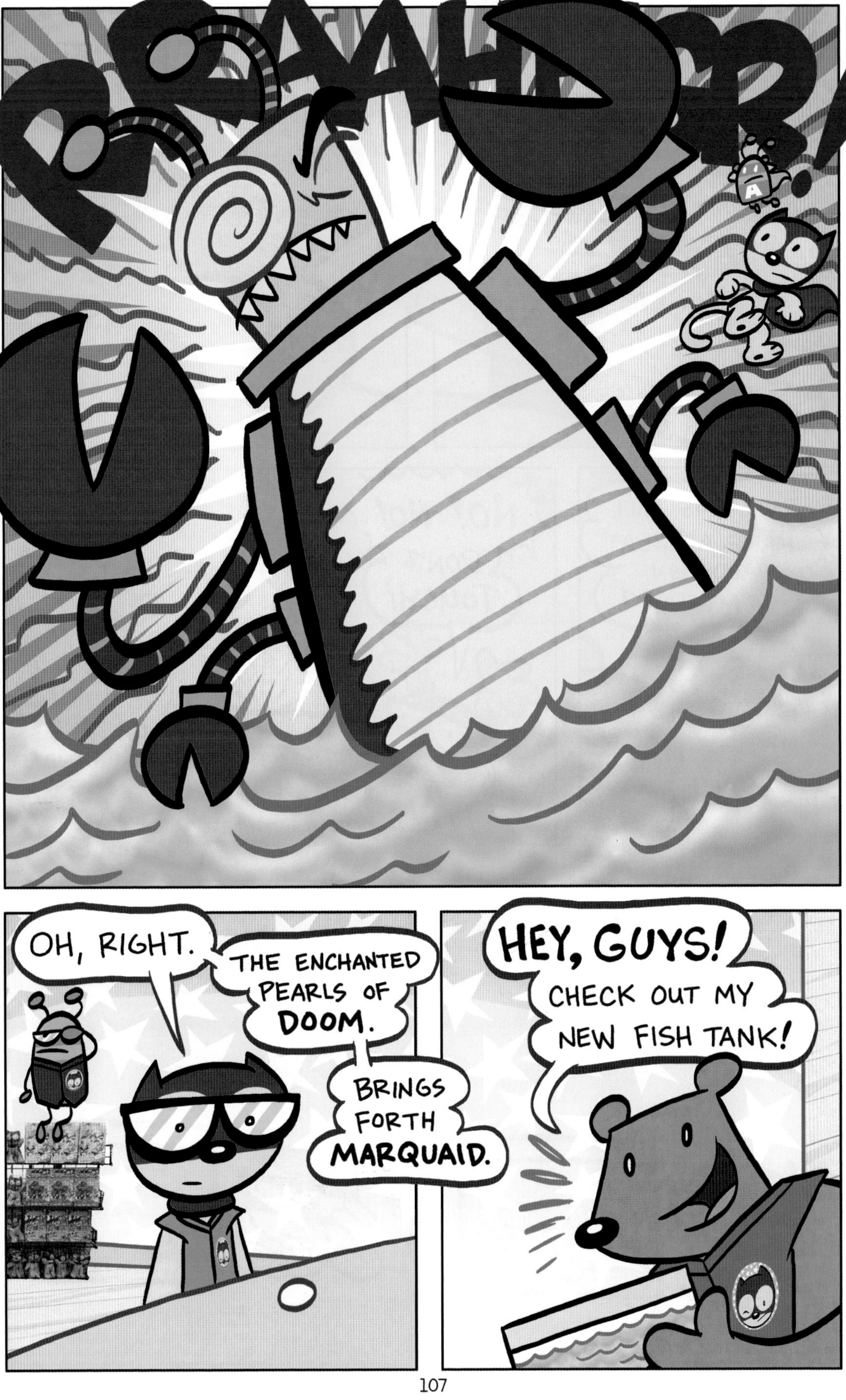
OH, RIGHT.
THE ENCHANTED PEARLS OF DOOM.
BRINGS FORTH MARQUAID.
HEY, GUYS!
CHECK OUT MY NEW FISH TANK!

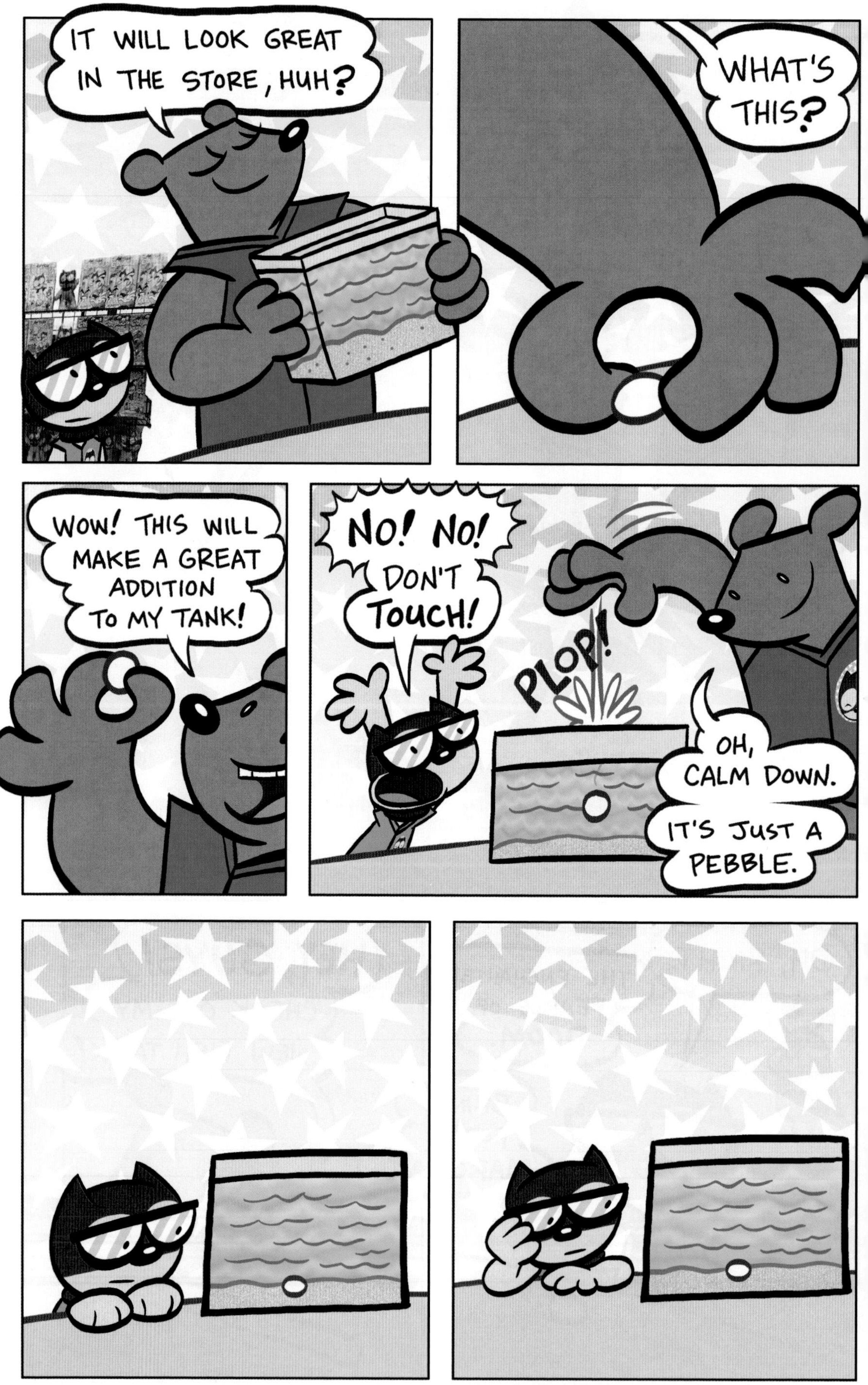
IT WILL LOOK GREAT IN THE STORE, HUH?
WHAT'S THIS?
WOW! THIS WILL MAKE A GREAT ADDITION TO MY TANK!
NO! NO!
DON'T TOUCH!
PLOP!
OH, CALM DOWN.
IT'S JUST A PEBBLE.

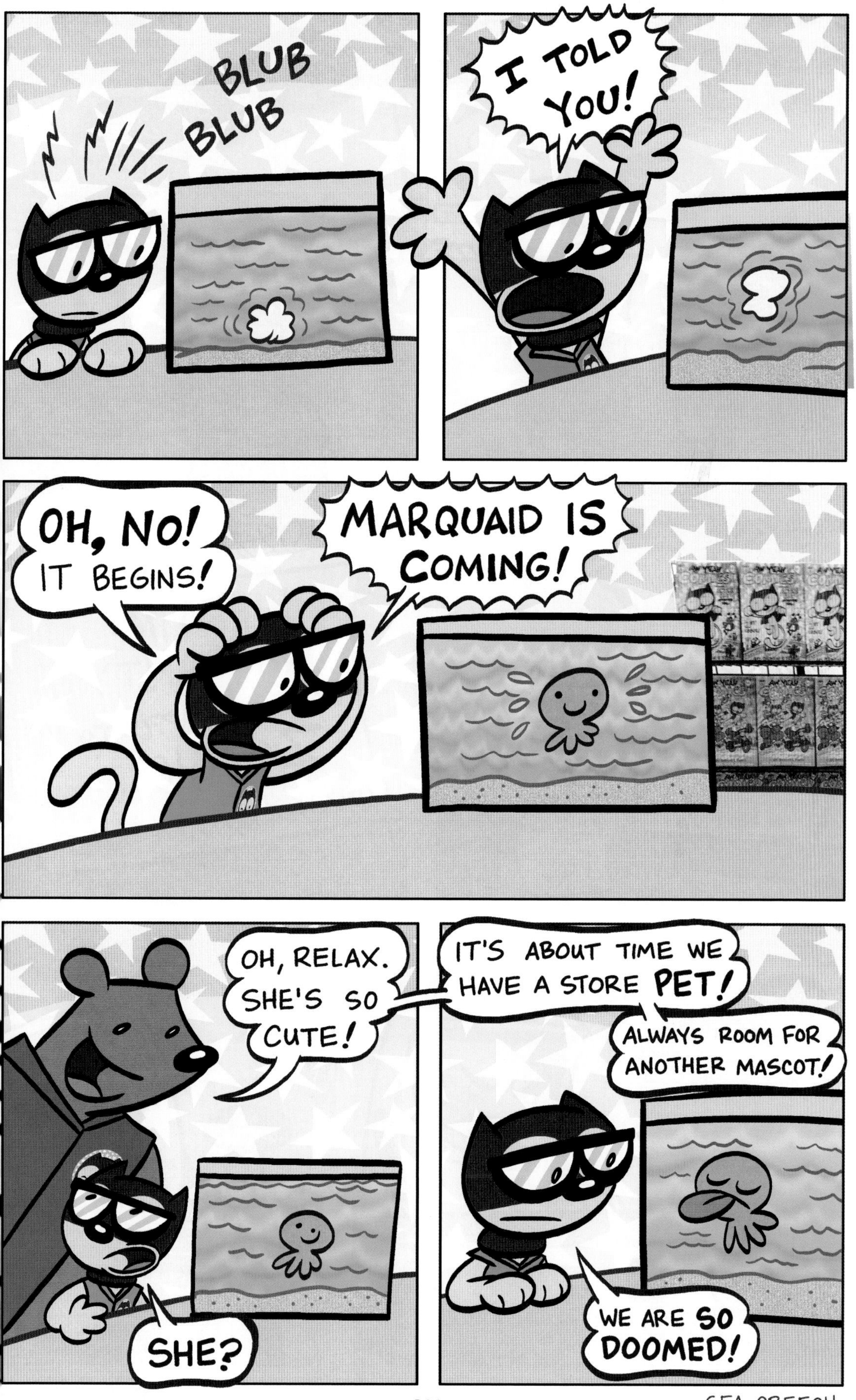
BLUB
BLUB
I TOLD YOU!
OH, NO! IT BEGINS!
MARQUAID IS COMING!
OH, RELAX. SHE'S SO CUTE!
SHE?
IT'S ABOUT TIME WE HAVE A STORE PET!
ALWAYS ROOM FOR ANOTHER MASCOT!
WE ARE SO DOOMED!

-SEA CREECH.

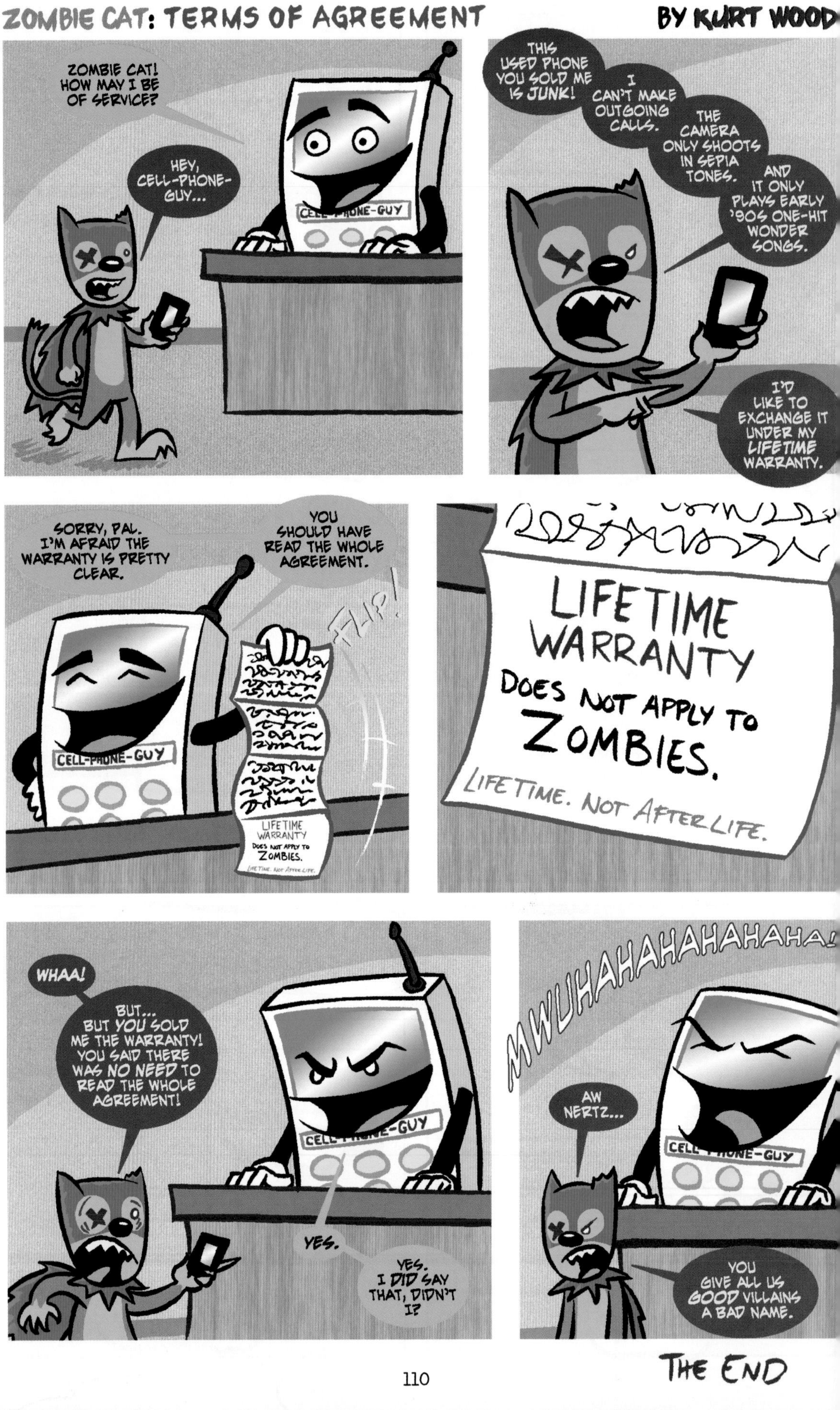
ZOMBIE CAT: TERMS OF AGREEMENT
BY KURT WOOD
ZOMBIE CAT! HOW MAY I BE OF SERVICE?
HEY, CELL-PHONE-GUY...
CELL-PHONE-GUY
THIS USED PHONE YOU SOLD ME IS JUNK!
I CAN'T MAKE OUTGOING CALLS.
THE CAMERA ONLY SHOOTS IN SEPIA TONES.
AND IT ONLY PLAYS EARLY '90S ONE-HIT WONDER SONGS.
I'D LIKE TO EXCHANGE IT UNDER MY LIFETIME WARRANTY.
SORRY, PAL. I'M AFRAID THE WARRANTY IS PRETTY CLEAR.
YOU SHOULD HAVE READ THE WHOLE AGREEMENT.
FLIP!
CELL-PHONE-GUY
LIFETIME WARRANTY DOES NOT APPLY TO ZOMBIES.
LIFETIME. NOT AFTERLIFE.
LIFETIME WARRANTY
DOES NOT APPLY TO ZOMBIES.
LIFETIME. NOT AFTERLIFE.
WHAA!
BUT... BUT YOU SOLD ME THE WARRANTY! YOU SAID THERE WAS NO NEED TO READ THE WHOLE AGREEMENT!
YES.
YES. I DID SAY THAT, DIDN'T I?
MWUHAHAHAHAHAHAHA!
AW NERTZ...
YOU GIVE ALL US GOOD VILLAINS A BAD NAME.
THE END

★ CHAPTER FIVE ★

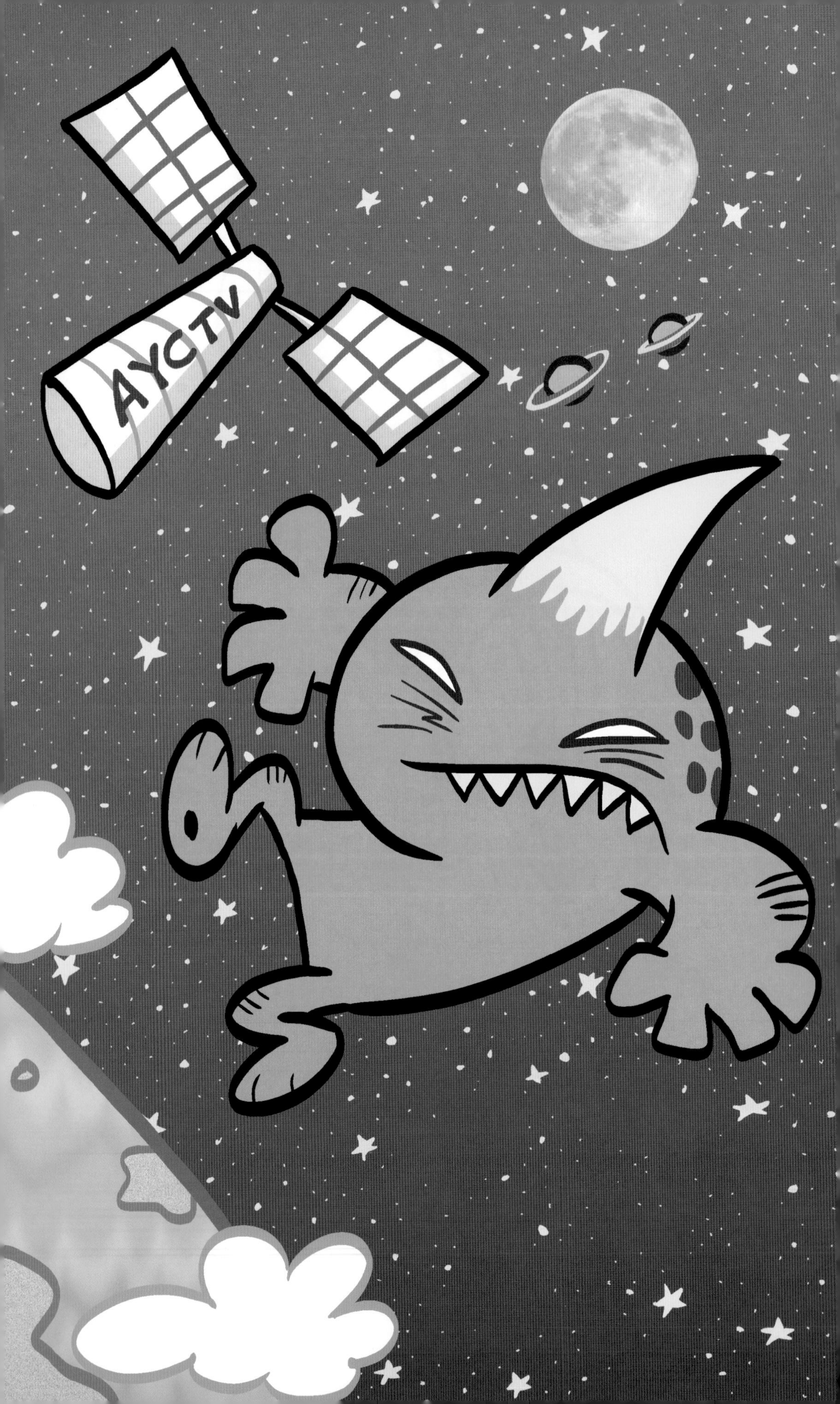
AYCTV

AW YEAH COMICS! PRESENTS...

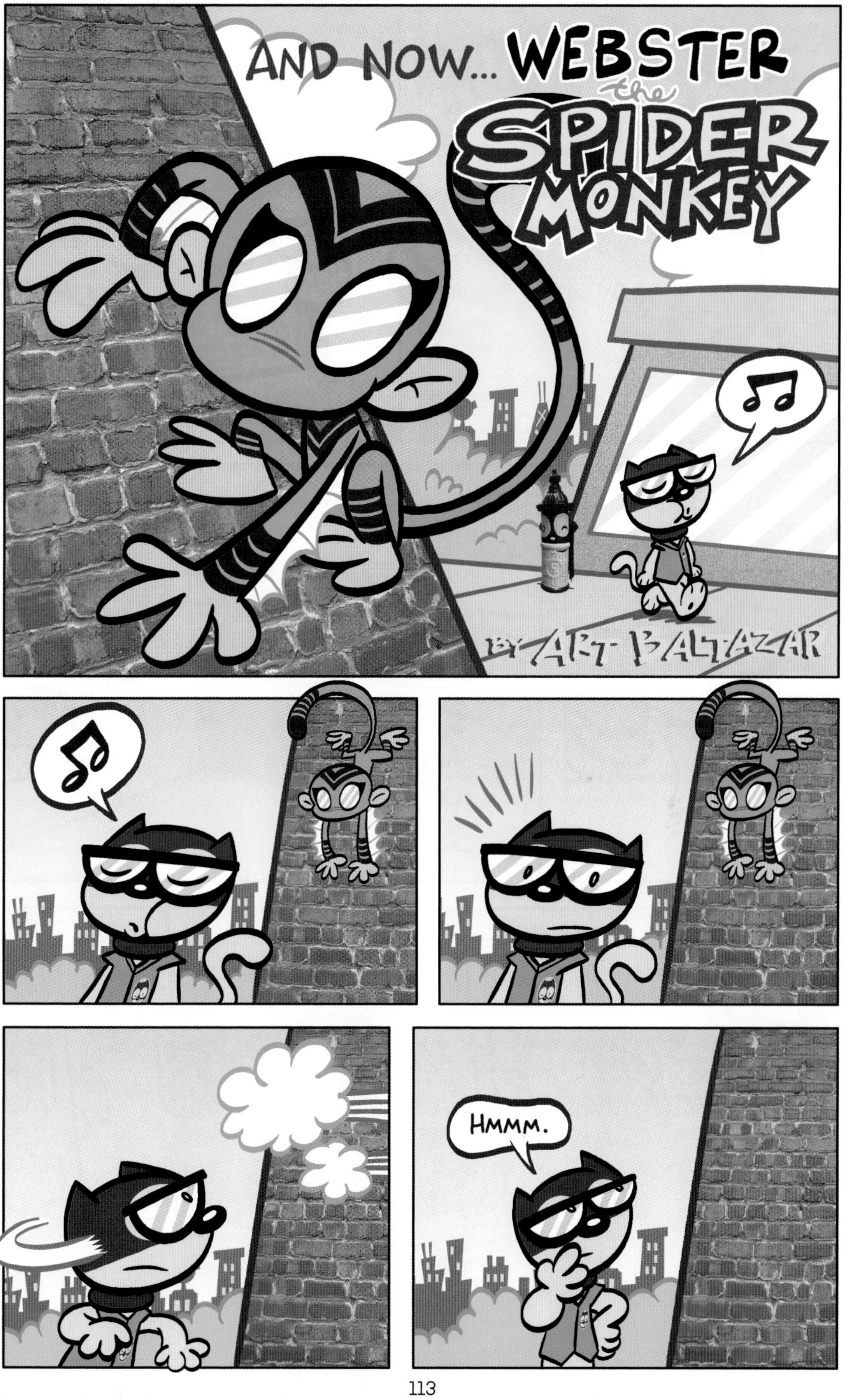

AND NOW... WEBSTER the SPIDER MONKEY
♫
BY ART BALTAZAR
♫
HMMM.

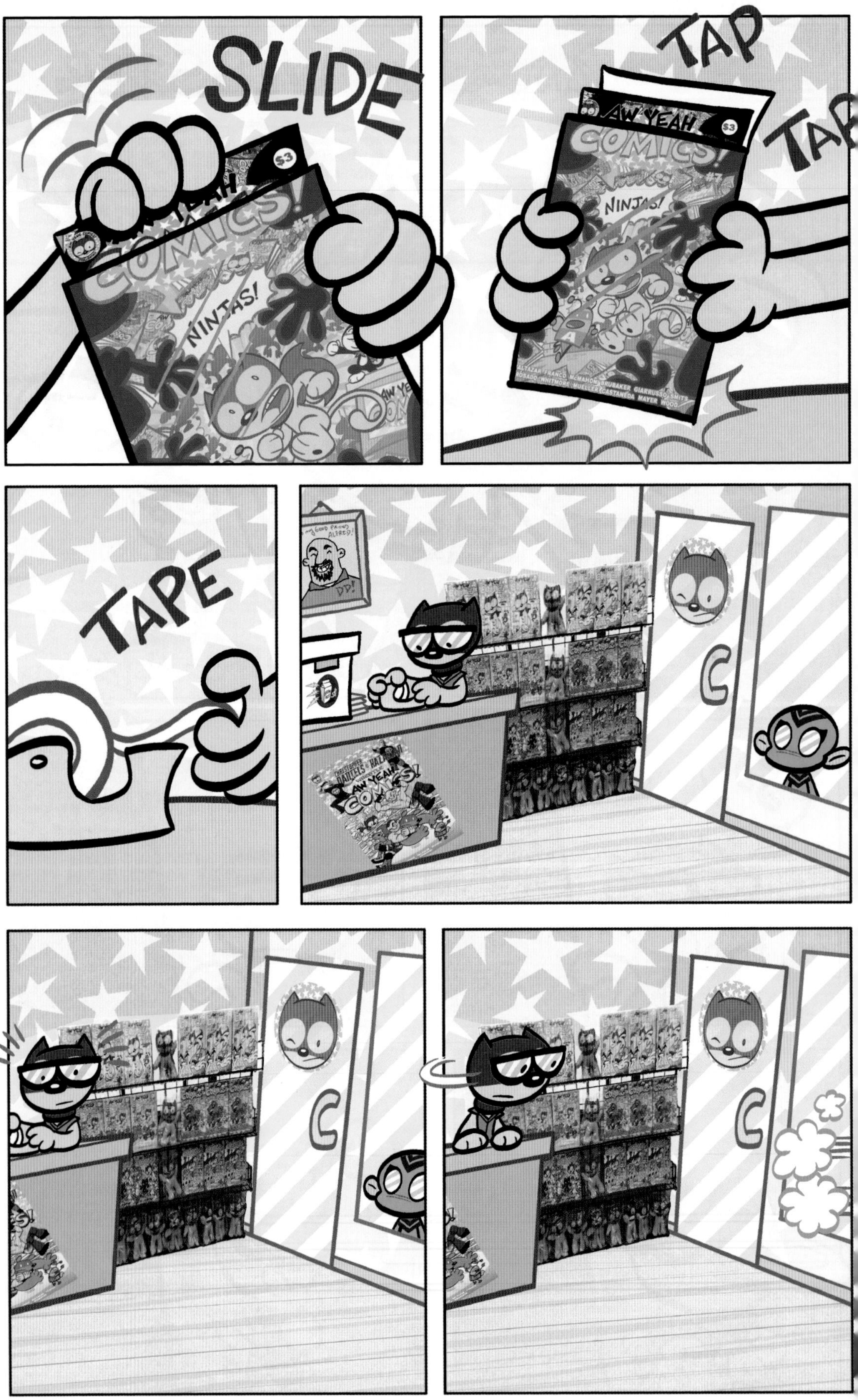
SLIDE
TAP
TAP
TAPE

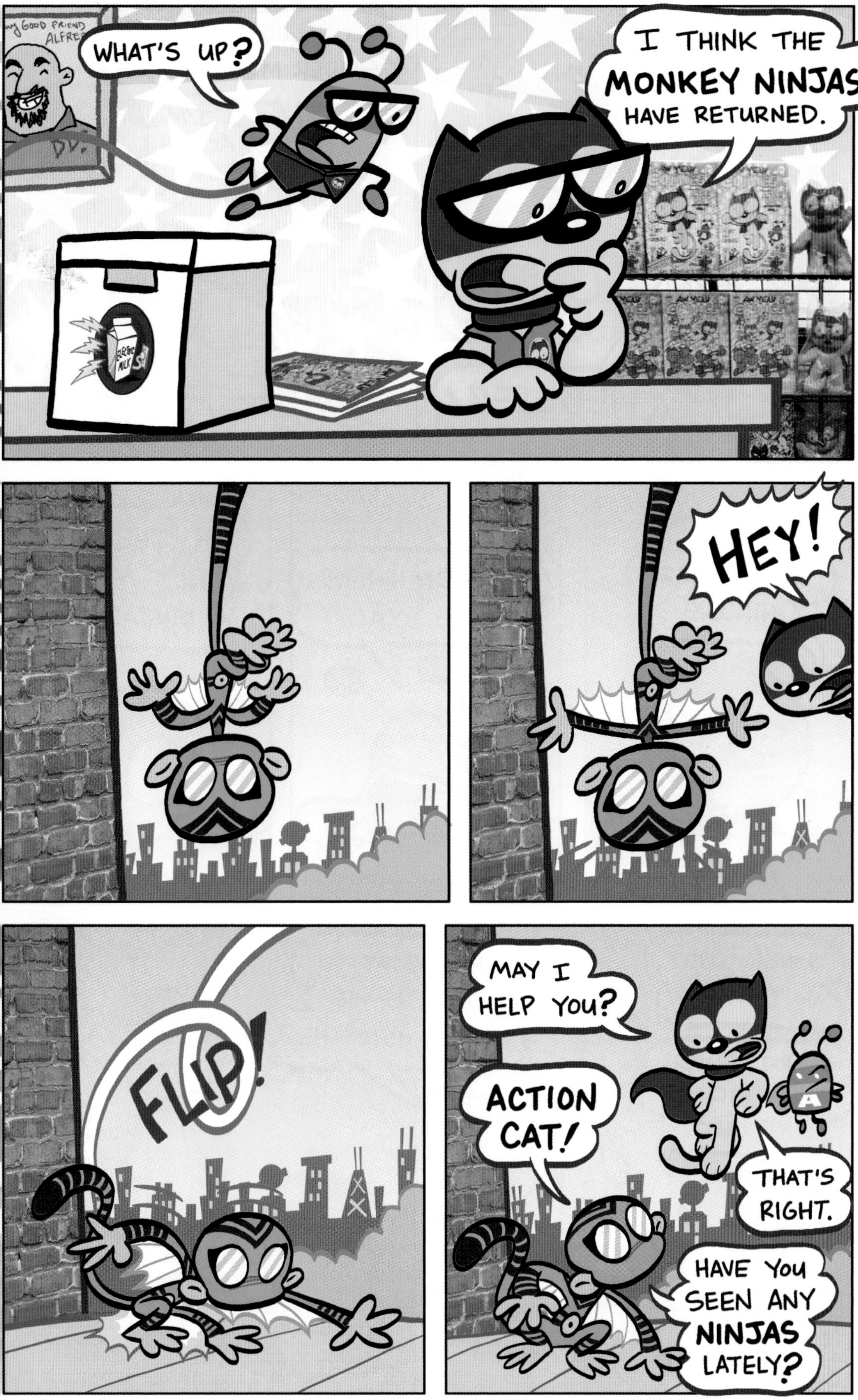

MY GOOD FRIEND ALFRE
WHAT'S UP?
I THINK THE MONKEY NINJAS HAVE RETURNED.
ELECTRO MILK
HEY!
FLIP!
MAY I HELP YOU?
ACTION CAT!
THAT'S RIGHT.
HAVE YOU SEEN ANY NINJAS LATELY?

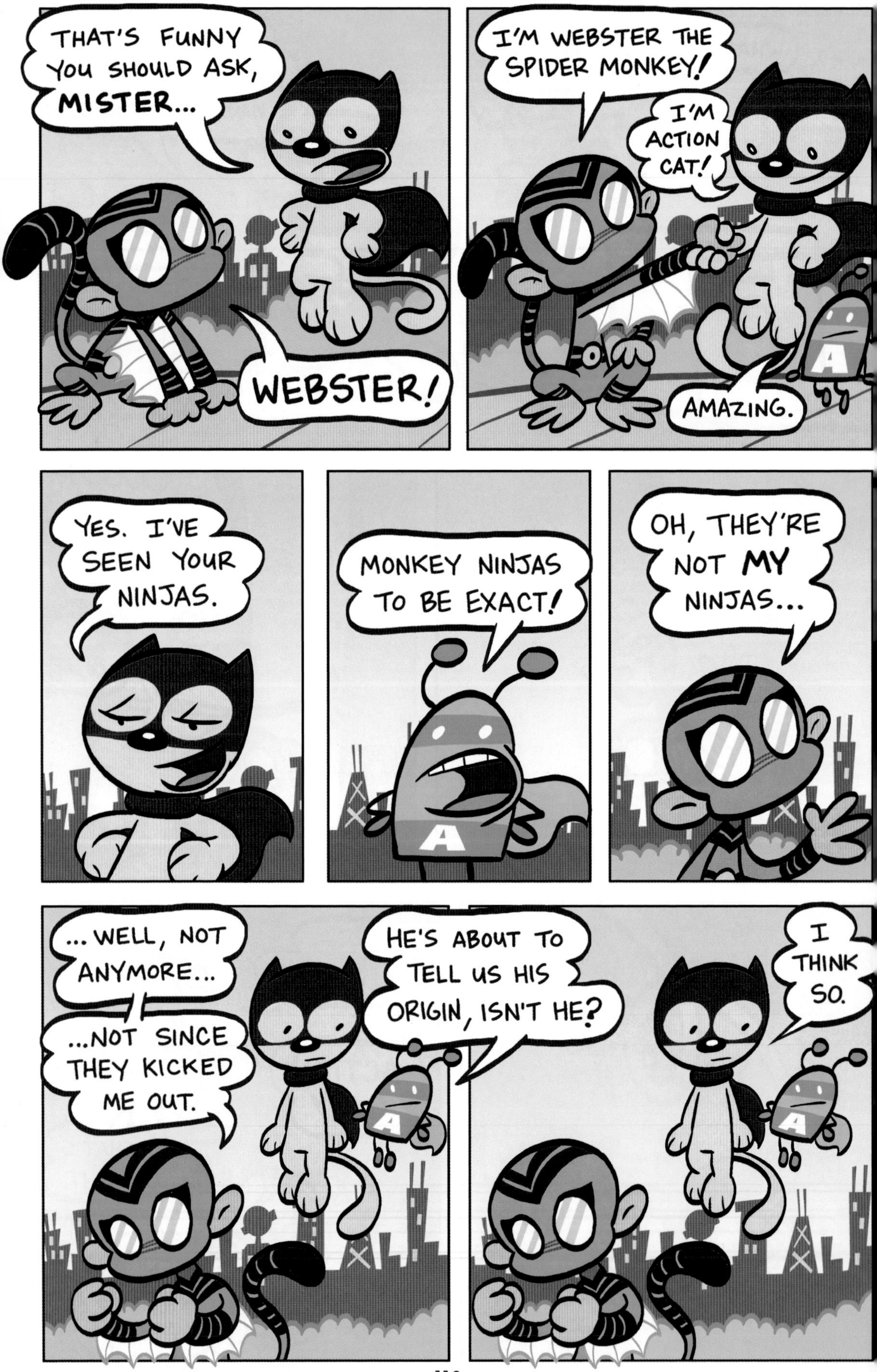
THAT'S FUNNY YOU SHOULD ASK, MISTER...
WEBSTER!
I'M WEBSTER THE SPIDER MONKEY!
I'M ACTION CAT!
AMAZING.
YES. I'VE SEEN YOUR NINJAS.
MONKEY NINJAS TO BE EXACT!
OH, THEY'RE NOT MY NINJAS...
...WELL, NOT ANYMORE...
...NOT SINCE THEY KICKED ME OUT.
HE'S ABOUT TO TELL US HIS ORIGIN, ISN'T HE?
I THINK SO.

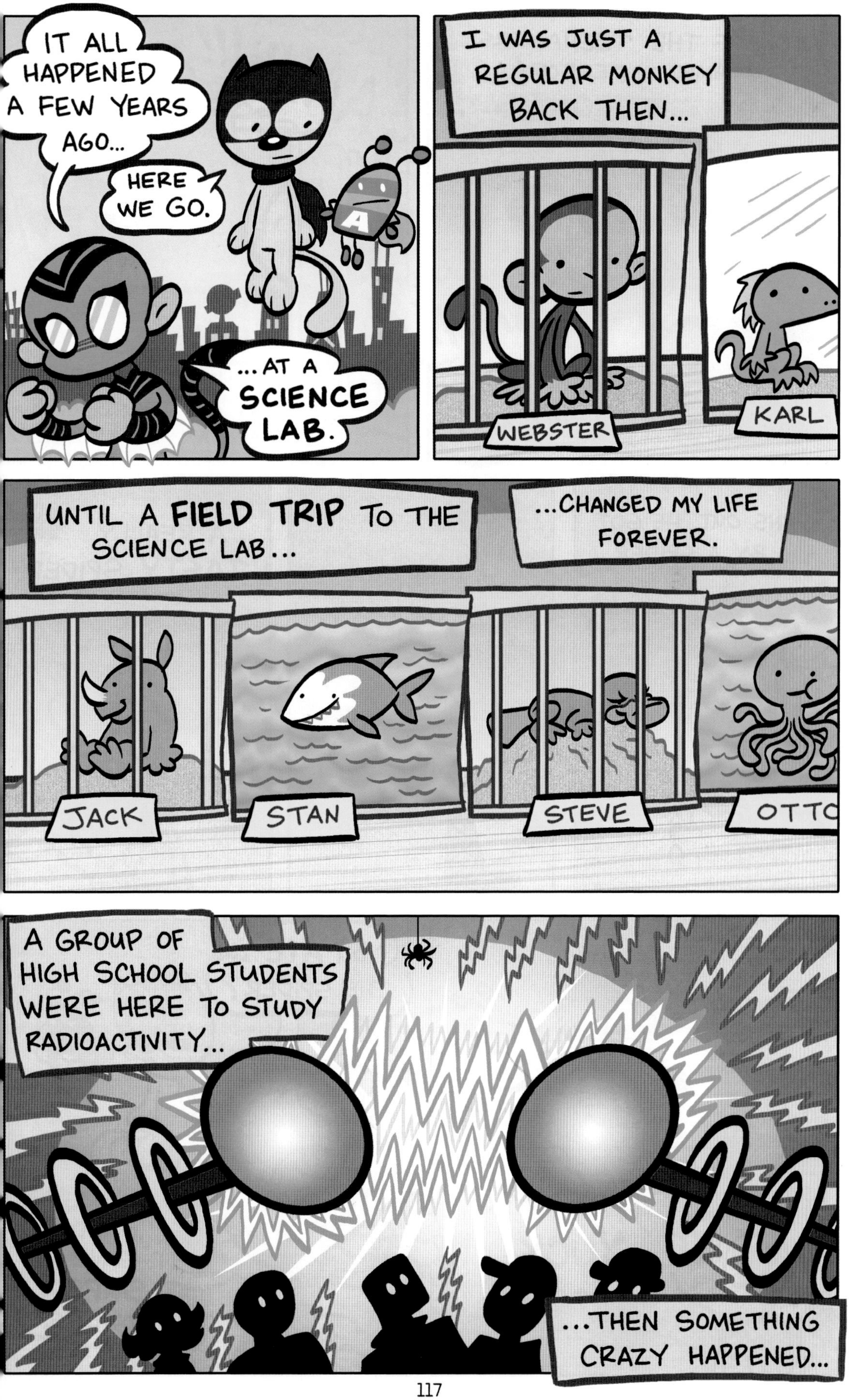
IT ALL HAPPENED A FEW YEARS AGO...
HERE WE GO.
...AT A SCIENCE LAB.
I WAS JUST A REGULAR MONKEY BACK THEN...
WEBSTER
KARL
UNTIL A FIELD TRIP TO THE SCIENCE LAB...
...CHANGED MY LIFE FOREVER.
JACK
STAN
STEVE
OTTO
A GROUP OF HIGH SCHOOL STUDENTS WERE HERE TO STUDY RADIOACTIVITY...
...THEN SOMETHING CRAZY HAPPENED...

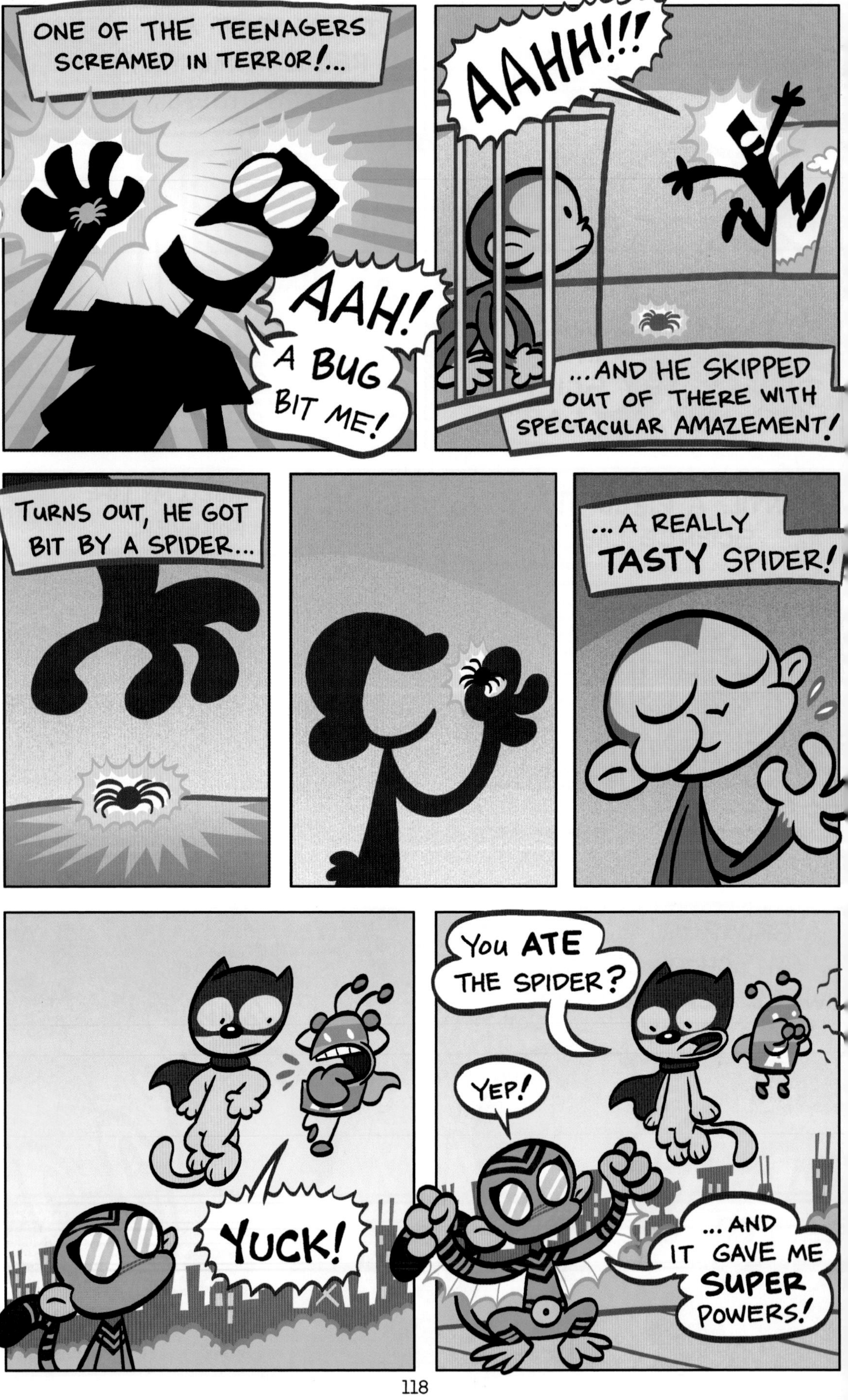
ONE OF THE TEENAGERS SCREAMED IN TERROR!...
AAH! A BUG BIT ME!
AAHH!!!
...AND HE SKIPPED OUT OF THERE WITH SPECTACULAR AMAZEMENT!
TURNS OUT, HE GOT BIT BY A SPIDER...
...A REALLY TASTY SPIDER!
YUCK!
You ATE THE SPIDER?
YEP!
...AND IT GAVE ME SUPER POWERS!

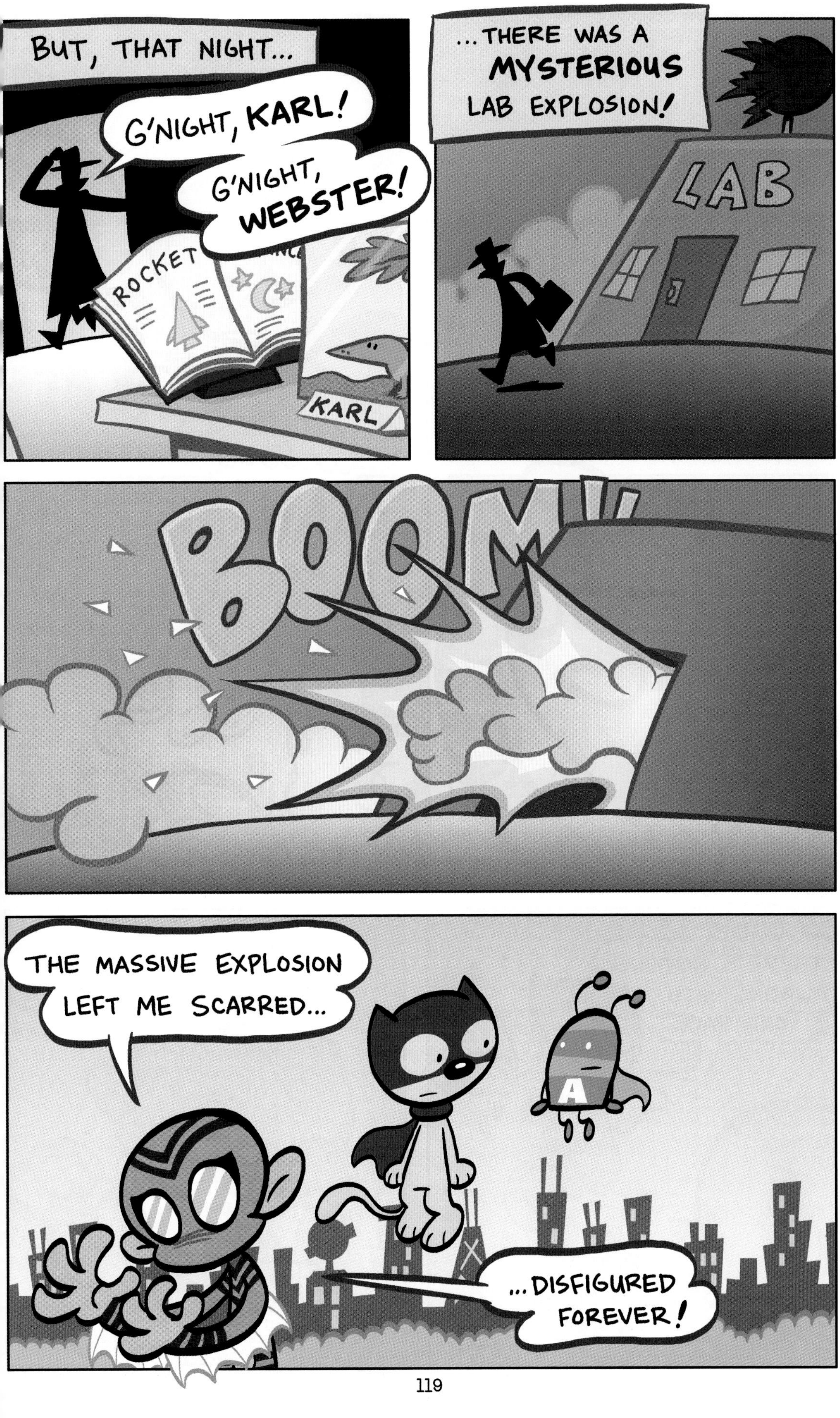
BUT, THAT NIGHT...
G'NIGHT, KARL!
G'NIGHT, WEBSTER!
ROCKET
KARL
...THERE WAS A MYSTERIOUS LAB EXPLOSION!
LAB
BOOM!!
THE MASSIVE EXPLOSION LEFT ME SCARRED...
A
...DISFIGURED FOREVER!

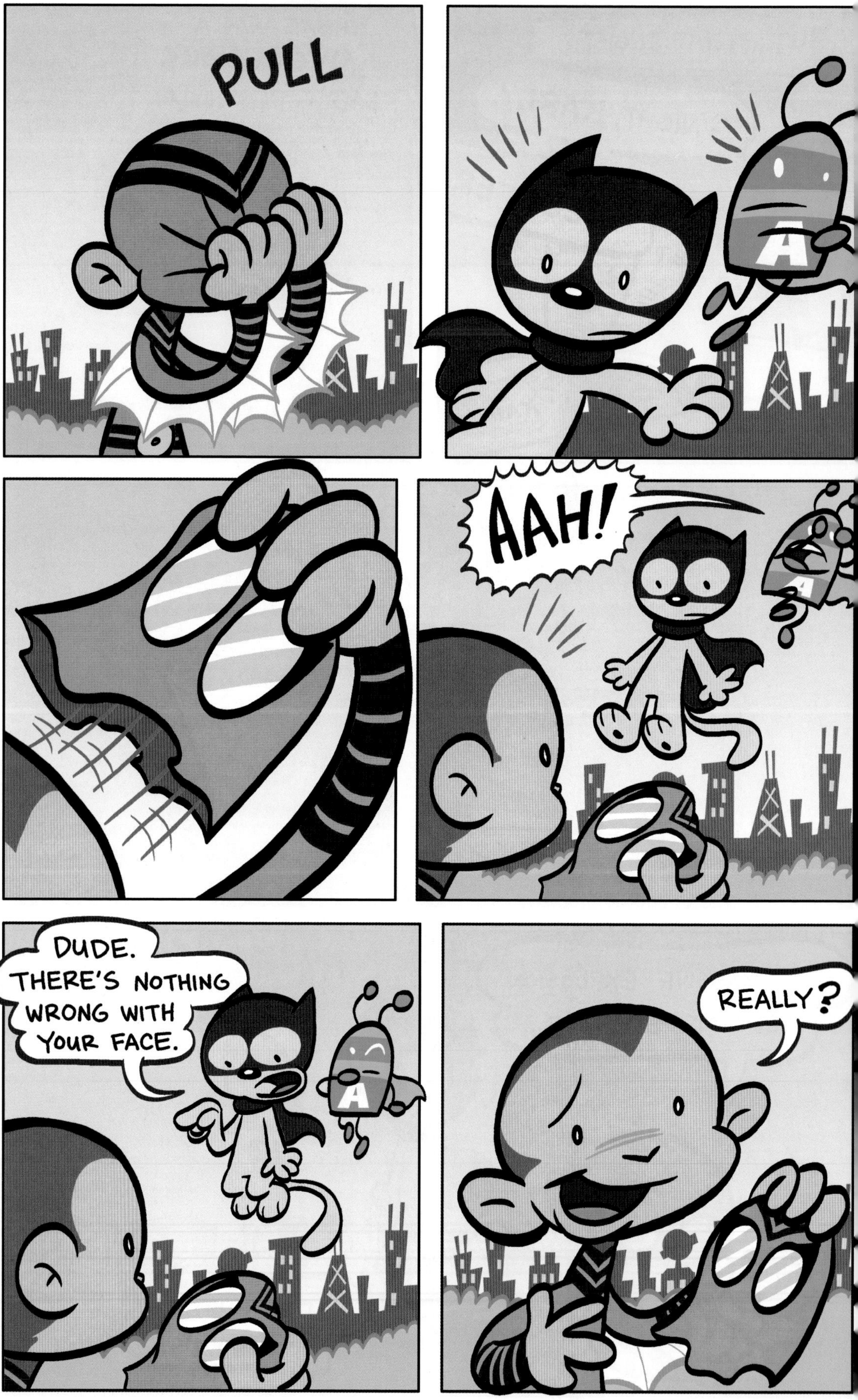
PULL
AAH!
DUDE. THERE'S NOTHING WRONG WITH YOUR FACE.
REALLY?

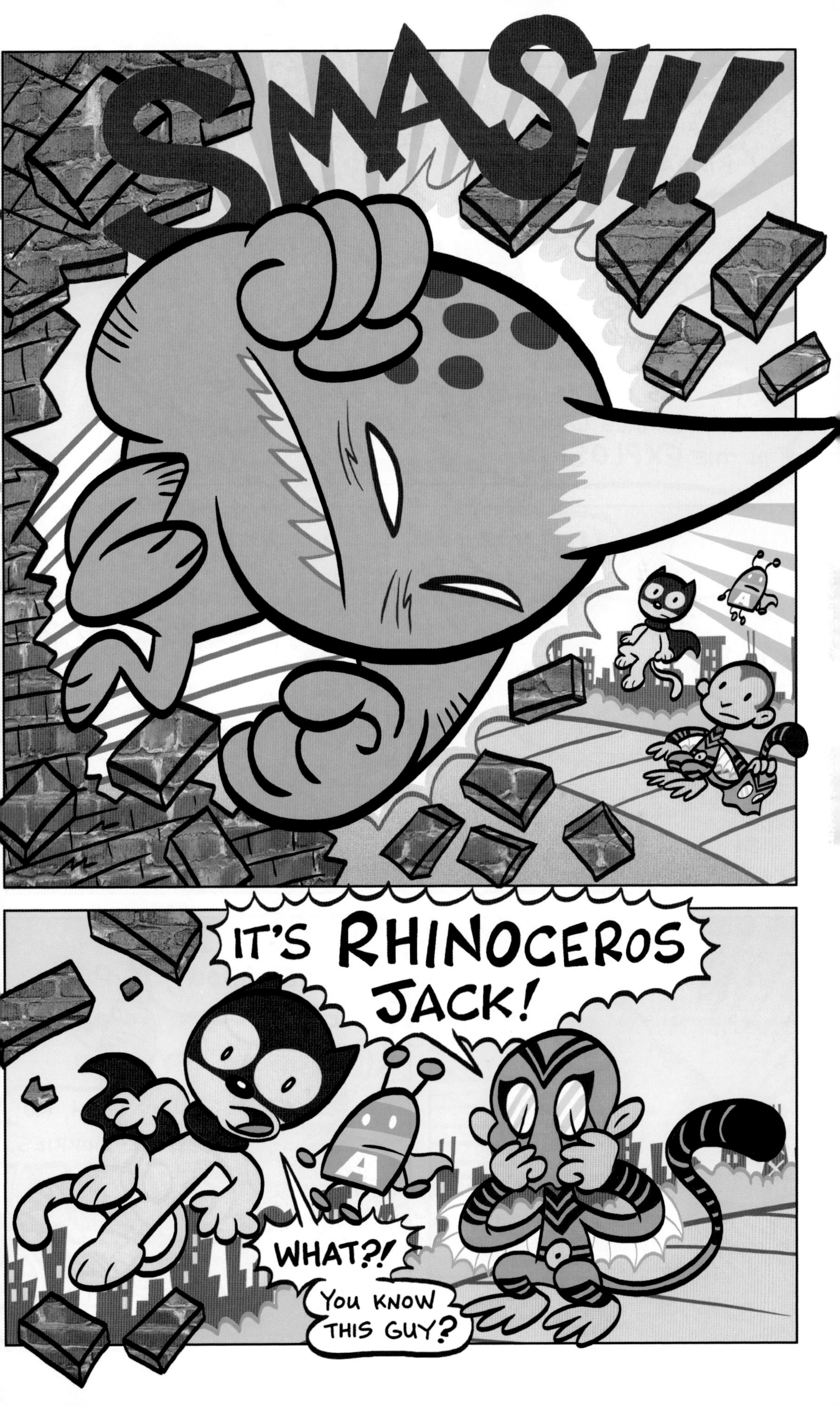
SMASH!
IT'S RHINOCEROS JACK!
WHAT?!
YOU KNOW THIS GUY?

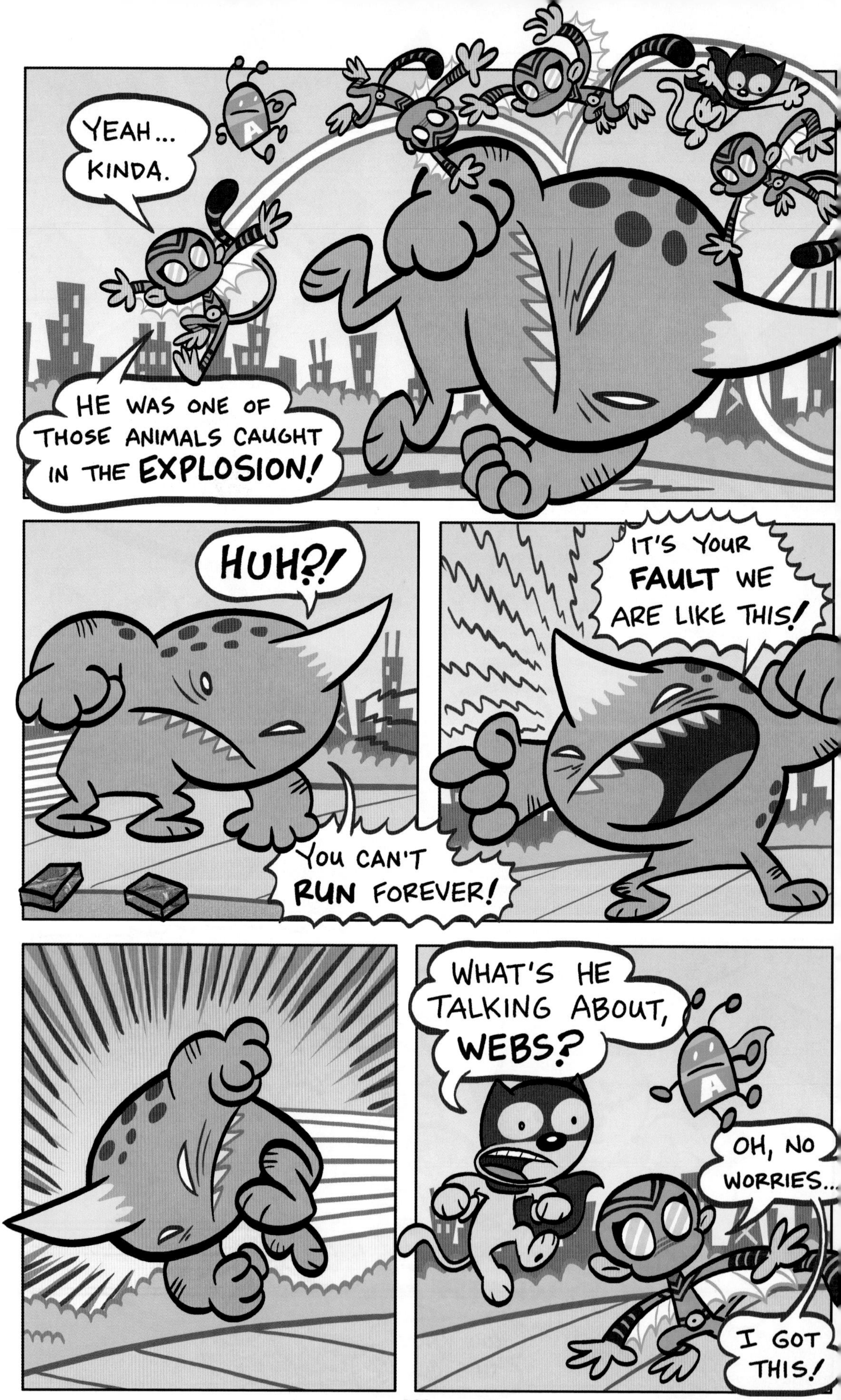

YEAH... KINDA.
HE WAS ONE OF THOSE ANIMALS CAUGHT IN THE EXPLOSION!
HUH?!
IT'S YOUR FAULT WE ARE LIKE THIS!
YOU CAN'T RUN FOREVER!
WHAT'S HE TALKING ABOUT, WEBS?
OH, NO WORRIES...
I GOT THIS!

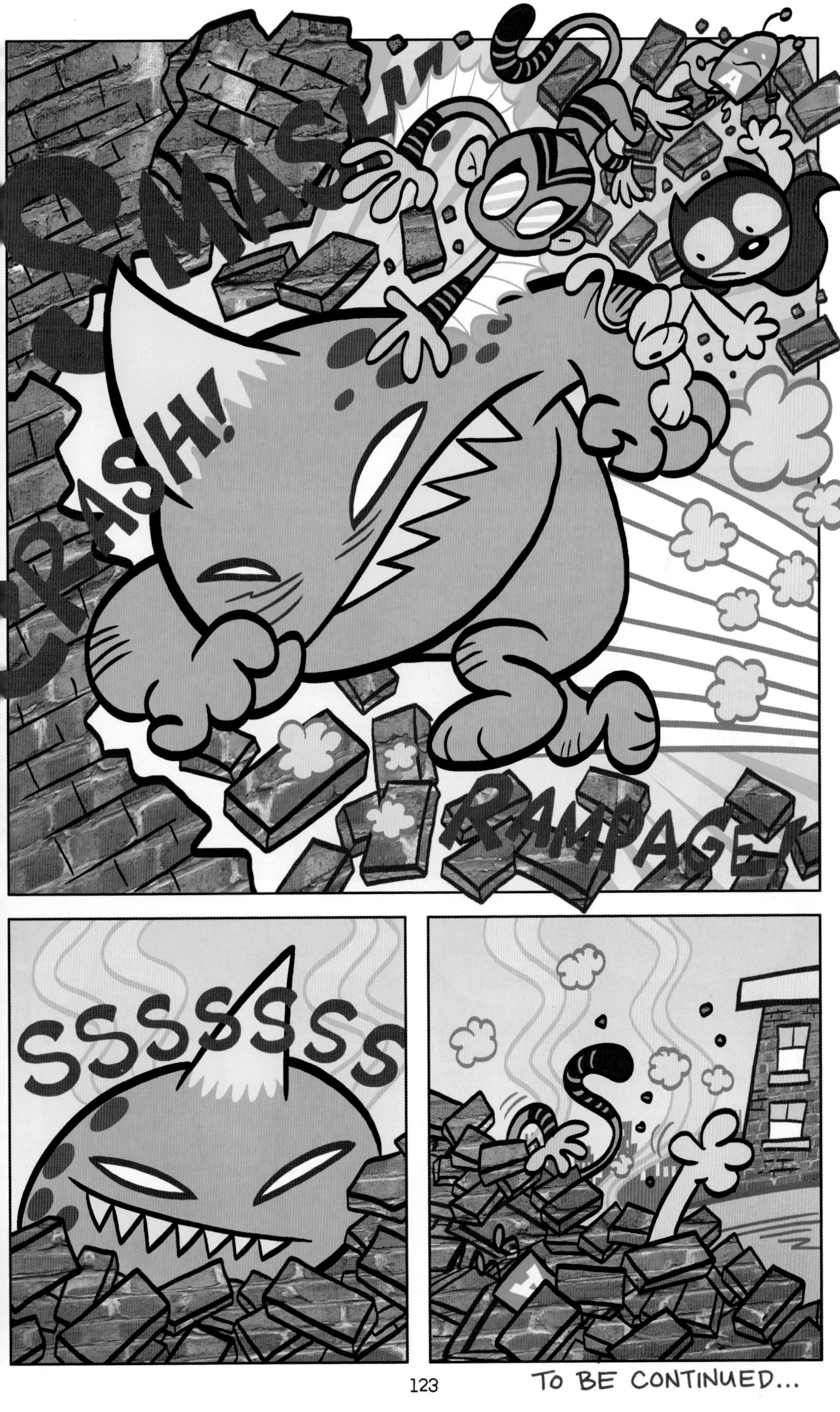
SMASH!
CRASH!
RAMPAGE!
SSSSSSS
TO BE CONTINUED...

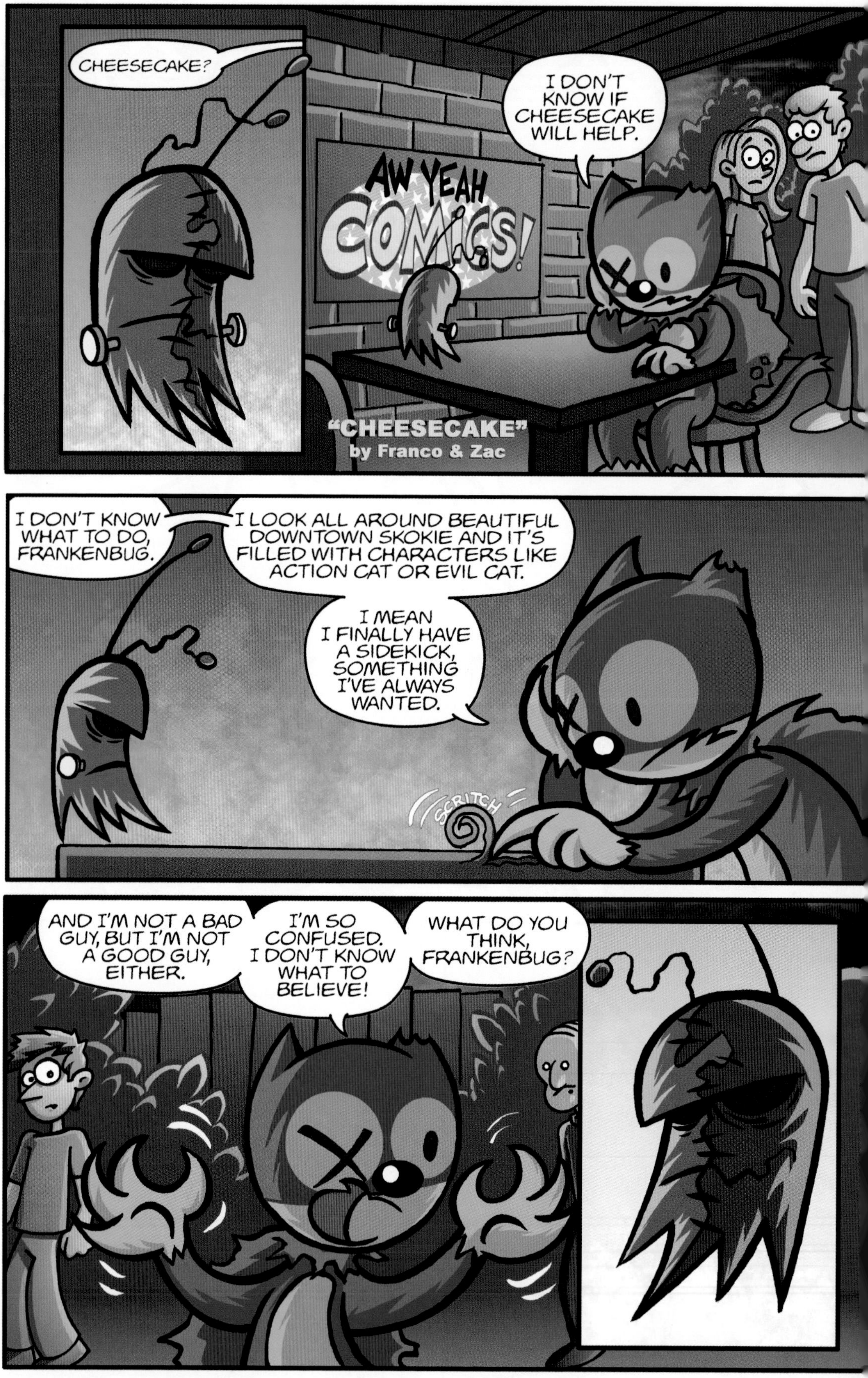
CHEESECAKE?
I DON'T KNOW IF CHEESECAKE WILL HELP.
AW YEAH COMICS!
"CHEESECAKE"
by Franco & Zac
I DON'T KNOW WHAT TO DO, FRANKENBUG.
I LOOK ALL AROUND BEAUTIFUL DOWNTOWN SKOKIE AND IT'S FILLED WITH CHARACTERS LIKE ACTION CAT OR EVIL CAT.
I MEAN I FINALLY HAVE A SIDEKICK, SOMETHING I'VE ALWAYS WANTED.
SCRITCH
AND I'M NOT A BAD GUY, BUT I'M NOT A GOOD GUY, EITHER.
I'M SO CONFUSED. I DON'T KNOW WHAT TO BELIEVE!
WHAT DO YOU THINK, FRANKENBUG?

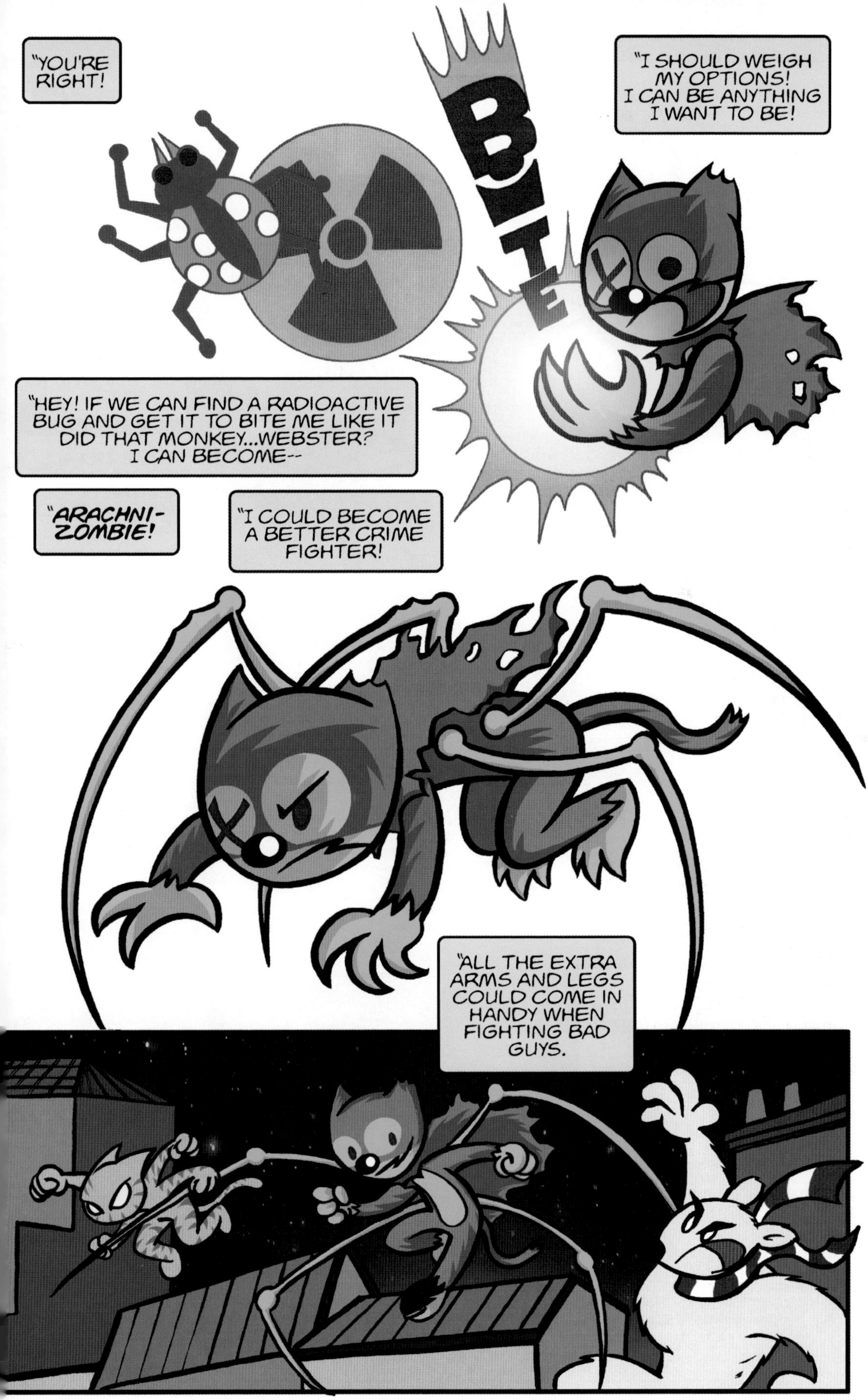
"YOU'RE RIGHT!
BITE
"I SHOULD WEIGH MY OPTIONS! I CAN BE ANYTHING I WANT TO BE!
"HEY! IF WE CAN FIND A RADIOACTIVE BUG AND GET IT TO BITE ME LIKE IT DID THAT MONKEY...WEBSTER? I CAN BECOME--
"ARACHNI-ZOMBIE!
"I COULD BECOME A BETTER CRIME FIGHTER!
"ALL THE EXTRA ARMS AND LEGS COULD COME IN HANDY WHEN FIGHTING BAD GUYS.

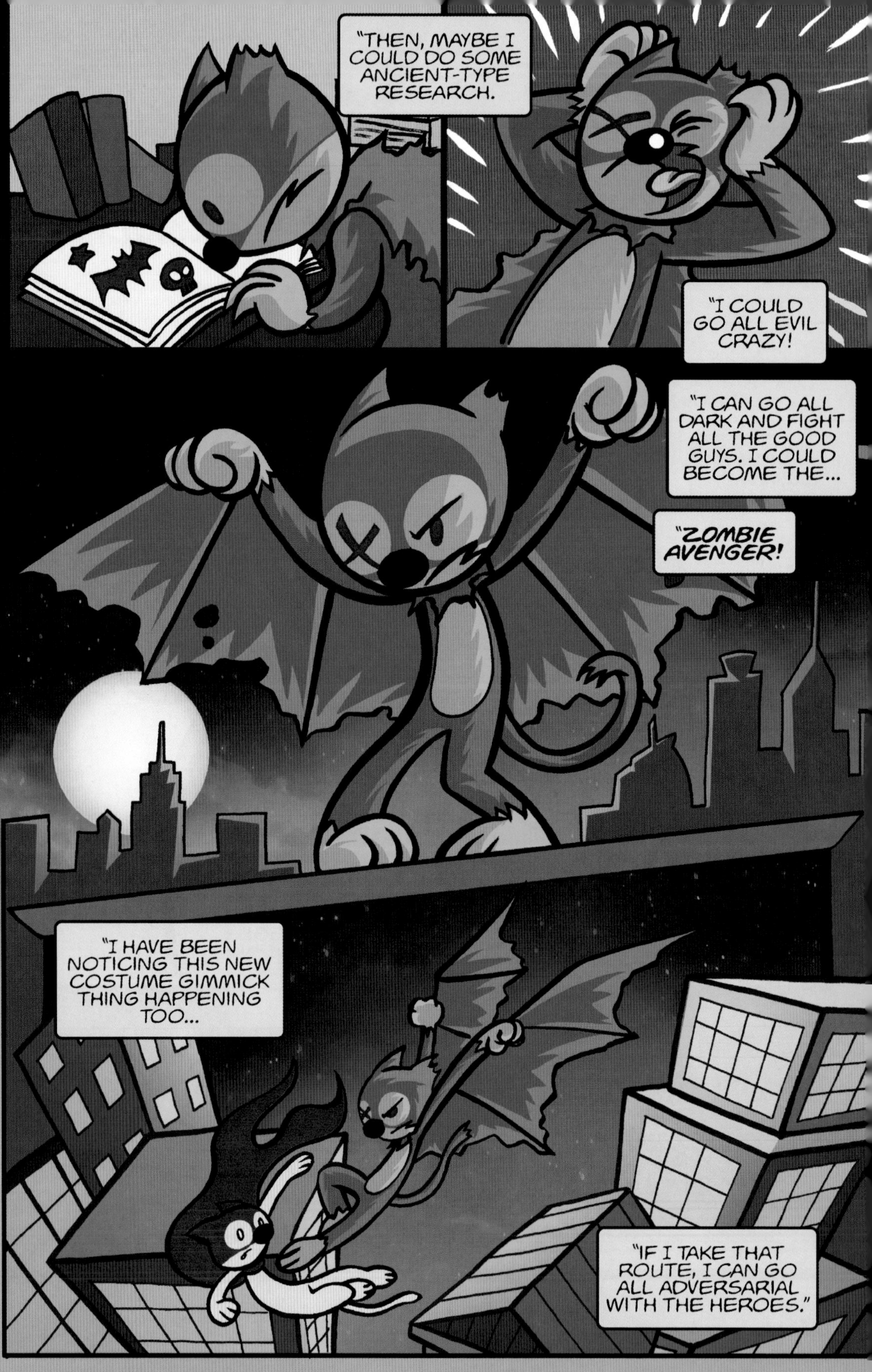

"THEN, MAYBE I COULD DO SOME ANCIENT-TYPE RESEARCH.
"I COULD GO ALL EVIL CRAZY!
"I CAN GO ALL DARK AND FIGHT ALL THE GOOD GUYS. I COULD BECOME THE...
"ZOMBIE AVENGER!
"I HAVE BEEN NOTICING THIS NEW COSTUME GIMMICK THING HAPPENING TOO...
"IF I TAKE THAT ROUTE, I CAN GO ALL ADVERSARIAL WITH THE HEROES."

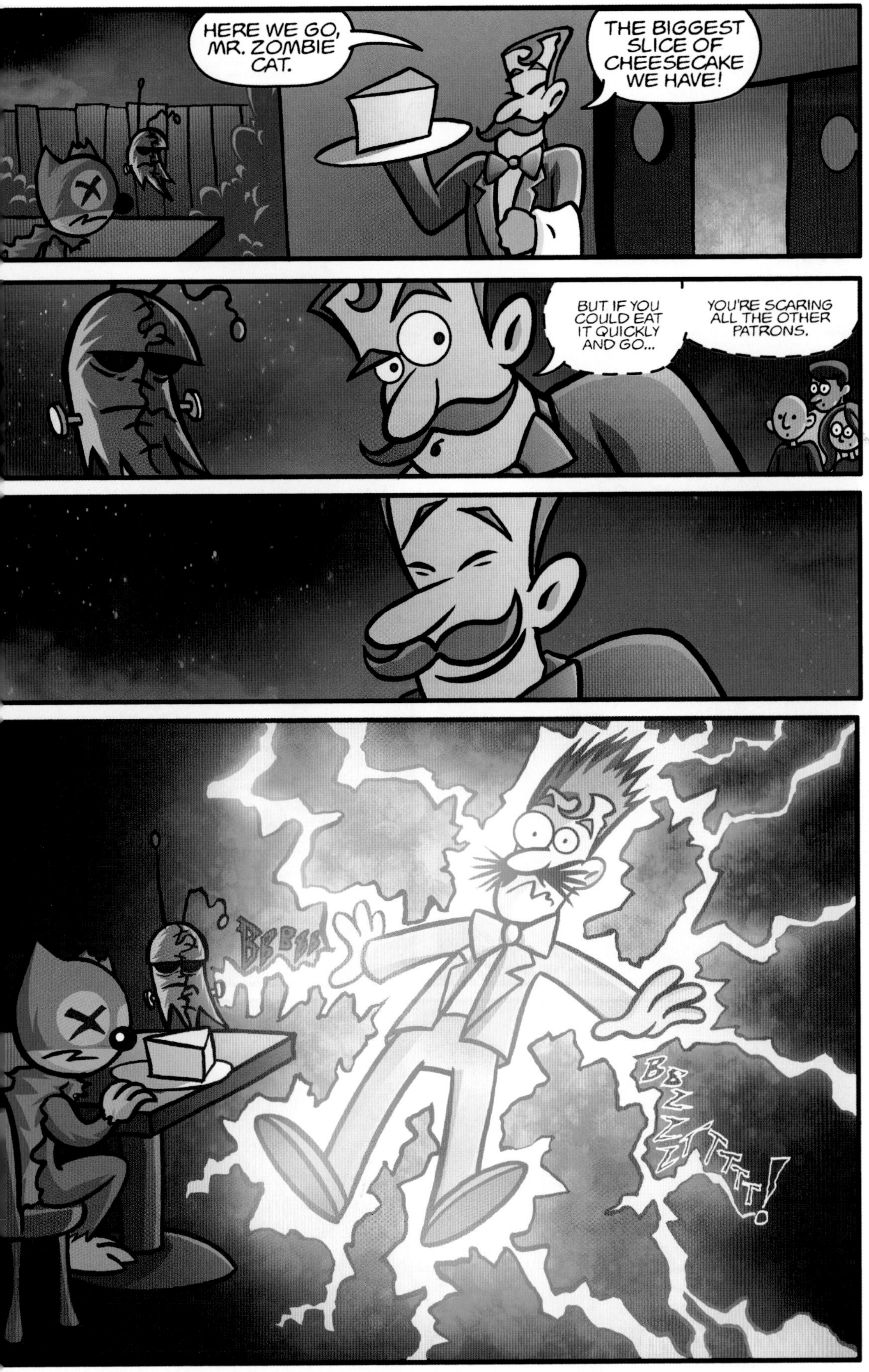
HERE WE GO, MR. ZOMBIE CAT.
THE BIGGEST SLICE OF CHEESECAKE WE HAVE!
BUT IF YOU COULD EAT IT QUICKLY AND GO...
YOU'RE SCARING ALL THE OTHER PATRONS.
BBBSS!
BBZZZTTTTT!

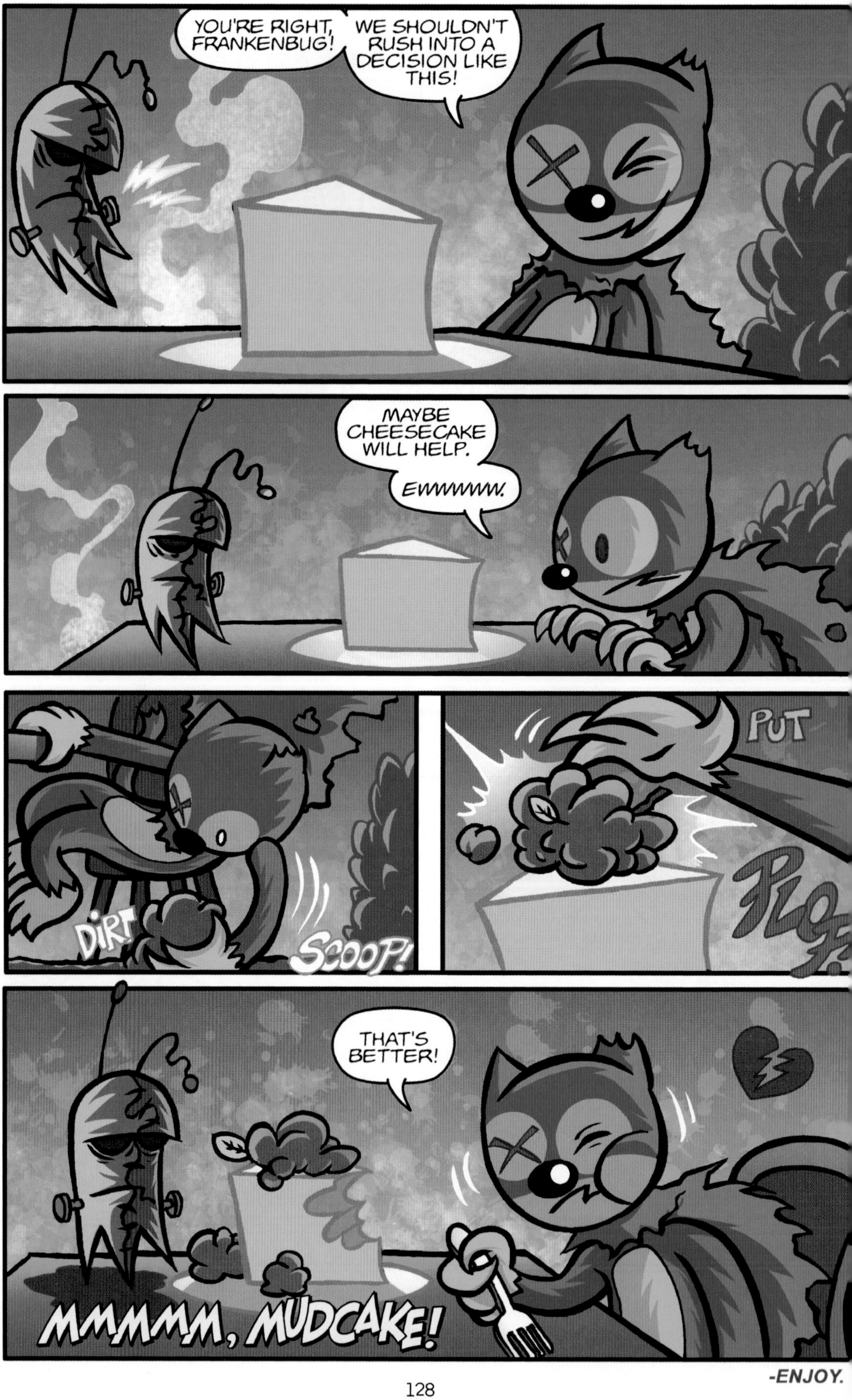
YOU'RE RIGHT, FRANKENBUG!
WE SHOULDN'T RUSH INTO A DECISION LIKE THIS!
MAYBE CHEESECAKE WILL HELP.
EWWWWW.
DIRT
SCOOP!
PUT
PLOP!
THAT'S BETTER!
MMMMM, MUDCAKE!

-ENJOY.

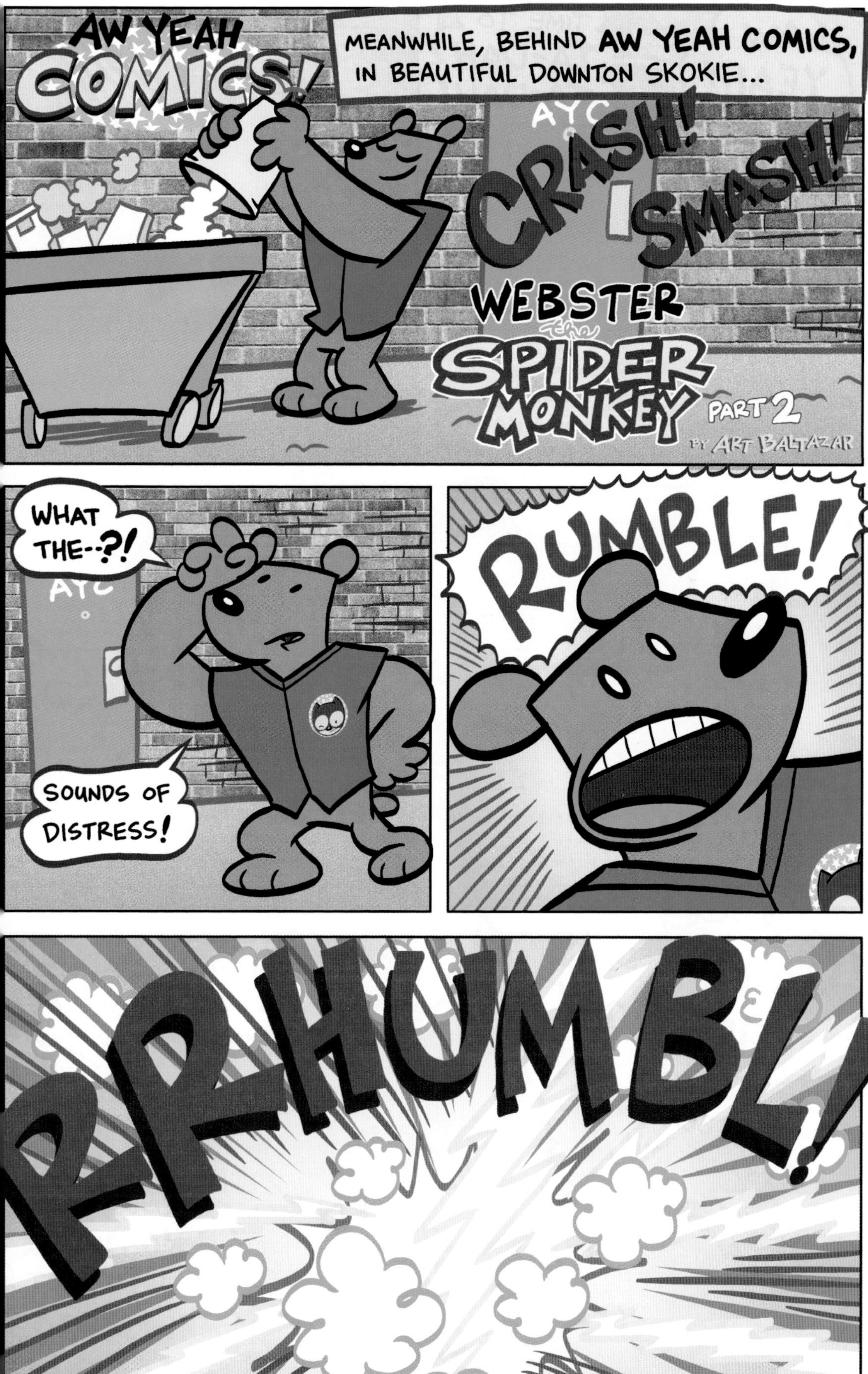
AW YEAH COMICS!
MEANWHILE, BEHIND AW YEAH COMICS, IN BEAUTIFUL DOWNTON SKOKIE...
AYC
CRASH!
SMASH!
WEBSTER the SPIDER MONKEY PART 2
BY ART BALTAZAR
WHAT THE--?!
AYC
SOUNDS OF DISTRESS!
RUMBLE!
RRHUMBL!

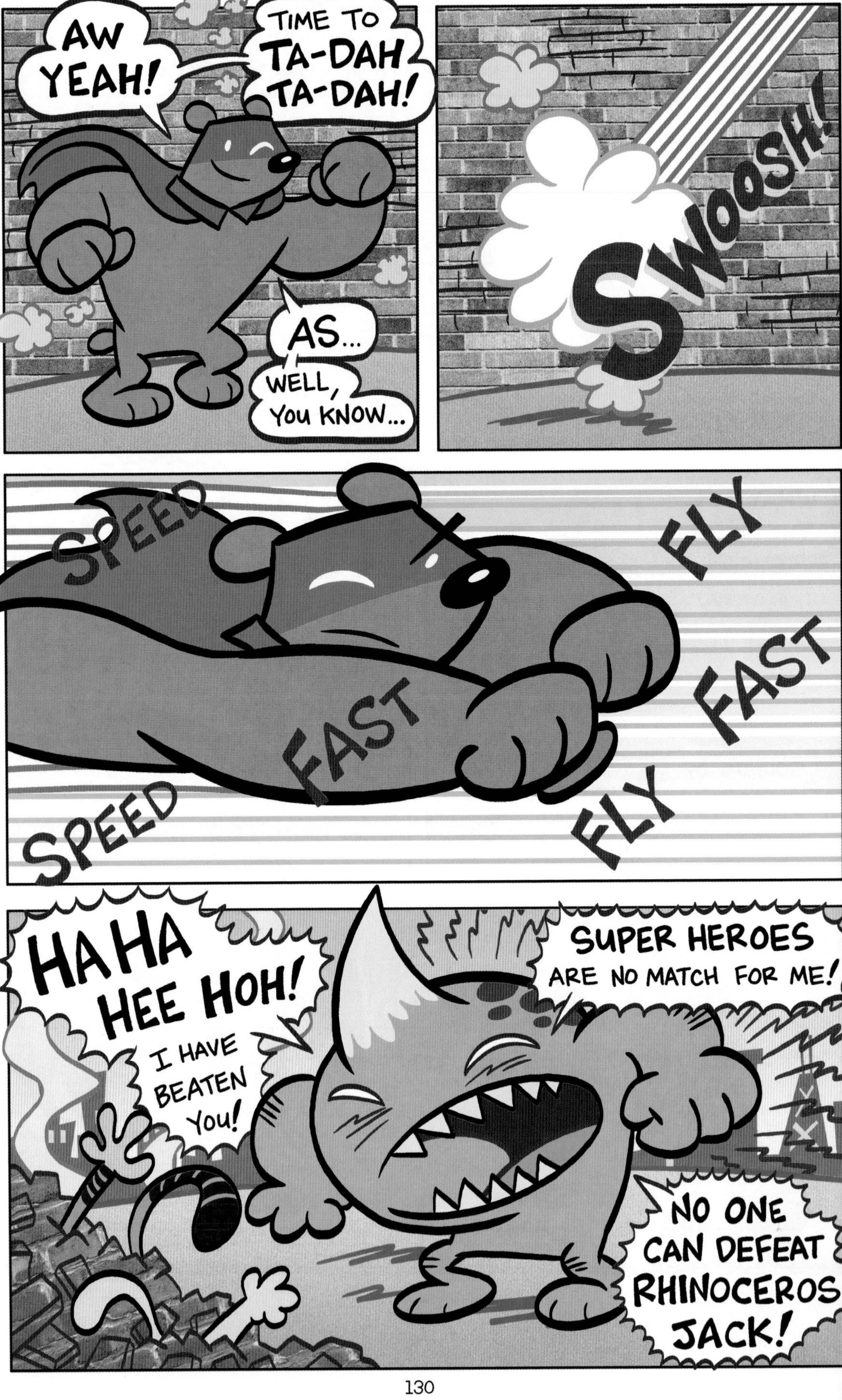

AW YEAH!
TIME TO TA-DAH TA-DAH!
AS...
WELL, YOU KNOW...
SWOOSH!
SPEED
FLY
FAST
FAST
SPEED
FLY
HAHA HEE HOH!
I HAVE BEATEN YOU!
SUPER HEROES ARE NO MATCH FOR ME!
NO ONE CAN DEFEAT RHINOCEROS JACK!

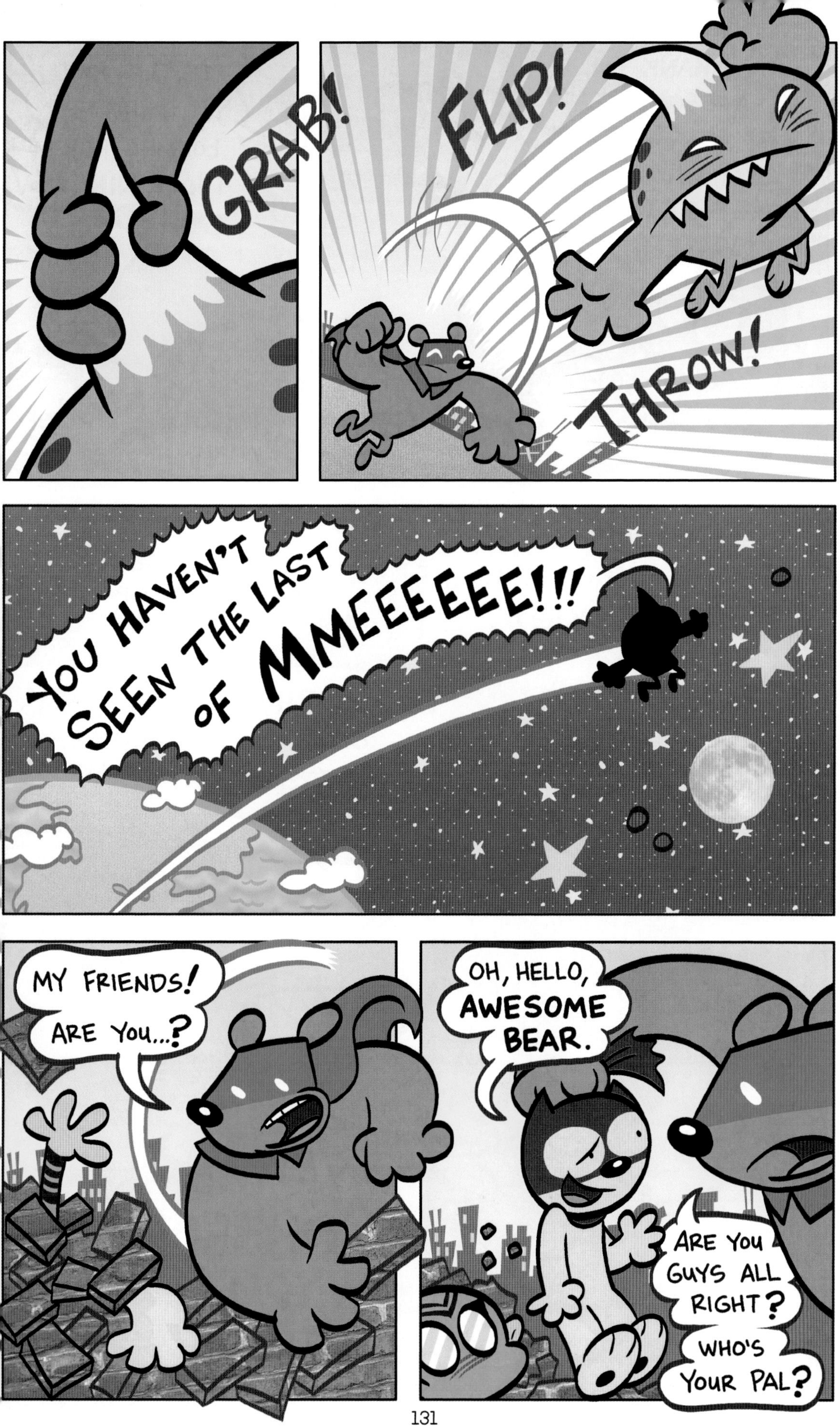
GRAB!
FLIP!
THROW!
YOU HAVEN'T SEEN THE LAST OF MMEEEEEEE!!!
MY FRIENDS! ARE YOU...?
OH, HELLO, AWESOME BEAR.
ARE YOU GUYS ALL RIGHT?
WHO'S YOUR PAL?

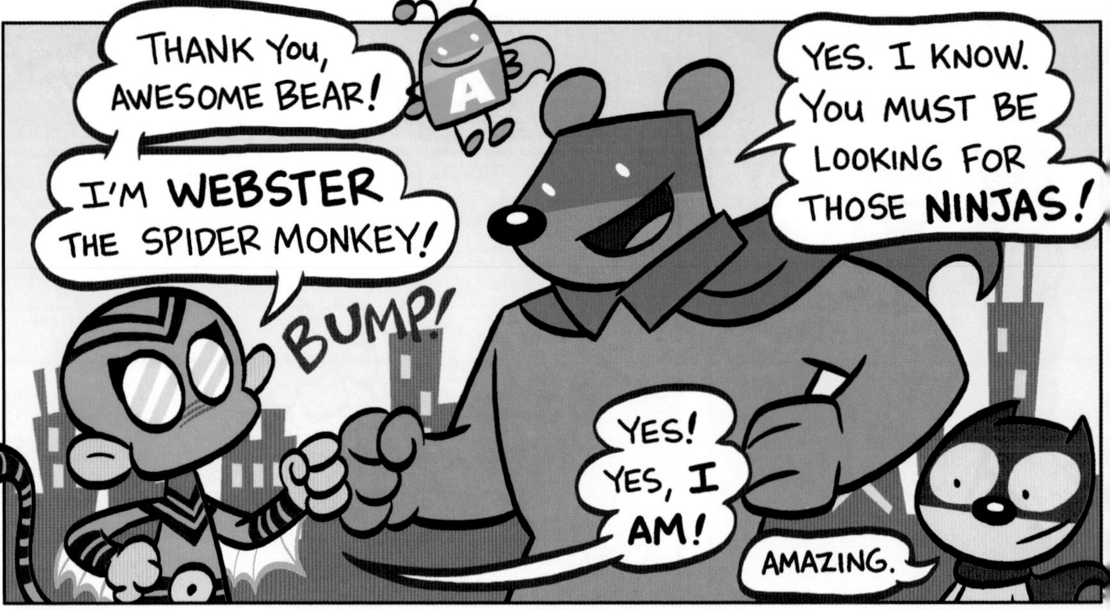
THANK YOU, AWESOME BEAR!
I'M WEBSTER THE SPIDER MONKEY!
BUMP!
YES. I KNOW. YOU MUST BE LOOKING FOR THOSE NINJAS!
YES! YES, I AM!
AMAZING.

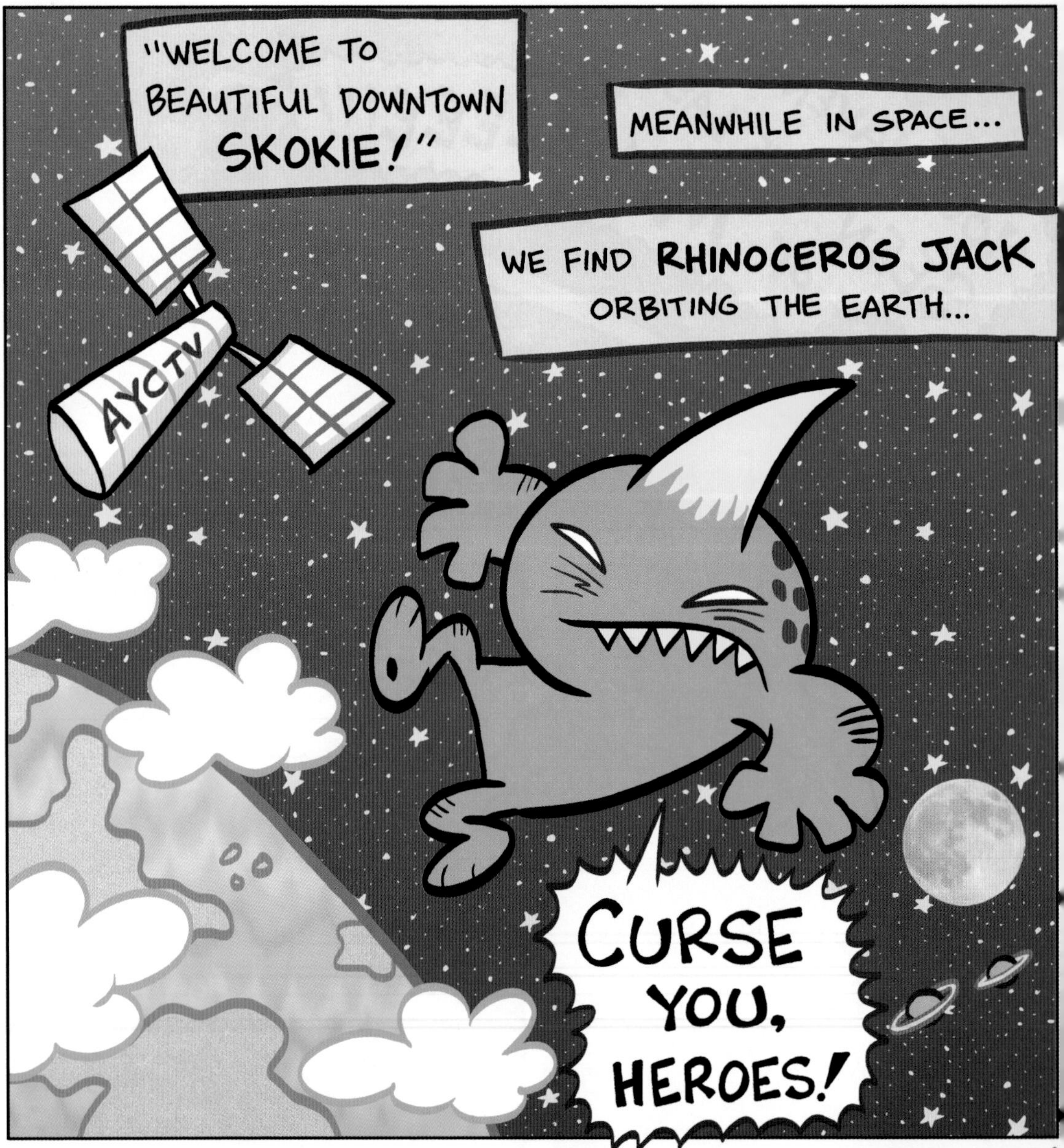
"WELCOME TO BEAUTIFUL DOWNTOWN SKOKIE!"
MEANWHILE IN SPACE...
WE FIND RHINOCEROS JACK ORBITING THE EARTH...
AYCTV
CURSE YOU, HEROES!

AW YEAH ORBIT!

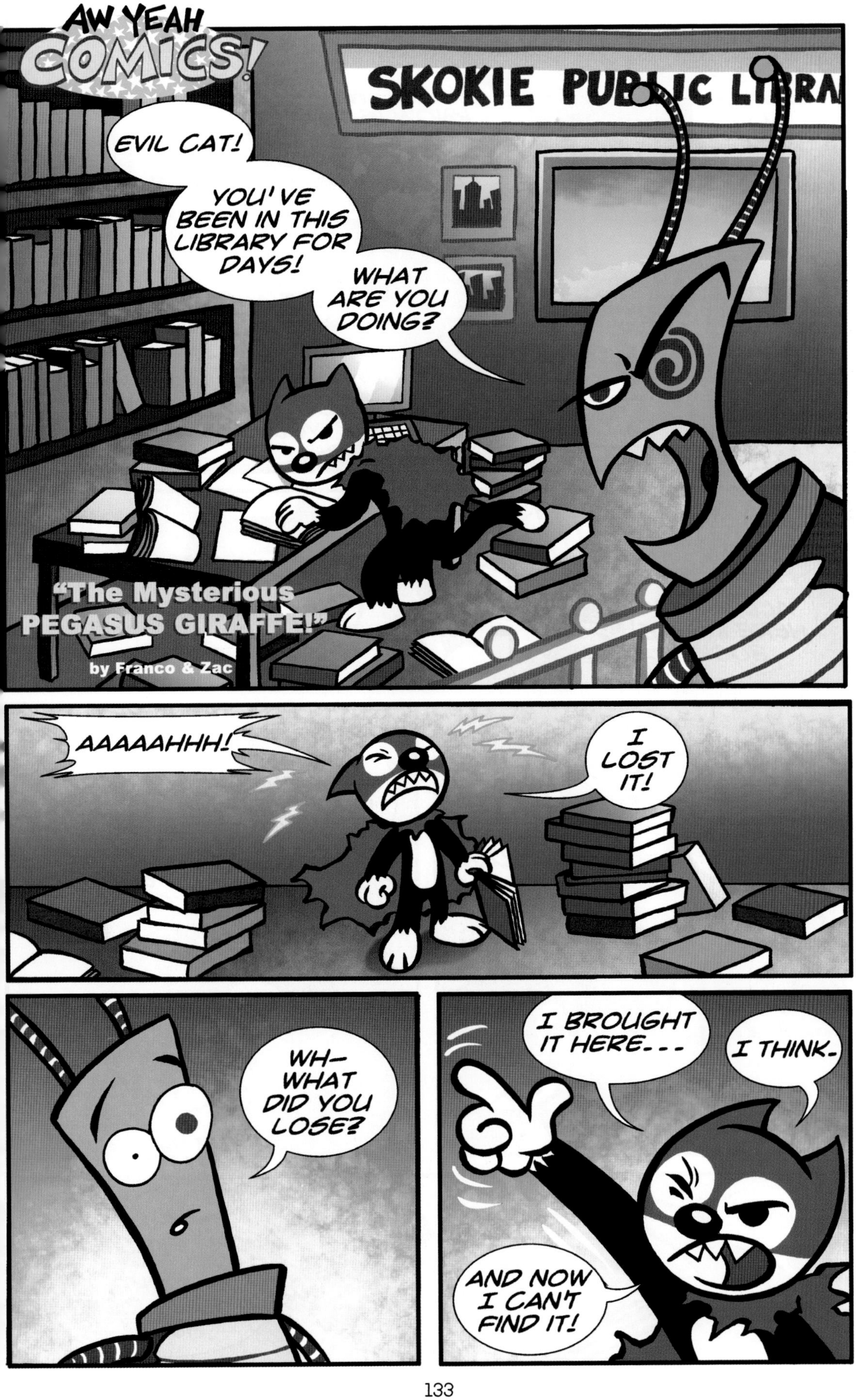
AW YEAH COMICS!
SKOKIE PUBLIC LIBRA
EVIL CAT!
YOU'VE BEEN IN THIS LIBRARY FOR DAYS!
WHAT ARE YOU DOING?
"The Mysterious PEGASUS GIRAFFE!"
by Franco & Zac
AAAAAHHH!
I LOST IT!
WH-WHAT DID YOU LOSE?
I BROUGHT IT HERE...
I THINK.
AND NOW I CAN'T FIND IT!

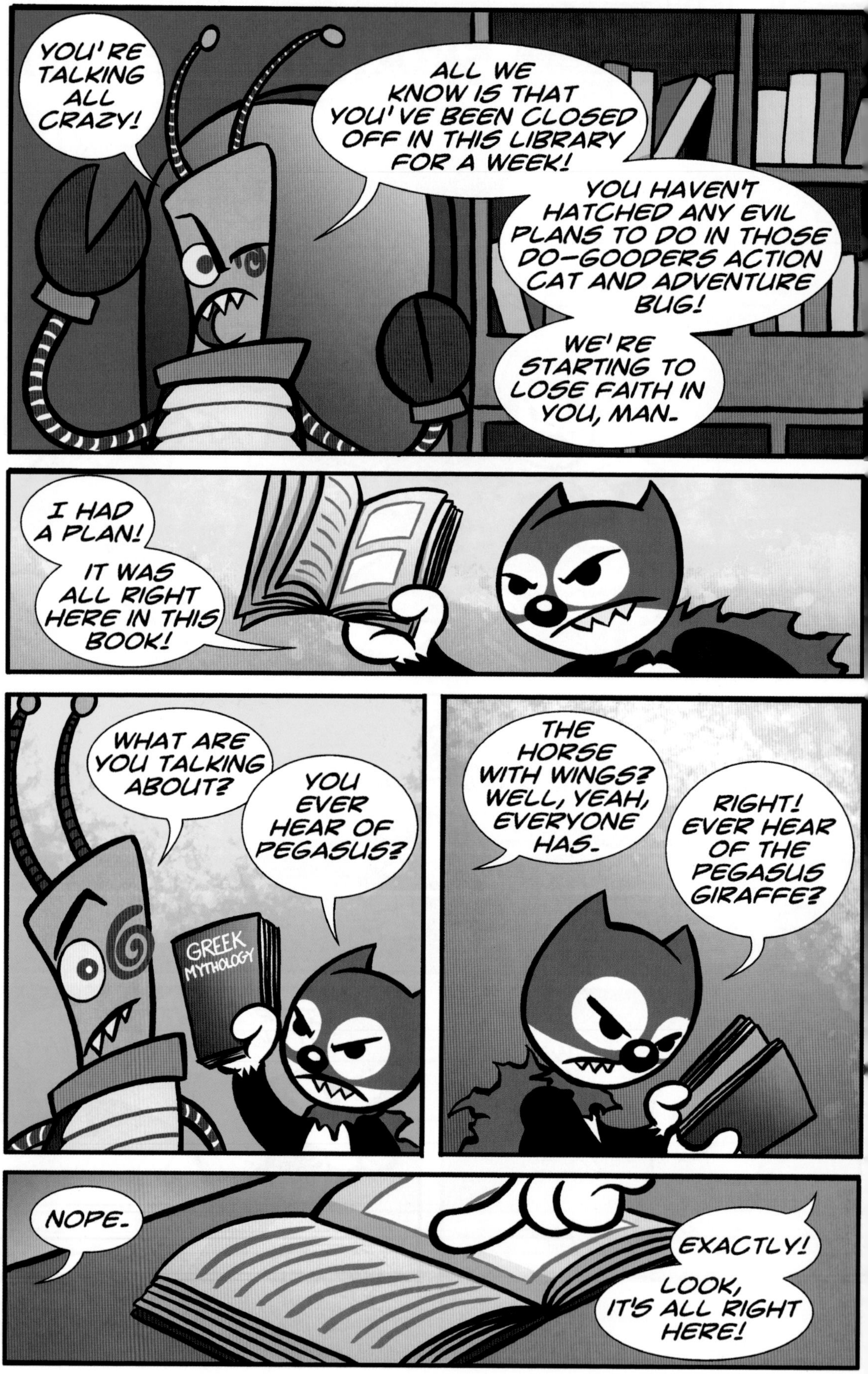

YOU'RE TALKING ALL CRAZY!
ALL WE KNOW IS THAT YOU'VE BEEN CLOSED OFF IN THIS LIBRARY FOR A WEEK!
YOU HAVEN'T HATCHED ANY EVIL PLANS TO DO IN THOSE DO-GOODERS ACTION CAT AND ADVENTURE BUG!
WE'RE STARTING TO LOSE FAITH IN YOU, MAN.
I HAD A PLAN!
IT WAS ALL RIGHT HERE IN THIS BOOK!
WHAT ARE YOU TALKING ABOUT?
YOU EVER HEAR OF PEGASUS?
GREEK MYTHOLOGY
THE HORSE WITH WINGS? WELL, YEAH, EVERYONE HAS.
RIGHT! EVER HEAR OF THE PEGASUS GIRAFFE?
NOPE.
EXACTLY!
LOOK, IT'S ALL RIGHT HERE!

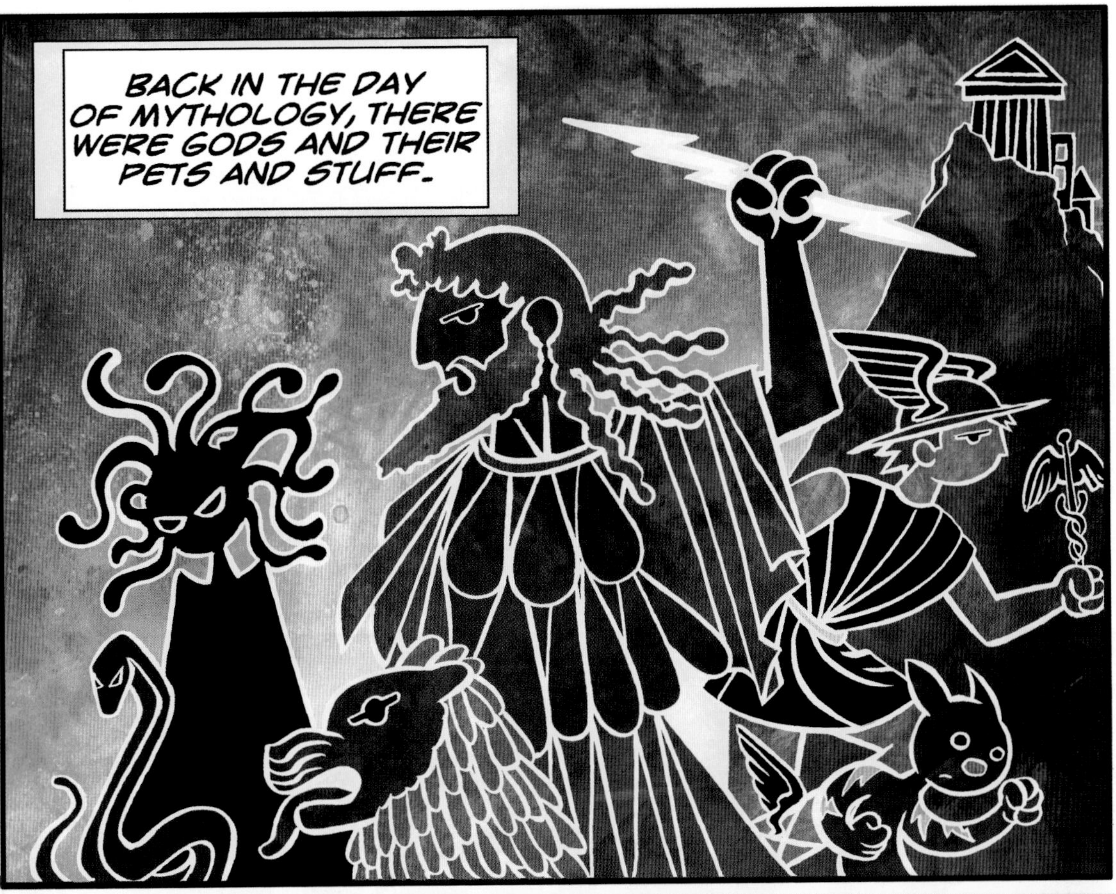
BACK IN THE DAY OF MYTHOLOGY, THERE WERE GODS AND THEIR PETS AND STUFF.

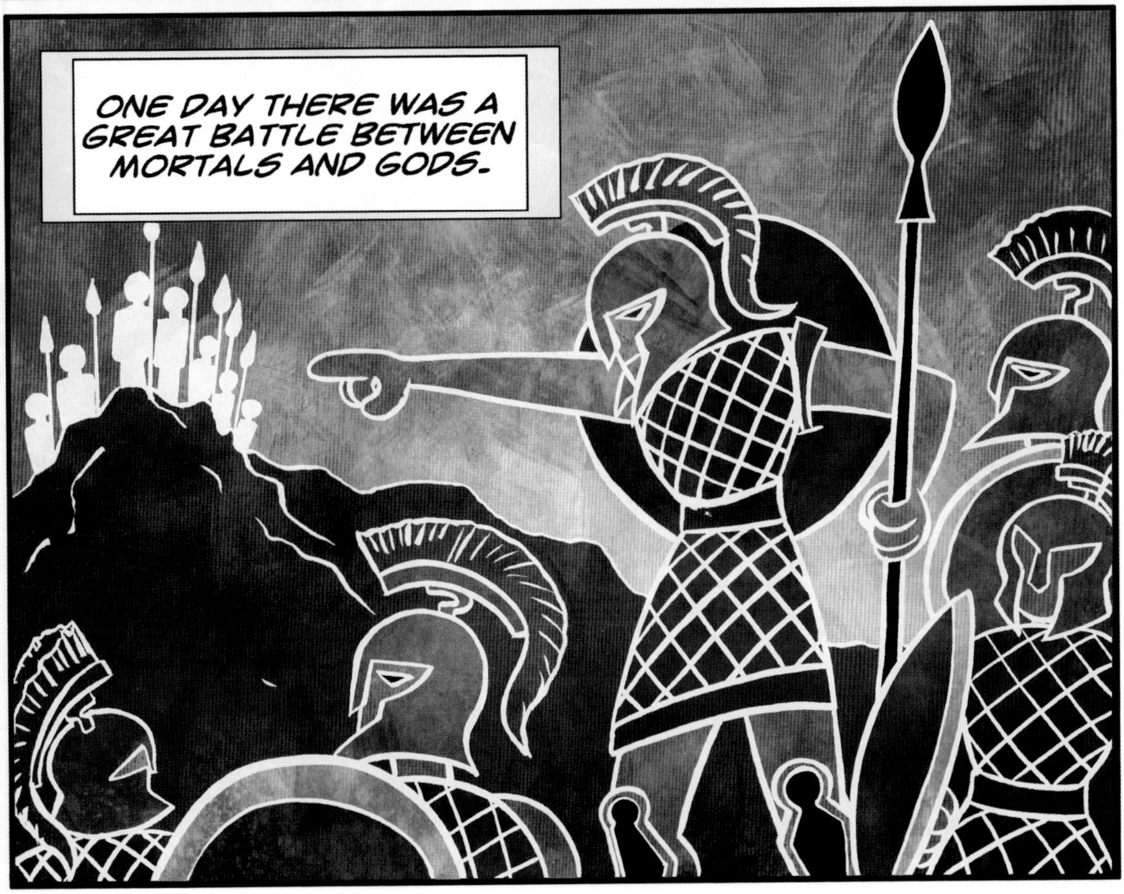
ONE DAY THERE WAS A GREAT BATTLE BETWEEN MORTALS AND GODS.

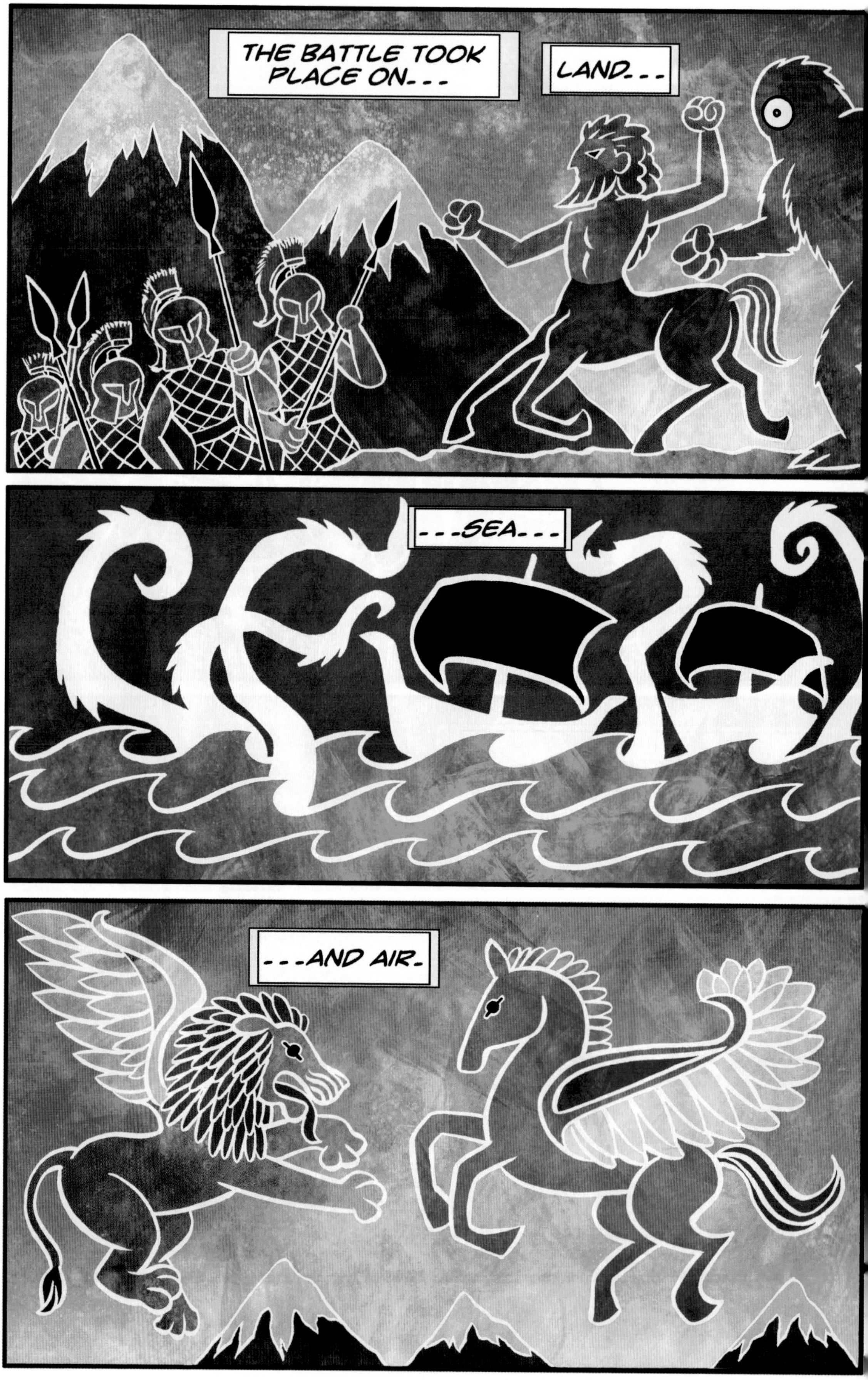
THE BATTLE TOOK PLACE ON---
LAND---
---SEA---
---AND AIR.

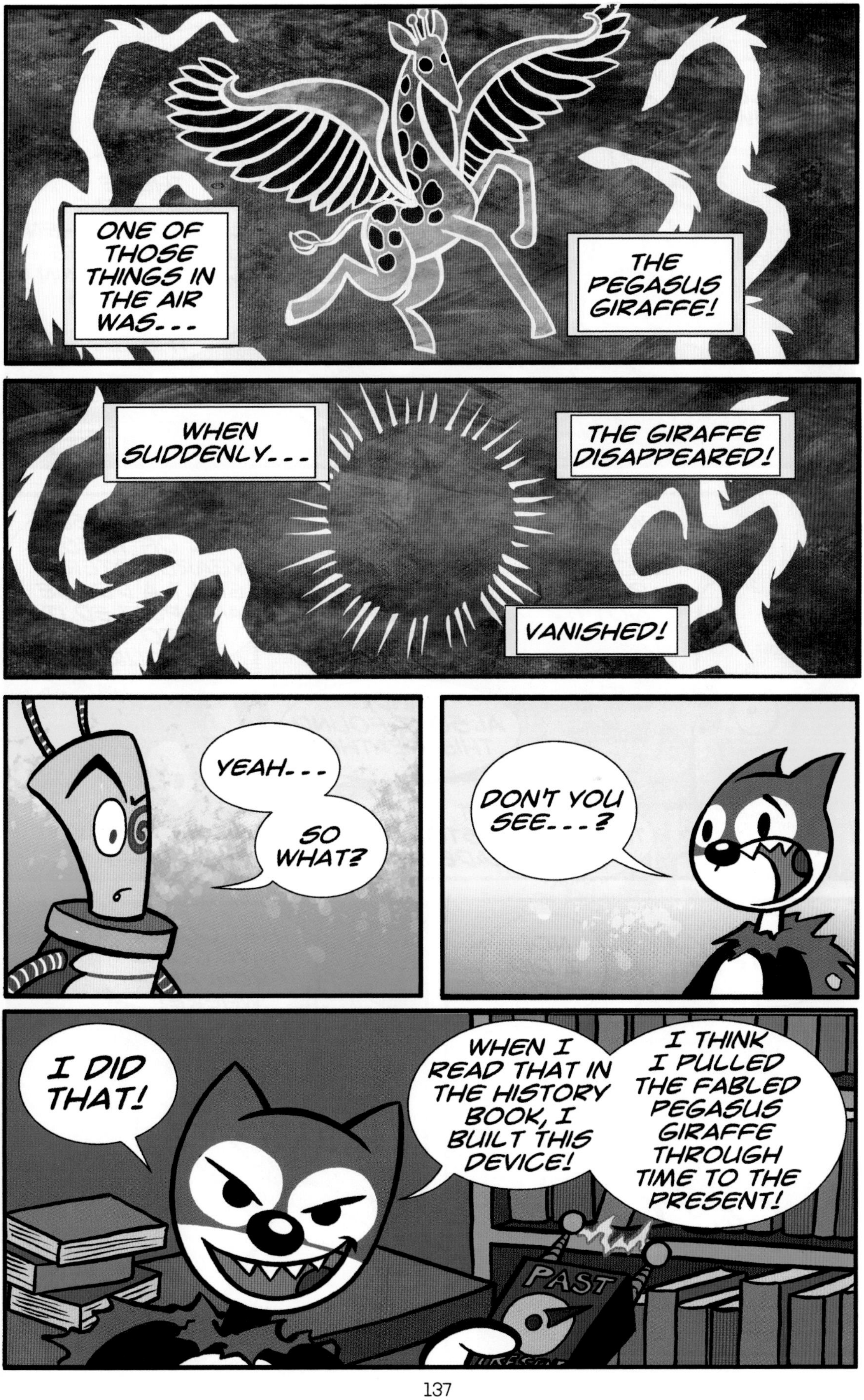
ONE OF THOSE THINGS IN THE AIR WAS...
THE PEGASUS GIRAFFE!
WHEN SUDDENLY...
THE GIRAFFE DISAPPEARED!
VANISHED!
YEAH...
SO WHAT?
DON'T YOU SEE...?
I DID THAT!
WHEN I READ THAT IN THE HISTORY BOOK, I BUILT THIS DEVICE!
I THINK I PULLED THE FABLED PEGASUS GIRAFFE THROUGH TIME TO THE PRESENT!
PAST

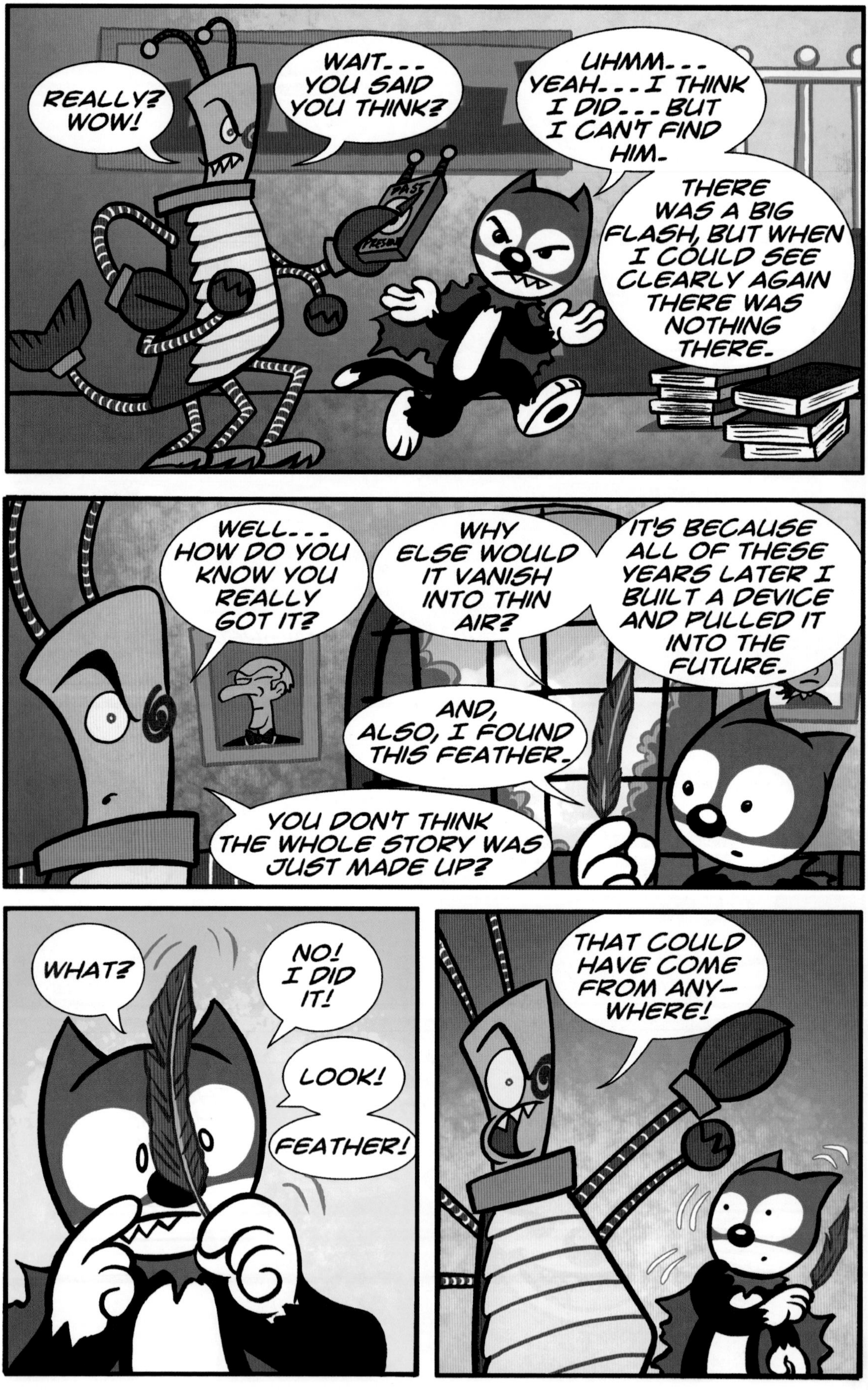
REALLY? WOW!
WAIT... YOU SAID YOU THINK?
UHMM... YEAH...I THINK I DID...BUT I CAN'T FIND HIM.
THERE WAS A BIG FLASH, BUT WHEN I COULD SEE CLEARLY AGAIN THERE WAS NOTHING THERE.
WELL... HOW DO YOU KNOW YOU REALLY GOT IT?
WHY ELSE WOULD IT VANISH INTO THIN AIR?
IT'S BECAUSE ALL OF THESE YEARS LATER I BUILT A DEVICE AND PULLED IT INTO THE FUTURE.
AND, ALSO, I FOUND THIS FEATHER.
YOU DON'T THINK THE WHOLE STORY WAS JUST MADE UP?
WHAT?
NO! I DID IT!
LOOK!
FEATHER!
THAT COULD HAVE COME FROM ANY-WHERE!

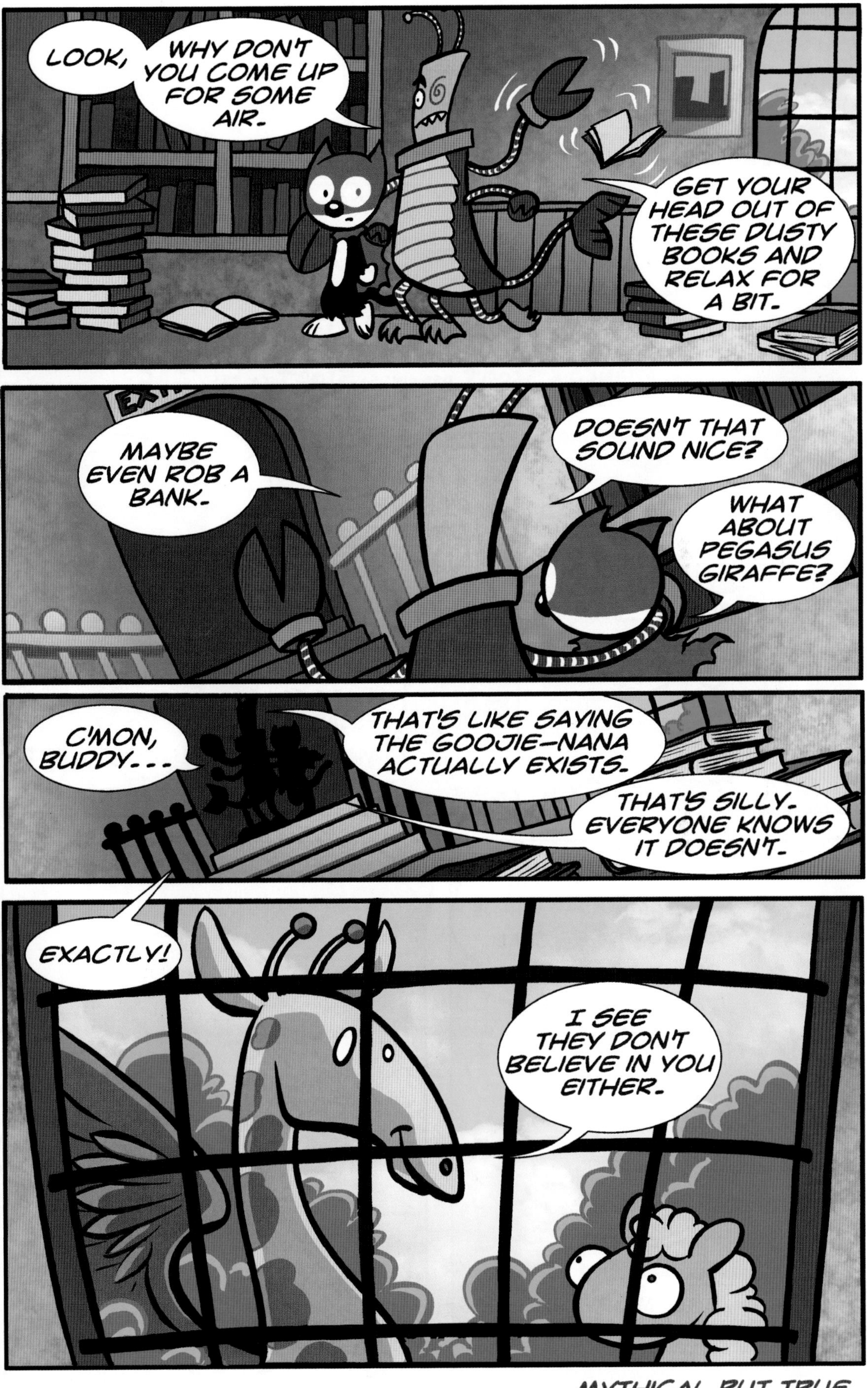
LOOK,
WHY DON'T YOU COME UP FOR SOME AIR.
GET YOUR HEAD OUT OF THESE DUSTY BOOKS AND RELAX FOR A BIT.
MAYBE EVEN ROB A BANK.
DOESN'T THAT SOUND NICE?
WHAT ABOUT PEGASUS GIRAFFE?
C'MON, BUDDY...
THAT'S LIKE SAYING THE GOOJIE-NANA ACTUALLY EXISTS.
THAT'S SILLY. EVERYONE KNOWS IT DOESN'T.
EXACTLY!
I SEE THEY DON'T BELIEVE IN YOU EITHER.

MYTHICAL BUT TRUE.

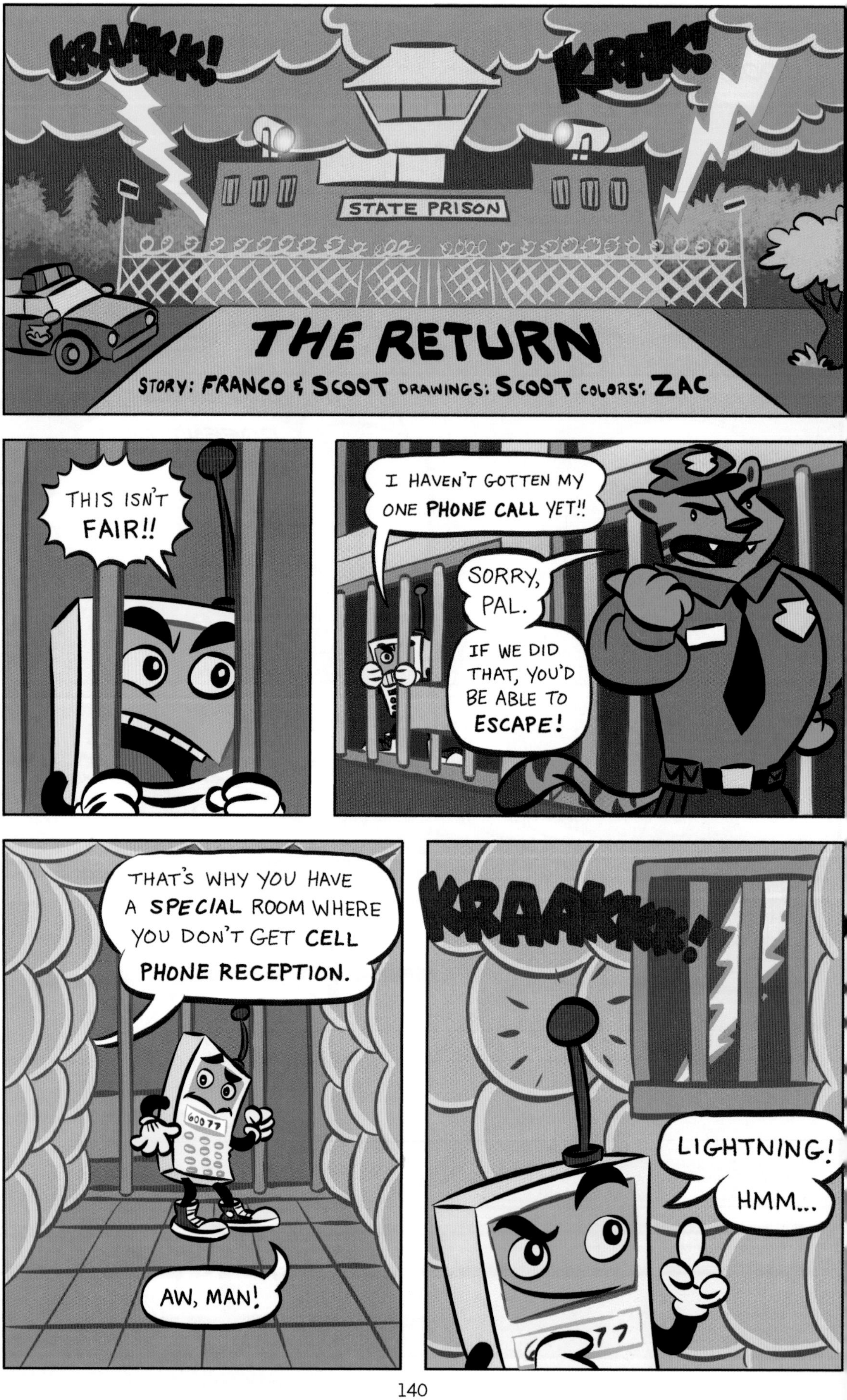
KRAAKK!
KRAK!
STATE PRISON
THE RETURN
STORY: FRANCO & SCOOT DRAWINGS: SCOOT COLORS: ZAC
THIS ISN'T FAIR!!
I HAVEN'T GOTTEN MY ONE PHONE CALL YET!!
SORRY, PAL.
IF WE DID THAT, YOU'D BE ABLE TO ESCAPE!
THAT'S WHY YOU HAVE A SPECIAL ROOM WHERE YOU DON'T GET CELL PHONE RECEPTION.
AW, MAN!
KRAAKKK!
LIGHTNING!
HMM...

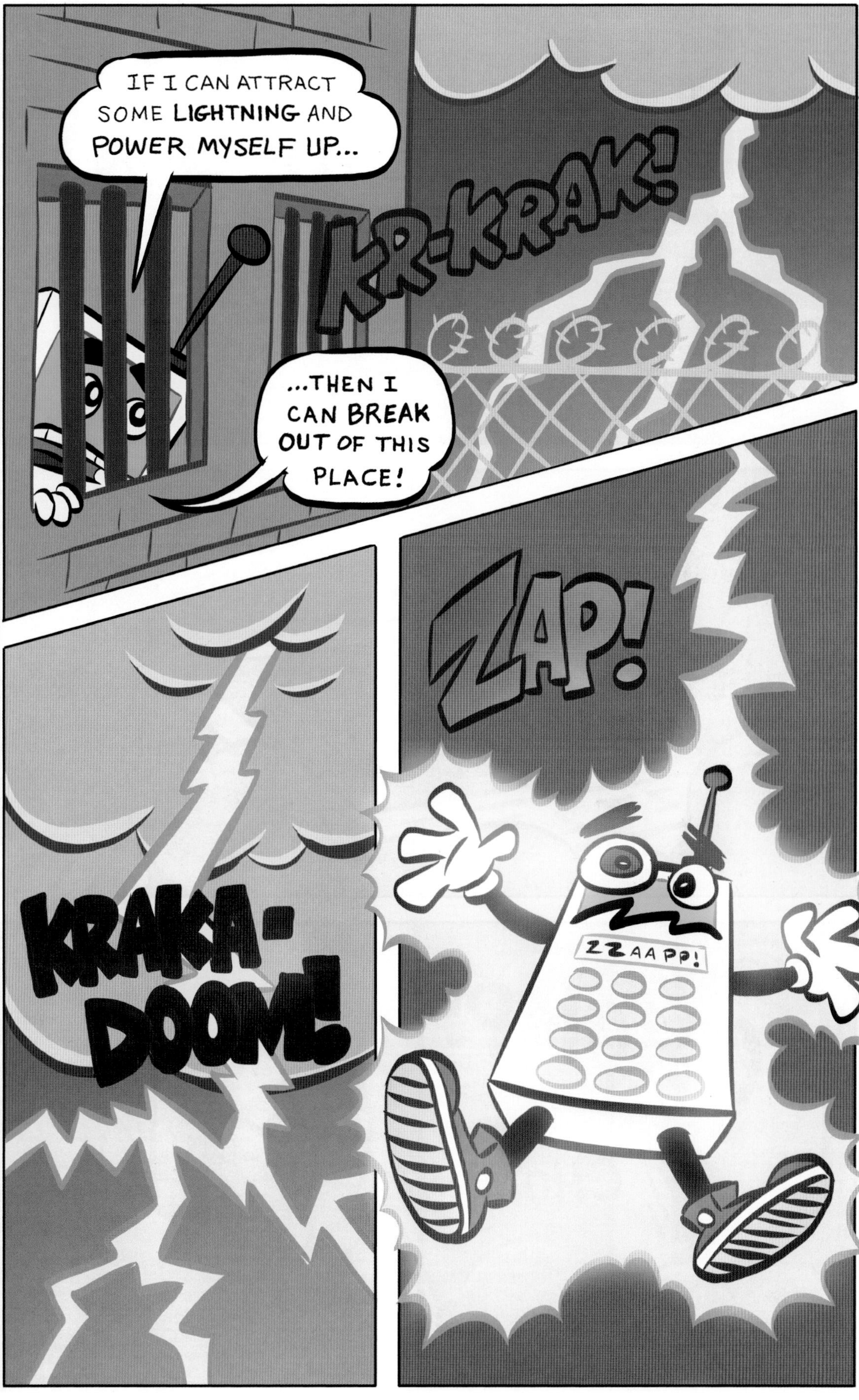

IF I CAN ATTRACT SOME LIGHTNING AND POWER MYSELF UP...
KR-KRAK!
...THEN I CAN BREAK OUT OF THIS PLACE!
KRAKA-DOOM!
ZAP!
ZZAAPP!

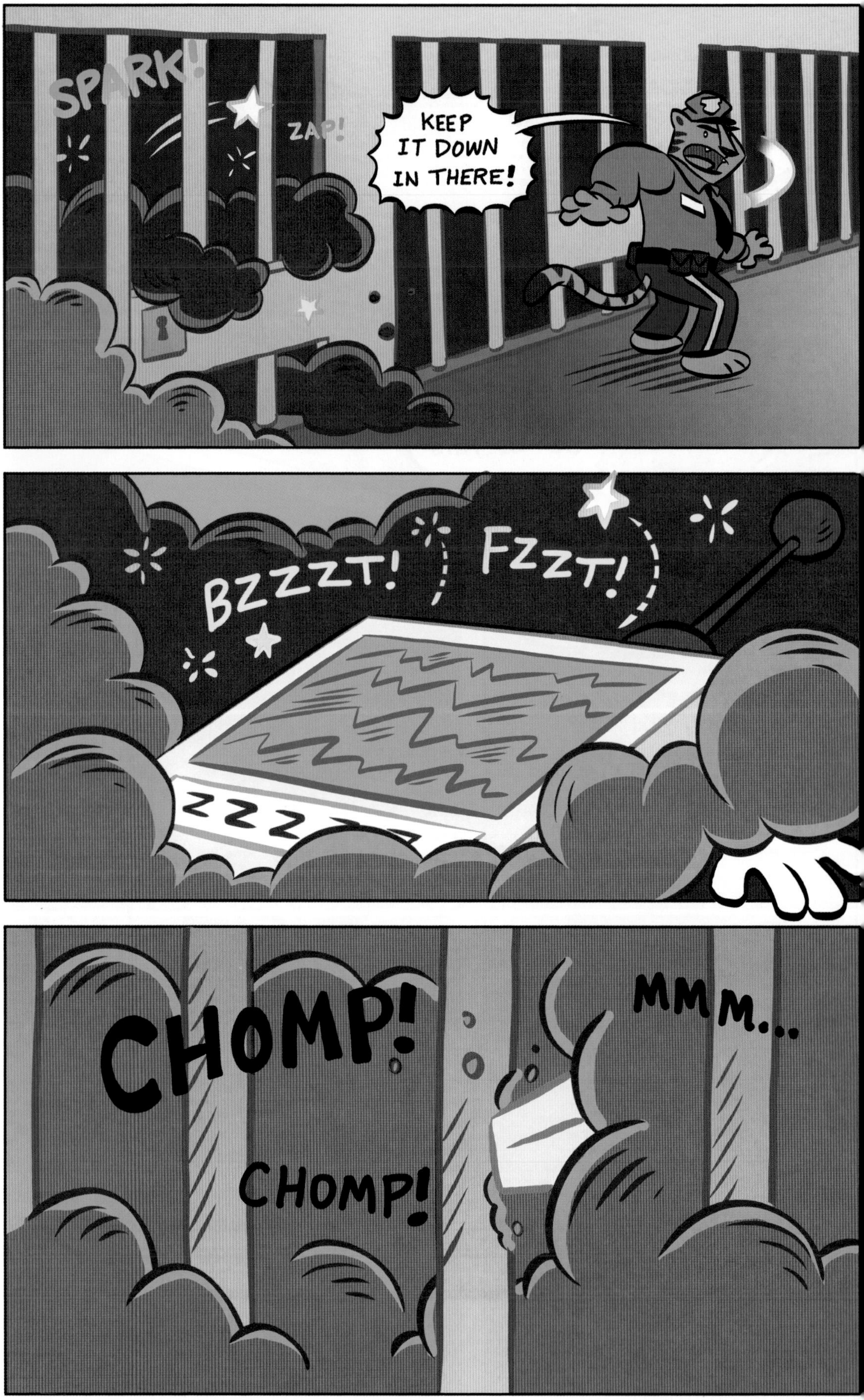
SPARK!
ZAP!
KEEP IT DOWN IN THERE!
BZZZT!
FZZT!
ZZZ
CHOMP!
CHOMP!
MMM...

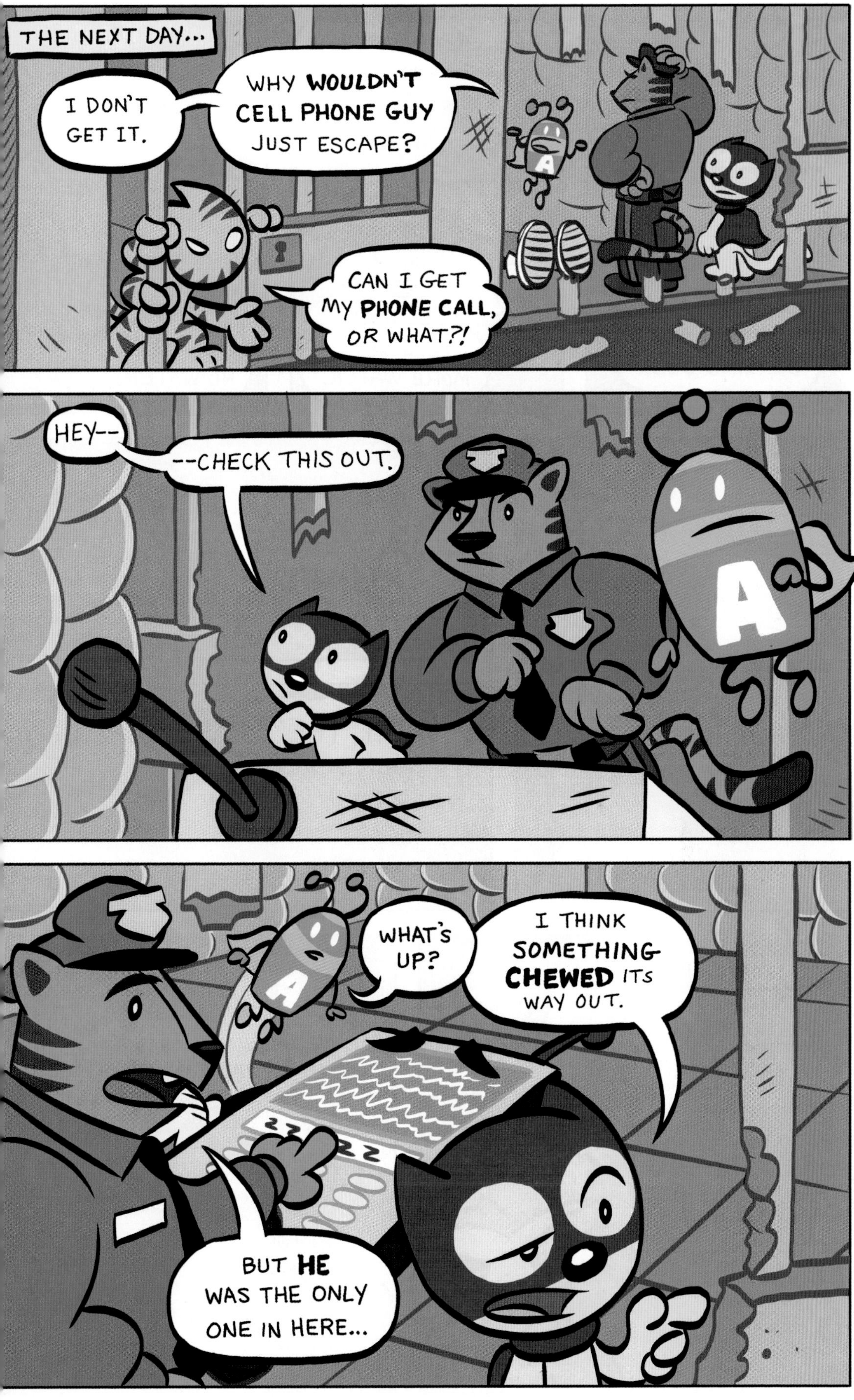
THE NEXT DAY...
I DON'T GET IT.
WHY **WOULDN'T** CELL PHONE GUY JUST ESCAPE?
CAN I GET MY **PHONE CALL**, OR WHAT?!
HEY--
--CHECK THIS OUT.
WHAT'S UP?
I THINK SOMETHING **CHEWED** ITS WAY OUT.
BUT **HE** WAS THE ONLY ONE IN HERE...

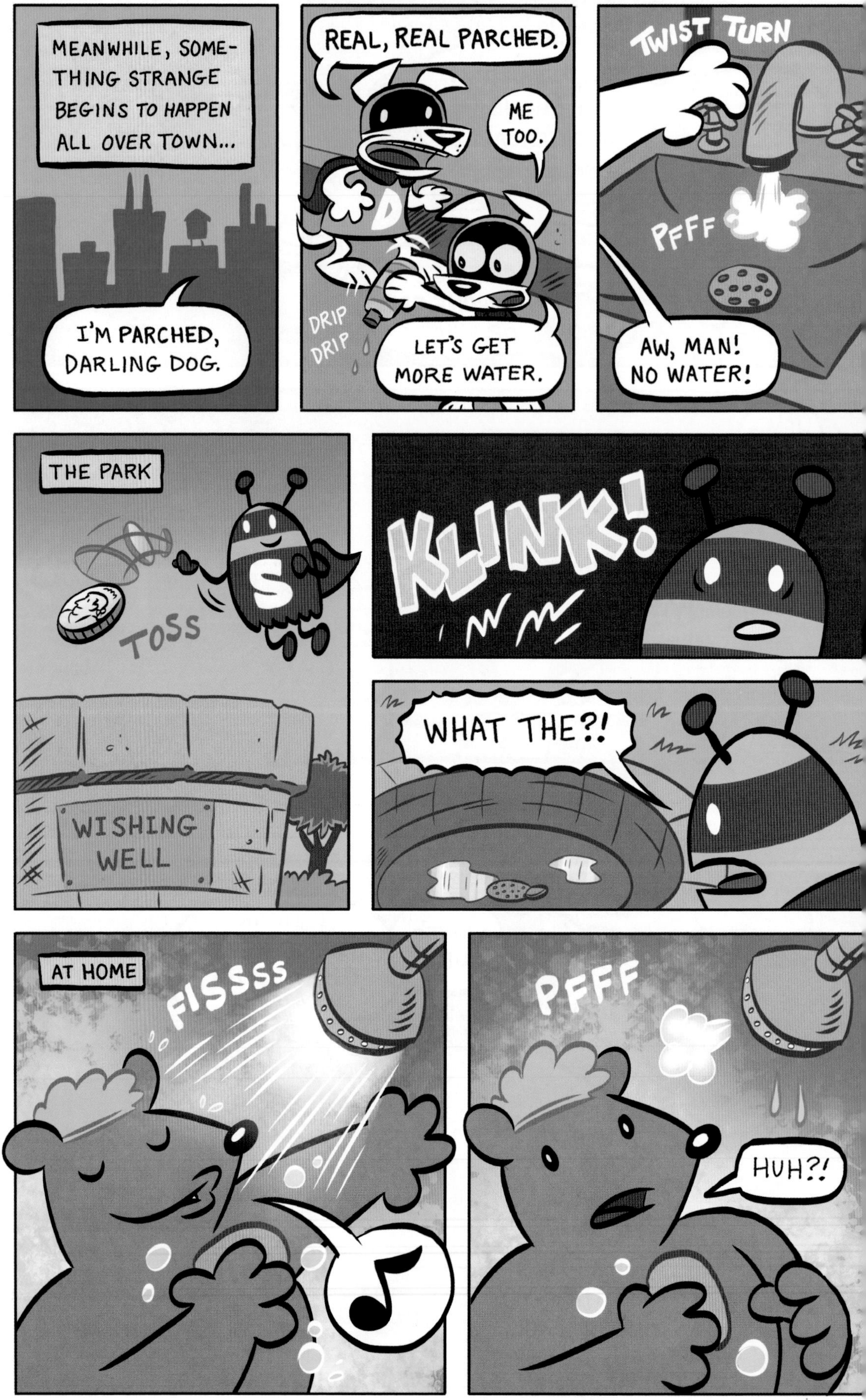
MEANWHILE, SOMETHING STRANGE BEGINS TO HAPPEN ALL OVER TOWN...
I'M PARCHED, DARLING DOG.
REAL, REAL PARCHED.
ME TOO.
DRIP DRIP
LET'S GET MORE WATER.
TWIST TURN
PFFF
AW, MAN! NO WATER!
THE PARK
TOSS
WISHING WELL
KLINK!
WHAT THE?!
AT HOME
FISSSS
PFFF
HUH?!

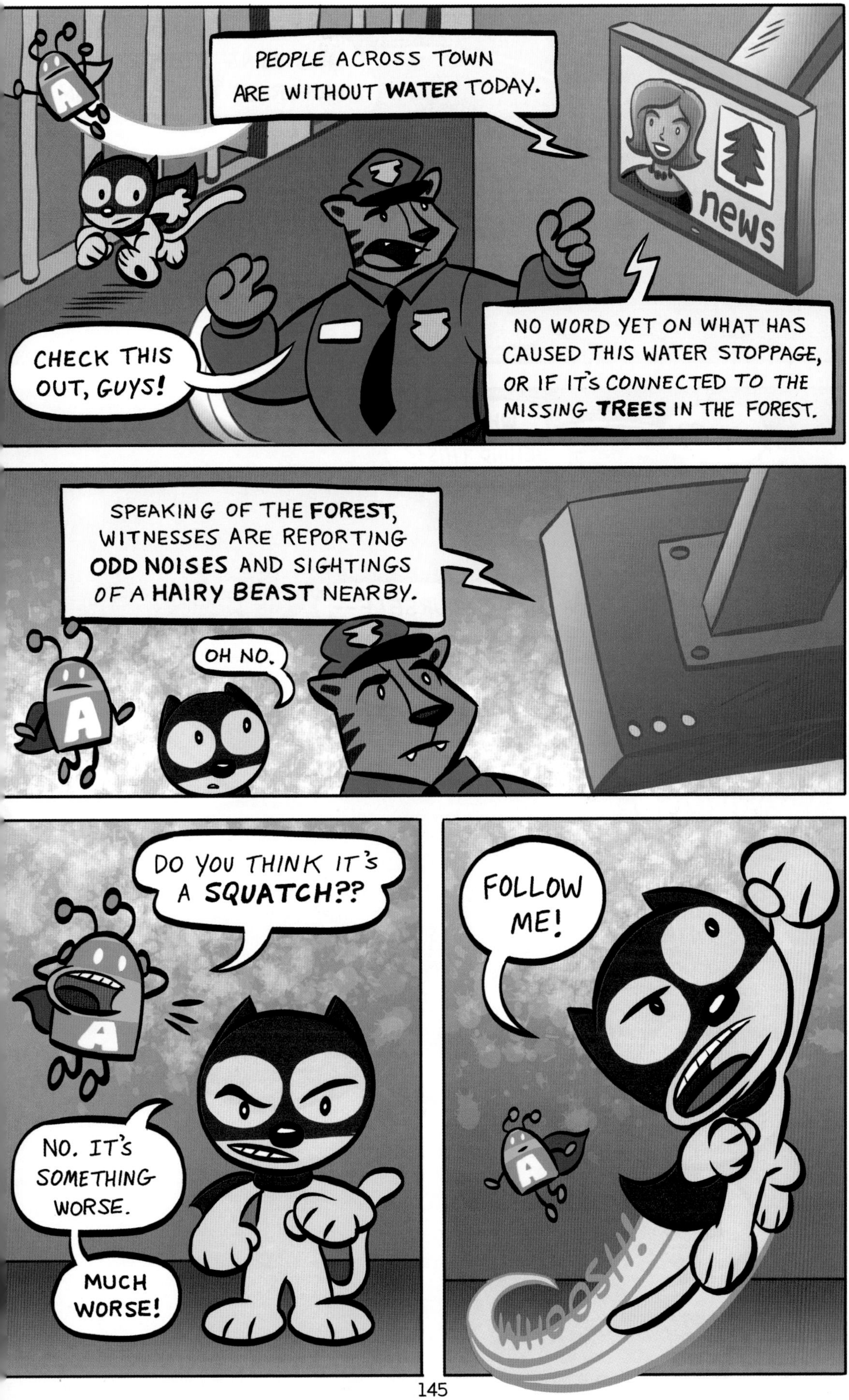
PEOPLE ACROSS TOWN ARE WITHOUT WATER TODAY.
CHECK THIS OUT, GUYS!
news
NO WORD YET ON WHAT HAS CAUSED THIS WATER STOPPAGE, OR IF IT'S CONNECTED TO THE MISSING TREES IN THE FOREST.
SPEAKING OF THE FOREST, WITNESSES ARE REPORTING ODD NOISES AND SIGHTINGS OF A HAIRY BEAST NEARBY.
OH NO.
DO YOU THINK IT'S A SQUATCH??
NO. IT'S SOMETHING WORSE.
MUCH WORSE!
FOLLOW ME!
WHOOSH!

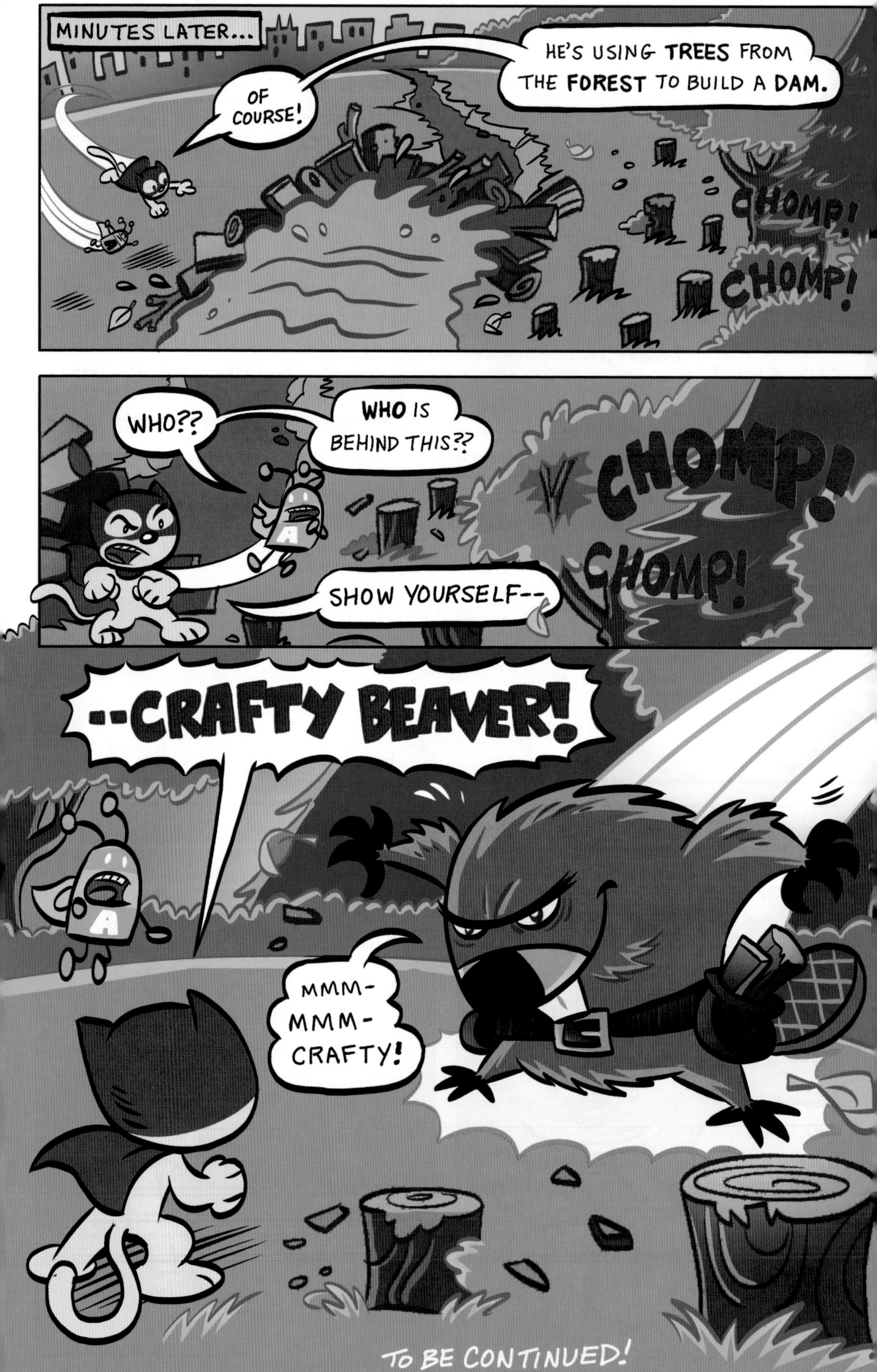
MINUTES LATER...
OF COURSE!
HE'S USING TREES FROM THE FOREST TO BUILD A DAM.
CHOMP!
CHOMP!
WHO??
WHO IS BEHIND THIS??
CHOMP!
CHOMP!
SHOW YOURSELF--
--CRAFTY BEAVER!
MMM-MMM-CRAFTY!
TO BE CONTINUED!

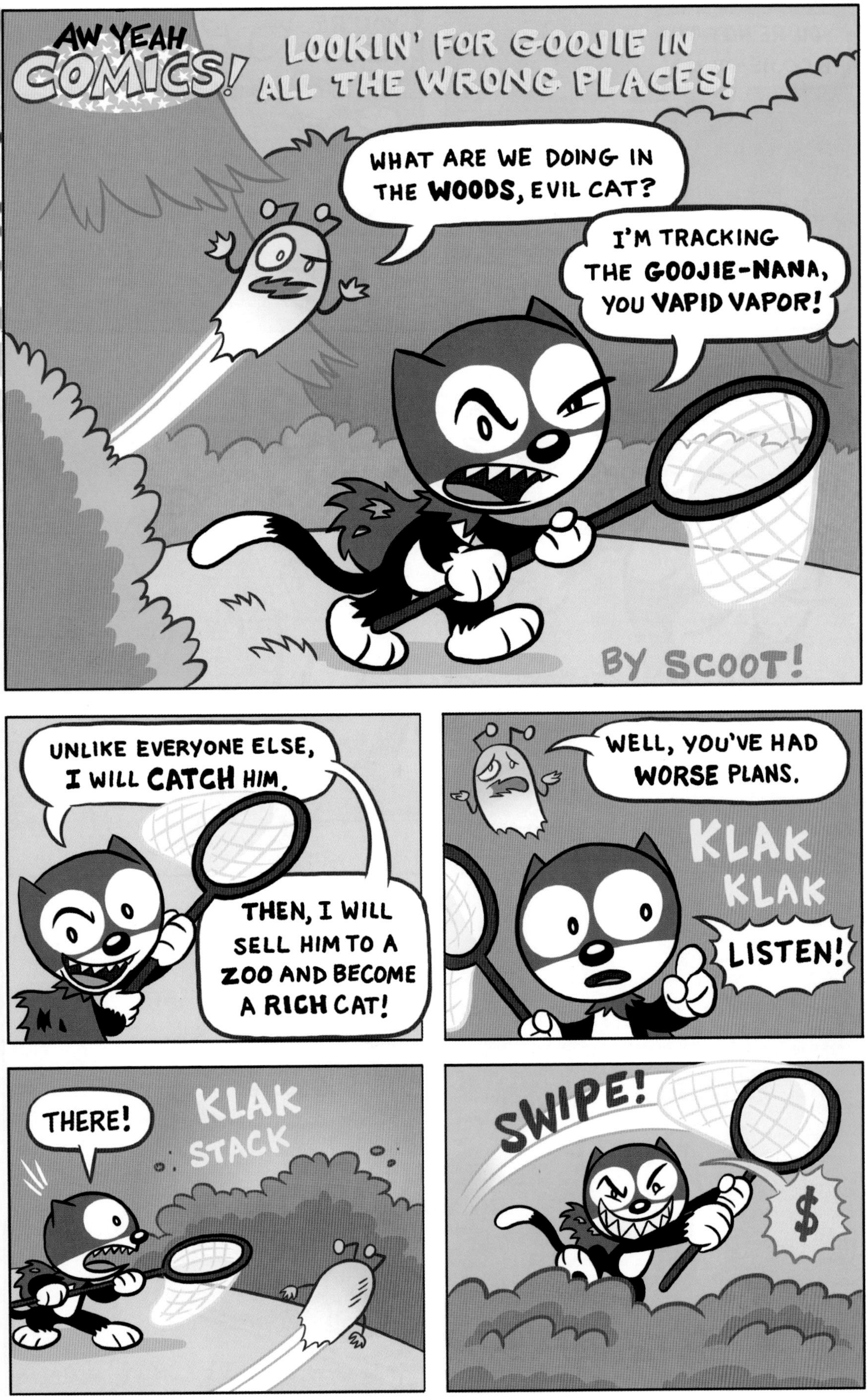

AW YEAH COMICS!
LOOKIN' FOR GOOJIE IN ALL THE WRONG PLACES!
WHAT ARE WE DOING IN THE WOODS, EVIL CAT?
I'M TRACKING THE GOOJIE-NANA, YOU VAPID VAPOR!
BY SCOOT!
UNLIKE EVERYONE ELSE, I WILL CATCH HIM.
THEN, I WILL SELL HIM TO A ZOO AND BECOME A RICH CAT!
WELL, YOU'VE HAD WORSE PLANS.
KLAK KLAK
LISTEN!
THERE!
KLAK STACK
SWIPE!
$

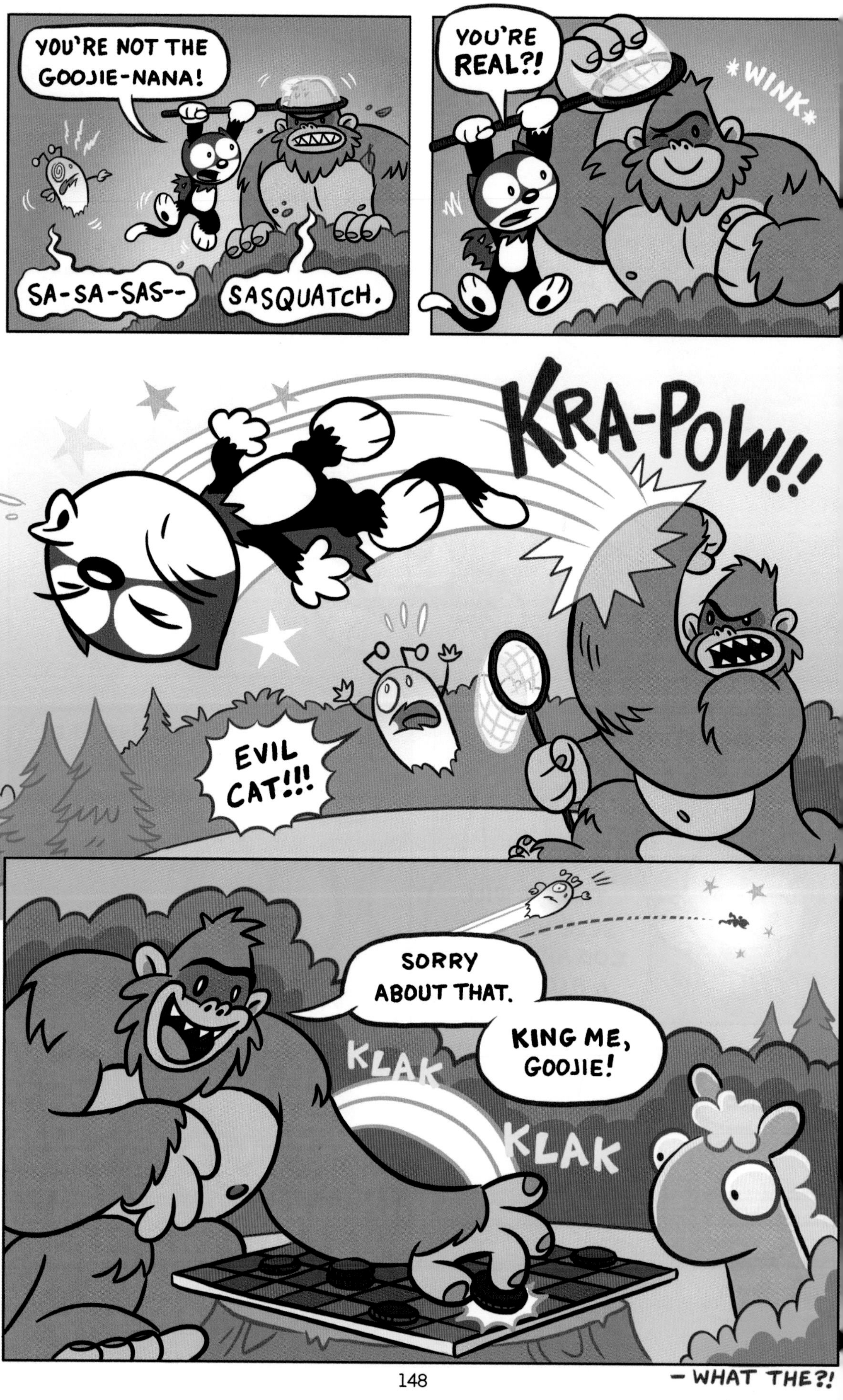
YOU'RE NOT THE GOOJIE-NANA!
SA-SA-SAS--
SASQUATCH.
YOU'RE REAL?!
WINK
KRA-POW!!
EVIL CAT!!!
SORRY ABOUT THAT.
KING ME, GOOJIE!
KLAK
KLAK
—WHAT THE?!

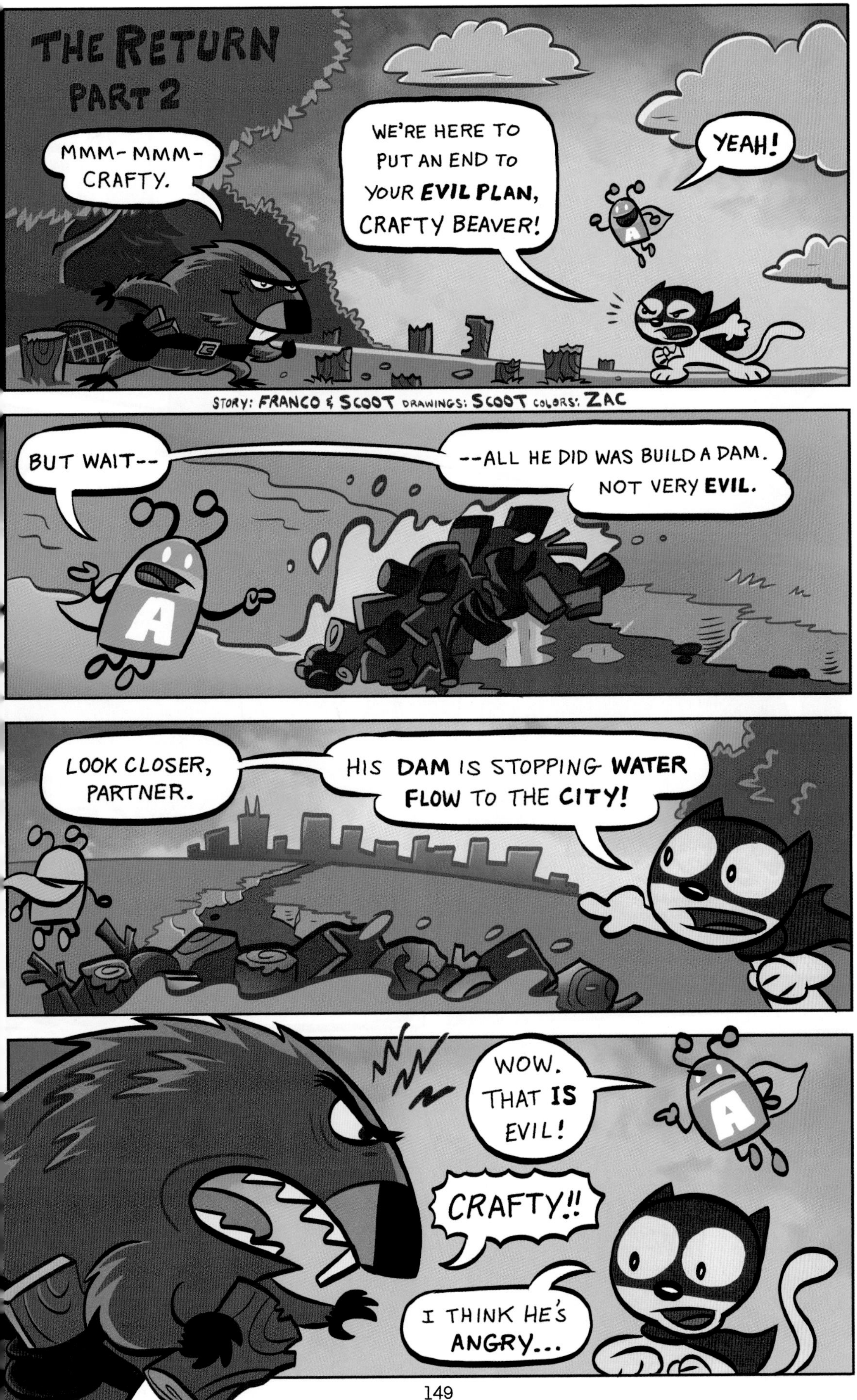
THE RETURN
PART 2
MMM-MMM-CRAFTY.
WE'RE HERE TO PUT AN END TO YOUR EVIL PLAN, CRAFTY BEAVER!
YEAH!
STORY: FRANCO & SCOOT DRAWINGS: SCOOT COLORS: ZAC
BUT WAIT--
--ALL HE DID WAS BUILD A DAM. NOT VERY EVIL.
LOOK CLOSER, PARTNER.
HIS DAM IS STOPPING WATER FLOW TO THE CITY!
WOW. THAT IS EVIL!
CRAFTY!!
I THINK HE'S ANGRY...

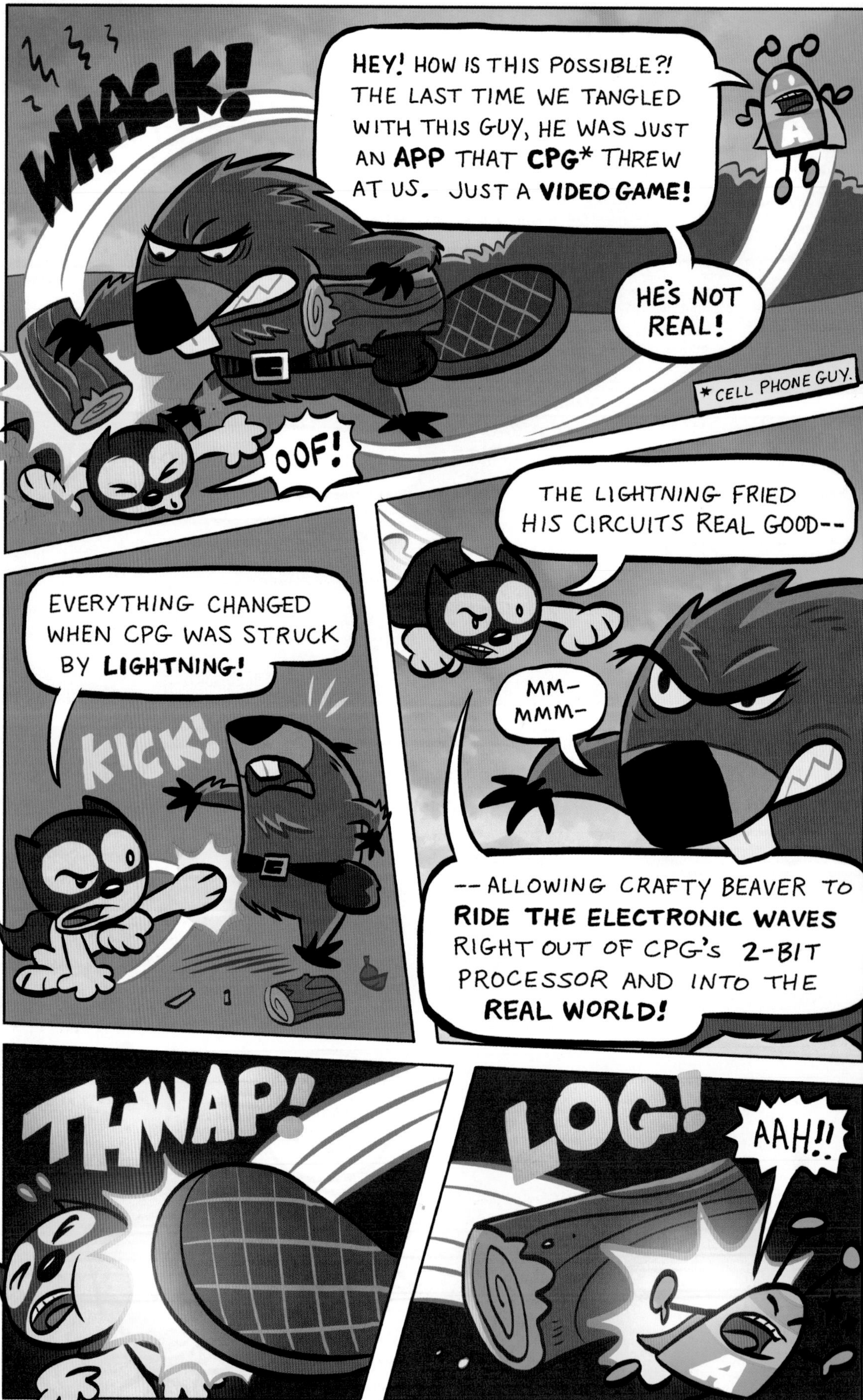
WHACK!
HEY! HOW IS THIS POSSIBLE?! THE LAST TIME WE TANGLED WITH THIS GUY, HE WAS JUST AN APP THAT CPG* THREW AT US. JUST A VIDEO GAME!
HE'S NOT REAL!
*CELL PHONE GUY.
OOF!
EVERYTHING CHANGED WHEN CPG WAS STRUCK BY LIGHTNING!
KICK!
THE LIGHTNING FRIED HIS CIRCUITS REAL GOOD--
MM- MMM-
--ALLOWING CRAFTY BEAVER TO RIDE THE ELECTRONIC WAVES RIGHT OUT OF CPG's 2-BIT PROCESSOR AND INTO THE REAL WORLD!
THWAP!
LOG!
AAH!!

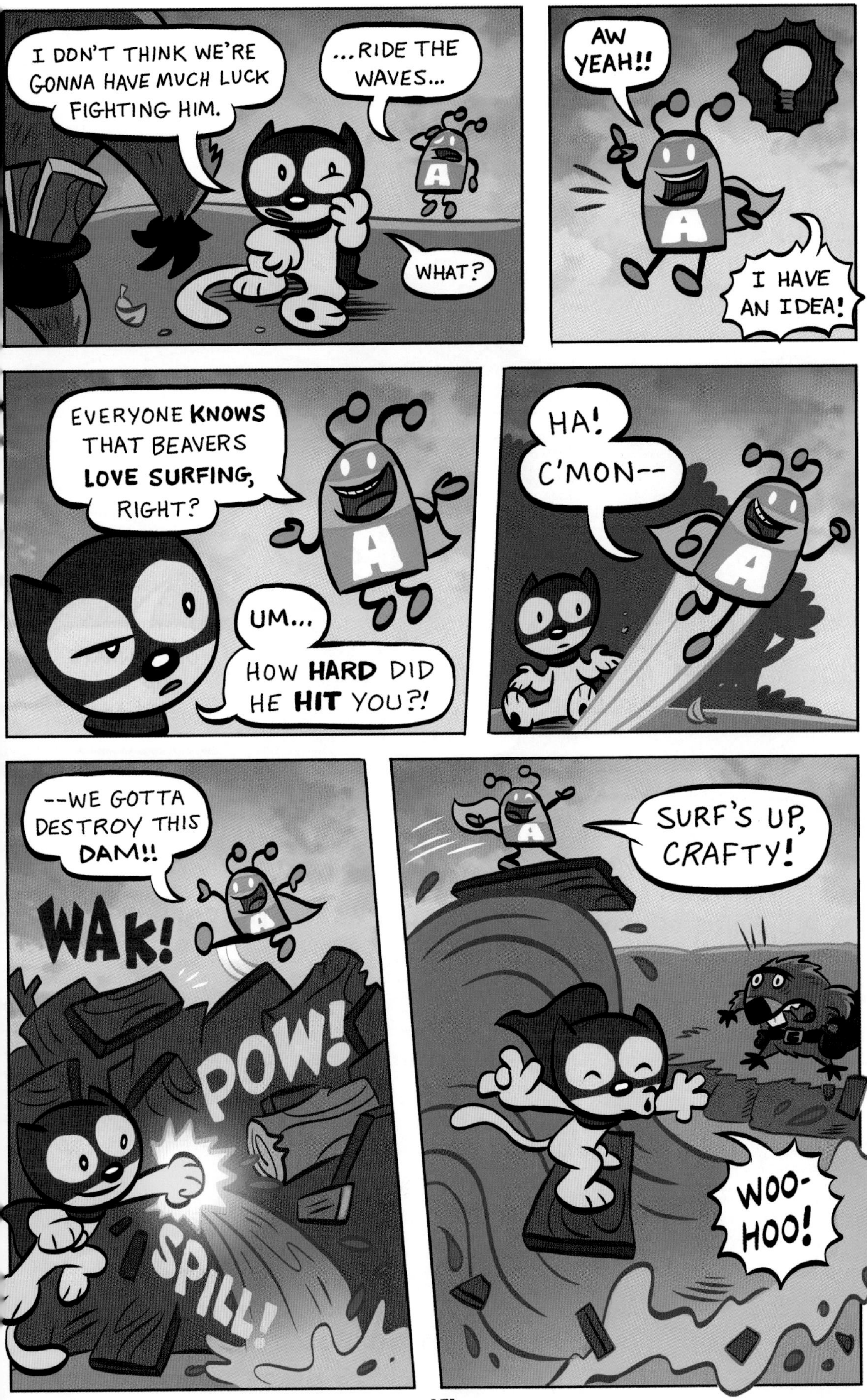
I DON'T THINK WE'RE GONNA HAVE MUCH LUCK FIGHTING HIM.
...RIDE THE WAVES...
WHAT?
AW YEAH!!
I HAVE AN IDEA!
EVERYONE KNOWS THAT BEAVERS LOVE SURFING, RIGHT?
UM...
HOW HARD DID HE HIT YOU?!
HA! C'MON--
--WE GOTTA DESTROY THIS DAM!!
WAK!
POW!
SPILL!
SURF'S UP, CRAFTY!
WOO-HOO!

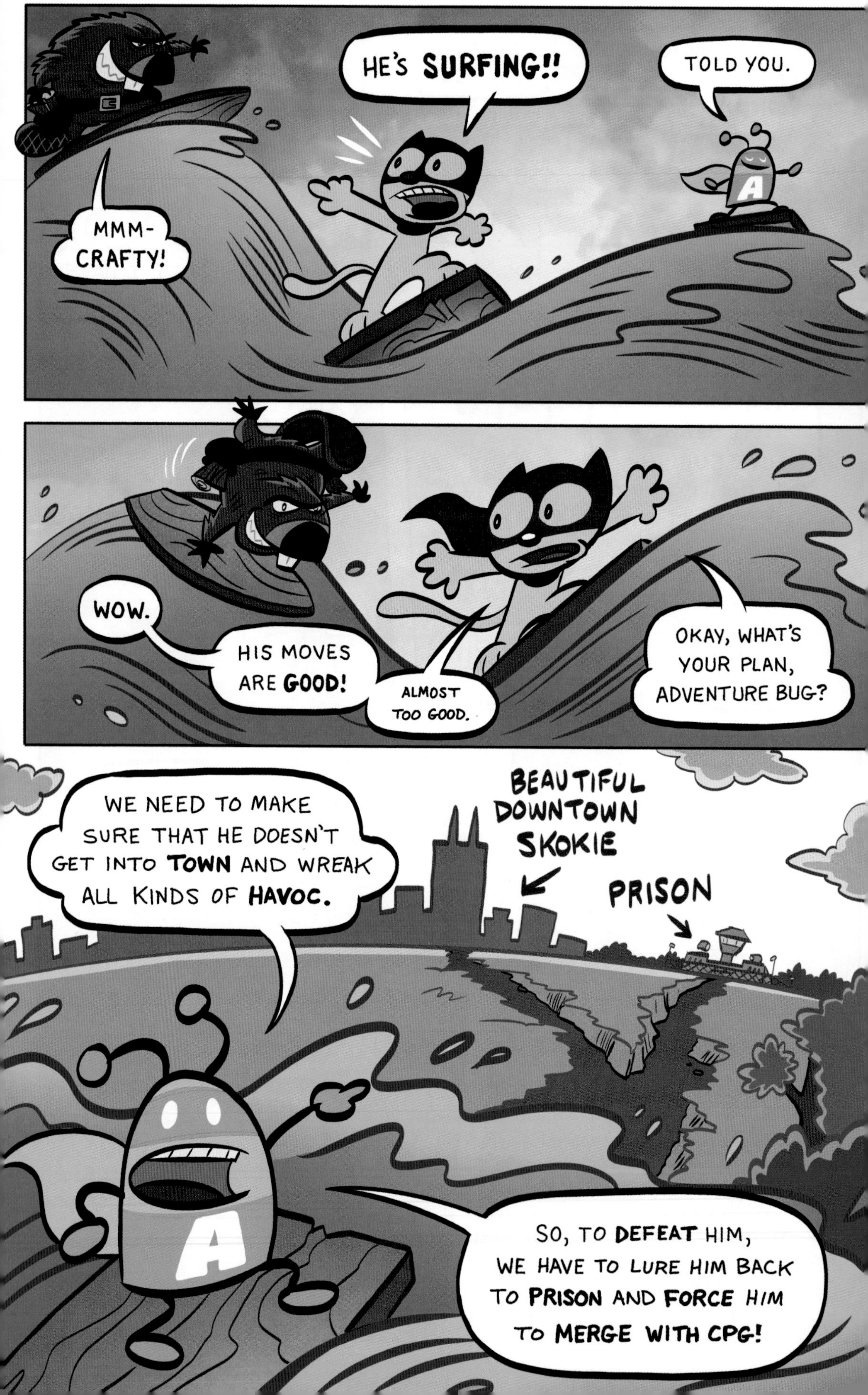
HE'S SURFING!!
TOLD YOU.
MMM-CRAFTY!
WOW.
HIS MOVES ARE GOOD!
ALMOST TOO GOOD.
OKAY, WHAT'S YOUR PLAN, ADVENTURE BUG?
BEAUTIFUL DOWNTOWN SKOKIE
PRISON
WE NEED TO MAKE SURE THAT HE DOESN'T GET INTO TOWN AND WREAK ALL KINDS OF HAVOC.
SO, TO DEFEAT HIM, WE HAVE TO LURE HIM BACK TO PRISON AND FORCE HIM TO MERGE WITH CPG!

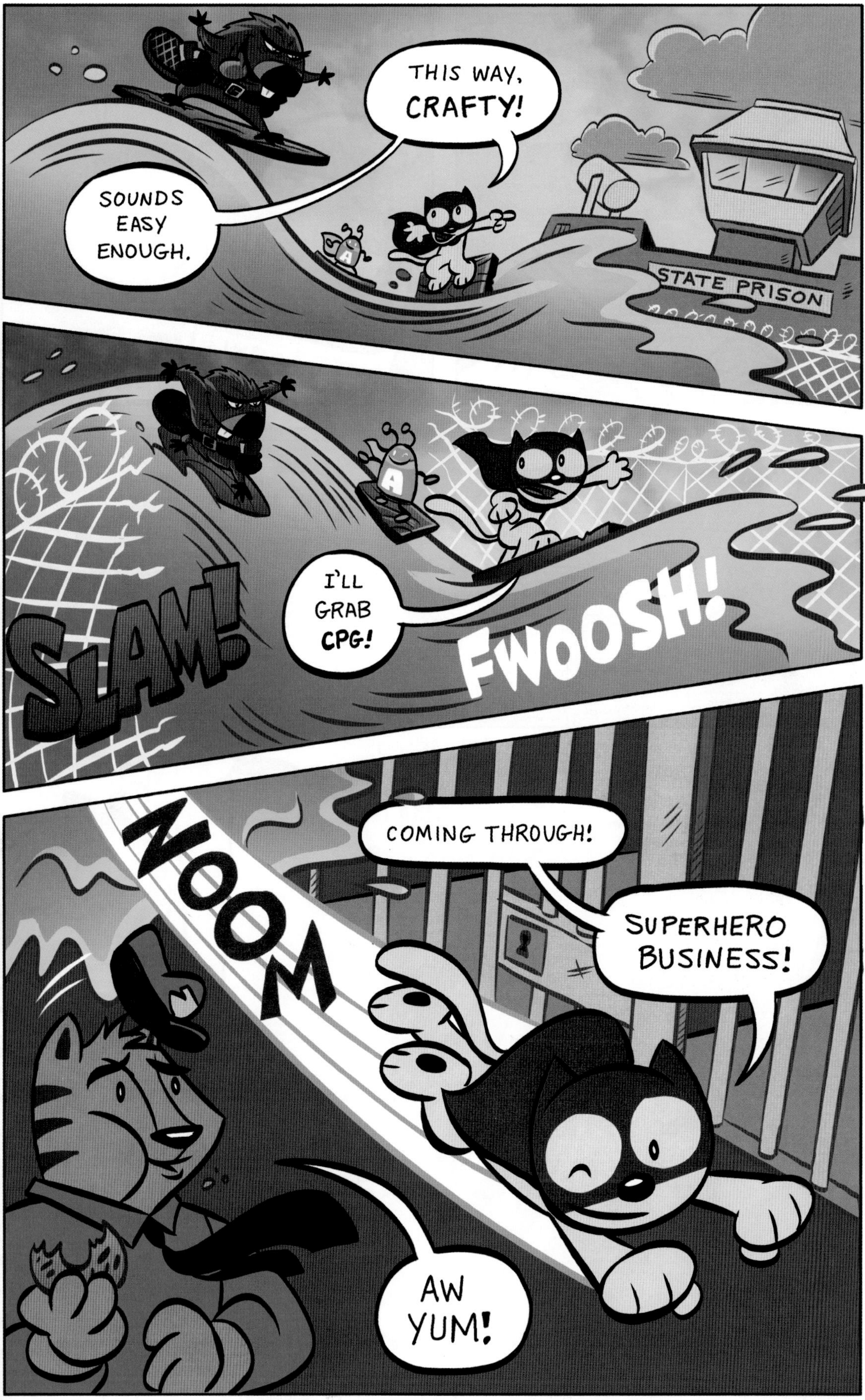
THIS WAY, CRAFTY!
SOUNDS EASY ENOUGH.
STATE PRISON
I'LL GRAB CPG!
SLAM!
FWOOSH!
NOOM
COMING THROUGH!
SUPERHERO BUSINESS!
AW YUM!

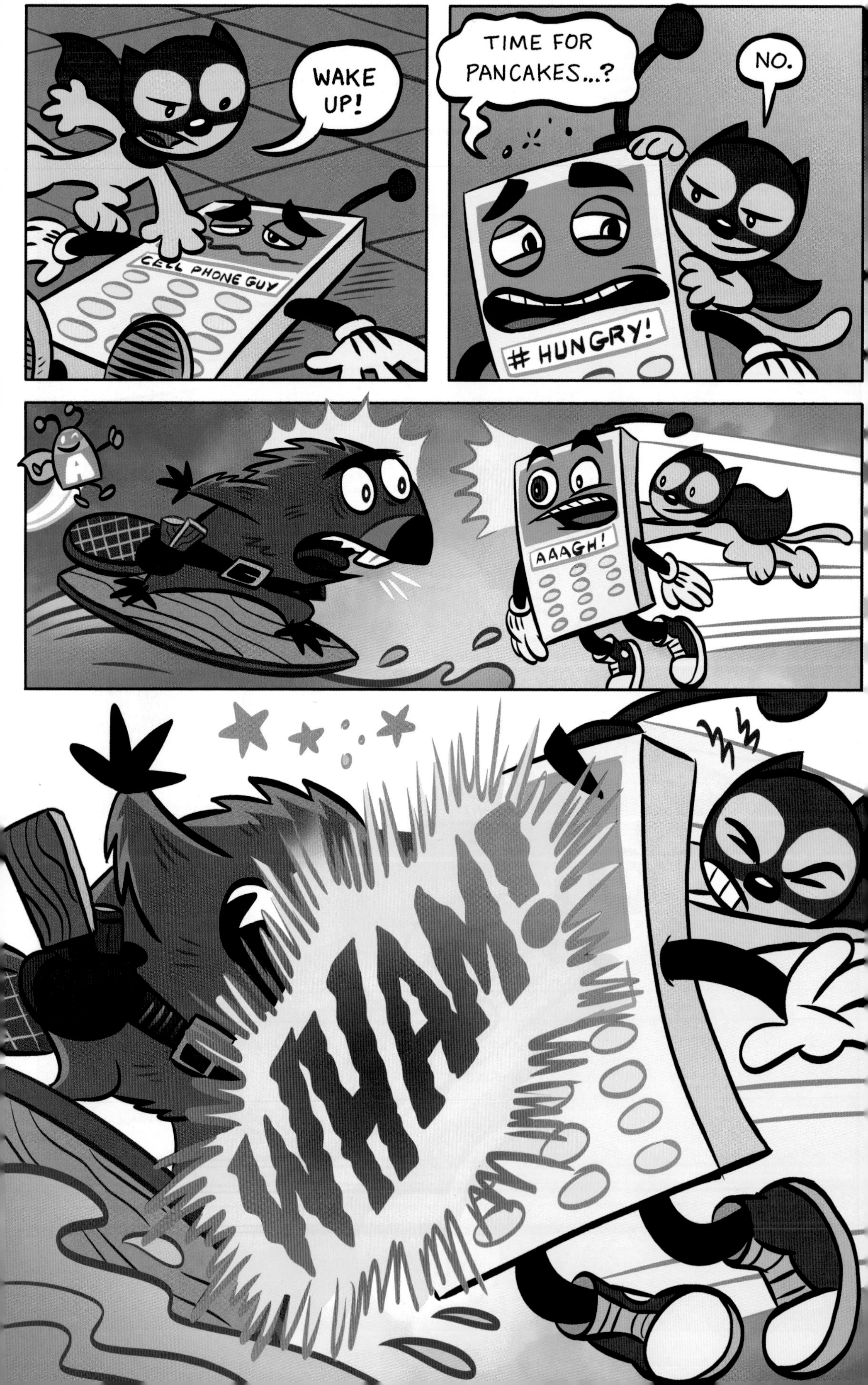
WAKE UP!
CELL PHONE GUY
TIME FOR PANCAKES...?
NO.
HUNGRY!
AAAGH!
WHAM!

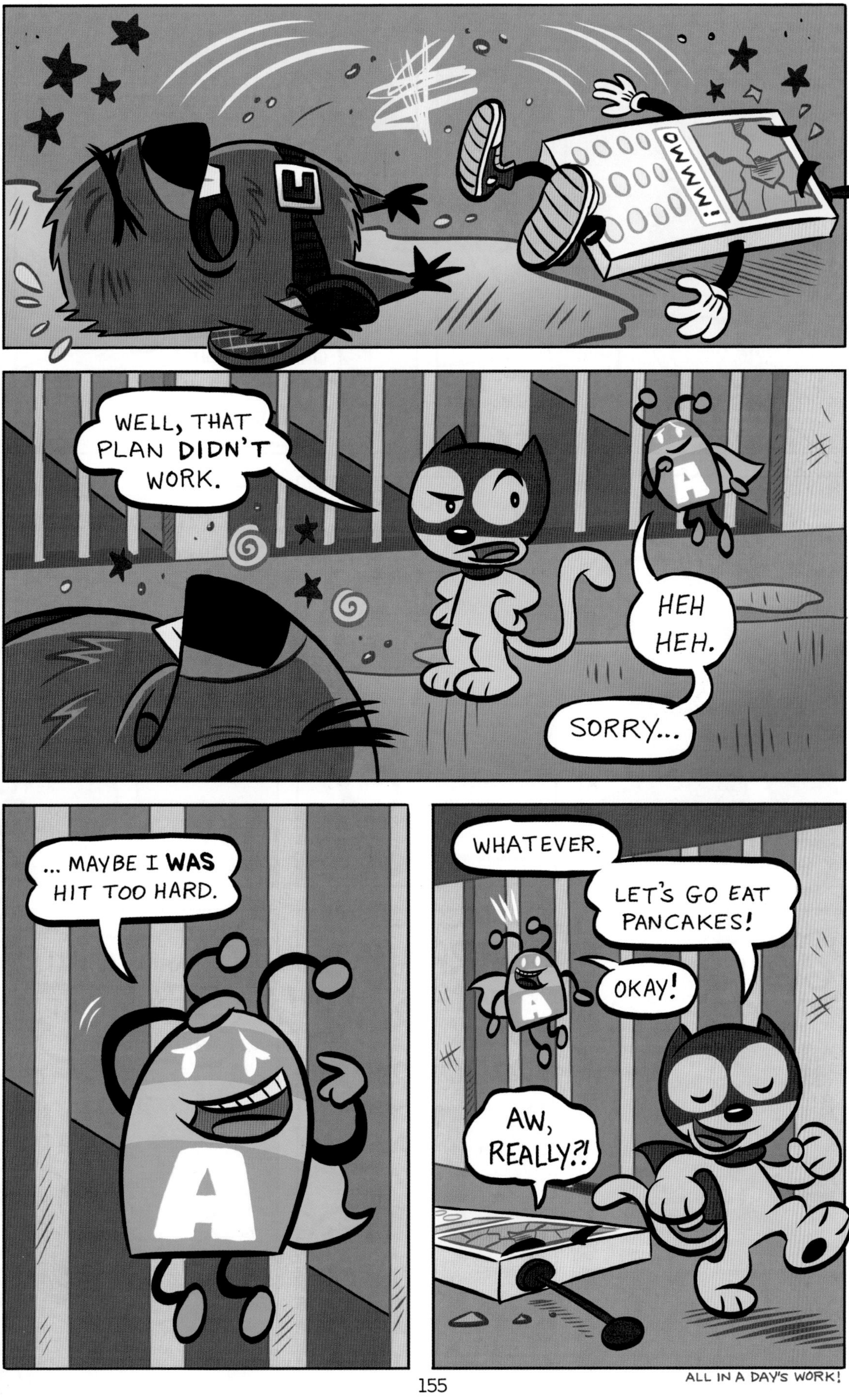
OWWW!
WELL, THAT PLAN DIDN'T WORK.
HEH HEH.
SORRY...
... MAYBE I WAS HIT TOO HARD.
WHATEVER.
LET'S GO EAT PANCAKES!
OKAY!
AW, REALLY?!
ALL IN A DAY'S WORK!

"NUCLEAR PLANT"

BY DAVID WOLFGANG VON EHRLICHER AND ART BALTAZAR

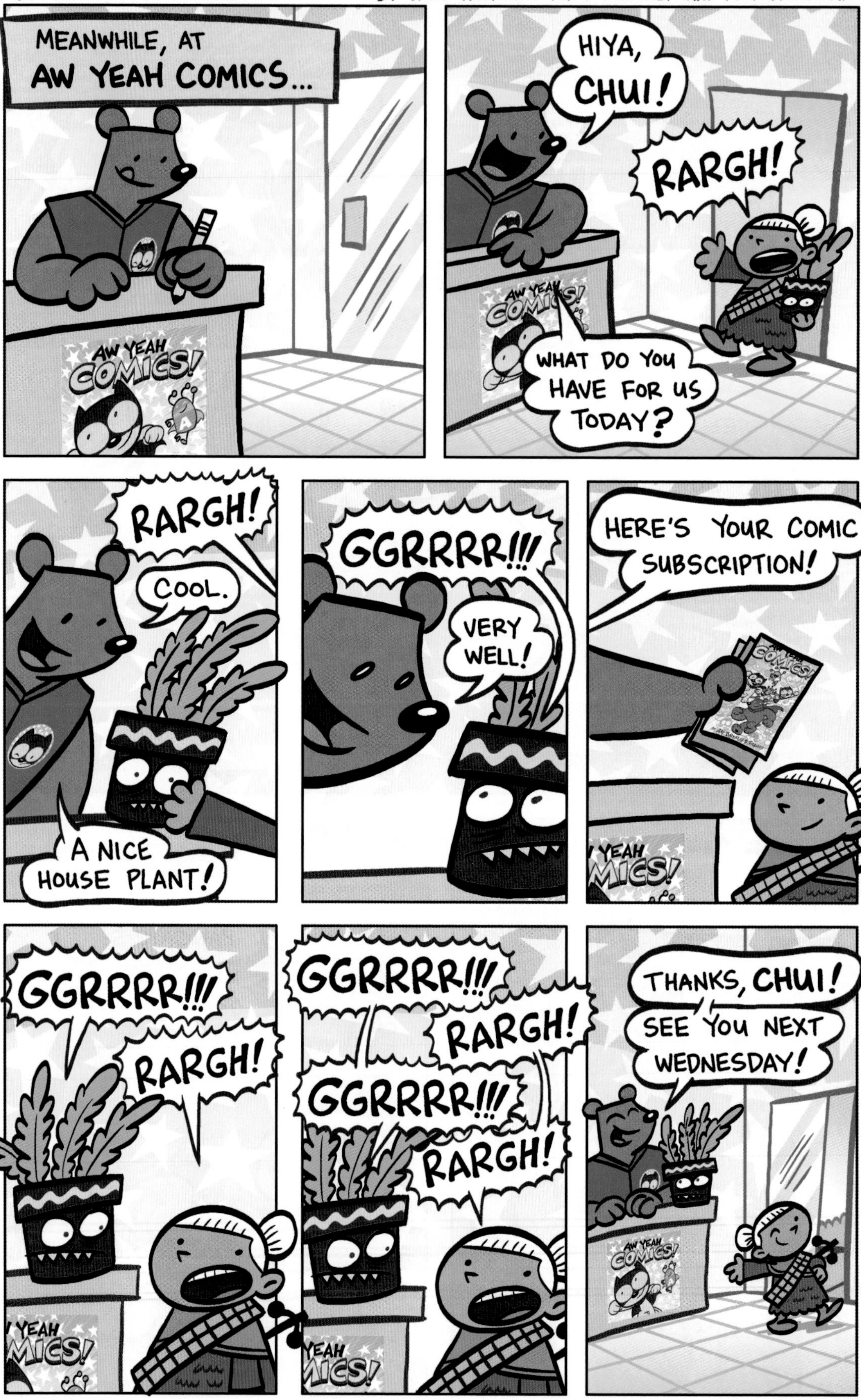

MEANWHILE, AT AW YEAH COMICS...
AW YEAH COMICS!
HIYA, CHUI!
RARGH!
WHAT DO YOU HAVE FOR US TODAY?
RARGH!
COOL.
A NICE HOUSE PLANT!
GGRRRR!!!
VERY WELL!
HERE'S YOUR COMIC SUBSCRIPTION!
GGRRRR!!!
RARGH!
GGRRRR!!!
RARGH!
GGRRRR!!!
RARGH!
THANKS, CHUI!
SEE YOU NEXT WEDNESDAY!

RARGH!

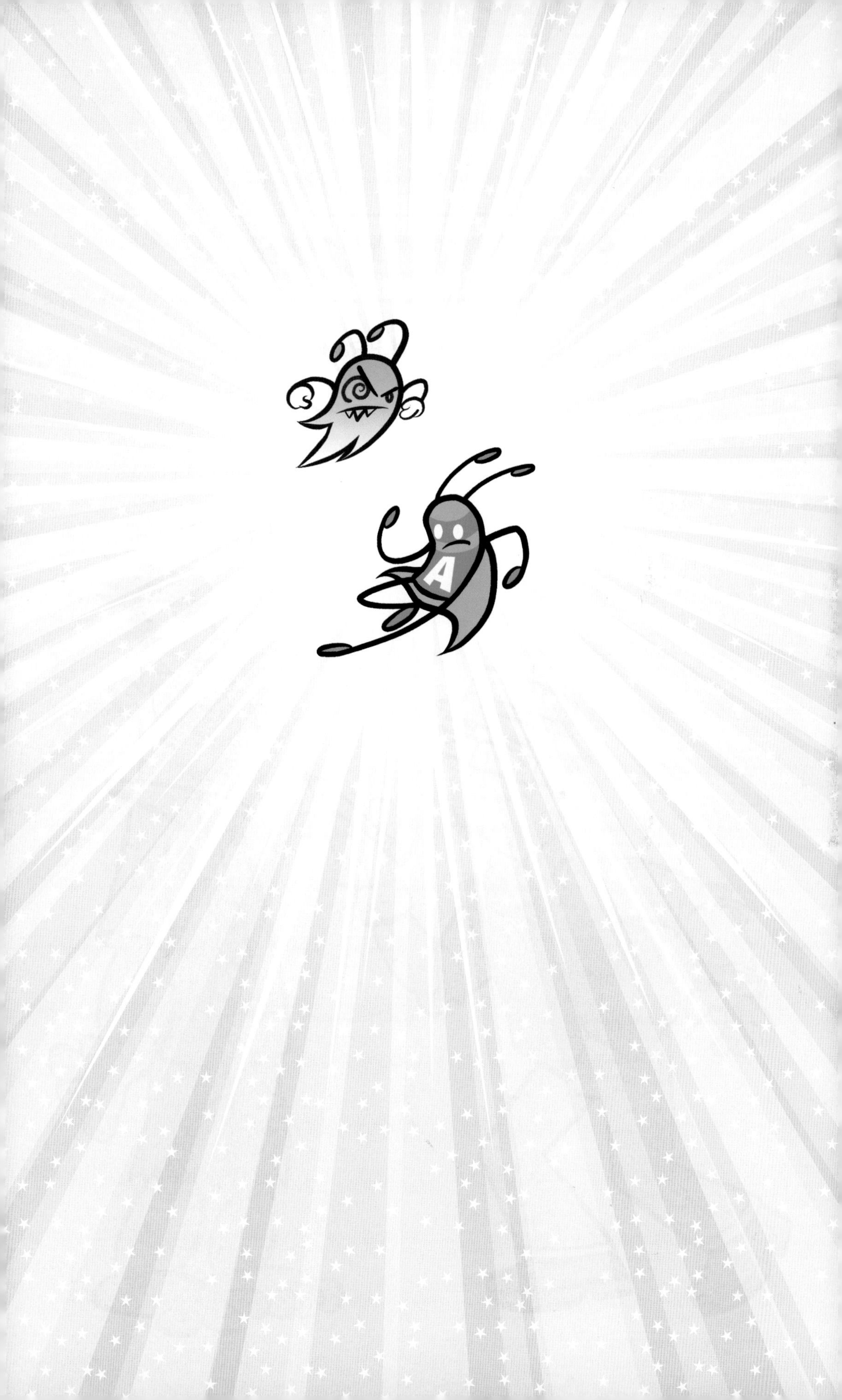

★ SKETCHBOOK ★

by Art and Franco

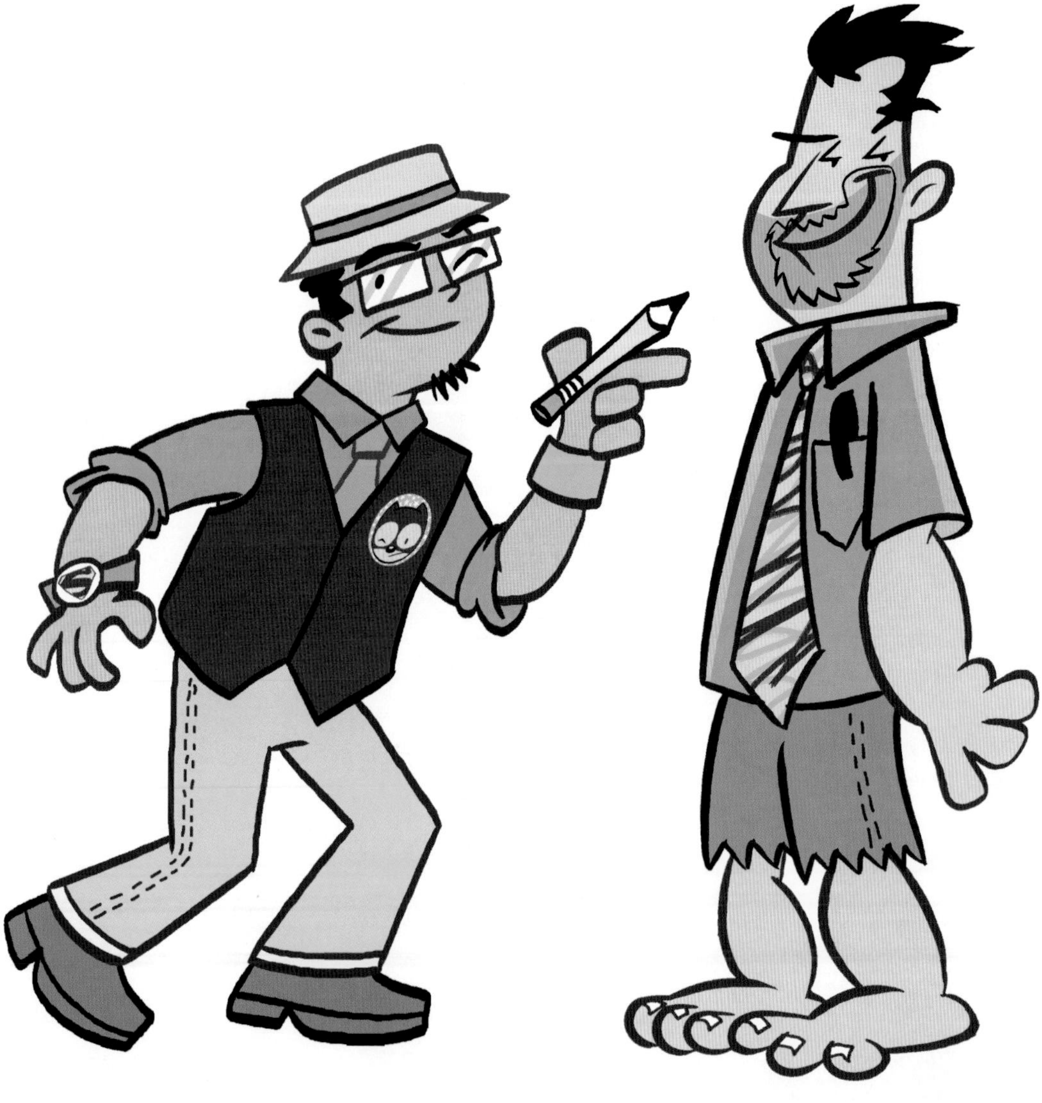

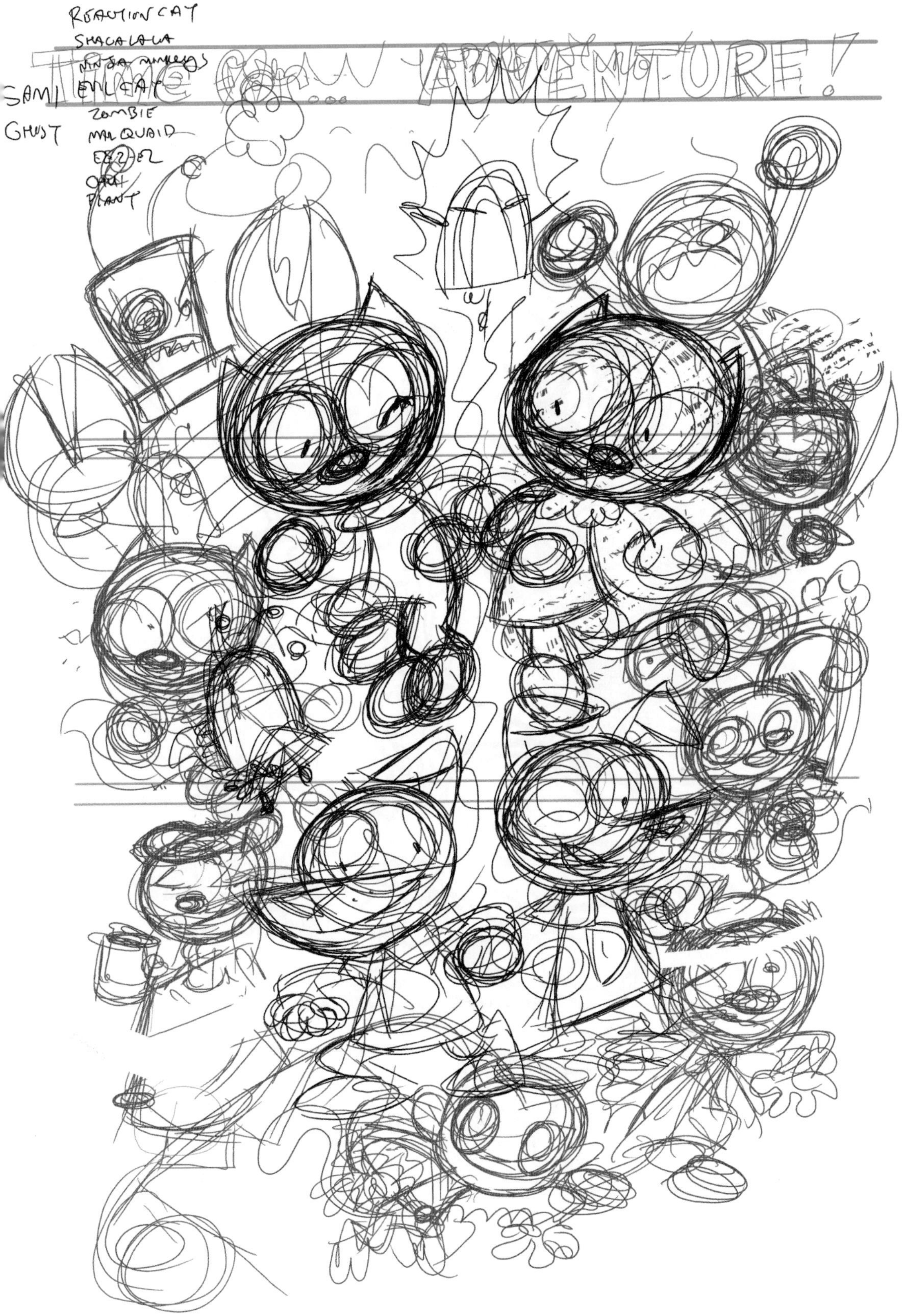
REACTION CAT
SHACALALA
NINJA MONKEYS
SAMI
EVIL CAT
ZOMBIE
GHOST
MALQUAID
PLANT
ADVENTURE!

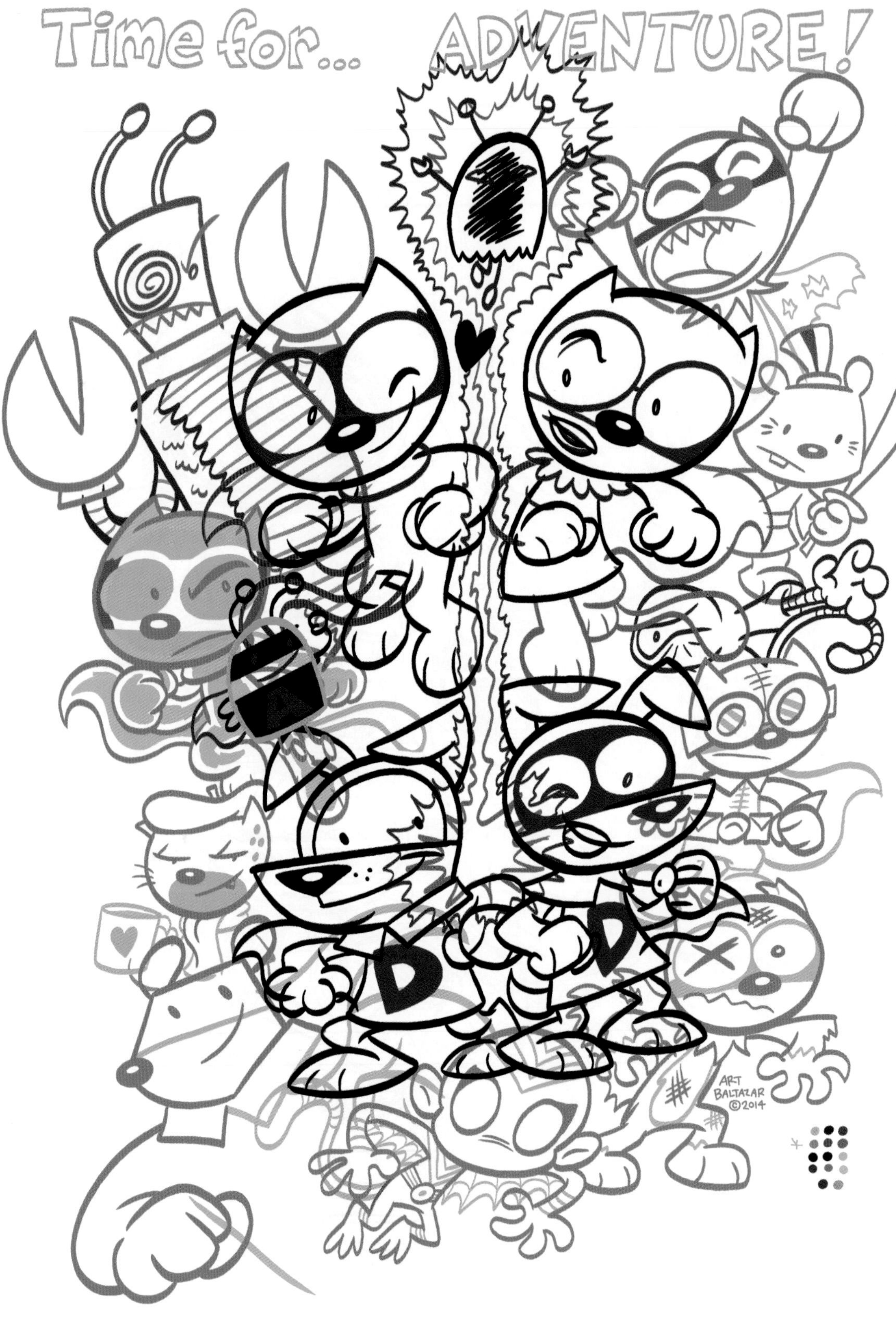
Time for... ADVENTURE!
ART BALTAZAR ©2014

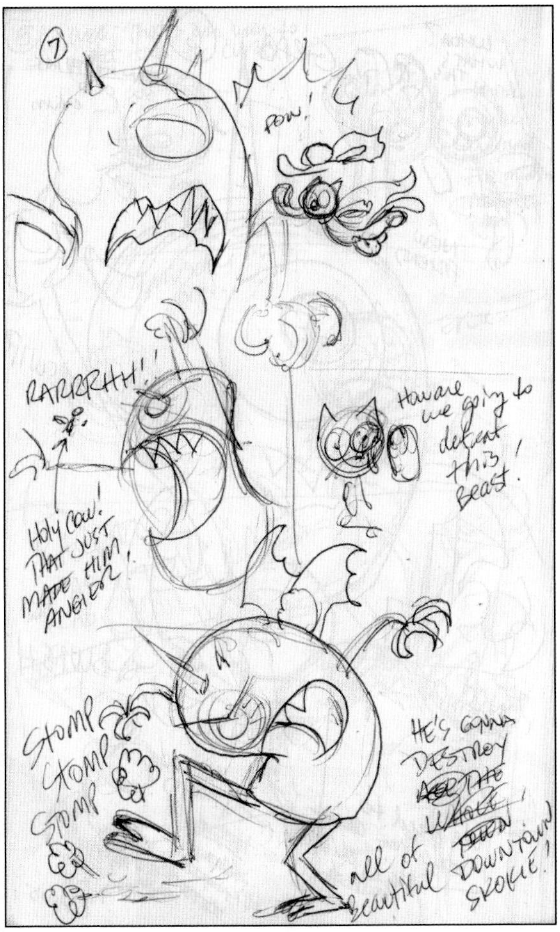
7
POW!
RARRRHH!
Holy cow! THAT JUST MADE HIM ANGIER!
How are we going to defeat this beast!
STOMP STOMP STOMP
HE'S GONNA DESTROY all of beautiful DOWNTOWN SKOKIE!

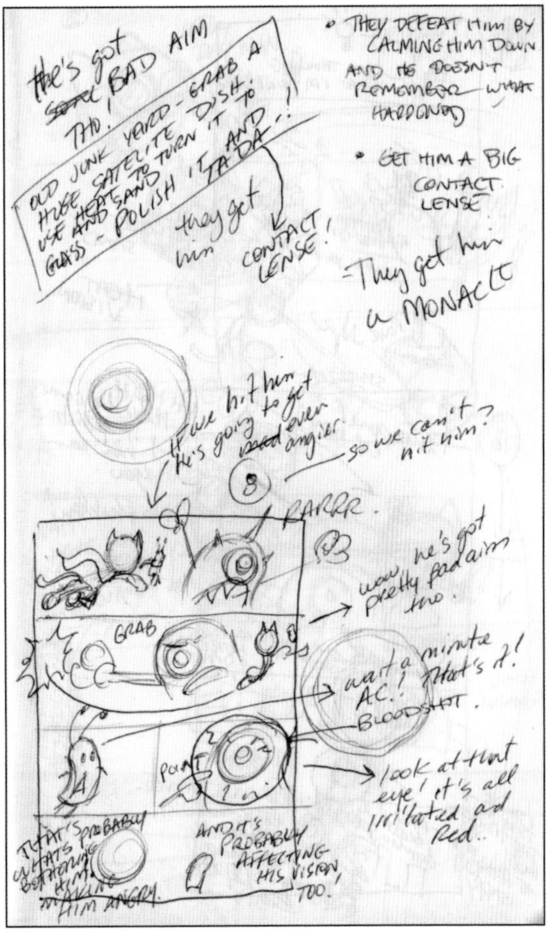
He's got BAD AIM THO!
OLD JUNK YARD - GRAB A HUGE SATELITE DISH USE AND SAND TO TURN IT TO GLASS - POLISH IT AND TA DA..!
they get him CONTACT LENSE!
• THEY DEFEAT HIM BY CALMING HIM DOWN AND HE DOESN'T REMEMBER WHAT HAPPENED
• GET HIM A BIG CONTACT LENSE
-They get him a MONACLE
If we hit him he's going to get even angier.
so we can't hit him?
8
RARRR.
wow he's got pretty bad aim too.
GRAB
wait a minute AC! That's it!
BLOODSHOT.
POINT
look at that eye! it's all irritated and Red..
THAT'S PROBABLY WHAT'S BOTHERING HIM
AND IT'S PROBABLY AFFECTING HIS VISION, TOO.

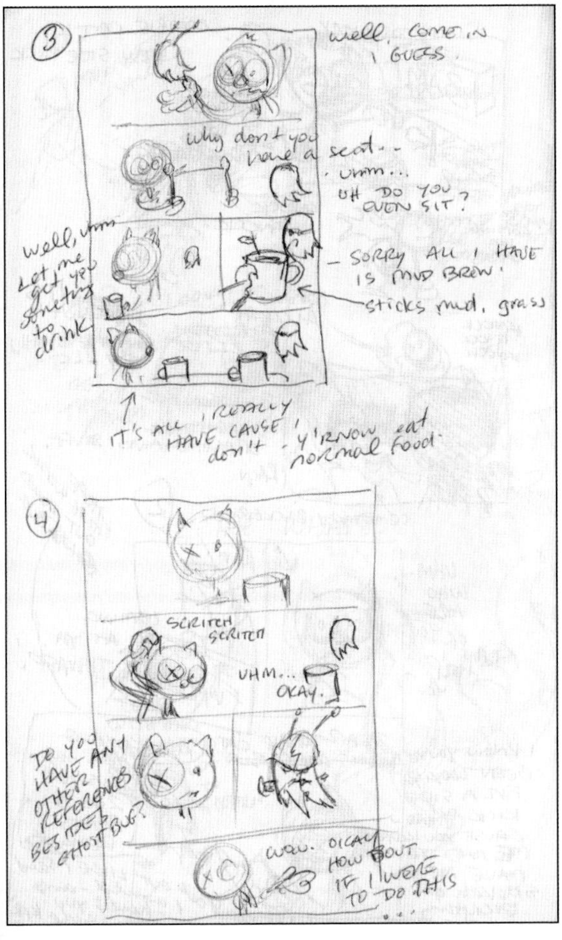
3
well, come in I guess.
why don't you have a seat.. uhm... UH DO YOU EVEN SIT?
well, uhm let me get you something to drink
- SORRY ALL I HAVE IS MUD BREW!
sticks mud, grass
IT'S ALL I REALLY HAVE CAUSE I don't - y'know eat normal food
4
SCRITCH SCRITCH
UHM... OKAY.
DO YOU HAVE ANY OTHER REFERENCES BESIDES GHOST BUG?
WOW. OKAY HOW ABOUT IF I WERE TO DO THIS

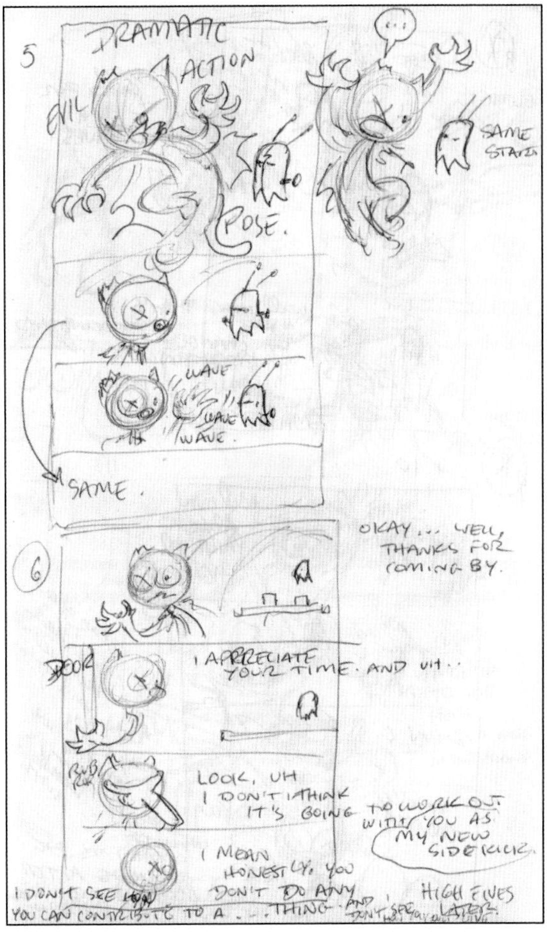
5
DRAMATIC EVIL ACTION POSE.
...
SAME STANCE
WAVE WAVE WAVE
SAME.
6
OKAY... WELL, THANKS FOR COMING BY.
DOOR
I APPRECIATE YOUR TIME. AND UH..
LOOK, UH I DON'T THINK IT'S GOING TO WORK OUT WITH YOU AS MY NEW SIDEKICK.
I MEAN HONESTLY, YOU DON'T DO ANY
I DON'T SEE HOW YOU CAN CONTRIBUTE TO A... THING AND
HIGH FIVES LATER

★ GALLERY ★

Cover art from *Aw Yeah Comics!* #1–#4

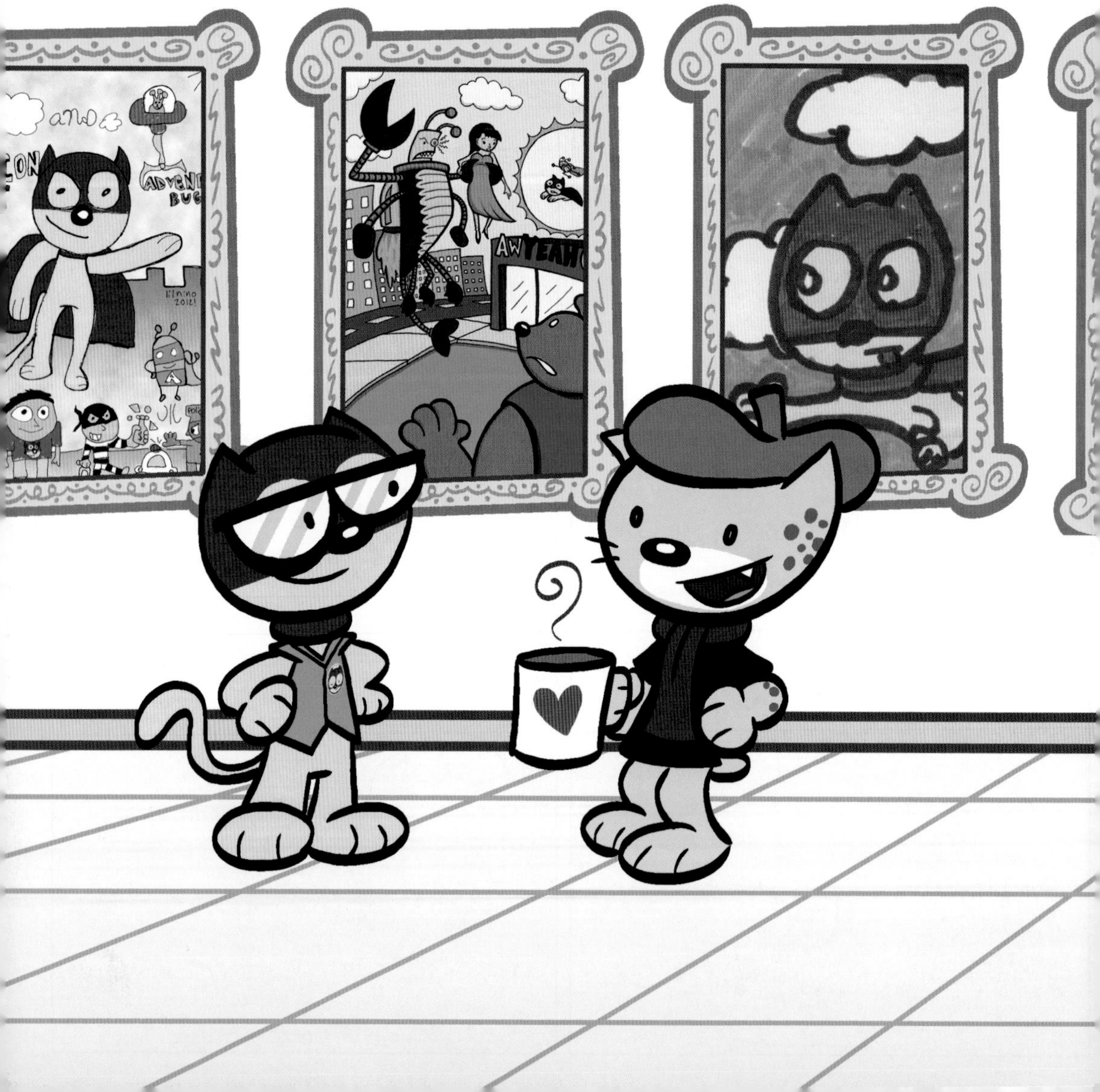
AW YEAH

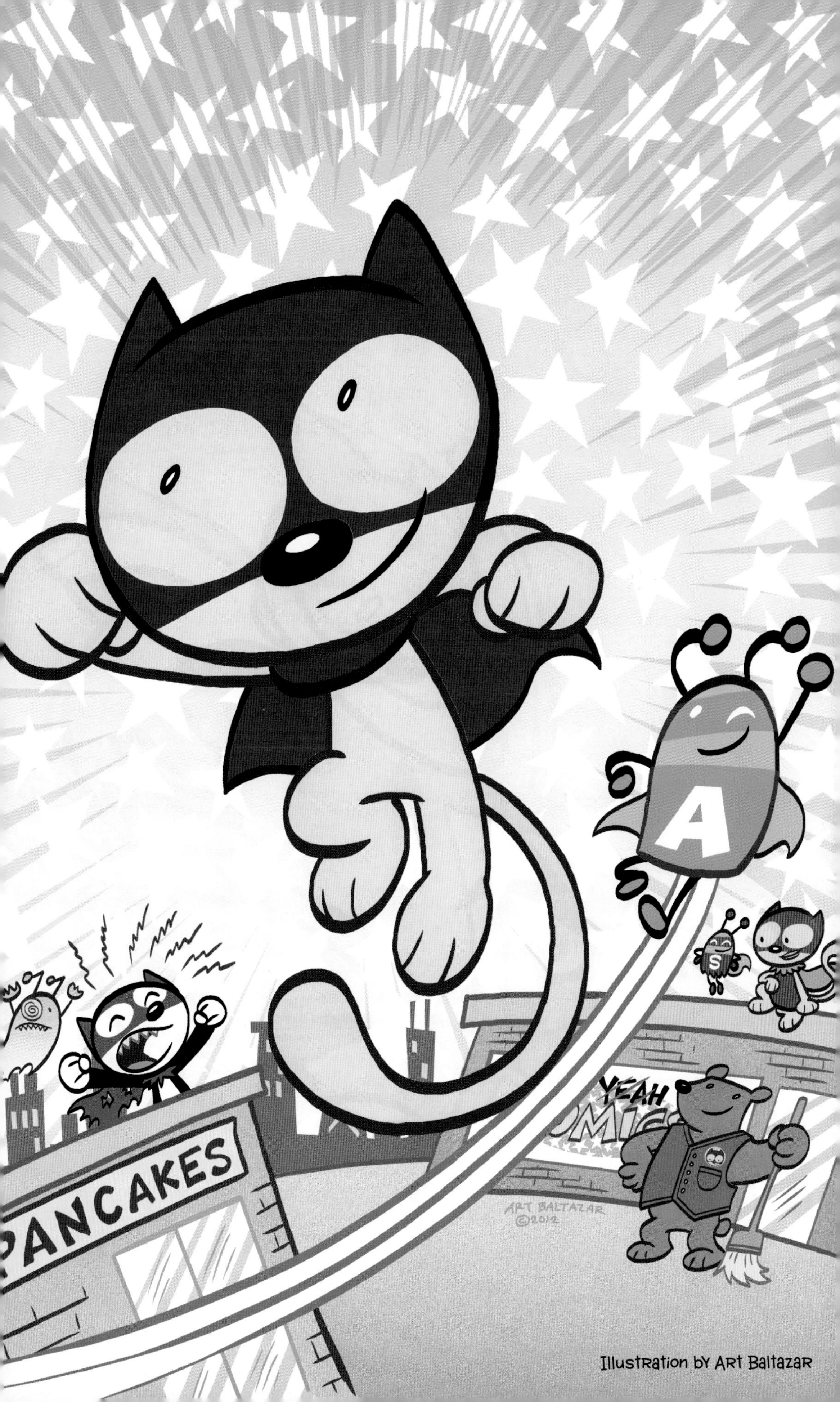
A
PANCAKES
YEAH
ART BALTAZAR
©2012
Illustration by Art Baltazar

Illustration by Franco

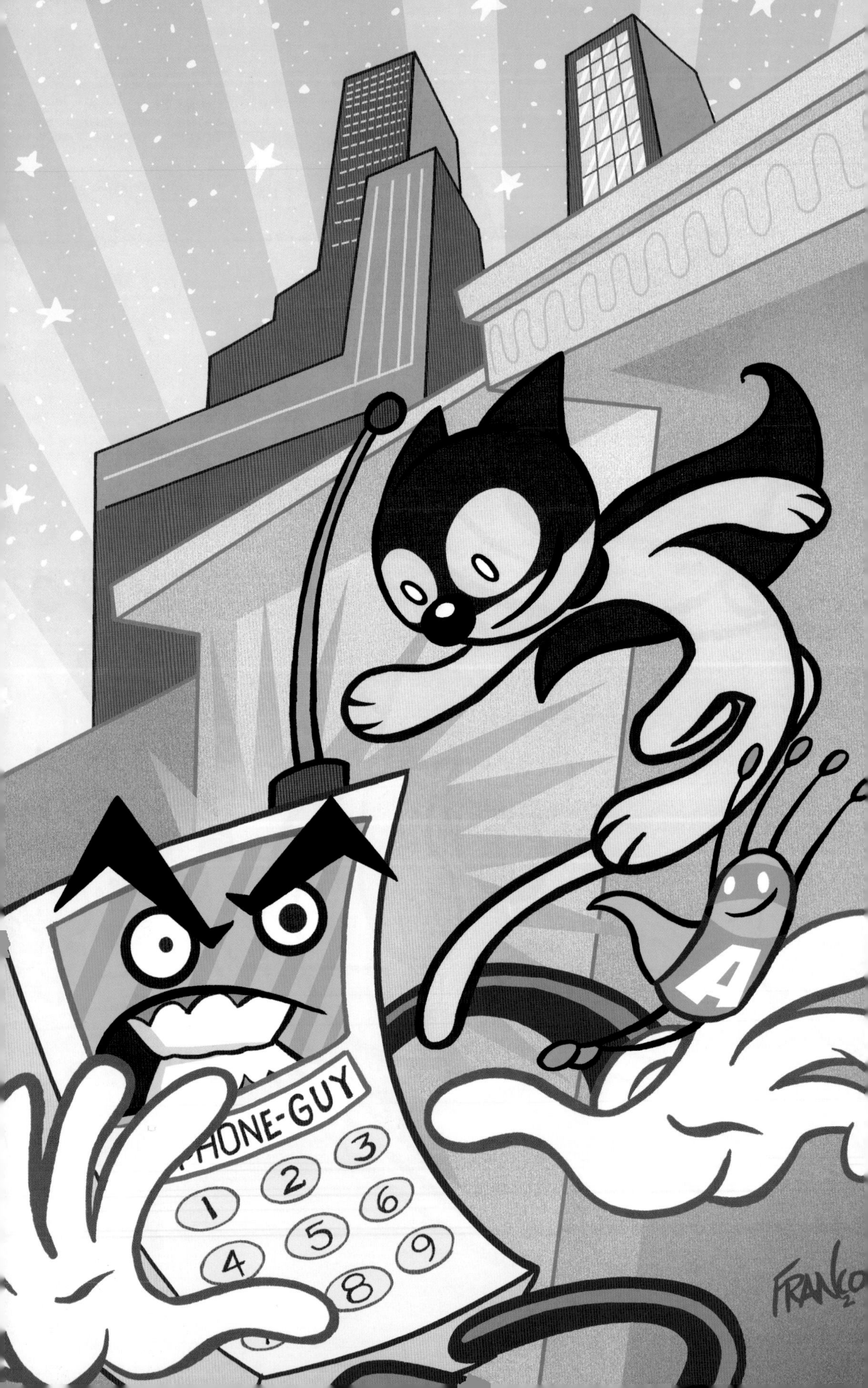
PHONE-GUY
FRANCO

Illustration by Art Baltazar

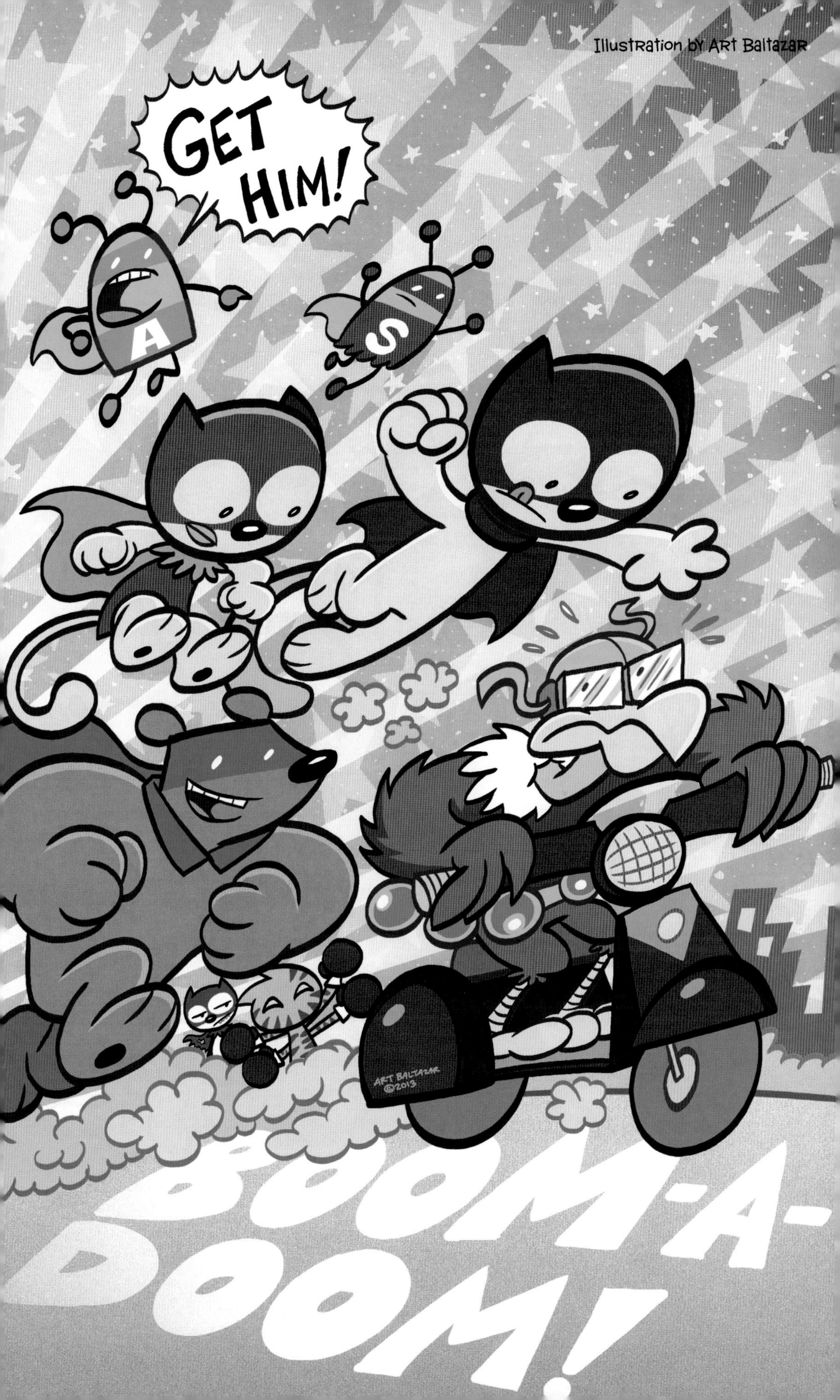
GET HIM!
A
S
ART BALTAZAR ©2013
BOOM-A-DOOM!

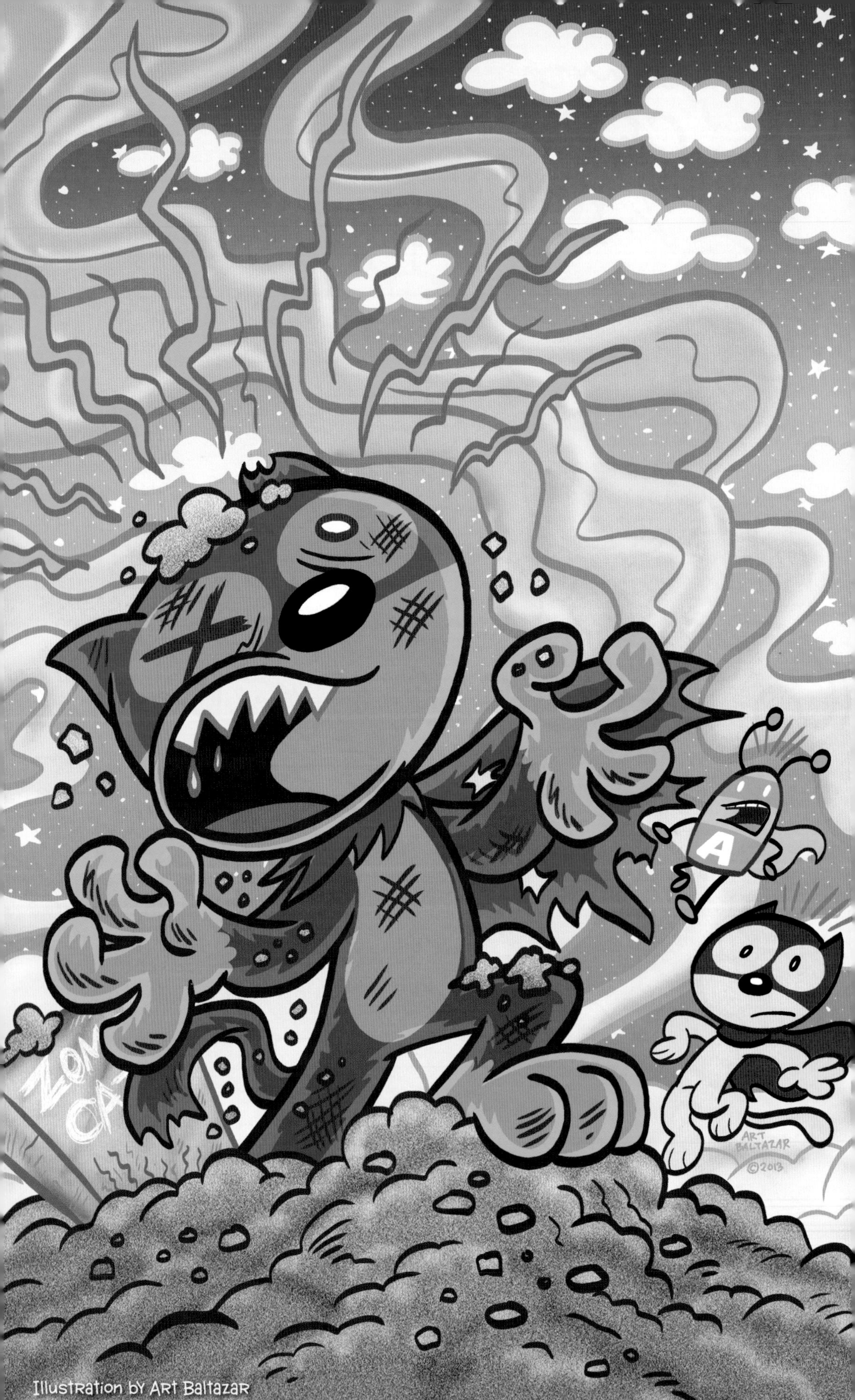
ZOM
CA
A
ART BALTAZAR ©2013

Illustration by Art Baltazar

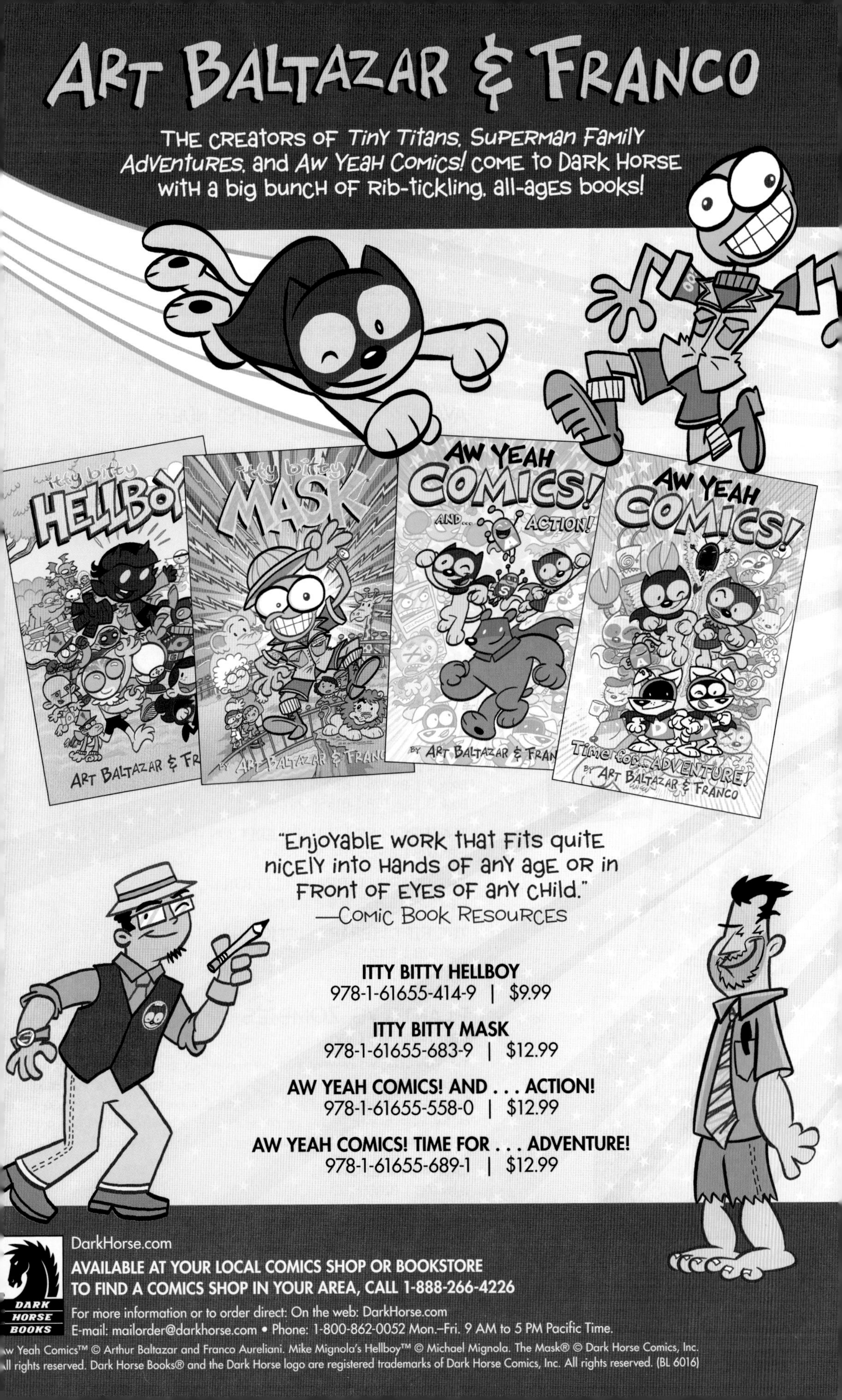
ART BALTAZAR & FRANCO
THE CREATORS OF Tiny Titans, Superman Family Adventures, and Aw Yeah Comics! COME TO DARK HORSE WITH A BIG BUNCH OF RIB-TICKLING, ALL-AGES BOOKS!
itty bitty HELLBOY
ART BALTAZAR & FR
itty bitty MASK
BY ART BALTAZAR & FRANC
AW YEAH COMICS! AND... ACTION!
BY ART BALTAZAR & FRAN
AW YEAH COMICS!
TIME FOR... ADVENTURE!
BY ART BALTAZAR & FRANCO
"Enjoyable work that fits quite nicely into hands of any age or in front of eyes of any child."
—Comic Book Resources
ITTY BITTY HELLBOY
978-1-61655-414-9 | $9.99
ITTY BITTY MASK
978-1-61655-683-9 | $12.99
AW YEAH COMICS! AND . . . ACTION!
978-1-61655-558-0 | $12.99
AW YEAH COMICS! TIME FOR . . . ADVENTURE!
978-1-61655-689-1 | $12.99
DARK HORSE BOOKS
DarkHorse.com
AVAILABLE AT YOUR LOCAL COMICS SHOP OR BOOKSTORE
TO FIND A COMICS SHOP IN YOUR AREA, CALL 1-888-266-4226
For more information or to order direct: On the web: DarkHorse.com
E-mail: mailorder@darkhorse.com • Phone: 1-800-862-0052 Mon.–Fri. 9 AM to 5 PM Pacific Time.
Aw Yeah Comics™ © Arthur Baltazar and Franco Aureliani. Mike Mignola's Hellboy™ © Michael Mignola. The Mask® © Dark Horse Comics, Inc. All rights reserved. Dark Horse Books® and the Dark Horse logo are registered trademarks of Dark Horse Comics, Inc. All rights reserved. (BL 6016)

★ OTHER BOOKS FROM DARK HORSE ★

THE ADVENTURES OF NILSON GROUNDTHUMPER AND HERMY
Stan Sakai

Swashbuckling bunny Nilson Groundthumper may have the brain of a fool, but he has the heart of a hero, and once he meets simple, innocent Hermy, the two won't stop until they find a quest to call their own! Together, the duo face thieves, witches, and monsters, and get lost everywhere they go!
ISBN 978-1-61655-341-8 | $14.99

AVATAR: THE LAST AIRBENDER
Gene Luen Yang, Gurihiru

The wait is over! Ever since the conclusion of *Avatar: The Last Airbender*, its millions of fans have been hungry for more—and it's finally here! This series of digests rejoins Aang and friends for exciting new adventures, beginning with a face-off against the Fire Nation that threatens to throw the world into another war, testing all of Aang's powers and ingenuity!

THE PROMISE TPB | $10.99 each
Book 1: ISBN 978-1-59582-811-8
Book 2: ISBN 978-1-59582-875-0
Book 3: ISBN 978-1-59582-941-2

THE SEARCH TPB | $10.99 each
Book 1: ISBN 978-1-61655-054-7
Book 2: ISBN 978-1-61655-190-2
Book 3: ISBN 978-1-61655-184-1

THE RIFT TPB | $10.99 each
Book 1: ISBN 978-1-61655-295-4
Book 2: ISBN 978-1-61655-296-1
Book 3: ISBN 978-1-61655-297-8

THE PROMISE LIBRARY EDITION HC
ISBN 978-1-61655-074-5 | $39.99

THE SEARCH LIBRARY EDITION HC
ISBN 978-1-61655-226-8 | $39.99

THE RIFT LIBRARY EDITION HC
ISBN 978-1-61655-550-4 | $39.99

PLANTS VS. ZOMBIES
Paul Tobin, Ron Chan

The confusing-yet-brilliant inventor known only as Crazy Dave helps his niece Patrice and young adventurer Nate Timely fend off a "fun-dead" neighborhood invasion in *Plants vs. Zombies*! Winner of over thirty Game of the Year awards, *Plants vs. Zombies* is now determined to shuffle onto all-ages bookshelves to tickle funny bones and thrill . . . *brains.*

LAWNMAGGEDON HC
ISBN 978-1-61655-192-6 | $9.99

TIMEPOCALYPSE HC
ISBN 978-1-61655-621-1 | $9.99